"The person I'm interested in is *you*, Monica...

"It's just I've never had much family to bond with. No one has ever been as important in my life as my father was. But that's not saying that someone else couldn't be."

Edward held Monica transfixed with his gaze.

His eyes met hers, and in the sparse light it was as if their energy closed the inches that separated them and became one constant, undeniable connection. "You do know what I'm saying, don't you?" he asked, his voice soft and husky.

She did know. The feeling was new and different and as exciting as it was wonderful. Edward made her feel cherished and appreciated. She loved this feeling.

Monica had worked hard to prove that she was determined enough to succeed with her career. But now, in the moonlight with Edward, she felt good about just being herself...a woman for all the right reasons. And someone special in Edward's eyes...

Dear Reader,

Diversity is a fact of life. Differences enrich our lives and help us to understand and accept varying cultures and traditions. Never is this more important than in the area of romance. I hope you enjoy exploring the journey of Edward and Monica, two people who come from different worlds and yet share common bonds that help them grow together in spite of adversity.

Both Edward and Monica made promises to people they loved, and both were determined to keep their word, even if it meant that doing so would disrupt their future together. Both were seekers of the truth, even if that truth was hard to believe in. But they persevered in the face of tragedy and never gave up supporting each other. Their mutual respect and admiration and, of course, a growing love, brought these two together to find the solution each needed. Edward found the family he'd never had. And Monica found the one man she'd always waited for.

Was it an easy journey? No. True love hardly ever is. But I hope the ending will bring a smile and a tear and a belief in dreams.

I love to hear from readers. Contact me at cynthoma@aol.com.

Happy everything,

Cynthia

HEARTWARMING

A Family Man at Last

—

Cynthia Thomason

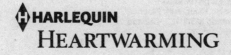

HARLEQUIN
HEARTWARMING

HARLEQUIN®
HEARTWARMING™

Recycling programs
for this product may
not exist in your area.

ISBN-13: 978-1-335-88974-4

A Family Man at Last

Copyright © 2020 by Cynthia Thomason

This edition published by arrangement with Harlequin Books S.A.

For questions and comments about the quality of this book,
please contact us at CustomerService@Harlequin.com.

Harlequin Enterprises ULC
22 Adelaide St. West, 40th Floor
Toronto, Ontario M5H 4E3, Canada
www.Harlequin.com

Printed in U.S.A.

Cynthia Thomason inherited her love of writing from her ancestors. Her father and grandmother both loved to write, and she aspired to continue the legacy. Cynthia studied English and journalism in college, and after a career as a high school English teacher, she began writing novels. She discovered ideas for stories while searching through antiques stores and flea markets and as an auctioneer and estate buyer. Cynthia says every cast-off item from someone's life can ignite the idea for a plot. She writes about small towns, big hearts and happy endings that are earned and not taken for granted. And as far as the legacy is concerned, just ask her son, the magazine journalist, if he believes. You can contact Cynthia at cynthoma@aol.com and cynthiathomason.net.

Books by Cynthia Thomason

Harlequin Heartwarming

Twins Plus One

Baby Makes Four
A Man of Honor

The Cahills of North Carolina

High Country Christmas
Dad in Training
High Country Cop

Visit the Author Profile page
at Harlequin.com for more titles.

This book is dedicated to two unique women—
my outspoken and loving sister-in-law from
England, Sally Anne Brackett, and my talented
and spiritual daughter-in-law from Israel,
Yafi Yair.

CHAPTER ONE

YESTERDAY HAD BEEN the longest day of the thirty-five years Edward Smith had been on this earth. And that included the months he'd spent in juvenile detention for assorted crimes and misdemeanors. And the times he'd gone thirty-six hours without sleep while studying for college exams. The longest day and the worst day.

Edward had driven down to Sweet Pine Key two nights ago to see his father. He came from Miami as often as he could, usually at least once a month. His weekends in Sweet Pine were a chance to unwind from his high-pressure job. No one could maintain an uncomfortable stress level in the Florida Keys. Here, life was laid-back, easygoing, warm and sunny.

And, of course, these weekends gave him a chance to visit with the man he most admired in his life—William Smith, a former judge and the man who'd changed Edward's life by adopting him, a foster kid who'd been kicked around the system until he faced a future as bleak as his past had been.

Edward had arrived at his father's large pine home in Monroe County around nine o'clock on July 3, a steamy Friday night. He'd found the judge sitting in his library sipping on a whiskey while he awaited the arrival of his only son. They'd talked for a couple of hours before Edward excused himself and went up to bed. They still had two days to catch up before Edward had to return to Miami and the patients that waited for him there.

A bit after dawn on Saturday, Edward had walked out to the dock of Smitty's In and Out Marina, the name his father had given the enterprise he'd purchased when he retired from the bench in South Carolina. Edward had been certain he'd gotten out of bed ahead of his father. He'd planned to have the rental boats gassed and ready for customers before William wandered out with his cup of coffee in his hand. Though Edward had never quite fit in with the Keys lifestyle, while he was here he liked to help.

It had been a beautiful morning. The sun slanted rays of promise over the Gulf of Mexico, and Edward looked forward to a day of calm water and warm breezes. What Edward hadn't planned to see was his father's body floating facedown in the Gulf of Mexico, his shirt torn and a fragment of it wrapped around a bolt supporting a piling under the dock. If not for that bit of cloth, William Smith might have floated off with the tide and been halfway to Texas by now.

And so, on that beautiful July morning in the Florida Keys, Edward had felt himself gut-punched and gasping for breath. He lifted his father's face from the murky depths and saw the lifeless eyes open and staring, the weathered skin of his cheeks suddenly colorless from overexposure to saltwater. He leaned over the dock and retched before taking his cell phone from his pocket and dialing 911.

Confusion and shock muddled Edward's brain. Clear thinking evaded him despite his being so closely connected to the Miami-Dade County Police Department. Something instinctive told him to avoid more contact with the body. "Don't disturb evidence," he said to himself. But why did it take so bloody long for the police to arrive?

The Monroe County Sheriff's Department sent a squad car and two cops to investigate. They were local guys who dealt mostly with neighborhood crime on Sweet Pine Key. Finding a body was a big deal to them, since murders were few on the quiet island.

They'd questioned Edward for a short while, then declared the death an open-and-shut case.

"No evidence of foul play," Officer Roland Patterson had said. "Of course, the coroner will have to validate that."

"I'd say the judge just slipped and fell off," his partner, Bobby Cashiers, said.

Edward wanted to shout at them, but common sense dictated that yelling at the lead investigators would be a mistake. But they'd come to this conclusion based on what? "That's it?" he said. "You're declaring this an accident?"

"That's the way it appears to me," Roland said. "No doubt this is a shame, but it's no secret that your father was known to tip a few. Yesterday being a Friday night and all, he might have been staring at the bottom of a bottle by the time the sun went down."

Sure his father drank a few on the weekends. He no longer worked on the bench, and he was exactly where he wanted to spend the rest of his life. Besides, who didn't drink in the Keys? But that didn't mean he was a sloppy drunk who would fall off his own dock.

"I didn't get here until almost nine," Edward said. "Dad was fine then. Yeah, he'd had a couple, but no one has ever even hinted that William Smith couldn't hold his liquor." Edward held his temper as best he could, but he desperately needed to find an explanation for the inexplicable.

"What time was it when you last saw your father after you arrived?" one of the officers asked.

"I went to bed around eleven."

"Is that the usual routine for you and the judge? Have a drink or two and then you leave him and go up to bed?"

"I guess so," Edward said. "Sometimes Dad went to bed before I did, but I wanted to be up early to get the rental boats ready."

"You never heard the judge go to bed?" Roland asked.

Most everyone on the key called William Smith "the judge." That was what he'd been for over thirty years, before he'd followed his dream to own a marina in paradise. And folks who didn't call him "the judge" called him "Smitty," after the name he'd given his beloved marina.

"I didn't hear him come up the stairs," Edward said. "Maybe he stayed up a while to read."

"Or other things," Bobby Cashiers said. His implication was clear.

"He wasn't drunk!" Edward proclaimed. "We had a perfectly normal, *sober* conversation for two hours. After our talk, he returned the whiskey bottle to the liquor cabinet. He wouldn't have had another drink."

"Then why did he come out on the dock?" Cashiers asked.

"I don't know why he would come out here after dark. Maybe to see the stars. Maybe to check on something. But I can guarantee you he didn't walk out here so inebriated he fell off a dock he'd been walking on for fifteen years!"

The discussion between the officers and Edward continued for over an hour. The officers kept insisting that the evidence, or what they referred to as "lack of evidence," pointed to an accidental death, possibly related to alcohol consumption. Edward insisted that his father was an excellent swimmer with much to live for. "Even if he'd had a fifth of whiskey, he wouldn't have been so drunk he couldn't have swum a hundred feet to shore."

"Maybe he passed out, hit his head," Roland pointed out.

"Not likely," Edward said. "But if such a ridiculous thing happened, the coroner will find a wound on his head."

"Look, you're not here for most of every month," Roland added. "I'm not sure how much you know about the judge's behavior the last few years, but if he wasn't at Tarpon Joe's in the evening drinking with his buddies, he was dang sure in his house drinking alone."

"I know enough about his behavior to say he didn't fall off this dock!"

Eventually the coroner arrived and the body was removed to the shore. An initial examination did not show any injury to the judge's head. Edward knew there wouldn't be a self-inflicted injury, just as he knew his father hadn't stumbled from the dock. An ambulance took William Smith's body to the small morgue at the sheriff's department. Later, the judge would be transported to Fisherman's Chapel and Funeral Home a few miles away. The coroner promised to look the body over carefully, and if he saw any reason to contradict the officers' conclusions, he would let Edward know.

But Edward wasn't satisfied. He sensed the coroner would be as quick to declare the death an accident. "Don't you have a homicide investigator in this department?" he asked the coroner.

"We do."

"Then let's get an expert here," Edward insisted. "I would think it's customary procedure in a case like this."

The coroner didn't look convinced that such action was necessary, but he nodded. "Don't guess it can hurt."

And so here it was a Sunday morning, more than twenty-four hours after Edward had found his father's body. Word had spread among the residents of the small island, and a few neighbors had stopped to offer condolences. Edward dealt with such comments as "Sure is a shame."

"A good man, the judge." He sat on the porch of his father's decades-old house and waited for the homicide detective to show up.

And as he waited his mind filled with memories. The first time he'd set eyes on the judge, Edward had been sixteen years old, a veteran of the foster-care system since he was three and a kid who always seemed to get into trouble. The court appearance he'd been at was worse than most. Edward had been picked up for stealing a car—again.

Judge Smith had given him a stern talking-to, but not before he'd heard Edward's story. One foster home after another. Unknown parents, no family, a high-school dropout. He'd asked Edward a number of questions, even smiled a time or two at the answers.

Ultimately, he'd sentenced Edward to six months in a juvenile-detention center, with release dependent upon Edward's earning a GED so he'd have a high-school diploma. And then the strangest thing happened. The judge visited Edward at the detention center. Not once, but several times. The visits became weekly occurrences. And despite a chip on Edward's shoulder the size of an oak tree, a bond between the two formed and grew.

The day Judge Smith offered Edward a room in his home in South Carolina had been the day Edward's life had experienced a rebirth. And the day the judge adopted the seventeen-year-old, Edward's future began.

Edward sighed and tried to swallow the huge lump in his throat. The homicide investigator wouldn't care about any of that. Judge Smith, the man who'd taken Edward from the gutter and given him hope, was now just a body, after all.

A bit of that oak-tree chip came back to settle on Edward's shoulder as he waited for the investigator to arrive. And when she did, Edward couldn't believe his eyes.

There must be some mistake, he thought. The officer who got out of a plain, dark gray midsize sedan was hardly what anyone would consider homicide-detective material—certainly not the *Law & Order* type. No more than five feet four inches tall, slender, with dark hair pulled back into a tight bun from a round olive-skinned face, the female coming toward him didn't look old enough or seasoned enough to deal with crimes of the worst sort.

Maybe the true homicide detective was busy and had sent someone from his office. But it wasn't so. The woman dressed in black slacks, a short-sleeved blue shirt and sensible walking shoes showed him her badge and said, "Good morning. I'm Monica Cortez, detective for the Monroe County Sheriff's Department, Middle Keys division."

Edward could hardly find the words. "You're the homicide investigator assigned to this case?"

Her dark eyes widened. She started to say something, but obviously thought better of it and extended her hand. "I'm the only homicide detective in this part of the Keys," she said. "I assure you I'm qualified to do my job."

Oh, jeez. She must have interpreted Edward's comment as a negative take on her stature, gender and appearance—just exactly what his first impression had been. He wasn't one to judge anyone based on appearance or any other feature. He'd learned that lesson the hard way, and yet he'd just made a judgment of this lady.

"I'm sorry," he said. "I suppose I'm just surprised to see a…" He stopped. He was only digging his gender-inequality hole deeper.

"A woman in this position?" she said for him.

"Something like that. But I meant no disrespect."

"Sure you didn't." She took a notebook from her shirt pocket and snapped her ballpoint pen into writing mode. "You're Edward Smith, I presume?"

"I am."

"I'm sorry for your loss." It was a clichéd statement, but she actually seemed to mean it.

"How much do you know about this case?" he asked.

"I've read the reports. Officers Cashiers and Patterson filled me in with the details." She looked away from the house and toward the dock. "Are you ready to answer some questions?"

From her tone, he almost got the impression she was going to interview him as a suspect. "Anything you want to ask," he said.

"I think we should start by going to the scene."

"Yes, of course. That would be fine." He led the way over lush Bahia grass to where water lapped against a pristine shoreline. Edward's father had made many improvements to the property in the years he'd owned it. The dock stretched one hundred feet into the blue Gulf of Mexico. At intervals, berths were occupied with the small fleet of boats owned by Smitty's In and Out. The gas pumps and a bait house sat a few yards down the shore. It was a typical marina setup, yet with a kind of tropical charm. Edward and his father had worked hard to make the property into what the judge had wanted—an oasis filled with flowers and palm trees.

Edward had almost forgotten the purpose for the walk to the dock, he was so caught up with memories of years past. He and his dad had attached mooring lines here, bumpers there. They'd worked together whenever Edward could get away from school and, later, his job. They'd laughed often, shared a few beers.

"Where exactly did you find the body?" Detective Cortez asked.

He stopped near the end of the dock and pointed down. "Right about here."

"The last time you saw your father alive was the night before?"

"That's right. Friday. We had about a two-hour conversation when I got in from Miami, and I went to bed."

"And when you found him the next morning in the bay, was he wearing the same clothes he'd had on the night before?"

Edward thought a moment. The other officers hadn't asked him that question, but it seemed an important one. "Yes, actually, he was. Which means this happened late Friday night and not Saturday morning."

"Possibly. The coroner will be able to give us an exact time of death."

She asked him other questions, some of them repeats of what the officers had asked the day before. *What was your father's state of mind? Did you notice any unusual behavior, nervousness, anxiety? Are you aware of anyone who might hold a grudge against your father?*

"There might be someone from his past," Edward admitted. "My father put a lot of people behind bars when he was a judge in South Carolina. But I doubt many of those people even knew he lived here on Sweet Pine. He hasn't practiced law in over a decade. When he bought this marina he was happy to leave that other life behind and run this operation."

"I'm familiar with this marina," Monica said. "My father used to work here. Perhaps you know the name. Juan Cortez?"

"Oh, sure, Juan. I remember him," Edward said. "Nice guy, hard worker. My dad depended on him. Where is Juan now?"

Monica looked away and tapped her pen on her notebook. "He passed away five years ago. A heart attack. I'm surprised your father didn't mention it."

Jeez, maybe he had forgotten. He wasn't involved in the day-to-day operation of the marina. "I don't mean to minimize Juan's value to my father," Edward said. "Five years ago I was still establishing my career. I wasn't here too often."

"Yeah. I've only seen you a time or two." She looked into the murky water. "Just a few more questions. Did you know many of your father's friends and acquaintances from around here?"

"Not many of them. I spend more time in Miami than I do in the Keys. My main employment is with Miami-Dade County. I do try to come down here whenever I can, though." He paused, thought about what he'd just said. "Though that will no doubt change now."

"So you had a good relationship with your father?"

"The best. I owe him…" This police detective wasn't interested in the sad tale of Edward Smith, so he cut short his explanation. "Anyway, yes, we did."

"And can you think of anyone here who might have reason to want your father dead?"

The question brought fresh anguish to Edward's chest. He took a deep breath. "No, no one," he answered. "If my father had any enemies here, he never discussed them with me, and I never observed any hostility between him and any other person. Look, my dad was happy here, happier than he'd been in years. He was always positive, cheerful, looking forward to living his golden years right in this house."

"And you never heard a local person speak ill of your dad?"

"No. I can only assume that the locals were glad to have him as part of the community. He was an honest, hardworking contributor to the economy. This business brought tourists to Sweet Pine from all over."

Monica Cortez stopped taking notes and gave Edward an intense stare. "I hate to bring this up, but I'm told you know the conclusion Cashiers and Patterson came up with, and you're not satisfied with it."

"I do. That's why I asked for a homicide investigator. My father drank, but so does most everyone in the Keys. I've never seen him drunk or unable to handle himself. The thought of him walking out on this dock and just suddenly tipping over is ludicrous." To further emphasize his case, Edward added, "And even if he had fallen in, which he didn't, he could have swum a few feet to reach shallow water, where he could have walked to shore with no problem."

"I know this is difficult," Cortez said. "It's human nature to want to find a reasonable explanation for something we don't understand."

"Do you, Miss Cortez? Do you really know how difficult this is for me?"

She didn't answer.

"Because I came here on Friday night to spend a weekend with my father, and Saturday morning I find him floating in the bay. This weekend started out no differently than any other in the last fifteen years. And yet, the man I owe my life to is gone. So, yeah, this is difficult for me."

"I understand that," she said. "My questions and comments are merely an effort to get to the bottom of this."

He hadn't meant to sound so harsh. He needed this woman's help. He needed someone to believe that his father hadn't just tripped on a board and fallen into the water. "I'm sorry. I'm just going through…"

"I get it," she said. "You need a minute?"

"No. Go on."

"How was your father's health the last few years?"

"Excellent. He was seventy-six years old

and didn't even take a blood-pressure pill. And he was still strong. Patched the roof on this house last year with just a ladder and some tar paper. And if you're wondering about his mental state, he was sharp as a tack."

Cortez put her notebook on a bench at the end of the dock and bent over. She examined the dock and the piling where the judge had been found. She unwound the fabric piece from the bolt, set it on the dock and ran her hand through the water to feel the wood around the piling. After a moment, she uttered a small sound. "Hmm."

"What?" Edward asked. "Did you find anything?"

Cortez stood. "Maybe. It's probably nothing, but I'm going to call for a diver. He should be here within the hour. I need to check a few things, like when high and low tides were last night and this morning."

Edward suddenly experienced a burst of relief. This detective, as inexperienced as he suspected she was, was taking him seriously. "Are you going to wait for the diver to get here?" he asked.

"Most definitely. If you have something to do…"

"No. Let's go up to the house. We might as well have a seat and get out of the sun."

They walked back to the house together. Cortez made her phone call. It was as short and efficient as everything else about her. But Edward was becoming more confident about her efficiency by the minute.

SHE'D SEEN HIM AROUND. Most everyone on Sweet Pine Key had seen him, talked about him, speculated about his supposedly mysterious past. But Monica had never met anyone besides the judge and the one guy who worked at the marina who actually knew him on a personal level. Of course, her father had known Edward, too, but since he'd been gone five years, she rarely heard Edward's name mentioned around the small settlement of Sweet Pine. Sometimes a neighbor might mention that Smitty's son was on the island. Most times not.

Maybe that was because Edward spent so much time in Miami. Maybe it was because he chose to stay separate from the Keys' lifestyle. He didn't hang out at the local watering holes when he was here. He didn't brag at the bait shops about his big fishing conquests. Whatever the reason, Monica was fascinated today by the slim, good-looking, six-foot-tall man with the sandy blond hair who looked nothing like Smitty, the judge.

She'd heard rumors that Edward was adopted. Seeing him close up today, she could believe it. The judge was a stocky five foot, seven inches with a thin ring of white hair around a bald pate, and had a thick, muscular torso and short legs. Edward was muscular, from tip to toe. Before the end of the day, Monica was determined to find out if Edward was biologically related to Smitty. If Edward wanted a homicide investigation, then she had to have all the facts.

They sat on the porch of the iconic Florida Keys home that the judge had purchased when he'd made a deal to buy the marina. Folks on Sweet Pine had admired the house for decades. Only a short walk from the dock, it seemed a perfect fit for a man who wanted to leave civilization behind and watch the sun set over the Gulf. As far as Monica knew, since the judge had moved onto Sweet Pine, he rarely took his old Pontiac out of the garage. He was content to ramble around in his two-thousand-square-foot home, play with his boats and walk to the convenience store and liquor seller. Folks said he had his necessities delivered from the nearest supermarket.

Sometimes he wandered down to Tarpon Joe's Bar and Grill if he felt uncommonly sociable. Monica had even run into him there and had a few brief conversations with him and the small crowd of senior citizens he attracted. A nice old guy, she'd thought. Friendly and pleasant. And he'd spoken fondly of his son, Edward, who lived and worked in Miami.

While they waited for the diver to arrive, Monica continued to question Edward. She asked about people the judge talked about, whether he had close friends on the island, whether he ever mentioned having a run-in with one of his neighbors. Yeah, Smitty talked about regular customers who came for bait, oddball tourists who rented boats. But, according to Edward, he'd never argued with anyone about more than the size of the shrimp he was charging ten bucks a dozen for.

She saw an opportunity to get to the bottom of Edward's story. "So what about the early years, when you were a boy and the judge was still on the bench in South Carolina? Do you recall anyone threatening him?"

Edward answered quickly and concisely. "I only met my father when I was sixteen," he said. "The judge adopted me."

So the rumors were true. "Oh, really? Do you mind telling me how that came about?"

"I suppose not. I was a troubled kid, growing up in the foster system. I got in some scrapes, broke the law a few times. My big break came when I was sent before Judge Smith in juvenile court."

"The judge pardoned your crimes?" Monica asked.

"Heck, no. He sent me to juvie for six months. But he didn't forget me. For some reason he took an interest. He visited me in detention, made sure I was getting an education, even gave me extra homework that he looked over himself."

"And you and he grew close?" Monica said. "I mean, he did adopt you. That must have been a big step."

"It was for me," Edward said. "The judge was waiting when I was released and he took me back to his home, where he lived alone with only a housekeeper. I stayed with him a couple of months, and then he made it official. I became his son."

"Just like that?" Monica said, not wanting to sound suspicious, but jeez, a successful judge taking a problem kid home to his house was not an ordinary occurrence. In fact, some people might say that Edward fell into a pot of gold.

"No, not 'just like that,'" Edward said. "I proved myself every day to my dad. I worked my butt off to show him I was worthy of his trust. I studied, didn't run around, broke off with all my old friends. I knew what a lucky break he was offering me."

"You even got an education, right?"

"Went to the University of Miami because they had an excellent program in psychology. It was tough at first. I missed my talks with my dad, but we communicated often, and I went home to South Carolina when I could. I worked on campus, and what I couldn't earn, the judge provided. Finally got my master's degree and a doctorate.

During that time the judge moved down here, so we were close again."

On the surface, Monica couldn't find any reason to believe that Edward didn't have fond and grateful feelings of this man who had given him his big break. Edward appeared successful in his own right, so he would have no motive to want to see his father dead for monetary reasons. And it appeared the judge was a thoughtful and caring provider.

"Did William have any other family?" Monica asked.

"No. His wife died before I met him. They'd had no children, and he never remarried."

Didn't leave many relatives to question, Monica thought. If she was going to investigate this case, she would have to find motives among the people the judge knew or had known.

The diver arrived, and Monica put away her writing tools. She and Edward walked with the diver to the end of the dock. He donned a wet suit and went into the water, concentrating especially on a particular piling where she had looked earlier.

After a few minutes, his head broke the surface. "Yeah, I see what you're talking about, Monica. There appears to be fresh gouge marks in the wood."

"Can you tell if the marks mean anything? Any pattern?"

"Not really. Looks like about a two-inch vertical line. I can't tell what it was meant to be. I'll come back after the tide goes out and get a better look."

"Thanks, Carl," Monica said. "Tide goes out at four fifty this afternoon. I'll meet you back here," she added. "But I guess that's it for now."

"I'm going to stay for a while," he said. "Might have a look around the bottom to see if I find anything."

"Okay."

Monica and Edward went back to the house to wait. Edward turned on the ceiling fans. The day was becoming typically hot and humid. Monica's clothes were beginning to itch. She took off her ball cap and brushed strands of damp hair from her forehead, but didn't loosen the sensible bun at the back of her head.

"Look, Edward," she said. "I don't know

if we'll find anything to corroborate your theory that your father was murdered. But I am truly sorry it happened. I'll do all I can to ease your mind about this loss."

He nodded. "Thanks."

"I really do understand what you're feeling. Like I said earlier, my father died five years ago."

"That's tough. Do you have other family?"

She stopped short of mentioning every one of her relatives—aunts and uncles and numerous cousins. And her brother. But she did tell Edward about her mother and her nephew, Emilio, both of whom lived with her in her small cinder-block house just up the road.

"My father thought a lot of the judge," she said. But then she stopped.

Carl was coming toward them. He reached the porch and handed her an object in a plastic bag. "Found this at the bottom sticking out of the sand."

Monica stared at the five-inch pocketknife with a carved marlin in the wood handle. She handed the bag to Edward. "Do you recognize this?"

His voice hitched. "I gave it to my father for Christmas last year."

"It doesn't show any effects of being in the water long," she said. "He could have dropped it Friday night."

"And he could have used it to carve whatever you and Carl found in the piling," Edward said.

Had the judge carved something of significance in the moments before he died? Monica couldn't wait to return after the tide went out so she could see for herself.

CHAPTER TWO

CARL CHANGED INTO shorts and a T-shirt, then tucked the bag with the knife into his duffel. He told Monica he'd see her later. Monica knew he would follow protocol and take the knife to Forensics. Not that much would be uncovered by examining it. The knife had been in the water almost forty-eight hours. The chances of finding identifying marks or fingerprints were slim. Besides, William Smith hadn't been killed by a knife wound. Monica still believed he'd died by drowning. But she was willing to consider other options.

Once Carl had left, Monica took out her notebook again and asked Edward a few more questions. He was cooperative, but his thoughts seemed a thousand miles away. Finding the knife—a gift—had been rough on him. She could relate to his grief. She had been closer to her father than to any person on earth, and it still hurt to think of him.

"Did your father always carry the knife?" she asked.

"As far as I know he did."

"What did he primarily use it for?"

"Any number of little jobs. There always seems to be a use for a knife at a marina."

"Where did he keep it when it wasn't in his pocket?" she asked.

Edward admitted that he wouldn't know the exact whereabouts of the knife twenty-four hours a day, but he offered his best guesses.

"I suppose you'll want to be here when Carl returns," she said. "You'll want to see the marks in the wood for yourself."

"I'll have to see them later. You said low tide would be around five o'clock. I have an appointment at the Fisherman's Chapel to discuss funeral plans for my father at that time." He shook his head slowly. "I still can't believe I'm talking about him dying." He stared into Monica's eyes. "I expected to have him around for much longer."

"I know, Edward. I'm so sorry."

"I wish I'd spent more time with him,"

Edward said. "Suddenly nineteen years seems like the blink of an eye. He was in my life for such a brief time—a time when I was concentrating on getting my degrees." He gave her an earnest stare. "I imagine you feel that way about your father. I'm sorry I didn't know him better."

"You would have liked him," she said. "Everyone did. Your father especially."

"I know my dad depended on him."

"Actually, Edward, my father had hoped to make the marina his life's work. You may know this, but the judge encouraged him by offering him a part of the business if he stayed on."

Edward seemed frozen in time. He seemed to have no recollection of this offer. "My dad intended to reward Juan with a percentage of Smitty's In and Out?"

"That's the way I understood it. Certainly not an equal share. I think it was ten percent. My dad told me there's a document somewhere that confirms this agreement. I don't have it, so it must be among the judge's papers."

She remembered her father telling her about the agreement. "The judge," Juan had said. "He is a good man. He will take care of us." But that was more than five years ago, and now there was no one left to take care of the Cortez family but Monica herself.

Monica stared out at the water. She didn't want to see Edward's face when she told him the whole story. After all, years had passed since Juan was supposed to get a share of the marina. Monica had worked her way up in the sheriff's department and was providing for her family. The judge's promise no longer mattered. Had William Smith made other promises that he hadn't kept? If so, maybe not everyone on Sweet Pine Key liked him unconditionally.

"But your father died before claiming his share?" Edward asked.

"That's one possibility," she said. "Look, Edward, I'm just bringing this up because it shows that there may be folks around here that held a grudge against your father. Not that my father did, but the judge never made good on his promise for whatever reason."

"And you think there may have been other broken promises?"

"I don't know."

"I get what you're saying, Detective…"

She looked at him then. "Call me Monica, please. In case you might have wondered, I haven't been a detective all that long. I'm just used to being called Monica."

"Okay, Monica. You're suggesting that my dad reneged on the deal he made with Juan?"

"Maybe. Maybe not. I don't know. The only people who do know can't tell us. Obviously my father didn't kill your father. But maybe there's someone else on Sweet Pine Key who had reason to. It's worth checking out. If you believe your father was murdered, I think you should give some thought to the validity of that."

"Okay. I've never considered that my father might have had an enemy here, but I will do as you suggest."

She gave him a look of sympathy. "You called for a homicide investigator, Edward. This is what you get—someone who is trained to look under all the rocks."

Monica stood. "I guess that's it for now. I'll see you tomorrow. I'll have pictures of the gouges in the wood. In the meantime, go to your appointment at the chapel. Try to get some rest." She smiled at him.

"I look that bad?"

She recalled her earlier assessment of him—tall, fair, nice-looking. "No, you don't look bad. But you've had a shock. If your father had a doctor in this area, you might want to consider a sleeping-pill prescription."

"That won't be necessary," he said. "I don't mind being awake. I like to remember, especially when memories are all I have left."

She nodded. She remembered her father every day and always would. She walked to her car and got in. In her rearview mirror she saw the big old house, and the lone figure on the porch staring at the water. In her job, she based her conclusions on facts, but she couldn't help having a strong emotional reaction to Edward Smith.

LATE SUNDAY AFTERNOON, Edward went to Fisherman's Chapel on Little Fawn Key, a few miles from Sweet Pine. The funeral director met him at the door. "Ah, Edward, I am so sorry for your loss," the man said. "I am Raul Gonzalez."

Edward figured it was Gonzalez's business to know the grieving people he served, even if he'd never met them. Raul's handshake was warm and solid, respectably demonstrating the profession he served. He wore trousers as black as his slicked-back hair and a muted floral shirt, which was his only concession to the Keys lifestyle.

"Is my father's body here?" Edward asked.

"Yes. He is in the restoration room. I think we can make him look very good. Very good indeed."

Edward's first thought was that unless his father was smiling and offering him a cold drink, there was no chance he would find him looking well.

"Did the coroner give you any details on my dad's passing?" Edward asked.

"Some. The time of death was determined to be around midnight Friday night. There was water in his lungs, too."

Edward had gone to bed shortly before midnight. While he'd been settling in, his father was outside facing his murderer. The thought made him shiver. "Were there any unexplained marks on his body?" Edward asked.

"None that I know of," Gonzalez said. "I

understand why you're asking. I've heard that you are questioning the officers' conclusions. You've called in our homicide investigator, Monica Cortez."

"Yes, that's right."

"Monica is such a sweet girl. I'm certain she sympathizes with your loss. If anyone will work hard to uncover the truth, Monica will."

"She seems very nice," Edward said, though he was still grappling with Monica's sweetness being appropriate for her job. "I am a bit concerned about her lack of experience."

"I don't think it will matter so much in this case. The judge, rest his soul, slipped and fell into the water. A terrible shame."

Those words were like a fresh stab to Edward's heart. Another person who assumed his father was a clumsy man whose drinking made him do stupid things.

"Shall we go into my office and discuss your plans?" Gonzalez suggested. "I'm thinking the funeral can be scheduled for Tuesday evening. That gives you enough time to invite out-of-town guests, family and so forth."

"Tuesday will be fine," Edward said, though there was no one he would notify. The judge had no family and neither did Edward. They were two loners who'd met due to circumstances of fate and ended up the centers of each other's worlds. "I'm thinking we can just spread the word around town that the service will be Tuesday," he said. "My father must have known everyone around here, and some will want to pay their respects."

"Yes, absolutely," Gonzalez said. "Speaking of Monica, I'm sure her family will come. Monica's father—I planned his funeral five years ago—was a close friend of the judge. Her mother, Rosa, knew him also. Little Emilio is too young to have met the judge."

"Emilio? That must be the boy Monica spoke of."

"Yes. She is raising her brother's child. Miguel didn't come to Sweet Pine often. I don't think Monica has seen much of him. Juan's death was hard on him, so soon after that other loss."

"What loss is that?" Edward asked.

"Miguel's sweetheart died in childbirth.

Many believed he never recovered afterward. And then his papa. He couldn't care for the child the boy's mother left with him, so he brought the infant to Monica." The director smiled. "Such a good boy, Emilio. Smart and well-behaved.

"Everyone in Sweet Pine admires the Cortez family. Juan was one of the first refugees who came to America during the Mariel boatlift. Juan Cortez was a good man through and through."

Edward and Gonzalez sat in the well-appointed office equipped with comfortable chairs and numerous boxes of tissues, and planned the last time anyone would see William Smith. Whatever Gonzalez suggested was fine with Edward. He just wanted to remember his father as the vital, giving man he'd been—the man who'd changed Edward's life.

The time was nearly 6:30 p.m. when Edward got back to the house. The hours loomed ahead of him—long and lonely. He didn't know what he would do to pass the time. He'd just pulled into the drive when an automobile with rental plates came in behind him. A man and a woman got out. Surely they'd seen the sad message draped on the gate and weren't here to make boat-rental arrangements.

They didn't look like typical renters. The man was dressed in nice jeans and a polo shirt. He was tall, muscular and oddly familiar-looking. The woman was pretty and of medium height, with blond hair. She wore a light blue dress, which fluttered around her legs in the Gulf breeze.

Edward waited on the porch as they approached the house. "If you've come to rent a boat, I'm sorry, but we're closed."

The woman stared at him as if taking in every aspect of his appearance. Maybe she thought, as Monica had, that he looked tired and strung-out. Well, he was.

"Not here for a boat," the man said. He extended his hand. "My name is Jeremy Crockett."

The name instantly rang a bell as it would with almost anyone who called themselves a sports fan. No wonder the man looked familiar. "*The* Jeremy Crockett?" Edward asked. "The receiver for the Carolina Wildcats?"

"Ex-receiver now," the man said. "But yeah, that's me. Are you Edward Smith?"

"I am. I can't imagine why you're here, but today is not a good time—"

"We saw your sign," Crockett said. "Did someone close to you pass away?"

"My father," Edward replied. "Two days ago."

The woman kept staring. Edward thought she might cry, though why she would shed a tear for someone she'd probably never known was baffling.

Crockett took the woman's elbow gently. "This is Brooke Montgomery, a friend of mine. We traveled from South Carolina today. She wanted to meet you."

The woman greeted him, but her hand shook. She swallowed. "Oh, Edward," she said.

Edward narrowed his eyes. "What's this about?"

"It's really you," she said.

"We've established that fact." Edward frowned.

"I'm so sorry about your father." Brooke's voice sounded hoarse as if her words were caught in her throat. If Edward hadn't considered her a complete stranger, he might have believed she really cared.

"Thanks, but why are you sorry?" This was another puzzling development in an already chaotic two days. A beautiful woman and her football-player boyfriend suddenly standing in his driveway. What was going on?

The woman sniffed. "I'm sorry because you're hurting. And also because I'm happy to see you that my tears are mixed up with so many emotions right now."

"You're going to have to give me more than that, Miss Montgomery," Edward said.

"How old are you, Edward?" she asked.

"Thirty-five. Why?"

She nodded. "Forgive me," she said. "I just can't believe…"

They all stood at the base of the porch, the woman looking as if she might explode with a cauldron of feelings, the man watching her intently, while Edward was caught in the middle, shaking his head.

"Edward, I was born thirty-two years ago, three years after you. I never knew you, but I have wanted to for so long. I've searched for you." She scrubbed a finger under her eye. "Edward, I'm your sister."

CHAPTER THREE

HIS SISTER? WHO was this woman trying to kid? Edward was caught between wanting to laugh with bitterness at the absurdity of her claim and wanting to tell her and her celebrity friend to get off his property. And on the very weekend he'd lost the only family he'd ever had.

He took a deep breath, then let it out slowly. "Look, lady, I don't know why you're doing this, but I already told you, I'm not in the mood for games."

"This isn't a game," Brooke said. "I have every reason to believe that you're my brother. Do you remember our mother? Her name is Marlene."

He could answer that question honestly and with disgust. "I don't remember anything about her. I don't know if she's alive or dead, but she's dead to me, period. I don't have any memories of my life before I was three."

"I thought that might be so," Brooke said. "I know quite a bit about you, actually. Our mother lives in Myrtle Beach now, close to Shadow Woods, where we lived when she gave birth to all of us."

"All of us?" Edward was dumbfounded. But he couldn't deny that he'd been born in South Carolina. That was one of the few facts he'd held on to for so many years. "There are more than just you and me?"

"I am a twin," Brooke said. "My sister is Camryn. She still lives in South Carolina. We were lucky. We were adopted as infants and grew up together. Our lives have been stable and happy."

"That's nice for the two of you," he said. "My life wasn't such a picnic."

"Yes, I know. But you met the judge and turned your life around. I'm so thankful."

"How do you know what I've done with my life?" he asked. "I changed my name—numerous times. I've never met you, never even had a clue that you might exist."

"I told you," Brooke said, "I've been searching for you for months, since I found our mother in Myrtle Beach and she let slip that Camryn and I had a big brother."

He shook his head. "Oh, I think I get it." He couldn't help his skepticism. "So, this sudden revelation is about our mother? What's her motive for sending you to me, sis—" He paused. "If, indeed, you are my sister, which, frankly, I don't believe for a minute."

The big wide receiver took a step toward Edward. "Hey, man, this is hard on everybody, okay? Why don't you let her say what brought her all this distance? Maybe you'll start to see things differently."

Brooke spoke calmly and softly. "Edward, I've learned you had a troubled past. Spent time in juvenile detention. Never adopted by a family and then you met the judge.

"Every time I learned a new fact about you, I tucked it in my heart because I realized it was just another stepping stone to finding you. And finally, a miracle happened and the missing clue came to me. I learned that the judge who sentenced you to your last months in detention adopted you and later moved to the Keys."

Her voice choked on her next words. She

looked up at Jeremy and said, "I had a special friend who believed in me and my determination to find you." She returned her gaze to Edward. Her eyes glistened with unshed tears. "And now I'm here standing right next to you."

Darn. This woman was good, Edward thought. But why should he believe a word of what she was saying? Maybe she was an opportunist who'd heard about his father's death and thought she might be able to scam a few bucks from his will. The Keys was filled with con artists who'd take a penny from a dead man's eyes rather than find an honest day's work.

But how did that explain the presence of Jeremy Crockett, star wide receiver for a pro football team, a man easily identified? No doubt, Crockett lent an air of authenticity to this cockamamie claim.

Suddenly Edward was just plain tired. He didn't want to have to think anymore, decide anything else, cope with any other surprises. He wanted these two off his property so he could go over the events of the last couple of days. He had a lot to think about, and being someone's brother just added another weight to what he already had on his shoulders.

"Okay, Brooke, I'll give you this much. Maybe I am your brother. Most probably I'm not. You have a few facts that support your story, but there are tests we can take to provide accurate proof—"

"Fine. We'll do a DNA test. Whatever you want," she said. "I know I'm right. Maybe I didn't know for sure until I arrived here today, but now there is not a doubt in my mind."

"Well, you might not have a doubt," Edward said. "And are sure. But I need time to process all of this. I've had a lousy few days, haven't slept, haven't eaten. I'm hardly in a state of mind to consider everything this means."

"Let us take you to dinner," she said. "We can talk then. Please, Edward…"

Now she was just making him angry with her badgering. Couldn't she tell he was at the end of his patience? He wanted to be left alone.

Maybe she didn't get the signals he was sending, but thankfully, Crockett did. He leaned close to her and said, "Let it go for tonight, Brooke. Edward needs to think things through."

She nodded slowly. "Of course, you're right, Jeremy." Looking at Edward, she said, "We'll go. We've booked rooms in Key Largo. We'll come back tomorrow. If there's anything I can do to help you with arrangements for your father..."

Crockett put his arm around her shoulders. "Brooke, honey, come on."

She dabbed a tissue at her eyes and let herself be led to the car. Thank goodness. Edward needed space. Of all the people he wouldn't have wanted to order off his property, his sister was definitely one of them!

RETURNING HOME EVERY day to 120 Lantana Lane was like an adventure for Monica. She never knew quite what to expect, but she was certain the basic ingredients of family that she depended on would be there. Love, comfort and tradition. And she would feel miles away from the responsibilities of the sheriff's office.

Her rise to detective had been a long and difficult one, but she'd been willing to do it to earn the extra money for her family.

She still had a lot to learn, but she knew the basics of forensics, crime-scene preservation, verbal investigations and detailed searches for clues. She was ready to apply all her knowledge to the case involving Judge Smith and help the grieving son with whom she'd felt an instant connection.

But this Sunday night she longed for some peace and quiet. She'd thought all day about Judge Smith, how he'd died and if she could prove his death was anything other than an accident. And she'd thought of his adopted son, Edward, who had been lucky enough to spend almost two decades with a father who loved him. Only Edward didn't feel lucky today. He was grieving, and Monica understood his loss.

She sighed with exhaustion as she pulled up to her house. The small truck belonging to her Aunt Lucy was in the driveway. Maybe Lucy had come alone, but most likely her husband, Horatio, was with her. Emilio's bicycle was on the front porch, and Monica was reminded that she needed to remove the training wheels and give him a lesson in balance and persistence. Delicious odors came from the open front door, but Monica wasn't hungry.

"*Tía* 'Nica!" Emilio rushed to open the screen door for his aunt. So much for some peace and quiet. She stepped inside the stifling-hot house and put her arms around the boy. His face was sweaty, his hair damp.

"Mama," Monica called. "Why isn't the air-conditioning on? It's like an oven in here."

"Yes, *chica*," her mother called. "The oven is on. Lucy and I are roasting vegetables to go with the black beans tonight."

"No, Mama, I didn't ask if the oven was on. I asked…" She stopped, recognizing the futility of her question, and adjusted the thermostat herself. Rising up on her tiptoes, she placed the flat of her hand as close to the ceiling vent as she could and was rewarded with a blast of cool air.

No matter how often Monica talked to her mother about leaving the old ways— the Cuban ways—behind, Rosa insisted on watching their pennies by refusing to turn on "all these modern devices." Besides, Rosa would tell her, the temperature was only too hot for Monica. The rest of the family thrived on the fresh air.

Fresh, humid, sweltering air, Monica would think and again remind her mother that they could afford to keep the air-conditioning on in the summer months.

Monica sat on the sofa and patted the spot beside her. Emilio claimed the seat. Monica asked him how his day was and he answered with a short but vivid description of everything he had done and with whom.

"He missed his *Tía* 'Nica," her mother said, coming from the kitchen. She kissed the top of Monica's head. "It's the Lord's day, Monica. You should spend it with family and not doing police work."

"I'm sorry, Mama. It couldn't be helped."

Rosa Cortez was a pretty woman. Thin and strong, with dark hair mixed with a few strands of gray, she had been courted by several men since Juan had died, but she'd turned them all down. "I think of myself as still married," she explained to Monica. "I always will be married to Juan."

Rosa's sister, Lucy, and her husband, Horatio, came in from the backyard. They greeted Monica warmly. Horatio told a funny story being a butcher at the local Cuban grocery store. Lucy wanted to hear all about the murder that had happened on Sweet Pine Key two days ago.

"It's not a murder, Aunt Lucy. Probably just an accident."

"Still a shock," Lucy insisted.

"Enough talk of death and tragedy," Rosa said, coming to the dining table with a platter of food. "Horatio brought us a beautiful pork roast. We should be grateful for family and all this bounty."

Monica couldn't help feeling conflicted. Usually these delicious scents made her feel like she was part of the customs that kept her close to her roots, but not tonight. Her mind was spinning with her desire to help Edward.

"I'm not hungry, Mama," she said. "I think I'll jump in the shower and take a walk. I'm sure I'll want leftovers later."

"Take a walk where?" Rosa asked. "It will be dark in an hour or so. A young lady shouldn't be out alone in the dark walking."

"Mama, I assure you I can take care of myself," Monica said. "I'm a police detective, remember?"

"Bah!" Rosa said. "You are no match for a grown man who might have intentions. Come, sit. Eat your dinner."

"I'll be fine, Mama," Monica repeated. Monica had told her mother many times that they lived in a safe place where crime statistics were low. This area of the Keys was the spot Juan had chosen for his family, where he'd had Monica promise she would keep them. "Please see that Emilio takes a bath and goes to bed by eight," she added.

Without waiting for her mother's reply, Monica hustled to the bathroom and started the water in the shower. Still, she heard her mother's grumbles in Spanish coming from the next room. Her Aunt Lucy tried to reason with her. "She's a young girl, Rosa. Let her go out sometimes. She needs to be with people her own age."

Thank you, Aunt Lucy, Monica thought as she scrubbed away the day's sweat. After a few minutes, she dried off and relished the feel of being clean and cool again. She dressed in a T-shirt, shorts and casual sandals, and stuck a few dollars into her pocket. She noticed the conversation at the dining table was pleasant and animated, so she quietly snuck out the front door.

With the sun going down, the air outside was beautiful. A typical, tropical Keys evening, certainly too perfect to have opted to use her car for the short distance. Monica took several deep breaths and walked down the main highway that traversed the entire distance of the Keys—from Key Largo in the Upper Keys, through the Middle Keys, where Monica lived, and ending in Key West.

She felt free, refreshed and alive. Not that she didn't love her family. She did. She loved her mama, her aunt and uncle, her cousins and, probably most of all, her nephew, Emilio. But for her brother... She'd lost respect for Miguel when he claimed he couldn't care for the boy and left him in Monica's hands. Although, only a few days later, Monica had realized the blessing Miguel had given her. Now her life was about providing for the three of them, as they lived in the small cinder-block house that Monica rented from a Sweet Pine native. And it was about watching Emilio grow up to be a fine man, like his grandfather had been.

After a half mile, the neon lights of Tarpon Joe's Bar and Grill drew her in. Monica would have something icy cold to wash away the trials of the day. She didn't drink much, realizing the foolishness of an officer driving an automobile after even one alcoholic beverage. But tonight she was walking and pondering the details of a difficult case. A beer would taste good.

The restaurant wasn't crowded this Sunday evening. Just a few locals usually found at the popular watering hole for most Sweet Pine residents. It was a welcoming kind of bar. The original owner, Joe Petrusky, had passed on almost twenty years ago. The new owner, Morris Goldstein, had kept the name Tarpon Joe's. A wise business decision, Monica had always thought.

She spoke to the people she knew, found a seat at the end of the bar and ordered a light beer.

When she'd had a few sips of her brew, she heard the front door open. Glancing back, she was shocked to see Edward Smith step into the bar. She had never seen him at Tarpon Joe's before, but then, she rarely saw him anywhere on the island. His routine seemed to be to visit his father without mingling with folks. Tonight, he looked tired but relaxed in shorts and a loose-fitting shirt with a palm-tree print. Monica quickly looked away. She assumed that Edward was here for a few moments' escape from the sadness that filled his home. She wouldn't interfere with his efforts to find solace in this difficult time.

She took another sip of beer, kept her head down and pretended to be occupied with the menu. But when the bar stool next to her scraped on the wood floor, she looked over.

"Is this seat taken?" Edward asked her.

CHAPTER FOUR

"UH...NO," MONICA REPLIED. "Have a seat."

"At first I didn't know if it was you or not," Edward said. "I mean, you look quite different when you're not in uniform."

That was an understatement. When he came into the watering hole, he'd taken a quick look around and decided to sit at the bar. That was when he saw the petite lady with the beautiful olive complexion and the long dark ponytail that hung past her shoulders. He thought she seemed familiar, but since he didn't know many women in the Keys, he figured her for a stranger. As he'd headed for a bar stool he'd finally gotten a good look. There was no doubt. The woman sitting by herself was Detective Monica Cortez.

Well, heck, he was here to have a beer, put the sadness and shock of the last two days into some sort of perspective—as if that was possible. Why not get closer to the lady who was deciding the fate of an investigation other officers had all but determined was closed? He hadn't come into the tavern to find conversation—in fact, his motivation was just the opposite—but he found himself drawn to her. There was something warm and approachable about Monica, especially dressed so casually in shorts and a T-shirt.

"I suppose I do look different," she said, sliding over a bit to give him room at the bar. "Obviously, I try to maintain a professional appearance when I'm on the job. But once I'm home, I'm just your typical Keys girl."

Other than her choice of casual clothes, Edward didn't think there was anything typical about her. Even without a lot of makeup she seemed to stand out in the neon glow of the bar. Her cheeks and lips were rosy, and her eyes snapped as if they held a dark mystery in their depths. And that hair... He'd had no idea that there was so much of it.

He smiled for the first time in a long while. "We've had quite a day, haven't we? I guess we both felt the need to decompress." He ordered a beer from the bartender.

"Funny, I've been coming to the Keys for years, but I've never been to this place."

He followed her gaze as she scanned the interior. Posters of fish and other aquatic creatures were tacked to the walls, along with giant catches that taxidermists had preserved for eternity. Mixed in were beer signs and framed portraits of musicians he assumed had performed on the minuscule stage in one corner of the bar. The stage was empty tonight.

The smells were typical of an established bar. Greasy food, beer, fried fish and even smoke left over from the days when the habit was allowed in public places. Now, the wooden bar was clear of ashtrays, and only lined with ketchup and vinegar bottles, as well as salt and pepper shakers.

She turned to face him. "Well, welcome to Tarpon Joe's. I suppose now you're realizing what you've missed."

"It's not the usual type of place I go to for a drink," he said. "But I like it. No one could deny the local charm." He picked up a menu. "Actually, anyplace would be preferable to the house. I couldn't stay there another minute. I felt like I was suffocating. You probably understand."

"I do. I've always admired that house. It's so beautiful, but it must seem especially gloomy tonight." She turned her beer glass in her hand. "Where do...*did* you and your father go when you went out down here?"

"We usually went to The Tender Trap in Little Scrub Key. My dad liked the seafood."

"I saw your father here a few times. I guess, since he was in the boat-and-fishing business, he wanted to hang out with the Tarpon Joe's crowd once in a while. Most everyone who comes in here is into fishing."

"Do you remember him talking to anyone in particular?" Edward asked. Maybe Tarpon Joe's was a good place to start examining the last few years of his father's life, the parts he didn't know much about.

"Not really. I know why you're asking, though. But people seemed to like him. I would be surprised if anyone in this tavern would have a motive to..." She let the rest of her sentence drop.

"That's good to know, at least." If his father had been murdered, Edward knew it was just as important to know who wouldn't

have done it as it was to know who would
have. Edward began looking at the selections
on the menu. Burgers, chicken strips, fried
grouper—just what he expected. He found
the salad choices and thought he might settle on a large spinach entrée with veggies
and cheese.

When he told Monica what he wanted, she
gave him a sympathetic look. "I can imagine you're not hungry," she said. "I couldn't
eat for days after my father died."

He shrugged. "This is one of those times
when a person has to remind himself to eat."

"Forgive me," Monica said. "I shouldn't
comment on your appetite or what you've
just been through. You're here to forget
about the events of the last days, and here I
go talking about the tragedy."

"It's okay. I'm sure there will come a
time before too long when I'll be comfortable talking about him. But it'll be a long
time before I can put the most unpleasant
aspects of his death behind me. His memorial service is planned for Tuesday evening,
and then there's the matter of his will and
personal property."

She nodded. "There are a lot of details

to take care of when someone dies. So, are you planning on staying in Sweet Pine for a while?"

"Maybe for a couple of weeks. I spoke to my supervisor in Miami and told him I needed some time. This morning, before I saw you, I took a long look around the house." He paused, remembering the hurt he'd felt viewing the things his father had cherished. Touching them, wondering about them. "I hate to admit it, but I wasn't aware that my dad had kept so much. I've never seen so many pictures and collectibles and printed material. Don't know why I hadn't noticed before."

The bartender stepped up to take his order.

"The spinach salad," Edward said. He hoped his appetite would return when he finished the beer.

"Fried grouper is the specialty," Monica suggested.

Edward thought a moment, then said, "Okay. I'll try it. Actually, it does sound good."

Monica smiled.

"I hate to eat alone…" he said.

She hesitated a moment, but then ordered the shrimp dinner.

When the bartender walked away, a customer came up behind Monica's bar stool. He was a gruff-looking guy in denim shorts and a T-shirt with the sleeves cut off. Edward wondered what he did for a living.

"Hey there, Monica," the man said before giving Edward a critical look. "What's going on? You slumming it tonight?"

"If I were slumming it, Hank, I'd be sitting with you instead."

The man hooted his appreciation of her candor. "One of these nights, sweetheart, you'll give me a shot. Just wait and see." After spearing Edward with one last look, the man wandered toward the bathrooms.

Monica took a sip of beer, turned to Edward and said, "And that was another example of Tarpon Joe's specialties."

"Funny," Edward said, admiring how she'd handled the guy. "I don't remember too many customers at Smitty's who looked like him. Most of our clientele came from Miami and points north."

"The classier crowd, eh?"

"I don't know about that. I guess most of

them looked at fishing as an adventure, not as a means to put food on the table."

"We have folks like that on Sweet Pine—people who depend on fishing for their livelihood. They provide catches for the local restaurants, as well as food for themselves."

Edward took a swallow of his beer. "Nothing wrong with that. Honest living. Guess I should ask you the question that's been on my mind all day."

"You want to know about the pictures Carl took, right? And his conclusion about the carving in the wood piling?"

Edward nodded.

"Neither of us could make any sense of the carving. It was almost a straight line, about three inches long. Looks like it had been gouged from top to bottom. But it was fresh. I'd say carved within the last few days."

"So that leads you to believe that Dad might have carved it in the moments before he died?"

"Very possibly. I wish I knew what he was trying to indicate by the line. It's not really much to go on."

Edward gave her a hard look. "Could it have been an initial? If it was, that means he was trying to give us a clue about who killed him."

"You're getting ahead of yourself, Edward." She spoke gently. "There is still no other evidence that the judge was murdered. Unless you've come up with someone who might have had a motive to kill him and his name begins with a letter that has a straight line. Your father, if he did carve that line, might have been trying to say 'help' or any number of other things."

"Or it could have been an initial," he repeated. Now was as good a time as any to question her about her brother. He'd been wondering about Miguel Cortez since the funeral director told him of the man's existence and his estrangement from his family. "Mind if I ask you something?"

"Of course not."

"Why didn't you tell me about your brother?"

"My brother?"

"Yeah. You mentioned your mother who lives with you and a boy named Emilio that you referred to as your nephew. Unless you have other siblings, I'm assuming that the boy is your brother's, and I'm curious about why you didn't mention Miguel earlier."

"How did you hear about Miguel? He's been gone from Sweet Pine for a long time. No one even talks about him much anymore."

He told her about the conversation with Gonzalez.

She stared into her glass, but a slight twitch of her eyes told him that his question had touched a nerve. "There's no reason to bring up Miguel here," she said. "We were talking about you and your father. My brother's been in the Miami area for five years. I never even see him."

That information was consistent with what Gonzalez had relayed to him. "But you're raising his son?"

"That's right." She paused just as the bartender set their food in front of them.

Edward unwrapped his utensils from a tightly wound napkin. "Actually, Monica, I do think there's a reason to mention Miguel."

"Oh, what's that?"

"You hinted that your father might have had a grudge against my father, something about a promise not kept."

She had speared a shrimp but refrained

from taking the fork to her mouth. She gave him an intense stare. "The point I was trying to make was that my father was *not* the kind to hold a grudge. I told you he was close to your father, well-liked—"

"I remember and I believe you. But if the fortunes of the Cortez family were tied to my father giving part of the marina to Juan, maybe someone else related had a reason to seek revenge for what they might have seen as an injustice."

"My brother? You're suggesting that my brother might have killed your father?"

She asked the question calmly, her expression calculating the logic of his words. There was no hint of upset or hurt in her voice. Either she was a cop in control, or she'd thought the same thing herself. "How did he accomplish this, Edward? There wasn't a mark on the judge's body, and the only weapon we know of at the scene, a pocket-knife, belonged to your father.

"And besides," she added, "the official conclusion is that the death was an accident."

"I know that, but I'm just spitballing here. As a homicide investigator, don't you want information on every theory out there?"

"Every *reasonable* theory," she said. "The notion that my brother would have waited five years to exact revenge for our dad, and then snuck into Sweet Pine to kill your father is not what I would call reasonable."

"Emotional crimes are not often reasonable, Monica."

"And they usually don't take years to concoct, Edward."

He didn't want to argue with her. He knew the criminal mind, and she knew investigative tactics. They weren't enemies. They should work together. Edward just wanted to eliminate Miguel as a suspect. Monica should be in favor of that. "You wouldn't mind if I talked to him, would you?" he asked.

If he thought his request would rattle her, he was wrong. She continued eating her dinner. After a few bites, she said, "Under whose authority would you be conducting this interrogation? I mean, you're not a cop. At least, I don't think you are. Based on appearances, you're a guy with a psychology degree living in Miami, most likely treating patients in an office. What do you know about questioning anyone about a possible murder?"

He had to tread carefully. He didn't want

her to think he was overstepping her. But his doctorate was in criminal psychology. He was an expert in unraveling the criminal mind. Or, he should be. "I know more than you might think. I'm employed by Miami-Dade County in the criminal-investigations department."

Her eyes widened. "So you are a cop?"

"Nope. I'm a criminal psychologist. I often question suspects to try and determine the truth of their statements and to come up with motives, if they exist. When I'm not at Miami PD, I counsel at the holding facilities. Suspects and convicted criminals make up the majority of my social circle these days. I'd really like to talk to Miguel."

She ordered another beer. Several minutes passed before she said, "I see."

"My intent to speak with your brother wouldn't be to accuse him of something. As a matter of fact, I'm hoping to eliminate him as a suspect. Some good does come out of my conversations with these guys," he said. "Not everyone I talk to goes to jail, Monica, or deserves to."

He waited while the bartender set down

her beer. When asked if he wanted another, he declined.

Edward finished his meal while Monica nursed her second beer. "What do you say, Monica?" he finally asked. "May I have your permission to talk to your brother?"

"It's not easy to reach him," she said. She pushed back her plate. "I don't even know his address. Are you willing to meet with him in Miami?"

"I'd rather talk to him here in town. Better yet, at my Dad's. Body language can be as important as words when a suspect is questioned at the scene of the crime. Perhaps your sheriff's department could request that he come to Sweet Pine since he knew my father. It's the truth, after all. Just tell him you're questioning everyone who came into contact with William Smith. That's also true."

"I know what to say, Edward."

"Great. Sure you do." He hoped she could tell that he appreciated the favor she'd just granted him. He liked her. She was fair, and he wanted her to feel the same about him. "We're working together on this, Monica. We both want to uncover what happened."

"And I hope we do, Edward, but I don't think it will come from the mouth of Miguel Cortez. He didn't kill your father. I would swear to that. But he is a liar and he's good at it. You should know that."

She pulled a few dollars from her pocket and started to set them on the bar.

"I'll get this," Edward said.

Those dark eyes flashed again. "No, you won't."

"But I want to."

"My meal, I'm paying." She set down the money and he didn't argue.

"Are you leaving now?"

"Yep. Got a half-mile walk up the road to my house."

"I walked from Dad's house. I could use more exercise. I'll walk you back."

"That's not necessary. Besides, the Judge's house is in the opposite direction. And I don't need a protector."

"I'm sure you don't. But I've already told you that I don't want to go home. Besides, I've kept you out longer than you were probably planning, and I intend to see you home. Let me do this, Monica."

She gave him a look that said she understood his gallantry was basically about him not wanting to go back to the Judge's house. She shrugged and headed for the door. Edward dropped a few bills on top of hers and followed.

CHAPTER FIVE

MONICA WASN'T AFRAID of the dark. But this lonely stretch of Highway 1 was about as dark as any patch of road anywhere. A few side lanes showed lights from a smattering of houses and trailers, but mostly this area was sparsely inhabited. Admittedly, she was glad to have some company.

She glanced at Edward's profile. Strong jaw, nicely shaped nose, just enough flesh in his cheeks to make him look healthy. He walked with his hands in his pockets, a slow, steady pace, and seemed to be keeping her shorter strides in mind.

After a minute or so he said, "Something really strange happened today."

"Isn't that more or less the story of your life lately?"

"You're right about that. Tragedy followed by a freakish sort of surprise, but this is the opposite of losing a family member.

A young woman showed up at the marina today. I've never seen her before." He took a deep breath. "She claims to be my sister."

Monica stopped in midstride, then lightly touched Edward's elbow. "No kidding? That is weird. Was she on the level? I mean, she showed up two days after your father died. Did she claim any connection to the judge?"

"I know what you're thinking," he said. "I thought the same thing, that she was after an inheritance, might try to convince me she was related to my father. But she was surprised to learn that my dad had died. And it was clear she didn't know him."

"So, she is related to your biological father?"

"No. She said we have the same mother, not that it's anything to brag about."

"Interesting." Monica suddenly felt very protective of Edward and didn't want anyone to take advantage of him while he was grieving. Grief made a person vulnerable to all types. "Do you remember her at all?"

"No. I was put into foster care at the age of three. This lady and her twin sister were born at the same time my mother gave me up and were immediately put up for adoption themselves. To my knowledge I never lived in the same house with them."

"Her *twin*? You have two sisters?"

"I guess."

"And she expects you to take her word for this?"

"Maybe she expected me to, Monica, but I wouldn't do that."

"Right. Okay, you're a smart guy, I get it. I hate to be suspicious of people's motives, but I can't help it. You should be careful. She still might have an angle she's working to get something from you."

"She had a few facts that check out. And she's willing to submit to a DNA test."

That was a good sign. "Then do it," Monica encouraged. "You can't be too careful. Because the timing is just so coincidental."

He nodded. "I almost hope she's wrong about everything. This sounds odd, but after just losing the only family I ever had, I'm not too keen on taking on any new ones, even if she is on the level. I need some time to sort out everything with my father. I can't even imagine adjusting to a sibling relationship with…complete strangers."

"I absolutely understand," Monica said.

"Is she sticking around Sweet Pine for a while? I can keep an eye on her."

"Don't do that. She doesn't seem threatening. I'm sure she's just visiting."

"Do you mind if I talk to her, though?" Monica asked.

"Why would you talk to her?"

She gave him a little smile. "Besides the fact that I don't want anyone taking advantage of you, it's only fair, isn't it? You're talking to my brother, so…"

He laughed, a low, husky sound from deep in his throat. She liked the sound. And she was happy to learn he could still laugh.

"I can handle talking to your brother," he said. "But thanks for the offer."

"Hey, you're an expert in criminal minds, body language, all that stuff. Call me if you need me, though."

She slowed and came to a stop. "This is it. I live up this lane. First house."

"I'll walk you the rest of the way."

She wondered what he would think of her pale yellow modest rental house. She'd worked hard to get it and worked hard every day to keep it, but compared to the judge's big old pine mini-mansion down the road, well… "That's not necessary," she said. "My mother is still up. The lights are on."

He took her elbow and turned her in the direction of the house. After a few hundred feet they were in her drive.

"Cute place," he said. "Looks like something you would have."

How could he possibly determine that? Did she look like the type who would grow morning glories and daffodils? She briefly stared at her yard, trying to see it through Edward's eyes. The porch light shone on her gardens with the various colorful blooms. One single queen palm tree shaded her bedroom window. The grass was clipped short and was a healthy green. Striped canvas awnings kept out the morning sun and added a touch of whimsy. Nine hundred square feet was hardly enough space for three people, but it was home to a loving family. Could he tell that, as well?

"Thanks," she said. "And thanks for walking me home."

"No problem. Glad to do it. Considering what I'm going back to, I wish you lived farther."

And then he took her hand in his and held

it for a few seconds. She was startled, but in a strange, pleasant way. His thumb lightly massaged her knuckles.

"Thanks for listening to me tonight," he said. "I promise not to take up so much of your time with my family saga."

"Anytime," she said. Her eyelashes fluttered as she focused on their clasped hands. "I should go in."

"Sure," he said.

"Monica!" Her mother's voice came through the screen door. "Is that you?"

Monica instantly dropped Edward's hand. "Yes, Mama. I'm coming."

"Thank the Lord," Rosa said. "I was just about to call the sheriff's office."

Monica chuckled at the absurdity of her mother's threat. "That's family for you," she said to Edward. "Think long and hard before you add a couple of sisters to your family tree."

She took a few steps toward the house.

"Monica?"

She stopped and turned back to look at Edward, who hadn't moved to leave yet.

"I'm glad I'm working with you," he said. "I'm sorry that we share the same sort of heartbreak—our fathers passing. I feel comforted since you understand what it means."

She nodded. "I do. Get some rest, Edward. Tomorrow will be a better day."

A LOUD BANGING on the front door awakened Edward from the first sound sleep he'd had in two nights. "What the...?"

He sat up in bed, tried to glimpse outside his window, which showed the barest signs of daylight. "Hang on," he called. "Be right there!"

He threw a T-shirt over his head and stumbled downstairs in his comfy pants and bare feet. When he reached the first floor, he saw his visitor through the open front window. He recognized the guy his dad had hired to help at the marina. "What are you doing here, A.J.?" he muttered to himself.

The young man gave a brief wave through the glass. "Hey, there, Edward. Thought you might want to open up today."

A. J. McGinnis had worked for Edward's father for over a year. The judge's previous assistant had taken a higher paying job in Key West with a charter fishing boat company. Desperate to find a replacement out of the limited Sweet Pine labor pool, William had hired A.J. And despite the fact that A.J.'s language appeared to have gotten fouler and his clothes greasier in spite of his employment at Smitty's, he showed up for work every day. Bottom line, he was a good boat mechanic and a dependable employee. Between the two of them, and Edward when he was around, the judge managed to keep his business running and boats rented.

Edward opened the door. "I'm not renting anything until after the funeral," he explained.

"But we've got bookings today," A.J. said. "Just a few, but the folks are coming all the way from Homestead."

"I called them and canceled. Everyone expressed their condolences and rebooked for a couple of weeks from now. There were no hard feelings." Except for A.J., Edward thought. The young guy would lose tips today. "I'm sorry I forgot to let you know."

The stark reality of the moment made Edward realize that he'd have to get someone to come in and manage Smitty's. Maybe A.J. could take care of reservations and payments, but Edward would have to train him and then find someone to do A.J.'s job. His to-do list just got longer, and he considered closing the marina for an extended period.

"That's just great for you," A.J. said. "But I was counting on working this weekend, not to mention today. I respectfully stayed away until this morning, giving you time and all, but I need the pay, Edward. This will be my third day without a salary."

Now the guy was just being insensitive. Obviously, nothing in the last couple of days had been "great" for Edward. He managed to hold his temper.

Edward knew his father paid A.J. on a daily basis. Perhaps he didn't really trust the guy to show up every time he should. Money at the end of a workday was usually a good incentive. "How much do you need, A.J.?" Edward asked.

"If you open up on Wednesday, after the judge's memorial service, a hundred bucks should do me for now." He squinted at Edward. "You are going to open up, aren't you?"

Edward had only canceled reservations through Tuesday, but he supposed it was time to think of the coming days. "I'm going to be here, anyway," Edward said. "So, yeah, plan on working Wednesday." He opened the wallet he'd left on the credenza by the door and took out five twenties.

A.J. palmed them and turned away. "See you at the service and then bright and early Wednesday," he called over his shoulder. He claimed a bicycle he must have leaned against the property fence. In a moment he was pedaling down the road, his thin, light brown ponytail flying out behind him. Edward didn't know where the man was going. Some nights, especially rainy ones, he slept in the bait house farther down the shore, unless he found someone to offer him a couch.

Edward stared at the sun rising over the water to the east. No sense going back to bed, he thought. He'd make a pot of coffee and begin the task of going through his father's belongings. A sad and arduous chore, but his father had told him that everything he owned would be left to Edward. So if Edward was going to consider selling the business and the house, he had to know every scrap of paper his father had left behind. "Just exactly what have you left me, Dad?" he asked the silent house.

Edward was onto his second cup of coffee and third trash can of miscellaneous junk from kitchen drawers and cabinets when the phone rang. He hoped the call wasn't from a potential customer. He was tired of explaining the reason they were closed. And it hurt every time he went over the cold facts.

"Smitty's In and Out," he said.

"Good morning, Edward," a soft but strong female voice said. "It's Brooke. I hope it's not too early to call."

He closed his eyes and pictured the cute blonde lady who'd insisted she was his sister. Was he really in the mood to go over her claim today? But it wasn't too early. Eight thirty was a respectable time to call. "No, it's okay," he said. "I am pretty busy, though."

"Sure, I understand," she said. "Again, I'm so sorry about your father. But I'd really like to talk to you. Just you and me this time. Jeremy is staying at the hotel."

"How much time do you need?" he said, knowing he sounded like an impatient clod. But he didn't have a lot of time. The funeral was tomorrow. The business was reopening on Wednesday. He and Monica were in the middle of an investigation. The thought of her calmed him. He wondered if she was working on the case today.

"You have to eat, don't you? How about meeting me for breakfast? There's a nice little diner a few miles north of you called Harry's. Do you know it?"

"I know it. Okay. I'll meet you there in an hour if that works for you."

"Perfect. See you then."

EDWARD ARRIVED AT Harry's Good Eats at nine thirty after an easy five-mile drive from Sweet Pine. Monday mornings were usually quiet in the Keys in the summer. Weekenders had gone home and locals were gearing up for the workweek. He wondered again what Monica was doing.

When he pulled into the parking lot he saw the same rental car that his supposed sister had arrived in yesterday. He parked a few spots away and walked to the door of the restaurant. Before going in, he spotted her in a booth. She was facing the door, her face turned slightly to look out the near window. He took a moment to study her, trying to find similarities between the two of them.

He decided that if a person was looking for details in common, it might be possible to find them. They both had blond hair, though his was darker than her sunny color. Both had natural waves, hers bound into a casual knot at the back of her head, his still slightly mussed from sleeping. And their eyes. He'd noticed the day before that hers were as blue as the bay water, probably brighter than his, but still close.

He went inside. She turned at the sound of the door, spotted him and smiled. "I'm so glad you came," she said.

"No problem," he replied, though in truth meeting her did take time from several chores he had on his list—ordering flowers for the service, finding a few pictures of his father to display and arranging for some food to be brought to the house. He didn't know how many people would come. There were still doubts in his mind as to how many friends his father had made in Sweet Pine.

Edward slid into the booth across from her. She already had a coffee mug in her hands, but he offered to buy her breakfast.

"I had a muffin with Jeremy this morning," she said. "But you go ahead."

Her mention of the football star opened up a casual line of conversation. "So how did you two meet?" he asked, and then worried that he was coming across as invasive, especially if he didn't end up being her brother.

She didn't seem to mind and told him a story about her job at a television news network in Charleston and Jeremy's attempt to become the next anchor there. "He worked hard, but to tell the truth, he had a few flaws, mostly with regard to his on-air demeanor. In the end he decided to become a sports broadcaster—" she paused, and smiled "—and to marry me. I'm becoming a wife and a mother at the same time."

"You're pregnant?" he asked.

She laughed. "No. Jeremy has two children. Their mother died in a skiing accident."

"That's rough," Edward said, all too aware of the cost of losing a parent at any age.

The waitress brought him a coffee. He mixed in a teaspoon of sugar, took a sip and tried to soothe his jangled nerves. He could be staring at his very own sister. The idea was freaky. And yet, somehow intriguing. He'd never considered that his mother had

had more children. Until the judge adopted him, Edward's life had been a party of one. As was his custom growing up, he refused to allow himself to contemplate a happy ending, family-wise.

"Tell me about your life," he said. "Were you raised in Charleston?"

She briefly filled him in on details of a life of privilege in a historic Charleston home with two loving parents. She ended with an emotional retelling of needing to find her roots. And when she discovered from their biological mother that Edward existed, she'd set about trying to locate him.

"Edward, I don't want to give you any false impressions of our biological mother. She doesn't want to have anything to do with any of us. It hurts, but that's the way it is.

"I have no interest in trying to reach out to her," he said.

"And Edward," Brooke continued, "I know you're not convinced, but I am your sister. When I saw you yesterday, I knew I'd found my brother."

"I suppose DNA and blood tests will confirm that," he said.

"Of course. We should do that. But may I ask you a question?"

"Sure."

"Does the name Jerry Miller mean anything to you?"

He almost choked on his coffee. Jerry Miller was one of the many aliases he'd used during his troubled teen years. He used a different name every time he was caught doing something illegal. "Maybe," he said.

"I know you used that name when you were brought in front of a judge. I also know you had dark hair then and the beginnings of a chin beard. You were quite adept at disguises."

Once again she was spot-on. He'd invested a lot in hair dyes back when he was in trouble. "It wasn't much of a beard," he admitted. "I was all of fifteen at the time. And it was easy to obtain a box of Just for Men."

"You were on your own then?"

"Yeah. And believe it or not, I liked it that way. No one to answer to, no rules to live by, no foster parents threatening to toss me out." He'd always said those words, but inside he faced too many lonely days. "And then I met

Judge Smith, and he convinced me that my time as 'King of the Road' was over."

"I'm sorry your life was like that," she said. "I wish I had known you then. I wish you had known my adoptive parents. Your life would have been so different."

Yeah, like her rich parents would have taken in a runaway with a record. "I don't look back, Brooke. My life began in earnest when Judge Smith took me under his wing." He nodded at her. "But maybe a new chapter is opening now."

"You believe me?"

"I still want the DNA test, but yeah, you present a convincing argument."

"I'm so glad you're willing to explore this, Edward," she said. "Tell me about your life after meeting your father?"

He told her about getting his high-school-equivalency diploma and registering at the University of Miami to study psychology. She listened as if every word he said was life-changing. That time of his life had certainly been life changing for him.

"I can't wait for you to meet my... I mean *your* sister—Camryn," she said. "We're very different, she and I. I'm the driven overachiever and she's Mother Earth. But I love her dearly and I bet you will, too. And you are uncle to two beautiful girls."

She began to give details of Camryn's life, including the mention of her husband's two boys who now called Camryn their mom. Edward held up his hand. "Maybe we should slow this down a bit," he said. "Let me adjust to one new family member at a time." He wanted to let himself believe in this fairy tale, but it was all happening so fast. And fairy tales had never been a part of his life before the judge.

"Absolutely. We'll take it slow."

He called for the check just as the door to Harry's opened and Monica walked in. She was in full working garb today—dark slacks and blue shirt, a ball cap covering that luxurious hair. She had a few pounds of equipment on her belt. She went to the cashier, spoke a few neighborly words and ordered a coffee to go. Then her gaze wandered around the restaurant and stopped when she saw Edward.

She smiled, lighting up the room and softening the stark appearance of her uniform. For just a flash, Edward remembered what she'd looked like last night, her hair in a cute ponytail, her olive skin tanned and healthy against her white shorts. And he remembered holding her hand.

She walked over to him and then focused in on Brooke. "Oh, I'm sorry to disturb you," she said. "I didn't know you were with someone."

Edward stood. "It's no problem, Monica. Can you stay a while?"

"No. I'm on duty. Just needed a little mid-morning pick-me-up."

He introduced Monica to Brooke. "This is the lady I told you about," he explained. "Looks like we might be related after all. At any rate, we're getting to know each other."

Monica gave Brooke a top-to-bottom scan. Then she held out her hand. "Wow, this is exciting for Edward."

"It definitely is for me," Brooke said. "You don't know how long I've been searching for this guy."

"And to think you found him in Sweet Pine Key."

"Yes, it's strange. I suppose it proves that one should never give up. I never knew where to look until I heard about a judge adopting him and moving to the Florida Keys. But I'm so glad we've found him."

A waitress delivered Monica's coffee to her in a cardboard cup. Monica slipped her a couple of dollars and returned her attention to Edward and Brooke. "I'll leave you two alone to catch up on the years you've missed. Nice to see you, Edward, and nice to meet you, Brooke."

Still standing, Edward said, "Wait, Monica. Mind if I talk to you for a minute?"

"Not at all."

He walked her toward the door. "I had a thought last night. It's about A.J., the local guy my father hired to work at the marina."

"What about him?" Monica asked.

"He sometimes sleeps at the bait shack on the property. If he was there on Friday night, I thought maybe he might have seen something. Might be worth talking to him."

"I agree," she said. "That's why I spoke with him this morning."

"You did?"

"I saw him riding his bicycle and I stopped him. He claims he stayed in his tent Friday night. He sometimes sets it up on the shore in a remote area of Sweet Pine. We don't bother him, though camping on the beach is a misdemeanor."

"Oh." Edward was disappointed, but not in Monica. She'd recognized a lead and followed it. "One other thing..."

"Sure."

"I'm just curious. Have you contacted your brother yet?"

"I've got the number and am planning to call him on my lunch break," she said. "I'll let you know if he agrees to be interviewed."

"Okay, thanks. I'll let you go. Talk to you later."

After Monica had left, Brooke waited for Edward to sit again. "What was that all about?"

Edward thought a moment and decided it wouldn't do any harm to tell Brooke what was going on. "Monica—or Detective Cortez—and I are working on the case involving my father's death. She's the homicide investigator for this part of the Keys."

"Homicide?" Brooke sat up straighter. "You think your father was murdered?"

"I think it's possible, but so far I'm the only one who thinks so. Everyone else down here has been quick to call his death an accident."

Her eyes narrowed. "Why is that so? And why do you disagree with them?" She smiled. "Maybe those questions are too pushy, but I'm a television-news producer. I can't help myself."

He briefly explained his concerns, then said, "At this point I mostly have a lot of questions."

Brooke reached across the table and covered Edward's hand with hers. "Oh, Edward, be careful. If there's a murderer in the area, you don't know what he could do to you."

"In fact, I do." He told his sister about his education and his position as a criminal-psychology consultant. "Believe me, I've had lots of experience with the criminal mind, and I can handle myself. But thanks for your concern."

He left a few dollars on the table and stood to leave. "I've got a long list of things to do before my dad's service tomorrow," he said.

"If you don't mind, I'd like you to add one more thing to that list."

"If I can. What?"

"Ask your detective friend if she can get

one of those official DNA kits. We might as well settle this sooner rather than later. Like you said, you don't like living in the past, and I'm looking forward to a future with you in it."

"I can do that," he said.

"One more thing…"

He waited.

"Will you include my name as a guest at the service? I'd really like to be there."

He didn't explain that there wasn't an official guest list. But if there had been, he wouldn't have minded adding her name. Yes, she'd been a complete stranger yesterday. But today, he felt differently. Albeit, he still wasn't sure about all of these people popping up in his life right now, but the first one he'd met had come across as legit, and more. Besides, it might be nice to have a sister…or two.

"Sure. Fisherman's Chapel is about ten miles south of here. Six thirty."

"I'll be there," she said.

CHAPTER SIX

MONICA DROVE TO a local beach for her lunch break. She needed a few moments to compose herself, and a view of the turquoise water usually did that for her.

The parking lot was nearly empty, so she chose a spot, left the air conditioner on in her car and took out the sandwich she'd brought from home this morning. Before she opened the plastic container, she thought about her reaction at seeing Edward with a young woman this morning. Not just any woman— a classy, well-dressed, pretty woman.

She'd been surprised—no, shocked—to see him sitting in a booth with her. After all, just the night before, Edward had held her hand and looked into her eyes. She'd felt they connected somehow, but not romantically, exactly. She'd only known him for less than a day. But an emotional jolt had passed between them. The sensation had left Monica restless and wondering. Had Edward felt it, too? Surely a man as handsome, educated and sophisticated as Edward seemed to be had experienced many such jolts in his life. The feeling was new to Monica.

Monica wouldn't have approached them in the diner, but once her eyes had met Edward's, she had to go over and speak to him. When he introduced the woman as his sister, the one he'd told Monica about the night before, her heartbeat had slowed to a normal rhythm and her breathing returned to normal. Silly. She and Edward were just acquaintances, two people searching for the truth.

Monica dated…enough. She'd never found the right man for her, but she hadn't given up hope. Her goal with regard to finding a man she could spend her life with was complicated by having Emilio in her care. The right man for her had to be the right man for Emilio, too. So Monica never allowed her own needs, or any thought of a lonely future, to influence her relationships. When the right guy came along, she would just know. And one day was certainly not enough time to start thinking about having Edward in her life.

She turned her thoughts to Emilio, so she took her cell phone from her pocket and punched in the speed-dial number for her brother. She spoke to Miguel on occasion, maybe six times a year since he'd left his son with her and their mother. Sometimes she had a question for Miguel. Sometimes he called to see how his son was doing—not to say he was coming to visit, though. That was just fine with Monica. Emilio knew he had a father who lived in another city, but so far he hadn't asked many questions about this stranger who never showed up in his life. Monica had answers prepared for when he did.

After four rings, Miguel answered in a sleepy voice. "Mon, is this you?"

"Yes, it's me. How are you, Miguel?"

"I'm okay. Still working in the body shop, if that's why you called. You need money? I don't have much extra right now."

"No. We're fine." He sometimes asked this. She'd never taken any from him so far and didn't intend to in the future. Selfishly, she didn't want him to have ties to Emilio, especially monetary ones.

"The kid okay?"

"He's great. Enjoying summer camp."

Miguel yawned. "So why did you call? Mama okay?"

"She is, but I have to tell you something." She paused. Miguel remained silent. "There was an unexpected death in Sweet Pine a few days ago."

"No kidding? You doing some real police work now, eh, Mon? Who was it?"

"Judge Smith—you remember, the man who owned the marina?"

Several uncomfortable seconds passed until Miguel finally processed what she'd said. "How could I forget? He screwed our father out of a future. No big loss if somebody finally did the old guy in."

"Preliminary findings point to an accidental death," she said. "But the judge's son suspects foul play. He's asked me to investigate."

"What does that have to do with me?"

"Nothing. At least, that's what I want to believe."

"*Want* to believe?" Miguel's voice rose. He was obviously waking up enough to listen intently. "What does that mean?"

"The son, his name is Edward, knows about the judge's promise to our father. He also knows the promise was never kept."

"He should know it," Miguel said. "Maybe he will do something to make it right."

"That's not the point, Miguel. The promise was made to our father, not us." She decided to tell Miguel the whole truth. He had a right to know. "The man is compiling a list of suspects," she said. "Anyone who might have had a grudge against the judge."

"Hope his pen doesn't run out of ink. Could be a long list. As far as I'm concerned, Smitty was a class-A jerk—"

"I'd advise you to keep such opinions to yourself, Miguel. You sound like you did have a grudge against William Smith. Anyway, the son wants to talk to you."

"Is this guy a cop?"

"No, he isn't. He's just wanting to get to the truth."

"So exactly how does this guy know about my feelings, Mon? You tell him?"

"I mentioned it, yes. It's no secret. You were only too happy to tell everyone you met how you felt about the judge."

"That was a long time ago, Monica. It's been years since I was in town. If I was going to off the judge, I would have done it before now."

"I'm not sure there's a time limit on the kind of hatred you felt for Judge Smith," Monica said. "At any rate, Edward wants to talk to you, and I think you should plan to come down here and answer a few questions. I'm confident this matter can be cleared up if you just speak to Edward."

Miguel chuckled with bitter sarcasm. "Thanks, but I'll pass."

"That would be a mistake, Miguel. One day out of your life and you can be eliminated as a suspect. Otherwise Edward will track you down in Miami, maybe even come to the body shop. You don't want that, do you?"

"Sounds to me like this friend of yours is going to a lot of trouble...and yet you say he's not a cop."

"Anyone would. The judge was his father."

"I didn't kill the judge," Miguel said.

"I don't think you did."

Miguel breathed deeply a couple of times while Monica waited for him to make the right decision.

"Thanks for that, anyway, Mon."

"So you'll come?"

"Looks like you've roped me into it.

Thursday is my day off. I can be there about ten o'clock. I'll give this guy an hour and then I'm out of there."

"Okay. That's fair."

"Maybe I'll see Mama and the kid while I'm in town," he said.

"You want to see Emilio?" Monica took a deep breath and tried to remain calm. He hadn't seen his son since he'd dropped off the infant in Sweet Pine. Deep down, Monica hoped her brother would change his mind, but would that be fair to Emilio? Maybe Emilio should meet his father and have at least a visiting relationship with him. One thing was for certain—she would be present when they finally met for the first time.

"Yeah, sure," Miguel said. "I'd like to see Mama, too. I'll stop at your place when I get to Sweet Pine, before this interview."

"Emilio is in camp, but I can keep him home that day." She made a mental note to take Thursday off from work. She wasn't going to be absent from the house when Miguel showed up. Maybe he'd made a change in his life. A couple of years in the Dade Correctional Institution should have changed him, rehabilitated him. Maybe his years of stealing cars and stripping them at a Key Largo chop shop had taught him a skill, one that he was now using at the legitimate body shop.

On the other hand, maybe Miguel hadn't changed at all. She would know in just a few minutes on Thursday if he was still the self-centered hothead he'd always been. One thing she didn't ever want to consider was Miguel deciding to take back his son. She refused to picture Emilio in that kind of environment. Wait. No, that would never happen. A child was a responsibility and Miguel avoided responsibility at all costs.

Monica disconnected with Miguel and called Edward.

"Hi, Monica," Edward said. His tone was hopeful. "What's up?"

"My brother will be coming here on Thursday and he's agreed to talk to you." She let the news sink in, then added, "For what it's worth, Edward, I don't think my brother had anything to do with your father's death."

"You should stand behind him, if you can," Edward said. "He's your brother. For your sake I hope you're right. I hope I can agree with you that Miguel is innocent."

"He should be at the marina by noon," she said.

"Okay. Thanks for doing this, Monica. By the way, what did you think of my half sister?"

"She seems nice," Monica said. "And again, for what it's worth, she seemed like she could be legit. You should give her a chance."

"That's what I decided, too," he said. "She and her fiancé are coming to the service tomorrow night. That reminds me…are you coming?"

"Planning to."

"Great. Any chance you could bring a DNA test kit?"

"Uh…okay."

"Thanks. I appreciate you're coming to the funeral. I'm not saying we'll uncover any clues about the people who attend, but it would be nice to have two investigative minds there."

"Just what you need, Edward, a working funeral."

"Yeah, I know, but maybe it will be therapeutic. I need something to occupy my mind. These last few days have been tough."

"My mother and I are both coming," Monica said.

"You'll come to the chapel and back to the house later?"

"Yes. That's fine."

"I've got about a hundred things to do between now and tomorrow night," he said. "But it's good to be busy, even if all my errands are directed toward saying a final farewell to my dad. I'll look forward to seeing you again, Monica. You could be the only bright spot in an otherwise gloomy evening."

"See you then." Monica disconnected, packed up her sandwich container and backed out of the parking spot. Edward's last comment had taken some of the sting from having to speak to her brother. She'd head to the sheriff's department now and see if Forensics had come up with a report on that pocketknife yet.

By 6:00 p.m. the following night, the food Edward had ordered for after the service had arrived, and he was making final arrangements for the people who showed up at the house. He'd told folks in Sweet Pine to tell anyone who might have known his dad about the service, but he had no idea if anyone would come. He hoped the dining-room table in his father's house could support the weight of several large baking dishes and numerous appetizer platters. Better to have too much than too little, he concluded, knowing that this gathering was also a chance for him to get a better sense of the local residents who might show up.

Besides the investigation he was quietly conducting, he wanted people to come and pay their respects. In the last few years Edward hadn't spent a lot of time with his dad, and he reasoned that he would feel more at peace about his dad's life here if he'd had friends.

"Everything looks fine," he told the representative from a local restaurant. "Please come back around ten to pick up your supplies."

Edward headed the five miles down the road to the Fisherman's Chapel and arrived well before six thirty. A few people had already gathered in the parlor. Edward walked past them to the open casket. He hadn't wanted the lid to be raised, but Raul Gonzalez convinced him that this was a tradition in the Keys. Edward went up to the coffin and took a last long look at the man who had changed his life. He'd known this phase would be difficult, however, seeing his father like this—pale and unnatural-looking—was harder than he thought it would be. After just a minute, he walked away to introduce himself to the assembled guests.

Gonzalez stayed close by his side and filled in details about people as they came into the chapel. "This is the handyman many folks in the Keys hire to do assorted jobs," he said of a young, burly fellow. "I assume your father hired him, as well."

He went on to tell Edward about the supermarket manager, the local postman and several owners of retail establishments. Edward tried to remember names so he could have a conversation with each person before the night was over.

In the back of his mind was the constant thought that one of these people might have killed his father. If so, Edward was trained to uncover motives.

His father's marina employee, A.J., was the first person Edward immediately recognized. A.J. brought his bicycle into the chapel, claiming that he couldn't trust "these people on Sweet Pine" not to steal it. To his credit, A.J. had combed his hair and cleaned his beard. He had on a decent shirt with conch shells printed on it, nice shorts and leather sandals.

Brooke and Jeremy arrived just before six thirty. She came immediately to Edward and wrapped him in a warm hug. "How are you doing?" she asked.

"Okay, I guess." Confiding his feelings to this woman, as nice as she was, wasn't easy. He glanced at the door again, hoping to see Monica come in. After a moment, he said, "I got the DNA kits from my detective friend," he told Brooke. "She left them at my house this afternoon."

"Great. I'll follow instructions and leave my kit with you so you can handle the followup. I assume you'll be more comfortable doing that than having me take them back to Charleston. This way the results will come directly to you."

She smiled at him warmly. "I can't say it enough. I'm certain that you're my brother and I can't wait for you to meet our sister and all the children. I guarantee you'll be greeted with love, Edward."

Edward thanked her, but couldn't wrap his mind around meeting another sister and numerous kids. "I have to get through these next few days first," he said. "But maybe soon."

"Do you still think your father was murdered?" she asked quietly.

"I do," he said. "Though I'm probably the only one around here that thinks so."

She touched his arm. "Please be careful, Edward. I hate to think of you associating with anyone who would do such a thing. I want you in my life for many years to come."

Jeremy expressed his condolences and he and Brooke took seats in the parlor.

And then the Cortez women entered. Rosa Cortez, Monica's mother, was first. She wore a long black skirt and white blouse, and a fine lace mantilla over her dark hair. Monica walked behind her and nearly took Edward's breath away. She was dressed in a sleeveless, knee-length black dress with a high round collar and flared skirt. Her hair was pulled back and flowed past her shoulders. A simple moonstone and silver pendant hung against her chest. She was so unlike the no-nonsense police detective he'd met and more like an elegant lady going to a big theater opening.

So many sides to this woman, Edward thought. The serious officer in uniform, the sun-kissed Keys gal in shorts and a T-shirt, and now this—a woman who burned a new and powerful image into his mind with worldly beauty. He didn't wonder which Monica he preferred. He liked them all.

Rosa approached him first. "Oh, my poor *querido*, I am so sorry for your loss. I did not know your father well, but he and my husband were once close. This is a sad day for sure."

Edward smiled at her reference to him as a small boy. He had not been called a boy for more than thirty years. Maybe he never had. Running away from one foster home after another, and later learning to survive in a detention center, matured a person quickly. He was practically a man when Judge Smith took him in.

"If there is anything I can do…" Rosa said.

"No, thank you. I'm glad you came to-night."

She walked to the casket, kneeled in front and made the sign of the cross. Her lips moved, and Edward assumed she was saying a prayer for the man she could believe had cheated her husband.

Monica came up to him next. She placed her hand on his upper arm. "How are you holding up?" she asked.

"I'm okay. Just want to get this over with."

She gave him a smile of encouragement and the dimly lit room seemed to glow with the light of her compassion. "Some people believe we need these formal services to say goodbye to the dead," she said. "I'm not convinced. I preferred to say goodbye to my father in quiet, more personal ways."

Edward didn't need pageantry, either. He had said goodbye to his father in the solace of the home they had spent time in, in his father's library among all his books, on the porch where he spent his evenings. His goodbyes were almost finished now. He had other important work to do.

"Thank you for coming, Monica," he said.

"I don't mean to take advantage of you after hours, but…"

"Don't be silly. I'll be doing exactly what you are doing, looking at the people here, talking to them, trying to uncover some little clue, no matter how small."

"Will you stay at the house after everyone leaves? Maybe we can compare notes."

"Of course. I'll just run Mama home and come back. We'll talk as long as you like."

At this moment, surrounded by strangers, Edward had the sense that talking to Monica about anything for hours, days, even longer, would not be enough. He hardly knew her, but she had been, and still was, an anchor during this troubling time.

The service was short and simple. Edward and Raul were the only people in the family row of chairs. Edward gave the eulogy, which seemed well-received. A few others spoke of the judge's kindness and generosity to people who lived on the Key. Some said they would miss him. And then Edward invited everyone to his home. Of the fifty or so people who had attended, all said they would come. Edward waited until they had all left. He walked Rosa and Monica outside, and then returned to the coffin to say a final goodbye.

His words were only a quickly spoken expression of what he was feeling, but they came from his heart and soul. "I will miss you, Dad. I loved you, and thank you for allowing me to be your son. I promise I'll get to the bottom of what's happened. I won't stop until I find the answers." He touched the smooth wood at the side of the coffin. "Just rest, Dad. I will never forget you or my promise tonight." He turned and left the parlor knowing his father would be buried in the Middle Keys Cemetery, a spot his dad would have liked.

In the parking lot, Monica stopped Edward and spoke softly. "Are you okay?"

"I think I will be," he said.

"I hope you find answers, some closure for all of this."

"I hope so, too," Edward said, wondering how her thoughts had so closely mirrored his in the chapel. "And, Monica, thank you so much for all you've done. Coming tonight, arranging the interview with your brother."

"Edward?" She looked into his eyes and slowly shook her head. "Really, Miguel didn't do this. I understand why you want to talk to him, but I'd like him to leave Sweet Pine as soon as possible. My brother isn't a good man. I don't hold any illusions about that. But he gave me Emilio to raise and keeping the two of them as far apart as possible has been my main goal for a long time. Now, they're going to meet, and I won't rest until Miguel is on his way back to Miami."

She spoke with such passion that Edward was taken aback.

"Miguel is going to see his son?"

"He has asked to, not that I want it to happen. But I can hardly keep him from seeing his family. I'll take the day off so I can be at the house the whole time."

She was suddenly in police mode, making plans, being protective of her family, and Edward had to respect her desire. But he wondered. What had Miguel done to this family?

CHAPTER SEVEN

MONICA DROVE HER mother home around ten o'clock. "Edward is a nice man, 'Nica," Rosa said in the car. "And a gentleman. He walked you home the other night. A mother notices such things. What do you think of him?"

"The same as you, Mama. Edward is a nice man. But don't let one walk home lead you to believe in a future that doesn't exist."

"Bah. It could exist, 'Nica. I saw how he looked at you tonight. He finds you pretty. If you dressed more often like…"

"I'm a police detective, Mama. I don't start my days thinking about which pretty dress to put on."

Rosa stared at her hands clasped in her lap. "That's for the daytime, 'Nica. I'm talking about when you're not working. You don't have many pretty dresses. Spend a little money on yourself, *hija*. Buy pretty things, maybe some jewelry."

Monica sighed. "I will, Mama. Soon. Please don't worry about me. When the right man comes along, I'll know it. And if he doesn't, that'll be just fine, too. I have you and Emilio. I'm happy."

"I already had two children when I was your age, Monica. I was married to a wonderful man. I only want the same for you." She reached across the front seat of the car and twisted a strand of Monica's hair around her finger. "Sometimes I don't think you know how lovely you are, 'Nica. Beautiful inside and out. So you should think about settling down with the right man, sometimes I fear you wouldn't even know if he came along."

Monica smiled at her mother. "You're beautiful, too, Mama, and I'm not worried."

Rosa blushed. "You always know what to say."

They pulled into the driveway, and Rosa got out of the car. "Lucy and Horatio will be glad I'm home," she said. "I hope Emi wasn't any trouble."

"Get some sleep, Mama," Monica said through her lowered window. "I'll be home late. Edward and I have to talk."

Rosa gave her a sly look. "That's all? More talk?"

Monica closed up her window. "Good night, Mama!" she called out and reversed onto the street with a smile on her face. Family traditions affected her life in so many ways. Rosa believed that a woman had to be married to be happy and complete. She had to have children. A career was secondary. Monica knew differently.

But then Monica's thoughts landed on Sunday night, when a nice gentleman had walked her home and held her hand. Monica grinned. It wouldn't be so bad if they did more than talk, but she couldn't consider getting romantically involved now. Edward was grieving. She had promised to help him. Still, she hadn't gone inside her house and changed into shorts and sandals. She drove back to Edward's in her best black dress.

When she was almost at the marina, Monica glanced in her rearview mirror. Okay, she was pretty enough, she supposed. But Edward was a man for whom Sweet Pine Key was an occasional weekend away from the city. Monica had never really been interested in Miami. She'd visited there a few times and knew the city was full of vibrant and varied people, but she was happy in Sweet Pine Key with her mother and Emilio.

When Monica got back to the judge's house, a truck from a local Italian restaurant was leaving. Lights were on in the first floor of the big home. She hoped Edward had had a chance to relax and put some of the sadness of the night behind him. He stepped onto the porch when she pulled up. Like her, he still wore the clothes from the funeral service—a light blue shirt and black trousers.

"I'm glad you came back," he said. "I thought maybe the stress of the evening was enough for one night."

She smiled. "Funny. I thought the same about you." She came up the three steps to stand in front of him.

"And yet here we are," he said.

"Yes. Here we are."

He took her elbow and led her to a chair under the porch light. "Did I mention how pretty you look?" he said. "How nice that dress is?"

She fingered one of the folds of the skirt. Maybe her mother was right. "Thank you,

Edward, but I doubt my wardrobe was the most important thing on your mind."

"More's the pity. It should have been. If you and I had met under different circumstances, I'm sure the evening would have been all about that dress."

Her face flushed with an unfamiliar warmth. She was grateful the light was too low to give her blush away. Edward pulled a chair close to hers and sat.

"So, I thought everything went very well," she said. "Your eulogy was perfect."

"Thanks. It was difficult to write because I never expected to be giving it so soon."

"I don't think we're ever prepared to say parting words to someone we've loved." She cleared her throat. "What about the guests tonight? Did you have enough opportunity to talk to them?"

"Yes. Having everyone back here after the service gave me the chance I needed."

"And did you come to any conclusions?"

"Only that the people who came to my dad's service seemed to admire him. Many of them spoke about his contributions to the community and his various charitable efforts."

"That may not help you solve a murder, but it must make you feel good to know he was respected."

"It does. What about you? Did you uncover any clues that would support my theory?"

"I didn't. But then I already know everyone here. I didn't expect to discover any surprises. You may have to face it, Edward. That your father's death was very likely accidental. I know it's not what you want to believe…"

He gave her an earnest stare. "I *can't* believe it, Monica. My dad was agile, smart, steady on his feet. I would have noticed if his faculties were diminished in any way. Darn it, Monica, he didn't just fall off that dock and not even try to save himself."

Edward was silent for a moment. "I have something I want to show you," he said.

"Okay. What is it?"

He stood. "I'll be right back. It's in the house." He looked down at her. "I don't know about you, but I could go for a glass of wine."

"Sounds nice," she said. "Maybe just the one."

He returned with an open bottle and two glasses. After setting them on a table, he poured a few fingers of red liquid into each glass. He handed Monica one glass and tipped the other toward her. "Thanks for your help," he said and clinked his glass against hers.

When they'd both taken a sip, he took an envelope out of his back pocket.

"Before you show me whatever that is," Monica said, "I want to clear up any issues about the pocketknife we found. Forensics was able to discern a few smudged fingerprints. As we assumed, they all belonged to your father. He was definitely the last person to touch that knife."

"Pretty much what we thought," Edward agreed.

Monica took another sip of wine. She enjoyed a nice red vintage once in a while. This bottle was especially fruity and semi-sweet. She settled back in her chair.

Edward took a piece of paper from the envelope. "I found this among some things in my father's desk." After unfolding the paper, he handed it to Monica. She set down her wineglass and read the document.

At first she experienced the same pangs of loss and loneliness she always felt when reminded of her father. His name jumped out at her in all three paragraphs of the letter. It was written by the judge six years before—a year before her father died. The signature at the bottom said Judge William Smith, but it wasn't notarized.

"Then it's true," she said. "The judge did promise part of the marina to my father."

"More than you even guessed," Edward confirmed. "Twenty per cent, offered to make sure your father would stay on at Smitty's. My dad obviously recognized Juan's value to the ongoing success of the business."

The paper shook slightly in her hand. "I wonder if my father knew about this, about the percentage, I mean. He would have been so grateful. My hunch is that the judge never had the opportunity to tell him."

"That's possible. He might have been waiting for an occasion to tell Juan, but then, your father passed away."

Monica read the letter again. "I'm glad you showed this to me, Edward. If nothing else it reaffirms my belief that the judge and my father had a close relationship."

"Since there doesn't seem to be anything formal that legally passes the property from one man to another," Edward said, "my guess is that your father died before mine had a chance to complete the transaction."

"So the promise was made, but isn't worth more than the paper it's printed on," Monica said.

"I'm sorry, Monica. Unless I can find something more binding…"

"It doesn't matter now," Monica said. "Even if your father had given this share to me or Mama, we wouldn't know what to do with twenty percent of a marina."

"I'm wondering what I'll do with it myself. We're going to open tomorrow. A.J. and I will run things for a while, but I have to get back to work in Miami, so I have to make a decision."

He took the letter from Monica and returned it to the envelope. "But this letter does make me think," he said.

She clasped her hands in her lap. "I know what you're going to say. My father could have told Miguel about this even if the document wasn't legal yet. The letter could point to my brother, provide visible proof of a motive, either revenge or greed. Miguel might have tried to convince the judge to give him part of the marina."

He nodded his head. "And my father could have denied him."

"But why would he act now?" As soon as she asked the question, she knew the answer.

"He was incarcerated for several years, right? Maybe this was his first opportunity to confront my father about the promise."

"My brother didn't do this, Edward. Miguel has his flaws, but murder? No. He wouldn't."

Edward reached over and covered Monica's hands with one of his. "I hope he didn't, Monica, really, I do. I'll know more on Thursday after I talk to him."

Monica felt her eyes burn. She wasn't a crier. Even when her father died, she'd remained stoic while the others in her family sobbed their grief. But this... "It would kill my mother to find out that Miguel did such a thing."

"Monica?"

She raised her face, looked into his eyes.

"Why are you afraid of your brother?"

HE KNEW HE was right. Monica slowly shook her head, trying to deny what he now acknowledged to be true.

"I'm not afraid of Miguel," she said,

though the twisting of her hands told him otherwise.

"Well, something's going on," Edward said. "From the moment I mentioned talking to your brother, you kind of closed down. I deduced that you didn't want him coming to Sweet Pine."

"Because of Emilio, that's all."

"Really? Because if you've had Emilio for his entire life, I can't see that Miguel has any real fondness for his son. Maybe he can come here and talk to me without ever seeing Emilio."

"No. Miguel wants to stop at our house before he comes to see you. He claims he wants to visit Mama and Emilio. If I deny him a chance to be with his son, I don't know what he would do."

"I'm sorry, Monica," Edward said. "I had no idea this would be so hard on you. If you like, I'll change the arrangements. I had wanted to talk to your brother at the scene of my father's death. Often guilt can be determined by an uneasiness in a suspect, or a slip of the tongue. But if this is going to upset you, I'll go to Miami and talk to Miguel there."

"That's not necessary," Monica said. "I've

known that this moment had to come some-time. Emilio knows he has a father. The fact that I don't want Miguel anywhere near his son is no reason to hide the truth."

"That's not all that's bothering you, Monica. Men have spent time in prison and come out to be good, caring fathers, but you seem very certain that this isn't the case with Miguel." Edward gently loosened her hands, felt the tension in her fingers and clasped the hand securely. "Tell me what Miguel did. Did he hurt you?"

"No, nothing like that."

"Then what, Monica? You can tell me. I'd like to help you with your relationship with Miguel, but you have to talk to me."

"Miguel was always a wild kid," she said. "He was often in trouble. At the beginning, his mistakes were small, childish things that many do, but as he grew up, he changed, became more obstinate, resentful of rules.

"Mama stood up for him, talked my fa-ther out of disciplining him. She said Miguel would mature and look back on his mistakes with regret. But he never did."

"So his crimes became more serious?" Edward said.

"Eventually, but never anything violent." She sought comfort from Edward's gaze. He gave her an encouraging smile.

"He started driving to Miami almost every night. Got involved in stealing cars for their parts, doing minor drugs. He was always asking Mama for money, and then, one day he stopped asking. He'd rented an apartment. Mama told herself he had a good job, but I knew he was getting money elsewhere. I tried to talk to him—he was beyond listening."

"And then he got caught, isn't that what happened?" Edward asked.

"Yes, but not before he met Ellie. She was from a traditional Little Havana family. When she became pregnant, she and Miguel kept it a secret from both sets of parents. Miguel's life might have turned out so differently if he and Ellie had begun a life together. He truly loved Ellie. She would have kept him on a straight path."

Edward had heard such stories many times—stories where an odd twist of fate decided a person's fortunes or turned him or her in the wrong direction. But Monica's story, told in her soft, clear voice with such emotion, made him wish he could take away her sadness. He wished he had known her then, when her family needed help.

"Ellie is Emilio's mother?" Edward said.

Monica nodded.

"What happened to her?"

"They had no insurance, so Miguel took her to a midwife for the baby's birth. There were complications with the pregnancy. Infection spread through Ellie's body and she couldn't fight it. When she died, Miguel's world was shattered. He brought the baby to me. I said I would keep him, and Miguel said he never wanted to see the baby again. He got back in with his old crowd in Miami and eventually went to prison."

"And Emilio has been with you ever since his birth?" Edward asked.

"Yes."

"Does he call you Mama?"

"No. I'm his *Tía* 'Nica. He knows his mother died, and he knows he has a father who doesn't live around us. Emilio hasn't asked for details, but I'm sure he will someday." She squeezed her eyes tight for a second. "I just hadn't planned on *someday* being Thursday."

"So this is all about Emilio?" Edward said. "You're afraid for your nephew, not yourself?"

"That's right. So long as Miguel leaves us alone, everything will be okay. He doesn't deserve to be in Emi's life."

Edward thought for a moment. Part of him wanted to cancel the plans to interview Miguel, but he was so confident of Miguel being a prime suspect. He couldn't just pretend it wasn't important. "I have an idea," he said. "What if Emilio didn't see his father on Thursday? What if Miguel came directly to my house?"

"Miguel has made up his mind. He'll have to drive by my house to come to yours. I can't keep him from stopping."

"Didn't you tell me Emilio went to summer camp?"

"Yes, but I've arranged to keep Emi home that day. I can't deny Mama the chance to see her son, even though she has unrealistic dreams of Miguel connecting with us again and all of us living together."

"That's never going to happen," Edward said.

"No. But it has been too many years that

Mama has seen her son—not since Papa's funeral. She's always imagining a transformed Miguel, and even though I know she'll be disappointed, I don't want to keep her from seeing him. And I can't deny Miguel the opportunity to see his son." She gave Edward a sharp look. "I don't know what Miguel would do if I told him he couldn't see Emilio." She sighed. "And I don't know what I would do if Miguel did anything to separate me from that boy. My heart would break. It's as simple as that."

"Would Miguel really try to take Emilio away from you?"

"Not logically. I don't think there's room in Miguel's life for a five-year-old boy. So I'm willing to take the chance on Thursday. I just hope and pray…"

"What, Monica? What do you hope for?" Edward took her hand again and held it tightly. It was such a small hand, considering all the responsibilities this woman had. A small, delicate hand that soothed a young boy's mind before he went to sleep, as well as protected her family when she had to.

"It's not something we should talk about now, Edward. Basically I just hope you are convinced as I am that Miguel didn't do this. Then he'll go on with his life and our lives will continue as they have."

Edward moved closer to her and smiled. "If that's what you want, then that's what I want for you. I'm not a dad, and I don't know many children, but I can sense your love for this boy. He's a lucky little guy to have you."

"I'm the lucky one," she said.

"I'll keep my conversation professional with Miguel. Don't worry. It'll be okay."

"I trust you."

"And I trust you. We have that going for us, Monica. It's a trust I sensed the first time I met you."

Her eyes widened and caught the moonlight in their black depths. "Me? All I'm doing is trying to satisfy you about what happened to your dad. And most of the time I'm wondering if I'm doing such a good job at that."

He cupped her cheek with his hand. "You're doing more than just a good job," he said. "In your kind, gentle way, you calmed me when I was stuck in the eye of the storm that was losing my father. You've helped me see reason. You even convinced me that family should be everything, and I've opened communication with my sister. And now you've shown me how a woman can give her all for one small boy."

"I'm afraid you're giving me too much credit," she said.

He gently stroked her cheek. "Accept my gratitude, my admiration. I've never met anyone like you."

His desire to kiss her was strong, but he sensed it wasn't the right time. She leaned back. "Too soon?" he said, his tone light and teasing.

"For a kiss?"

"That's what I was thinking."

She smiled. "I can't say I wasn't thinking about it, too. But maybe it is too soon. Besides, tomorrow is a working day, and I should go home."

She stood. He locked his hand with hers and walked her to her car. "Thanks for coming tonight. And thanks for sharing your story."

She opened her car door and turned to look at him. "You owe me your story, Edward. I'm sensing there's much about you that I don't know. Yet."

"I'll tell you anything you want to know, the good and the bad."

She got in her car. He watched her drive away and released a long, satisfied breath, one that a few minutes ago he wouldn't have believed he was even capable of right now. He would sleep tonight, more soundly than he had in days. He'd forgotten to tell her that she'd done that for him, too.

CHAPTER EIGHT

"WHY ISN'T EMILIO going to camp this morning, Monica?" Rosa said Thursday morning. "Is he ill?" She placed her palm on his forehead. "He feels cool."

Emilio looked at his aunt over his bowl of cereal. "Why aren't I going to camp, *Tía* 'Nica?"

Monica hadn't told her mother and her nephew about Miguel's visit. First, she half suspected that Miguel would back out of the agreement and not show up. She didn't want to disappoint the child or her mom.

But Miguel had called a few minutes ago from the road. He was on his way. "One hour, 'Nica, that's all your cop friend gets from me," he'd said.

She hadn't called Edward a cop, but she didn't correct Miguel on the phone. She hadn't told Miguel about Edward's true profession as a criminal psychologist, either. If

Miguel had known he was seeing a doctor he would have refused for certain.

Miguel would arrive soon. It was time to prepare her family.

"You're not going to camp, Emilio, because we are expecting company this morning."

"Company?" Rosa asked. She picked up her duster and began wiping the furniture. "Help *Abuela* put your toys away, Emilio."

"Oh, Mama, you don't need to do any of that," Monica said. "The house looks fine, and this particular guest won't notice if a few toys are on the floor."

"Who's coming?" Emilio asked.

Rosa had been hovering over the kitchen table, but Monica told her to have a seat. When her mother had settled, she said, "Miguel called, and he's on his way."

Rosa gasped.

"Who is Miguel?" Emilio asked.

"He's…someone our family has known for many years," Monica said.

"Mui hijo," Rosa said. "My son is coming. He has changed his ways, just as I've always prayed."

Monica wasn't surprised that Rosa considered a visit by her ex-con son a miracle.

The only times Rosa and Juan had argued was when they had a disagreement about Miguel's bad behavior. Rosa always defended him. Juan always told her to face the truth.

"Miguel should be here by ten o'clock," Monica said. "He can stay for an hour or so, but then he has an appointment with Edward."

"Why would Edward want to talk to Miguel?" Rosa asked.

"I don't want you to be upset, Mama, but Edward wants to talk to anyone who might have had a grudge against his father."

Rosa jerked upright in her chair. "What? A grudge about that marina? That is the past, 'Nica. Miguel would not carry such venom in his heart for so long. Besides, he has paid his debts. He has learned his lesson."

Monica patted her mother's hand. "Mama, if it makes you feel any better, I don't think Miguel had anything to do with—" she glanced at her nephew, who had taken an obvious interest in the conversation "—the incident," Monica said.

"You are right, *hija*," Rosa said. "You know Miguel would never do such a thing. Everyone at the service said that the judge slipped and fell. And you are a police detective. You would know if that weren't true."

Ignoring her mother's overzealous statement of confidence, Monica explained, "I had to agree to this for Edward's sake. He's hurting and he needs answers. He and Miguel will talk for an hour and then Miguel will leave. That will be the end of it, so I don't want you to worry."

"No, no, I won't worry. Edward is suffering. Whatever he needs to ease his pain, we must do."

"This man, Miguel," Emilio said. "If he's *Abuela*'s son, then he's your brother, right, *Tia* 'Nica?"

"Yes, darling. He's my brother, and I haven't seen him in quite some time. You can meet him soon."

Satisfied with an explanation of someone he didn't know, Emilio finished his cereal.

The next hour passed in a whirlwind. By ten o'clock, the little cinder-block house was a cool seventy-five degrees. The toys had disappeared from the living-room floor. Rosa was wearing one of her Sunday dresses, and her hair was pulled back into a neat bun.

Miguel arrived a few minutes past ten

in an old pickup truck whose engine could have woken the neighborhood. Rosa was at the front door, waiting.

"Mui hijo," she said as she went down the steps and met him by his truck. "How I have missed you."

"Hello, Mama. I've missed you, too."

"You could have come. We haven't seen you since your father…" Her words trailed off, and Monica joined her.

"I know, Mama. And you know why I haven't come." He stared at Monica as if she was primarily responsible for sending him to prison.

He looked good. He wore a pair of jeans, a plaid shirt and boat shoes with no socks. He was tanned, no doubt due to his love of fishing.

There was no sentimental embrace between brother and sister. "Hello, Miguel. You seem well," Monica said.

And then his gaze wandered to the door of the house, where Emilio stood. "So, there he is," he said. "A fine boy."

"Yes, he is," Monica said. "But Miguel, I hope you won't tell him just yet that you are his father. I hope you'll let me lead into that conversation."

"Whatever you say." Miguel passed her on the driveway and walked to the house. "Come here, Emilio. Let me see you." He lifted the boy in the air and spun in a circle. "A strong, sturdy little man you are. It's about time we met."

"You're my uncle, right?"

Miguel set Emilio down carefully. "We are all related here, *querido*," Miguel said. "We all have the name Cortez."

"I didn't go to camp today so that I could meet you."

"I hope you won't be disappointed," Miguel said, passing a glance at his sister. "I hope *Tía* 'Nica told you good things about me. I feel like we already know each other since 'Nica tells me a lot about you."

"She doesn't tell me much about you," Emilio said.

"Maybe that will change now that we know each other," Miguel said.

Rosa beamed. "Let's all go inside," she said. She came to Miguel's side and took his arm. "Maybe we can talk about you coming back to Sweet Pine more often. It could be a fresh start. Nothing would make me happier."

"We'll see, Mama." She walked him inside the house with Emilio trailing behind, but Monica could still hear her chatting. "You can get a job here, *hijo*. Now that you have skills. We would be a family again."

Please, no, Mama, Monica silently wished. *He'll bring trouble with him*. She entered the house prepared to talk Miguel out of such a foolish move. But he had already crushed their mother's dream for the future.

"Ah, no, Mama." He put his arm around Rosa's shoulder. "I won't come back here permanently. You know I wouldn't be here today if 'Nica hadn't set up this meeting. I had nothing to do with what happened to the judge, Mama. You believe me, don't you?"

"Of course, *hijo*, and so does 'Nica. She told me so." She gave Monica a look of such longing that Monica almost wished that happy family her mother dreamed of could be a reality. But she knew better.

"Isn't that right, 'Nica?" Rosa said.

"Yes, Mama."

They all sat at the table with platters of eggs and pork sausage. Miguel ate heartily while Rosa kept offering him more. Miguel teased Emilio, who laughed at his funny stories.

When the meal was complete, Miguel asked to see Monica outside. They went into the backyard, while Rosa cleared the table and Emilio sat at the window waiting for more time with his new relative.

"He likes me," Miguel said. "He's probably the only good thing besides Ellie that ever came into my life. I now regret not being with him."

Monica wondered if that was really true. "How could you have been with him?" she said. "You couldn't be a father while you're in jail."

"I'm not in jail anymore, 'Nica. Emilio is five years old. He should know the truth."

"Why? So you can take him to Miami, where he'll live how? And who knows where?" Panic began to increase Monica's heartbeat. The erratic thumping sounded in her ears. This couldn't be happening.

"You brought him to me when he was only a few days old, Miguel. You wouldn't even look at him. You asked me to raise him, and I have."

"And you've obviously done a wonderful job…"

"I've been there for him every day. Looked after him every day through good times and bad. What have you ever done for him?"

"Not much, I know. And I'm grateful to you."

"I don't want your gratitude, Miguel. I just want you to stay out of Emilio's life. He's happy and healthy, and in a good place. You're still unreliable, untrustworthy. What kind of existence will that be for him?"

Miguel chuckled, but it was not a happy sound. "He's my son, 'Nica. Mine. I can take him to the far corners of the earth if I want to."

"You wouldn't do that. You know you're not equipped to raise this child. You also know…" Her voice cracked as a sob tore from her throat.

"Know what, 'Nica?"

"That in just a few weeks, the novelty of having a son will wear off and you'll see him as a constant reminder of your past. You'll be miserable and sorry for having taken him from Mama and me. In this house, he feels safe and knows love, and that he can count on us."

Monica worried. Had she gone too far?

Instead, Miguel merely chuckled, as if this were all a joke. "You're getting worked up over nothing, 'Nica. I never said I would take him. I only said I could. You're probably right. I would screw up his life just like I have my own."

She closed her eyes, blocking her view of Miguel's face for a calming moment.

"But I want him to know I am his father. I want to be able to see him. What's so wrong with him knowing? It's the truth, and haven't you always been about the truth? Isn't that why I'm here today? So your friend can know the truth about what happened to his father?"

He was right. She had always put truth above nearly everything else in life. And she hadn't lied to Emilio. She told him his mother died and his father lived away from Sweet Pine. Emilio had never asked much more, and she had been grateful he was a happy child and they maintained their family, the three of them. Miguel was right again that she had agreed to him coming to town so that Edward could get to the truth—either the one he needed to believe, or the one he eventually must believe.

Yes, she wanted Emilio to share her same values about the truth. "Never lie, *chico*," she'd said to him. "The truth is always better than a lie. Nothing is so bad that the truth can't fix your problems."

Here she was, now faced with a truth she had avoided, thinking she would not have to confront it until Emilio was much older and better able to accept who his father was. Miguel was right about another thing, too. Emilio did seem to like him, but what could a child understand after knowing a person for a few minutes? All these thoughts ran through her head, but maybe Miguel had listened to her. Maybe his years in prison had changed him so he could finally think of someone besides himself.

She could tell Emilio the truth, though maybe not the part about his father being a criminal.

"All right, Miguel," she said. "Give me a few minutes to talk to Emilio. I'll tell him you're his father." Monica grasped his arm. "But you must leave him here. You can see him from time to time, but this is Emilio's home. This is where he belongs."

"Look, 'Nica. I just told you. I admit I'd

be lousy at raising this kid. But it can't hurt for him to know that there's someone else in his life that cares about him. You always say there is nothing more important than family. The more, the merrier, right?"

"But Miguel, you can't be his father just for today. That would be cruel. You must maintain contact with him. And with Mama. You can't walk out of their lives again."

"Okay, I get it. If you can't tell by now that I've changed, I don't know what else to say to you. Now go in and tell him. I'm supposed to meet with your cop friend in fifteen minutes."

She started toward the house, but stopped and turned back. "Just so you know, Miguel, Edward is not a cop. I told you that before. Why didn't you believe me?"

"I figured because you're a cop, that you uniforms stick together."

"Well, he's not one. He's just a son wanting to know what happened to his father," she said.

"SIT DOWN, EMILIO. I have to talk to you."

The boy sat at the kitchen table. Rosa

stared wide-eyed at the two of them and leaned against the sink.

"Miguel will be leaving soon," Monica said. "And it's important that you know the truth about him."

"He's nice," Emilio said. "And funny. He knows lots of funny stories."

"Yes, he can be funny," Monica said. "But he is much more to you than just an uncle who teases you and makes you laugh."

"What do you mean?" asked Emilio.

Monica took a deep breath and glanced at her mother, whose mouth had dropped open. "Remember, *chico*, when I said you had a father, but he lives some distance away?"

Emilio nodded and sat forward in his chair. He seemed so small and innocent, so incapable of understanding what she had to tell him. Monica prayed she would say the right words.

"The truth is, Emilio, Miguel is your papa."

"My papa?"

"Yes, sweetheart. Your mommy died soon after you were born, and Miguel asked Grandma and me to raise you."

"My papa didn't want me?" Emilio asked.

"It wasn't like that, Emi. Your father was

very sad because your mommy had died. He loved both of you, but he couldn't forget the sadness enough to give you all the love a papa should give to his son. So he did a wise thing. He gave you to two people who could love you night and day with their whole hearts."

"Then why is Papa here today?" Emilio asked the question with an innocent skepticism in his voice. He wanted to believe, but he couldn't quite make himself yet.

"He's here on business," Monica said. "But also to see you. He wants you to know that he's your papa and he didn't mean to hurt you in any way. He was just so sad." She lifted Emilio's hand and held it tightly. "He couldn't be your papa then, and Grandma and I wanted you so badly. We still do."

"I'm not sure I want him for a papa now," Emilio said. "I could have made him not so sad. I could have made him happy again."

Monica smiled. "Yes, perhaps you could have. You certainly make Grandma and me happy every day. But now maybe you have a chance to help your papa."

"Is he going away again, after his meeting?"

"Yes, but he'll be back. And you can talk

on the phone and maybe use the computer sometimes to talk to each other. I'll show you how."

Emilio thought for a moment and chewed on his bottom lip. "So, I'm staying here, just like always?"

"Yes, *chico*, you're staying right here."

"That's good. It's okay that I know something about my papa, but I don't want you and Grandma to be sad."

Monica stood, came over to Emilio and gave him a strong, secure hug. "I love you, Emi. So much."

She called Miguel inside the house and met him at the back door.

"Did you tell him?" Miguel asked.

"Yes, he knows," she whispered. "But Miguel, you must remember your responsibility to Emilio from now on. You must promise to call and visit sometimes, and you have to keep those promises. Emilio is a sweet, sensitive boy. If you want to be in his life, you have to accept what it is to be a papa. Remember what our father was like, how giving of himself."

Miguel nodded. "All right, 'Nica. You can

quit lecturing me. Can I have a minute to say something to Emilio now?"

"Of course." She watched Miguel walk into the front room, where he asked Emilio to sit with him. They talked a few minutes, and then Miguel said he had to leave. Monica came into the room and sat next to Emilio.

"When will you be back, Papa?" Emilio asked him.

"Soon. I will see you soon." He ruffled the boy's hair and kissed him on top of his head. "Be a good *muchacho*, Emilio."

"I will."

Miguel said goodbye to Rosa and Monica. "I hope your friend appreciates that I came all this way," he said as he left the house.

When he'd pulled out of the driveway, Monica dialed Edward's number. He answered quickly. "Monica, hello. How's everything going? Has Miguel upset you?"

More than you can ever know. But to Edward she said, "All's well. Miguel's on his way. I hope you won't push him too hard, Edward. He made a few giant steps forward today, but I'm still uncomfortable with how he'll react if you accuse him of something."

"Don't worry, Monica." Edward's voice was soft and measured. "This is my job, remember, talking to convicted criminals like Miguel every day. I just want to get to understand what happened and who may be involved, or not. I wouldn't do anything to hurt you or Rosa or Emilio."

His words calmed her. She had thought of him so often since they'd almost kissed two nights ago. She remembered the feel of his hand on her cheek. It had been a sweet moment that had made her heart beat so strong. She wanted Edward to find out the truth that he was seeking. But not at the expense of her family. Even after so short a time, she believed she knew Edward. That he would handle this situation with skill and compassion, and she believed he would never purposefully upset her. Still, doubts crept into her mind. She didn't trust Miguel. She didn't know what he would do for sure. But she hoped that nothing would disturb the balance of her little family.

CHAPTER NINE

EDWARD WENT OUT on the porch to await Miguel's arrival. Though he was eager to question Miguel, his thoughts were on Monica. She was worried about his speaking with Miguel, and he didn't want to be a source of concern for her. In just a short time she had come to mean so much to him. A hardworking cop who'd studied to move herself up the ladder to become detective, she was also tender enough to love a little boy who wasn't hers, and fair enough to consider a stranger's needs since his father had died. He would handle this meeting today with care.

Edward had liked and respected her from the first time he'd met her. But these growing feelings he had for her were taking things to a whole new level.

A.J. sauntered up to the porch, disturbing the trail of Edward's thoughts. Edward had agreed to open the marina again, although his heart hadn't been in the work. Yet A.J. seemed happy. He would have a paycheck coming to him and he'd be kept occupied in a meaningful way. Edward knew A.J., albeit not well. He'd seen the disheveled young man on several weekend trips to Smitty's, but he'd never had a real conversation with him.

Climbing the porch steps, A.J. swept a kerchief off his head and wiped the sweat on the back of his neck with it.

Edward glanced at his watch—12:15 p.m. His time with Miguel had already been cut by fifteen minutes. He didn't want to be interrupted with rental customers while A.J. was out to lunch.

"Could you get your lunch and come back here to eat it?" he asked A.J. "I'm expecting someone any minute, and I really don't want to be disturbed. I'll be in the house if you need me, but I'd appreciate you handling things around here for the next hour or so. You can take off an hour early, and I'll hose off the afternoon rentals when they come back."

"No problem," A.J. said. "Who's coming by? Is it something to do with the judge?"

Edward certainly didn't think his appointment with Miguel was any concern of A.J.'s, but he answered politely. "Everything I do these days is something to do with my father."

"Yeah, I'll bet that's true," A.J. said. "I've noticed you making piles of Smitty's belongings. Is all that stuff going to charity?"

"Yes. I'm keeping a few things, but maybe someone can use the others I'm letting go," he explained. "And by the way, if you see anything you like, go ahead and take it. I know my dad would have wanted you to."

A.J. nodded and drifted off toward the marina.

Just then, a pickup truck pulled into the marina parking lot. A man got out and approached Edward. He assumed the man was Miguel: he could detect a number of features similar to Monica's.

Miguel came onto the porch. "You Edward?"

"Yes, that's right." Edward held out his hand. Miguel didn't shake it.

"I gotta leave at one o'clock," he said.

"Have stuff to do in Miami. What did you want to talk to me about?"

"I appreciate you coming all this way, Miguel. I'm trying to find some closure on my father's death by talking to anyone who knew him."

"People with prison records, it looks like to me," Miguel said.

"Not at all." He led the way down the porch steps toward the dock. "Mind walking with me?" Edward's training had taught him that clues to a person's guilt or innocence could often be detected at the scene of the crime. Miguel fell into step beside him.

"I barely knew the judge," Miguel said. "Saw him a few times around Sweet Pine, Tarpon Joe's and here at the marina when I'd come to pick up my dad."

"Ever talk to him much?"

"No. Didn't have anything to say to him."

"You're like a lot of people around here. I'm having trouble finding folks who knew my dad on a personal level."

Miguel emitted a harsh croak from deep in his throat. "Your father wasn't a Keys guy. He wasn't like the rest of us. Kept to himself mostly."

They'd reached the end of the dock. "This is where it happened," Edward said. "Water is probably only about six feet deep at high tide, less when the tide is out. Seems odd to me that my dad would have drowned in such shallow water." He studied Miguel's face for some sign of agreement.

"People can drown in just a few inches of water," Miguel said. "Maybe the judge couldn't swim."

"Actually, he was an excellent swimmer."

"Maybe he had a heart attack," Miguel offered.

"No. Nothing like that. The autopsy would have found evidence of that." Edward looked over the water, hoping to relax Miguel by diverting attention from him. "You can see why I'm puzzled," he said. "I need to talk to people who have lived in this area for a time, see what they might know."

"You think your father was murdered, despite all the evidence?"

"I don't know. Maybe. As you look around this dock, what do you think, Miguel? Is it logical that a man would fall off his own dock and drown?"

"How would I know?" Miguel said. "I guess you've talked to the cops about this."

"I have. But I'm not satisfied with their conclusions."

"Monica's the homicide detective, and she thinks it was an accident. Why don't you believe her?"

"I believe that she believes it," Edward said. "And I have tremendous respect for your sister. I appreciate that she's helping me find the truth."

"Seems to me the truth has been laid out in front of you," Miguel said.

"Sometimes the most obvious clues can be overlooked." Edward stayed calm despite the obvious cat-and-mouse game.

Miguel squinted at Edward. "Monica tells me you're not a cop."

"That's right."

"Seems like you're doing a cop's work."

"I'm doing a son's work. Like I told you, I just want to know the truth."

Edward switched into confidant mode and asked Miguel a few questions about his background—where he was born, how long he'd lived in Sweet Pine, what jobs he'd had. They were two guys talking…and getting nowhere. But this was one of the methods in a criminal psychologist's toolbox.

"Let's get out of the sun," Edward suggested. They went back to the porch. Edward brought out two glasses of icy cold water and prompted Miguel to sit. Edward took the seat next to him. "Here's my problem, Miguel. I haven't found many people who were friendly with my dad. In fact, I've discovered that a few Sweet Pine residents didn't like him, period." That wasn't technically true, but again, it couldn't hurt to make Miguel feel like he wasn't alone with his resentments.

"You won't get an argument from me," Miguel said. "I suppose Monica told you how the judge conned our dad out of his share of this marina."

"Actually, your father was never the owner of any part of the marina, so it would have been impossible to con him out of it."

"You know what I mean," Miguel said. "He promised my dad a share of this property, and he never gave it to him."

"I'm still grappling with that," Edward said. "I've always thought of my father as a fair man. There must have been a good reason why the shares were never passed to Juan."

"I'll tell you who was a fair man," Miguel said. "Juan Cortez. And he didn't deserve to be treated like that."

"No, I suppose not."

Miguel remained silent for almost a whole minute. Finally, he looked at Edward. "I know what you're trying to do. You're trying to find out if I hated the judge enough to have killed him."

"Did you?" The question was a criminal psychologist's trick. Ask bluntly and watch for reactions. Miguel stared hard at Edward but didn't speak.

"I know you thought my father was unfair to your family," Edward began. "It could be motivation for a crime."

"Well, I didn't kill him." Miguel smirked. "But that doesn't mean I'm not sorry he's dead."

Edward took a deep breath. That last comment had been like a fresh stab wound to his heart. *Stay calm*, he warned himself. *You promised Monica.* "Miguel, if you didn't kill him, then you won't mind telling me where you were when he died. It was last Friday night."

"I'm starting to mind this whole conversation," Miguel said. "But if it will get you off my back, I'll tell you that I was in Miami."

"Can anyone verify that?"

Miguel set his glass on the table and stood. "This talk is over except for one thing. I want to know exactly what you do for a living. You probably had life handed to you from a rich judge with no strings attached. But something's going on here."

"You couldn't be more wrong," Edward said. "In fact, if you compared your early life with mine, before I met the judge, you'd be surprised and probably grateful for the family you did have once."

"Okay, so you're not a rich spoiled guy. You can still answer my question. Who are you?"

"I'm a criminal psychologist," Edward said. "I talk to guys who've gotten in trouble. I try to figure out what made them do the things they did. And I help them, if I can."

Miguel dropped his forehead to his palm. A string of epithets came from his mouth.

Finally, he looked Edward in the eye and said, "I know what this is really all about."

"You do? What is it about, Miguel?"

"You work with cops so you must have taken a good long look at my record. You know that Judge Smith helped put me behind bars."

In fact, Edward had not looked at Miguel's record, but to admit that he hadn't would not help him uncover what he wanted to know. He addressed the second part of Miguel's accusation. "My father had already retired from the bench when you went to prison. And he only worked in South Carolina. How could he have influenced your sentence here in Florida?"

"I bet judges talk to each other. Know people in common. What if Judge Smith called my judge and recommended a tougher sentence for me? I probably never stood a chance. But you know that, don't you?"

"I can't imagine that would have happened," Edward said. "It would be unethical." He wasn't sure what to say about Miguel's guesswork and suppositions at this point. He wanted to believe in the judge, but then, there was that promise to Juan that never materialized, either.

"I'm out of here," Miguel said. "Knew I shouldn't have come down to the Keys. Knew I shouldn't have trusted Monica." He stomped off the porch and turned toward Edward.

"I didn't kill your old man," he called out. "And I'm not going back to prison for something you *think* might have happened. You're not going to railroad me."

Edward watched Miguel drive away, his back tires spitting gravel. Edward was glad he didn't have many boats out this afternoon. He wanted time to make notes and think about his conversation with Miguel. Something about the conviction in the man's voice convinced him that he was innocent of killing the judge. Edward wanted to tell Monica his conclusion right away. Not only that, but he also wanted to see her to put her mind at ease. A phone call wouldn't work. He would take her to dinner.

FORTUNATELY, ONLY TWO boats went out that afternoon. Edward was able to give A.J. an hour off and still have enough time to contact Monica. While he waited for the boats to come in, he made notes about his conversation with Miguel. He was quite certain that Miguel had committed the crimes that put him in jail, but he was not a murderer.

After the last boat returned, Edward hosed it down and went in to take a shower and change his clothes. Feeling better, he called Monica on her cell phone. When she answered, she sounded breathless.

"Hi, Monica. It's Edward. How would you like to catch a late dinner with—"

She interrupted his invitation. "What happened at your place?" she demanded.

Her tone surprised him. "Just what I told you would happen," he said. "We talked for about forty-five minutes and then Miguel left."

"No, it was more than that," she said.

His heart beat fast. "What's wrong, Monica? Why are you upset?"

"He's gone, Edward. Emilio is gone. Miguel took him."

Edward shook his head to relieve a sort of brain freeze that threatened to numb his ability to reason. "What are you talking about? How could Miguel have taken

Emilio? Weren't you home like you said you would be?"

"For all but an hour, still, you don't know Miguel like I do. Despite all your talk of psychology, you don't understand what people are capable of." She was sobbing openly now.

"I'll be right there," Edward said. "We'll figure this out together."

He disconnected and ran from the house. In a little more than five minutes, he was pulling in front of the cute house on Lantana Lane. The driveway was full of vehicles, including Monica's gray sedan. She came from the house when he got out of his car.

Edward's heart ached for her. Her eyes were red and swollen, her face blotchy.

Edward was confused. He was certain that his interview with Miguel had gone well. Yes, the man was angry. Yes, he had a chip on his shoulder. But when he'd left the house, Edward was certain Miguel was headed back to Miami. Alone.

He approached Monica slowly. When she didn't back away, he took her in his arms. "It'll be okay, Monica," he said, leading her to a wrought-iron bench near the driveway. She sat and released a deep sigh.

Edward sat beside her. "Tell me what you know."

"I went to the station for no more than an hour this afternoon to catch up on some paperwork. When I left, Mama was home and Emilio was outside playing with his trucks." She glanced to where several toy trucks had been left on the lawn. "I got back around four o'clock. When I didn't see Emilio, I assumed he was in the house."

"But he wasn't?" Edward prompted.

"No. I asked Mama where he was. She looked puzzled and said she had just checked on him. He was still playing on the lawn." Monica twisted on the bench and lowered her head. "I knew right then. Something told me. I couldn't breathe. I ran outside and drew enough breath to start calling Emilio's name. Mama came outside and asked me what was wrong.

"When I told her I couldn't find Emi, she began to cry. 'He was just here,' she said.

"I asked her if Miguel had come back to the house. She said he hadn't." Monica scrubbed a tear from her cheek. "That she knew of, anyway."

Edward formulated a timeline of events in his mind. Miguel had left the marina a little after one, supposedly to go to Miami. Monica discovered Emilio missing around four. What had Miguel been doing for those three unaccounted hours? He asked Monica if she had a theory about where Miguel might have been, what he might have been doing.

"Miguel has always been unpredictable," she said. "He could have been anywhere. I checked Tarpon Joe's, a former hangout of Miguel's, but he hadn't been there. I can only assume now that he was somewhere thinking of a way to get what he wanted. I've never felt pain like this before, not even when my dad died." She looked at Edward then. The hurt in her beautiful eyes was almost his undoing. He would have willingly taken her pain upon himself if he could have done so.

Thinking to calm her, Edward made practical suggestions. "Have you called Emilio's friends?"

"Of course. I went to every house near us where Emi plays and even drove to the neighborhoods of his school friends. No one has seen him."

"What about the people who live on this street, the ones who don't have children? Did you check to see if they saw anything unusual?"

"Yes. No one saw anything." She twisted her fingers together. "That makes me think that wherever Emi went, he went willingly. No one heard any screams or cries. I called the sheriff's department and informed them of Emi's disappearance. They issued a missing-children's bulletin immediately."

Edward took her hands in his. "Monica, are you thinking that someone you don't know took Emilio?"

She nodded. "I did at first. The thought terrified me. But then I got a voice message from Miguel."

"Just a message? What did he say?"

"He said..." Monica nearly choked, but after a deep breath she was in control enough to continue. "He said he never should have trusted me."

She broke into fresh tears. Edward put his arm around her and held her tight. "You've tried calling him?"

"Incessantly. His phone just rings until it goes to voice mail. I've left a message every time. I've begged him…"

Edward tried to make sense of the chaos in his brain. He hadn't accused Miguel of anything. Still, he was angry about a lot of things, especially how his life had turned out, and he felt the world had betrayed him. But he wasn't a killer.

"Have you told the sheriff's department that you knew it was Miguel who took Emilio?"

"Yes. I called them right away, told them it was a kidnapping and gave them a description of Miguel's truck. They put out an APB on the truck, but said they couldn't call it a kidnapping. They said it appears that Emilio went with Miguel of his own free will. And, besides, Miguel is the boy's father, and by all rights—"

"But it isn't that simple," Edward said.

"I know that, but in the eyes of the law…"

Edward gently rubbed her knuckles with the pad of his thumb. "Look, Monica, I don't know Miguel. I admit that, but from what I saw of him, he won't hurt Emilio. Violence is not a core feature of his makeup."

She stared up at him with bright, luminous eyes. "But you thought…"

"I know. But I would want to interview anyone who might have had a motive, and Miguel did. But he didn't kill my father. I'm almost sure of that. He took Emilio to punish you, but he won't hurt him."

She put her cheek against his shoulder. "Thanks for saying that, Edward." After a quiet moment, she stood up from the bench. "I've got to go back inside. There could be a call on Mama's phone. Miguel has her number as well as mine."

"I'm going with you." Edward followed her to the house. From the doorway, he heard people chattering intensely and crying. He and Monica stepped inside and he was awed by the number of people in the small home.

Monica made an attempt to introduce Edward. Some names and faces stuck, others he tried to remember, but he could see how worried they all were, how much they cared about Emilio, and he felt for them.

Edward wondered at the kindness shown to him by all of Monica's family. No one seemed to blame him for what had happened, although he would have understood if they had. He blamed himself. What had he said that sparked Miguel's actions?

He recognized a few Spanish phrases, ones that identified the person who was responsible for the fear and sadness today. Miguel. And yet, for Monica's sake, Edward wanted to make this right.

Two hours passed. At this point, Emilio had been gone for more than five hours. The family had taken to the sofa and the few chairs in the room. They all tried to comfort Rosa while following Monica's every move.

"I wish I could do something else," she said repeatedly. "This waiting is such agony."

Edward understood. She was a cop. She acted. She solved problems. Only this time, she couldn't solve her own.

Shortly after nine, Monica's phone rang. She jumped up from the sofa, her eyes fixed on the digital screen. "It's him," she said. "It's Miguel."

She answered the call. "Where are you, Miguel?" she asked. "How is Emi?"

She paused while her brother spoke.

"Of course. I'll do anything you say. Just

tell me what you're going to do with Emilio. And please, Miguel, let him come home."

She disconnected. Everyone in the room waited with rapt attention. She took a long breath and said, "Emilio is okay. Miguel is leaving him at a McDonald's in Key Largo. I can pick him up there."

The release of tension in the room was audible. There were tears of joy. Rosa said a prayer. Monica grabbed her car keys.

"Key Largo?" Edward said. "Isn't that at least an hour away?"

"Yes."

"I'm going with you."

"I was hoping you'd say that."

CHAPTER TEN

ONCE IN HER SEDAN, Monica called the police in Key Largo. "I need an officer at McDonald's on US One immediately. It's a case of child endangerment." She requested that an officer be sent to the restaurant to stay with Emilio until she arrived.

Edward listened to her calm, rational voice and wondered how she was able to keep her emotions in check.

"Can you make it a female officer, please?" Monica added. "This child will feel more secure with a woman."

When she disconnected, Monica turned on the flashing lights on the roof of her car and sped north on the highway. "That was a good idea," Edward said. "You understand a bit of psychology yourself."

"It's not psychology," she said. "I just know Emi." She then called the McDonald's.

"You have a five-year-old boy there alone. Please put him on the phone."

"Hello, *chico*," she said, her voice still in control. "How are you?" She told Emilio that she would tell the night manager at McDonald's to give him whatever he wanted to eat. "I'll be there in a few minutes," she added. "I'm in the really fast car with the lights on top." She said goodbye and seemed to focus entirely on the white lines of the road in front of her. The only sign that she was succumbing to her emotions was when she swiped a tear from under her eye.

Edward's admiration for her grew. She was a good cop, staying in control despite the desperation she'd felt only moments before. "Would you like me to drive?" he asked.

She glanced over at him and smiled. "No. I'm going to go fast. You might get a ticket, but I won't. Just hold on tight."

EDWARD WAS RELIEVED when he saw the Golden Arches glaring at them from farther down the highway. Monica slowed her car and pulled into the parking lot. She slammed the vehicle into Park and jumped from the seat. He followed, keeping up as best he could. She couldn't get inside the restaurant fast enough.

It was after ten o'clock. There were a few cars in the drive-through, but no customers inside. None except for a uniformed police officer and a small boy. Emilio pushed aside his paper cup and ran to his aunt. "*Tía* 'Nica, I thought you were never going to get here."

She hugged her nephew tight. "I came as fast as I could. You know I can't go over the speed limit." She grinned up at Edward.

"How are you, sweetheart?" She ran her hands down his arms, settled her palms on his face.

"I'm fine," he said. "But I'm glad you came and got me. I didn't know where Papa was taking me."

"I want you to tell me all about your trip with Papa when we get in the car, okay?"

He nodded. "It wasn't so much fun, really."

She led him back to the booth where he'd been sitting. "Finish your drink, *chico*. It's late and we have to go."

"Can I have another Happy Meal?" he asked.

Monica chuckled, a good sign. "How many have you had?"

Emi showed her two toys.

"That's probably enough for tonight."

When Emilio was occupied with a game on Monica's phone, Monica motioned to the female police officer to follow her. They were out of Em's earshot. "Thank you so much for sitting with him."

"My pleasure," the officer said. "I understand this was a child-endangerment situation and I was happy to help. Got a couple of little ones myself."

"This case has a happy ending," Monica said.

Edward went to the counter and asked to pay the bill for anything Emilio had ordered.

The young man at the register said, "Forget it. I'm just happy to see the little guy with his mommy and daddy. He seems like a nice kid."

Edward didn't bother to correct him about who were and were not Emilio's parents. At this point Edward was just glad that Emilio was okay. Several times during the harrowing drive from Sweet Pine, Edward had thought about other possible endings for this situation, and each went from bad to worse.

Monica and Emilio walked up beside him. "Everything settled up here?" she asked.

"It's on the house," the young man said again.

She thanked him, looked at Edward and said, "Let's go home. We've got a sleepy boy here."

They piled into Monica's car. Emilio crawled into the back seat, and Monica covered him with a department blanket she kept for emergencies. She turned the air conditioner on low, opened her window slightly, so fresh air could soothe the boy, and they left McDonald's. Within minutes, Emilio was sleeping soundly.

Driving at a safe speed now, Monica kept her eyes on the road. Edward figured she had to be as exhausted as Emilio was, both physically and emotionally. She'd been through a myriad of feelings since this afternoon.

They'd traveled a few miles when Edward spoke softly, expressing the concerns that had been bothering him. "Monica, I want you to know how sorry I am that this happened. You know that I never would have interviewed Miguel if I'd known he'd pull something like this."

She took a long, deep breath. "Of course I know that, Edward. But how could you know? I never thought Miguel would do this, either, and I've known him all my life." She half chuckled, half sighed. "Though not so well these last five years, I admit."

"But I promised you I wouldn't upset him, and obviously that promise was not kept."

"You didn't break your promise, Edward. You need to get to the truth. As a police detective, I understand that. We both want the same thing—the truth. You say now that you don't consider Miguel a suspect. I hope that's true."

"It's true," he said. "But it turned out to be a difficult path getting to this conclusion. Miguel was not what I would call a cooperative participant." He turned slightly to study her profile. Her hair was mussed and glossy in the dashboard light. She blinked rapidly, trying to stay alert. Her hands were gripped tightly on the steering wheel. But inside, he knew her heart was filled with joy. It seemed a miraculous thing, the love she had for this child. And alien to everything Edward had known in his own youth. He envied Emilio the utter devotion she showed him.

"Are you sure you don't want me to drive?" he said to her. "I promise I won't get a speeding ticket. And you can put your head back and rest…"

She made a sound that startled him, something between a cough and a hiccup, and he realized she was close to tears. She put on her blinker and pulled off the road into a deserted parking lot in what used to be a gas station. The lot was dark, the pumps abandoned.

"You're exhausted, Monica," he said. "Let me help you. I can at least drive."

She put the car in Park, then she turned to Edward. "You have helped. So much."

Her eyes spilled over with tears. Her lips trembled with the effort to stay strong. He couldn't stop himself. He held her tightly to his chest, letting her sob out her frustration and her relief. She'd been so strong and was only now showing the first signs of release.

"Edward, I was so scared. I've never been so frightened in my life. Emilio means…"

"I know," he whispered through her hair. "It's okay. I can't imagine that Miguel would ever do anything like this again. In fact, I think his conscience was getting to him. He proved his point but couldn't go through with whatever he had planned. Perhaps he really does care deep down about Emilio and all of you."

She nodded, burying her face against his neck. Her breath was warm on his skin. He smoothed her tangled hair, lifting her bangs from her forehead. When she calmed a bit, he stroked her arm and moved his thumb up to caress her cheek. She didn't pull back. She offered a teary smile, letting him comfort her. At the same time, he was comforted by helping her. He never wanted to let her down again.

When her body stopped trembling, he spoke again. "You're okay, Officer Cortez. You did good. And it's okay to cry. You don't have to be strong every minute." He cupped her face with his hands and she stared into his eyes. She didn't speak, and he didn't, either. He just leaned in and kissed her forehead, her swollen eyelids, her cheeks.

When she presented her moist, full lips to his, he kissed her deeply. His mouth moved over hers, his tongue found entry into her sweet mouth. They kissed like lost lovers who had just discovered each other again. Longingly, hungrily. Edward's admiration became something more, something intense and meaningful. He wanted to heal her pain. He wanted to be the one she turned to.

When they finally parted, both were breathless. He almost hated to look into her deep, dark eyes again for fear he would see regret or shame. But her eyes were wide and bright. She laughed softly. "I don't know what just happened here," she said. "But I suddenly feel much better."

He chuckled low in his throat. "I get it." He kissed her briefly one more time and got out of the car to go around to the driver's side. "Scoot over. I'm going to drive, and think about…well, why we both feel better. You close your eyes and let your mind wander to happy days ahead with Emi."

She nodded. "Thank you, Edward. I don't know what I would have done if you hadn't come to the house tonight. You may not realize this, but your presence kept me calm and hopeful. I am so—"

"Stop," he said. "I wouldn't have wanted to be any place but here next to you." He was almost embarrassed by her gratitude because his words just then had come from his heart.

He put the car in Drive and pulled out

of the empty gas station. In a half hour he delivered Monica and Emilio to their front door. Her family was waiting. Exclamations of joy and relief filled the small yard. Monica's relatives touched Emilio, brushed his thick dark hair and cooed their love for the child. Such displays of emotion were alien to Edward, who had never experienced such overt expressions of love with anyone. Judge Smith had loved him, but feelings between the two men were nothing like this. Their fondness for each other had been from mutual respect, not an outpouring of raw emotion. Emilio slept through his family's happiness at his return.

And Edward went home to the big house at the marina, where he pondered exactly what had happened tonight. And Monica... Her passion, when she had allowed herself to feel it, was also great, again almost beyond Edward's comprehension. But she had awakened a passion in him that he'd often believed did not exist.

ONCE EMILIO WAS tucked in bed and the small house on Lantana Lane was quiet once more, Monica went into the living room and

sat on the sofa next to her mother. The por-
celain clock on the mantel, one of the few
treasures Rosa had brought with her from
Cuba, ticked past the midnight hour.

"How are you, *hija*?" she asked her daughter. "This has been a terrible ordeal for all
of us, but especially for you."

"I never want to relive anything like this
again, Mama," she said. "I don't want to
upset you even more, but I have to tell you
that I don't care if I never see Miguel again."

"Oh, 'Nica, don't say something you might
live to regret. What Miguel did today was a
horrible thing, but he is family, and in our
hearts we must find a path to forgiveness."

"Mama, I can't."

"But 'Nica, he dropped our Emilio in
a safe place. He could have taken Emi to
Miami and we might never have seen him
again." She shivered as she often did when
talking of Miami, a place she believed was
different from their laid-back island.

Monica knew her mother's words held
some truth. Miami was a big city, and if
Miguel had wanted to, he could have kept
Emilio from his family if he chose to. What
Miguel didn't know was that Monica wouldn't

have stopped looking for her nephew. Thank goodness Emilio was safe in his bed tonight.

When Monica had joined the police force, she'd realized her destiny was in this small town. And then Emilio came into her life, and her purpose to protect her family became her guiding force. She would never betray her word to her father and move the family away from their secure little home.

She took her mother's hand. "Mama, I can't promise you that I'll ever forgive Miguel. I can't tell you that I will ever want Emilio to spend one hour with his father again. But I can promise you that if redemption is in Miguel's future, true redemption, I'll rethink my feelings then."

"I trust you, *hija*," Rosa said. "You are a good girl. You will do what's best for us."

Monica rested her head on her mother's shoulder. Her thoughts wandered to a few hours ago when she'd been in a deserted parking lot with Emilio securely asleep in the car, and Edward, strong and capable, holding her close. She and Rosa just sat that way until the dawn was almost breaking.

CHAPTER ELEVEN

EDWARD AWOKE EARLY the next morning. As he prepared the rental boats for customers, his mind returned to images of Monica, and the joy that he felt privileged to have shared with her.

Though the marina had been his father's dream, Edward took care to complete every chore, which, in the past, had usually seemed so tedious. He took a deep breath and released it. For a few minutes, he forgot the grief that had been weighing so heavily upon him. He'd never been all that fond of the Keys, but perhaps Monica was changing his attitude. Or perhaps she was changing him.

His cell phone rang as he walked back onto the porch. He didn't recognize the number. But he knew the area code originated in South Carolina.

"Hello."

"Hi, Edward. It's Brooke. I'm calling to

see how you are. I haven't talked to you since your father's service, which was quite nice, by the way."

Oh, yes, his half sister. He'd thought of Brooke last night, after he'd gotten home. And even wondered if he and his sisters might one day have a supportive relationship, like the one he'd witnessed at Monica's. He was beginning to see that kind of relationship as an important part of his life.

"Thank you," he said. "I'm fine. Doing as well as can be expected, as the saying goes."

"It will take time, Edward."

"Yes, I know. I'm keeping busy at the marina, going through my father's possessions, donating to charities, saving a few things."

"That's tough," she said. "I've been thinking about you, wondering if you received the results of our DNA test."

They had both sent swabs of saliva to the lab.

"No, not yet. I'm thinking maybe today. The lab said two or three days, at least."

"Great. I have to admit I feel like you're already my brother, and it'd be nice to have you as part of the family officially."

He didn't want to be unkind. But for some

reason this woman had placed a great deal of importance on adding him, or another thirty-five-year-old man who might fit the description, to her family tree. Edward wasn't desperate to belong to any family, but he had decided to give the idea a chance.

"I hope you hear today," she continued. "And here's why. My twin wants to come to the Keys to meet you. We're hoping for to-morrow. She's made arrangements for care of her baby. It will just be the three of us— Camryn, Jeremy, whom you already met, and me, of course."

Edward had planned to spend the week-end clearing out his father's belongings. He'd informed his office that he would be back to work a week from Monday. An im-promptu visit from his half sisters would put his schedule back at least another few days. He'd also hoped to see more of Monica while he was still in Sweet Pine Key. Assuming she wanted to see more of him.

"Edward?" Brooke's voice brought him back from where his thoughts had taken him. "Are you there? Are you sure you're all right?"

"I'm fine."

"We won't come if you don't have the proof of our connection yet. But if you do, we really would like to see you. Camryn couldn't come the last time, and we'll only stay one night. Maybe you can find a place for us to stay."

Edward glanced up at the three stories of Dade pine siding that soared above his head. The house had five bedrooms and three bathrooms. He only used one of each. Brooke had seen the house. She knew he had plenty of room for three people.

"You can stay here," he offered. Well, it was the right thing to say. "I'll let you know if the test results come in today so you can make your plans."

"That would be great. There are still seats available on a flight to Miami in the morning, but we'd need to book by tonight. I can't wait for you to meet Cammie. She's such a sweetheart."

"Okay, then," he said. "Perhaps I'll see you tomorrow."

"I hope so," Brooke said cheerfully.

BY FIVE O'CLOCK, Edward had boxes filled with donations of his father's belongings. He'd carefully packed a few keepsakes to take back to Miami with him. Included were the official adoption papers that made Edward the official son of William Smith. Tired but satisfied with the progress he'd made, Edward called Monica.

He was disappointed when she didn't answer. He was hoping to see her tonight, perhaps someplace quiet on the waterfront. All afternoon he'd pictured her in the moonlight, her long dark hair catching the glow of a candlelit table.

He left a message asking her to call him, then he showered and changed into shorts and a T-shirt. He headed for Tarpon Joe's. He would enjoy a good dinner that would only have been better with Monica across the table from him.

Without Monica's company, he chose the same bar stool he'd sat in the night he happened to meet the attractive homicide investigator at the tavern. Tonight, the bartender, Nick, immediately came over and asked what he wanted to drink. Edward ordered a beer.

It was nearly seven when the door swung open and Monica came inside. She wore jeans and a red-and-white plaid blouse. She looked like a dream to him, yet her down-to-earth, straightforward attitude and outlook on life captured his senses, too.

She came to the bar, nodded at Nick and sat next to Edward. "I'm glad I found you. When I tried the house, no one answered, and I took a chance that you would be here."

"I left you a message on your cell."

"Oh, right. I haven't checked it in a while."

He smiled. "Anyway, I'm glad you're here. Guess I'm becoming a predictable Tarpon Joe's patron."

She glanced around the bar. "Not too busy for a Friday night," she said. "Must not be many tourists in town."

"I don't know. I had all my boats out both morning and afternoon."

Apparently satisfied with their small talk, Monica slid an envelope along the bar top toward him. "I just got this from the lab. It's your DNA results," she said. "I knew you'd be anxious to see them."

"I am. Thanks for using your pull at the department to rush this through."

He opened the envelope. The results were not surprising, considering his half sister's confidence.

"Brooke and I are related," he said to Monica. "This is exactly what she predicted."

Monica's gaze connected with his with a sincerity he found comforting. "How about you? Is this good news?" she asked.

"I'm not sure. I suppose I'm still processing the notion that I have two sisters and numerous nieces and nephews. I've never thought of myself as part of an extended family, and that's been okay. All my life I've basically been a loner until the judge made me a member of a family of two."

"So how do you feel about all this now?"

He smiled. "It's funny, but now I'm getting used to the idea of a family. In fact, I'm kind of liking the notion. At least I'm looking forward to meeting the rest of them."

She nodded. "Families are complicated. You've seen mine. On some level, I love my brother, but I don't trust him to do right by us, or even by himself."

"I get where you're coming from," Edward said. "How do you go from skepticism to trust? Sixteen years of my life I didn't trust anyone, never even came close. I suppose that could have been my fault as much as the system's, but it was a habit I couldn't break. The judge was the first person I could relate to in any sort of stable way."

Monica's expression was so sincere, he felt his trust issues almost fade away. "I understand," she said. "I grew up knowing I had love and support all around me. Even Miguel was my protector at one time, though that has obviously changed. But it doesn't mean that trust has become any less a part of my life. I want the same feelings for you." She smiled. "I'm thinking these sisters will convince you that family can be an integral part of your life."

"I hope you're right. I've watched you with your family. Everyone is so supportive, and it's…nice. I guess on some level I want what you have, for so long I had no family at all. Then the judge showed me love and security can be found in the most unlikely place. The man who sent me to juvie was the man who gave me a future. Can I extend these feelings to a bunch of people I've only just heard about? I don't know. But you're slowly convincing me that I should try."

"I'm happy to hear you say that, Edward," Monica said. "Despite my problems with

Miguel, I still believe that family comes first."

Edward nodded. "I envy you, Monica." Envy? That was only one of the emotions he felt toward this woman, and they were growing every day. "Speaking of family, how is Emilio today?"

"Actually, he's great. I know he was scared, but he's decided to now look at the incident as an adventure. You gotta love the resiliency of a kid."

"That's for sure. Since my father died, I've learned that my bounce-back capacity is definitely limited."

"You'll get better, Edward. The human spirit is a remarkable thing."

"I suppose."

"It's good that you've decided to give this sister thing a chance," she said.

"It seems easier now that I've talked to you, Monica, but I don't have too much time to adjust. Got a call from Brooke this morning. She wants to come back here tomorrow with her twin, my other sister. She's pushing this togetherness factor awfully hard."

"What did you tell her?"

"We both decided to wait for the DNA

results. But now that they're in, I'll call her to give her the go-ahead to book flights."

Monica's joy in his decision shone in her kind, dark eyes. "Are you sure that's what you want to do?"

"No reason not to, I guess. If being a member of a family is in my future, why wait?" He gave her a wry smile. "Just hope I don't get too nervous waiting for them to get here."

"I get it. It's all so new. You need to relax, Edward," she said. "Let things happen. Don't be worried about expressing your concerns or how you're feeling."

"Sure, but I wish I had a plan, something that will keep my sisters occupied when we're not discussing the 'big issue' of what our lives will be like from now on. They're going to stay at the house. I guess I can take them out to dinner…"

Monica touched his arm, instantly calming him.

"If you think it'll help," she said, "I'll come over to your place tomorrow night. Maybe an evening where you're comfortable will be better for everyone. I'll bring the food. Good food, sangria and a few Cortezes that can usually make any gathering a party." She paused, looking thoughtful. "Of course, if you think that will only complicate things, I'll stay away. Your call."

Edward liked her idea immediately. He had no doubt that Monica's family would break the ice with their exuberance and love of life.

"That's a great idea," he said. "Thanks, Monica. Having you there with your relatives will be a good thing for all of us." He grinned at her. "I look forward to getting to know them better."

"Good. It's settled then. I'll bring Emilio, too. He needs a distraction from the episode with his father." She took a deep breath and a sip of the beer Nick had delivered. "Now I have something else to tell you."

"I'm listening."

"It's about the investigation into your father's death."

Edward sat back in his bar stool, every nerve suddenly alert to what she had to say.

"Have you discovered another possible suspect?" he asked.

"Maybe. Nothing concrete, but I heard about a couple of locals who had argued with the judge recently. One elderly man, Dave Cochran, was angry when the judge didn't allow him to berth at the marina dock. He said the previous owner had allowed it. So instead, he's got his little Carolina flatboat hitched to a tree off his property. It isn't ideal."

"Doesn't sound like too great a motive to me," Edward said. "All the guy had to do was explain his situation to my dad. I can't imagine my dad wouldn't have tried to help him out."

She smiled sympathetically. "I know, but any lead is better than none, right?"

He agreed.

"The other guy, Harvey Bradford, was in contention to buy the marina when the previous owner was selling. Your father outbid him by a substantial amount. Bradford tried to work a deal, but the judge had other ideas."

Edward nodded. "A better motive for sure, but again, murder? Seems a bit over-the-top."

Nick the bartender suddenly appeared in front of them. "Can I get you guys anything from the menu?"

"No. I already ate," Monica said. "The beer is fine."

Nick leaned in toward them. "Say, I couldn't help overhearing. How's the case going?" He gave Edward a sideways glance. "You still convinced your father was murdered?"

Edward supposed his doubts about an accidental death had become grounds for much gossip around the Key. He wasn't surprised that folks would ask. "Truthfully, Nick, I never was fully convinced. It was just that my dad wouldn't have been clumsy enough to drown in a few feet of water."

Monica asked, "How often would you say the judge came in here, Nick?"

"A few times a month. Maybe a couple times a week. He was known but wasn't a daily customer."

"How much would he usually drink?" Edward asked.

"Depended." Nick dried a glass. "Sometimes a lot. And if he drank too much, one of the other guys helped him home. Otherwise he walked."

"Are you saying he was unsteady on his feet?" Monica asked.

Nick stepped back, put the glass on a shelf. "I've only worked here a few months, but in that time I've seen locals who could hold their liquor and others who would wobble after only one drink." He stared hard at Edward. "Hate to be so blunt, Eddie, but in my opinion, your father was a wobbler after hitting the bottle too hard."

"And he was in here the night he died?" Edward said.

"In the early evening." Nick set both elbows on the bar. "It's a dang shame if the judge stumbled and fell off that dock." He shook his head. "But it wouldn't be the first death to happen in the Keys because of too much sauce."

Edward looked at Monica. "Still, I arrived at the house around nine, and Dad didn't seem drunk. Yeah, he'd been drinking. He told me that. And he had a glass in his hand when I got there, but he wasn't sloppy, wasn't slurring his words, and definitely wasn't stumbling around."

Monica patted his forearm. "I know this is hard, Edward, but we're not done looking into this. Let me question the two guys

I told you about tonight. I'll come back to you with the results."

He covered her arm with his palm, hoping she sensed his gratitude. She wasn't giving up. She wasn't telling him his suspicions were founded on nothing but shifting sand. She was definitely in his corner.

When he finished his dinner, Edward walked Monica to her car. "Thanks again for all your help," he said. He cupped her face with both his hands. "You're an angel, Monica."

"Oh, stop. Lots of people would disagree."

"I'm not one of them." He leaned in and pressed his lips to hers for a quick but meaningful kiss. He figured she wouldn't be comfortable with a longer public display of affection in her hometown, especially where so many knew her, so he drew back and rubbed his thumb over her cheek. Monica always left him wanting more.

Someday…

CHAPTER TWELVE

EDWARD WOKE EARLY on Saturday morning
even though he knew A.J. would be ready-
ing the boats. When he'd talked to Brooke
last night, she was delighted to hear the news
about the DNA results.

"Oh, Edward, that's great," she'd said.
"How do you feel about all this?"

"Well…"

"If this still seems like too much, too
soon, I understand. But once we're all together you'll see how wonderful it'll be to
have each other in our lives."

He wanted to feel the same excitement
she did, and last night, he'd taken a few
steps toward accepting his new family, but
he'd learned in his life that it was better to
wait and see than expect miracles. He'd already had one miracle, and maybe that was
more than any person should hope for. At
this point, he still didn't understand what

his responsibility would be as a big brother, uncle, brother-in-law. Would he see his new family only on holidays? Would he receive daily phone calls? How intimately did he want to be involved? He'd have to start getting used to the idea that he was one of a group, since the idea was becoming more appealing.

"Cammie and I will see you tomorrow," Brooke had said cheerfully. "I know. I'm going on and on. I'll stop now. Sleep well."

He'd hung up the phone and drawn in a deep breath, suddenly viewing his father's house as his visitors might. Stuff everywhere. Edward had made progress on clearing out his dad's collections of…well, everything from newspapers to old toys and books. The kitchen cupboards were still loaded with odd-looking cooking utensils that Edward didn't even recognize.

He'd taken one metal contraption from the cupboard and remembered his father telling him it was a "potato ricer."

"Who rices potatoes?" he'd asked last night and decided to add the thing to a donation box. By the time he finally went to bed, he'd made good headway on decluttering his father's space. It was a long and arduous process, though, because every time Edward stumbled upon an unusual item, it made him remember the judge and wonder why he'd kept it. Obviously, there were aspects of his dad's life he hadn't known about. There was the promise to Juan Cortez, for instance.

Funny, he'd never thought of his father as a secretive man, but didn't everyone have secrets? Some more than others. In Edward's work environment no one knew of his boyhood struggles, and Edward saw no reason to talk about it. He was fortunate. His life had turned out better than he'd ever hoped for.

Now that it was Saturday morning, Edward was busy picking up, dusting, running the vacuum, making the beds and checking for supplies of clean towels and sheets. He didn't think his father had ever hosted a party, but today, company was coming, and the place had to be ready.

In the early afternoon an SUV pulled into the marina parking lot. Edward went out on the porch to greet his family. He recognized Jeremy, the ex-football great, whom his sister Brooke was planning to marry. He recognized Brooke, of course, but not the other blond lady who got out of the back seat. She looked like Brooke, which made sense because they were twins, but she had a few characteristics that set her apart from her sister.

"This is Cammie," Brooke said proudly, her arm around her sister who smiled at Edward but refrained from giving him a hug. Her blond hair hung to her shoulders in a casual style. She wore blue shorts, a checkered blouse and flat sandals, perfect for a warm Keys day. When she shook hands with Edward, he noticed her fingers were calloused and the nails were short. Brooke had said Cammie lived on a small farm, and Edward smiled to himself and thought about how his sisters, on the surface, at least, couldn't seem more different.

"We're so happy to have found you," Camryn said. "Brooke is the one to thank. I didn't really believe we ever would, but now I believe that Brooke can do anything she sets her mind to. She's said nothing but good things about you since coming back home."

Edward smiled. "I agree. Brooke is the type of woman who, when she makes up her mind to do something, you need to just get out of her way."

Jeremy chuckled and Camryn nodded. "Determination is part of her DNA," she said. "So I expect you have it, too."

The two men shook hands and they all went up to the house. Edward brought lemonade outside. A cool breeze off the Gulf kept the temperature comfortable. An hour or so later, they would have to retreat to the air-conditioning.

"We have so much to discuss," Brooke began.

"That's fine," Edward said. "I hope you don't mind, but a friend of mine is coming over this evening with some of her family members. She's bringing authentic Cuban food so you can get a taste of Sweet Pine Key."

"Sounds like fun," Brooke said.

Each of the siblings talked about their backgrounds. Edward couldn't help noticing the vast difference between how he and his sisters had been raised. He'd gone from one foster home to the next before being sent to juvenile-detention centers. His sisters had been raised in a grand Civil War–era home in Charleston with parents who provided them with everything they needed and more. Brooke talked about her horseback-riding lessons. Camryn told stories about the stray animals she brought home and cared for.

Camryn was definitely the nurturing one, with two girls of her own and two boys that came with her husband. Edward could immediately see that she loved her life, her husband, her chickens and goats, her life in the country. And her sister.

Brooke, as Edward already knew, was the ambitious, workaholic one, who came out of college with her mind set on climbing the ladder in corporate broadcasting. She was stylish, outgoing and independent, and her upcoming marriage to Jeremy meant she'd also be caring for two children who'd sadly lost their mother. Brooke spoke of them with such love and devotion Edward decided she had the nurturing gene, as well.

After hearing their stories, Edward firmly believed that a strong bond existed between these different women. They were sisters in more than name only. He wondered if he would ever fit in with his two siblings. At this point he felt like the outsider he was, a man with a checkered past, and only sad memories in his mind until a kind judge rescued him from obscurity.

"Now what about you, Edward?" Camryn asked. "Tell us about your life."

He'd been avoiding this topic. There wasn't much to say. He'd never been hugely ambitious like Brooke was. He'd never formed any lasting relationships with either people or animals, like Cammie had, until he'd met the man who adopted him. He'd managed to get into one scrape after another until he ran out of luck with the law and started a serious rap sheet.

Despite his tough adolescence, once he started talking about his life to his new family, he found it easy to tell the truth and even add some humor to his experiences. They didn't criticize, they didn't judge, just as Brooke had never given up hope of finding this lost brother. Edward admired her perseverance.

"Being adopted is often a matter of luck," Brooke said when Edward paused from talking. "Camryn and I were lucky. We know that."

"And I was, too, once I was taken under

the judge's wing. He supported me from the day we met, and saw me through the worst times of my life." Edward's eyes misted over. The death of his father was still too fresh, too hurtful.

He stood, cleared his throat. "Let's go inside. It's getting pretty steamy out here. I'll show you guys to your rooms."

Jeremy said he'd be in later. He wanted to check out the boats and catches coming in. He went off in search of A.J.

The ladies were delighted with their rooms, and said they'd need time to freshen up before the party. "We want to meet your friend, Edward," Brooke said.

"You have already," he told them. "She was at the restaurant when we met for breakfast the last time you were here."

"Really? I'm not sure I remember."

"She's the cop who came over and spoke a few minutes."

"Oh, of course. I remember now. The brunette. Well, any friend of yours…" She let the sentence hang between them for a moment, then added, "Or maybe she's more than a friend?"

"No, just a friend." Edward suddenly felt

the weight of his little lie. He didn't kiss a friend like how he'd kissed Monica. A friend's kisses didn't make him feel like Monica's did.

"Okay, Cammie," Brooke said, turning to her twin, "let's get settled."

Edward went to shower. Monica would arrive soon with he had no idea how many Cortezes.

MONICA'S UNCLE, Horatio Vasquez, was the first to arrive at five o'clock. Edward had met him at Monica's house the night of Emilio's disappearance. A stocky, strong man with an abundance of dark, wavy hair, Horatio looked like the butcher he was. Edward could imagine his skill with cleavers and knives. He wore a fresh apron over his pants and white shirt, ready to practice his trade at the marina.

Edward approached him next to the van Horatio had driven. Quality Butcher was written on the side of the vehicle. "Hello, Horatio," Edward said. "Nice to see you again."

Horatio slapped him on the back in a jovial greeting. Edward remembered the easy, spontaneous emotion the man had shown the last time they were together, both when Emilio was missing and again when the boy was found. He was still in awe of how that family had come together for each other.

"Where do you want me to set up?" Horatio asked.

"Set up? What do you mean?"

"Tables, chairs—the pig's spit is a rather large cooker. Plus, we have platters of tostones, *bunuelos*, cassava root in *mojo* sauce, Cuban bread and, of course—" Horatio chuckled "—the finest Cuban rum made from sugarcane."

Edward's mind had practically made a full stop at the mention of a pig's spit. "Are you saying you brought an entire roasted pig?"

"Of course. What else?" Horatio laughed from his large belly. "This is a celebration. Our little Emilio is safe. Your new family has arrived. Tonight we will sing and party and toast our many blessings."

Edward thought back to himself and the judge celebrating various holidays and achievements. With only the two of them, events were meaningful, but low-key. Their celebrations usually ended with a chat by the fireplace or companionable times reading. "Did Monica know you were bringing all this?" he asked Horatio.

"No. I wanted to surprise her, too. She is wonderful, Monica. Her heart was broken when Emilio went missing. She needs a party. And she likes you, Eddie. I told her not to worry about anything. I would provide for a party."

Horatio shouted toward the van, "Enrico, Salazar—bring the spit!"

The back doors of the van were flung wide-open and two men jumped out. They lowered a ramp and began rolling a large table to the ground. A huge, well-used metal smoking pit appeared. Edward wondered how many pigs had been turned on the spit, though it hardly mattered. The pig he was most concerned about was the giant one currently hanging from the rod today.

As Horatio's helpers moved the pit closer to Edward, he picked up on the strong odors coming from the roasting animal. Pungent, smoky, richly charred smells filled the air. Edward knew instantly that the "crackling" of the pig skin was a delicacy that was included on today's menu.

"Over there," Horatio said, directing the

men. "In front of the house. Set it up so everyone can enjoy this masterpiece." He smacked his lips. "It will be perfect," he said to Edward.

Wow. This pig could feed an army, Edward thought. Obviously, this pig was a symbol of pride to Horatio. Meanwhile, Edward had never experienced the sight and smells of a roasting pit before.

Two more men carried tables and other gear to the area of the spit. Soon Edward's lawn looked like a bustling example of color, smells and delicacies.

And then the front door of the house opened, and Edward's sisters came onto the porch.

"Oh, look at that. It's amazing!" Brooke said.

Camryn didn't speak at all. Her jaw dropped as she stared at the pig.

Edward headed toward his sisters with the intent of explaining his own surprise at the extent of Horatio's preparations. He stopped when Monica's car pulled into the lot. All four doors opened and her family poured out—Rosa, Aunt Lucy, Emilio and two other little boys. Edward let his gaze linger on Monica for as long as he could. She was a vision of warmth and sunshine in a light blue dress with a floral print. Her hair was loose and hung in waves around her shoulders. She wore simple white sandals on her feet.

Monica waved to him. He held up one finger, indicating he would be right there. He continued his trek to his sisters, who were still agog at all the activity in the yard.

"That's an entire pig," Brooke said when he reached the porch.

"Yes, it is."

Camryn, the animal lover, blinked rapidly a few times. "I've never seen this before," she said.

"I hope it isn't too much," Edward said.

"No, no. It's fine," she insisted.

Edward wasn't sure it was.

"I'm just used to choosing a pork roast from the meat department at the grocery store. This is quite a new experience for me." Camryn shrugged.

"For me, too," Edward said, grateful that his sister was willing to give this traditional Cortez meal a chance.

By the time Edward looked back to Monica, other cars had pulled into the parking lot. He didn't know how many family members or friends Horatio had invited, but his eyes were only on Monica. She immediately came toward him, smiling the smile he'd been waiting for. Suddenly, he wished this big celebration wasn't quite as large as it was.

CHAPTER THIRTEEN

MONICA STARED IN complete shock at the commotion going on in Edward's front yard. Kids were running around, laughing and playing. Her mother was chattering to her sister and about a dozen cousins. A nearly hundred-pound pig was sizzling on a spit.

But Monica didn't hear anything specific except Horatio's shouts. "Set the dishes here! Wipe the pig belly so the skin will crack!" All things she'd heard before in her lifetime, but never expected to hear at Edward's place.

"You look very pretty."

Edward's voice was calm and reassuring. She snapped her attention to his easy smile and deep blue eyes.

"Oh, Edward," she said. "I thought he was bringing *arroz con pollo*."

"What's that?"

"Chicken and rice." She grimaced her surprise. "But this is too much. He brought an entire pig."

The smile never left Edward's face. "You noticed."

"It's kind of hard not to. My family usually saves a pig roast for special occasions," she said. "I had no idea he would invade your yard with all—" she grimaced "—this!"

"It's not a problem," Edward said. "My sisters are excited. And look at Jeremy. He's standing right by the pig. I wouldn't be surprised if he took a turn at the spit."

She gave him a look she hoped would convey that he was only trying to make an unexpected situation better. "Sometimes we can go overboard a bit," she said.

Edward took her arm. "Come on, Monica. We wanted a party and now we've got one."

Monica stared at all of Horatio's preparations. Colorful cloths covered the tables. Bottles, which she suspected were filled with Cuban rum, sat on top. Bowls filled with *mojo* sauce were spaced so that everyone could use the sauce easily to add to their food. The scents of lime and garlic competed for air space with the charred crackling. A buffet table held large aluminum pans, which she knew had *picadillo*, succulent green beans and fried rice.

Monica scanned the crowd, looking for Edward's sisters. She spotted them on the porch, talking in an animated way with each other. What were they saying?

She turned to Edward. "I'll bet you were expecting a simple barbecue with a few burgers."

Edward kept walking, dodging one person and another. "Truthfully, Monica, all I've been expecting is you. So, relax, okay?"

They went to the spit, where Horatio was beaming with pride. "Ah, my little 'Nica. You're finally here."

Horatio nudged Monica in her ribs. "I said to Lucy, 'nothing is too good for our little 'Nica.' She works so hard and she deserves the best for her new special friend's family.'"

What was Edward really thinking? A few kisses with her and he'd been made an official member of the Cortez family? She had always relished her family's open nature and welcoming attitude, no matter who came in their homes. Now she wanted to run behind the nearest palm tree so Edward couldn't see the blush burning at the roots of her hair.

But there was no escape. With his hand on her elbow, Edward led her to the porch, where Brooke and Camryn waited. Monica felt relieved when she saw them smiling.

She and Edward climbed the steps. "You remember Monica, don't you, Brooke?" Edward said.

"Yes, of course," Brooke responded. "We didn't get a chance to say much to each other that day in the restaurant, but it's nice to see you again."

"Same here," Monica said, extending her hand. Brooke looked cool and stylish even in the Keys heat.

Monica was impressed. "How was your flight?"

Brooke said that it was fine.

Monica asked how she liked the old house and the accommodations. It was an easy conversation starter, but in truth, Monica had always admired the tropical charm of the house.

"Edward's made us feel welcome," Brooke said. "Of course, my sister and I are so grateful to have found him—we would have been content to sleep in a tent."

Monica mentioned the obvious activity in

the yard. "I asked my uncle to arrange the food for this gathering," she said. "I think he may have gone overboard."

Brooke smiled. "Nonsense. It's charming. And looks interesting." She pointed to the crowd below. "That's my fiancé, Jeremy," she said. "I guarantee that he can't wait to have some of that roasted pig."

Jeremy joined them then. The man Monica learned was an ex-football player seemed to fit right in. He talked easily with Edward, joked with Horatio and said he wished he'd brought his two children with him because they would have loved all this excitement.

With his hand at the small of Monica's back, Edward introduced her to his other sister. "And this is Camryn. I've only just met her myself today."

The two women spoke a brief, sincere greeting.

Edward then pointed out some members of Monica's family that he knew. He indicated Emilio, who was in his shorts and T-shirt and running along the beach. He mentioned Rosa, Monica's devoted mother, and her Aunt Lucy. When he was finished, more relatives had arrived, and they all introduced themselves. Smiles and greetings from and for everyone. Monica could see he was trying hard to remember everybody's name.

Edward suggested they all go into the yard, where icy pitchers of drinks waited. Brooke and Camryn mingled among Monica's family. Jeremy rejoined the men at the spit. When Horatio announced that the pig was "perfectly cooked," everyone came to the two long tables and took seats.

Dinner passed with robust toasts and many compliments to the chef. The joining of the two families, new and old, led to a happy event. Jokes were told, stories shared.

By the time darkness fell over the marina, the food preparation area had been cleaned, the leftover food was taken away and sleepy children were carried to automobiles to be taken home to bed.

Jeremy, who had admitted to liking the rum a bit too much, went into the house. Brooke and Camryn followed, after thanking Edward for an enjoyable time. Soon the lights in the second story of the house were extinguished.

Only Edward and Monica remained.

The evening had turned blessedly cool. Edward took Monica's hand and they strolled down the beach to the bait house, which was dark except for a security light that came on each evening. It wasn't raining, so apparently A.J. wasn't bunking in the shed tonight.

It was a beautiful, quiet night. Monica had finally relaxed. The evening had gone well despite her worry about Uncle Horatio's exuberance. She had simply wanted Edward's transition to being a brother to go easily for him. She'd wanted to help him connect with his sisters. He'd lost so much in the last little while. Monica understood that a supportive family and friends were what he needed now. She wanted to be one of those friends. In truth, she wanted to be more. She gently squeezed his hand and was rewarded with a smile from him.

Their families were different, but tonight she had seen a connection between them, a connection forged by a united longing to help this man over his grief. His sisters cared, and so did Monica. Looking at Edward's profile now in the moonlight, she believed his heart was healing.

Edward stopped under the light and turned her to face him. He took both her hands in his. It was several seconds before she could look into his eyes.

"It was a great party, Monica," he said. "But you seem so thoughtful. You're not upset about something that happened tonight, are you?"

She smiled, admiring the deep blue of his eyes. "I'm not upset," she told him. "But at first, I thought my uncle's preparations would seem strange to your sisters."

"I think it was a new experience for them," Edward said. "But they both enjoyed themselves. Hey, it's you I'm worried about. You're so quiet."

She laughed softly. "Edward, someone has to be quiet after that party. My family's social, they tend to talk constantly."

He chuckled. "That's just a sign that everyone's having a good time."

"True. Just about everyone in my family was here, including many more relatives than I'd anticipated. Uncle Horatio must have invited everyone on his Christmas list."

"And I would like to get to know each and every one of them better."

She grinned at him. "Then you'd better plan to stay in Sweet Pine for a long time."

"Right now, that's a very appealing idea. But I'm less interested in your family and most interested in just one of you."

His gaze on her face was so warm and comforting. Her heartbeat accelerated. She took a deep breath. "What do you mean?"

"I mean Horatio," he said with a teasing hint to his voice. "I really think I should pay him for the cost of the pig." His lips turned up at the corners, and she hoped that despite what he'd said, he was definitely teasing.

"Don't even try to pay him," she insisted. "You'd only wound my uncle's pride if you did that. He's generous to a fault."

"All right. Fair enough. And it's *you* that I'm interested in, Monica. And Rosa and Emilio. You've become like family to me in the days I've known you."

He considered her like family? This confession warmed her heart. Not just because he was beginning to recognize the value of having a family, but because he was suggesting that she was important to him. "I'm glad of that, Edward. Nothing is as important as family…"

"I'm starting to believe that. It's just I've never had much family to bond with. You know how I felt about my father. No one has ever been as important in my life as he was. But that's not saying that someone else couldn't be."

He placed his palms gently on her face and held her transfixed with his gaze. In the sparse light it was as if the energy in their eyes closed the inches that separated them and became one constant, undeniable connection. "You do know what I'm saying, don't you?" he asked, his voice soft and husky.

She did know. The feeling was new and different and as exciting as it was wonderful. She felt radiant and beautiful in his gaze. Edward made her feel cherished and appreciated. She loved this feeling.

All her life she had known she was pretty…enough. Because the boys had always chased her, she had worked harder than everyone else to prove that she was determined to succeed. Getting her position in the sheriff's department had been tough. Keeping her little family together had been her goal in life and her promise to her father was everything to her. But now, in the moonlight with Edward, she felt good about just being herself.

When he bent to kiss her, she was ready and eager for his lips to touch hers. His kiss was soft and sweet, but she wanted more. She wrapped her arms around his neck, stood on her tiptoes and kissed him back with a hunger that surprised and excited her. It was as if a flame had ignited between them, and Edward held her against his chest as if he would never let go.

The flicker of the light from the roof of the bait house caused them to separate. She and Edward were breathless. She clung to him as if her knees might not hold her.

"Wow, Monica, I don't know where that came from, but I don't think I could ever get enough of you." He took a deep breath. "Monica, I'm…"

She swallowed, anticipating what he was about to say. Was she ready to hear the words? Was it too soon? What if she was wrong? Was he mistaking other emotions, like gratitude, for what he thought he was feeling? She was a police detective, an accomplished woman. Yet at this moment her insecurities made her uncertain of herself. "You should go back," she said. "Your sisters must be wondering where you are."

He stroked her cheek with his thumb. "I don't care."

She looked down at the ground. "Maybe I don't, either, but I have to work tomorrow—gotta get up early."

"You're working on Sunday?"

She smiled. "Crimes have been known to occur on Sundays."

"I suppose." His eyes brightened. "Hey, after my sisters leave, could I pick up Emilio and bring him here? I saw how he got a kick out of the beach today. I have kid-size snorkeling equipment and I thought I might introduce him to the sport. Just beginning breathing exercises, that sort of thing."

"He'd love that," she said. "But watch him carefully. I know you will, but it's water, and…"

Edward backed away a step. "Monica, if anyone knows the danger of water, it's me."

She hadn't meant to remind him of the judge's death. "I'm sorry. Of course, you'll be careful. I should have a new report on the investigation into your father's death on Monday."

"Thanks. I know you're doing everything you can."

She nodded. "See you on Monday. And it's fine to come by the house for Emilio. I'll let him and Mama know."

He kissed her again and together they walked to her car. She hesitated before getting inside, held his hand a bit longer than perhaps she should have. She hoped he would sleep well tonight, as she would if her thoughts and dreams would let her.

CHAPTER FOURTEEN

WHEN EDWARD PULLED into the gravel drive in front of the little house on Lantana Lane the next day, he discovered a hollow piece of his heart when he didn't see Monica's car. He knew she was working, but still, she seemed so much a part of this setting—the floral garden, the lacy curtains at the window and the neat lawn beneath a palm tree.

She'd said that crimes sometimes occur on a Sunday. He hoped she wasn't on a call right now. He hoped she was safe. And it would be nice if she was missing him just a little.

Rosa came out of the house with Emilio close behind her. She had on a colorful dress and wide-brimmed hat. Perhaps she was going to work in the garden when Emilio left.

"Hello, *Senor* Edward," she said.

"Just Edward, Rosa. And thanks a lot for last night."

"Our pleasure." She smiled warmly.

"Hey, Edward!" Emilio called out and raced down the steps to greet him.

Edward shook his hand. "Hey, Emilio. Ready for some fun?"

Emilio gave his grandmother a confident grin. "Yes, I can't wait."

Rosa waved. "Okay. Remember to mind your manners today. Edward does not want any naughty boy."

"Are we really going in the water?" Emilio asked. "*Tía* 'Nica doesn't take me too often. She's always busy."

"We are," Edward said. "We're going to practice breathing underwater."

"Like a fish?"

Rosa laughed.

"Very much like a fish," Edward said.

"Bring him home whenever you like," Rosa said. "I will be here. I know from experience that little boys can be a handful."

Edward wondered if she was referring to her grandson or her own son, Miguel. "We'll be fine, Rosa. Don't worry. I have prepared a picnic lunch for us, so don't expect us until the late afternoon."

Emilio ran back to the house and brought

out a backpack with a beach towel peeking out of the top.

During the drive to the marina, Edward explained a bit about snorkeling, saying that his own father had taught him the basics when he was a teenager. "Unfortunately, I haven't found time to do much snorkeling in the last few years. So this will be as fun for me as I hope it is for you."

With a classic little boy's enthusiasm, Emilio bounded out of the car, grabbed Edward's hand and raced toward the beach. Edward laughed. "Slow down, Emi. I'm not as young as you are."

He was happy to see the boy's excitement, but he still went slowly, having Emilio practice breathing through the mouthpiece before they went into the water. Then he fitted a small mask over Emilio's nose and eyes, and had the boy lower just his face into the shallow water and continue his breathing. Emilio's breaths were short and tense, but he soon was inhaling almost normally. Only then did Edward attach child-size fins to Emi's small feet and show him how to paddle in a smooth, fluent manner.

"I can do it, I can do it!" Emilio shouted with pride.

Edward didn't point out that he hadn't taken his hand from the child's tummy since they entered the water. He didn't want Emilio's enthusiasm to be crushed with this first lesson. But he was quick to point out that the boy was not quite ready for deep-water snorkeling yet.

"You're doing really well, Emilio," he said. "Being in the water can be fun, but it can also be dangerous. You must never go in the water without an adult with you until you're a big boy. Do you understand?"

Emilio nodded. "But you'll go in the water with me, won't you?"

"Whenever I can, but you'll have to remember to stay close to me for a while."

Emilio shifted his mask to the top of his head and let the snorkel hang around his neck. "Can we try one more time?"

"Yes, we can, but afterward how about some lunch?"

"Okay."

"I hope you like ham-and-cheese sandwiches," Edward said later when they sat at a table on the porch of the house.

"I like them. And chips."

"I just happen to have some chips, too," Edward said. "And fruit punch."

Emilio ate eagerly. "This is the best lunch I've ever had."

Edward smiled at him over his own sandwich. "That's fine, Emilio, but I'm sure your *abuela* has fixed you some good lunches, too."

Emilio nodded. "But she has never let me be a fish."

They remained silent for a few minutes, each enjoying their lunch and lost in their own thoughts. After a time, Emilio said, "I don't like to be alone."

Edward stopped eating and put down his sandwich. This was such a strange thing for a little boy who was so loved to say. "Are you ever alone, Emilio? Aren't *Tía* 'Nica or *Abuela* always with you?"

"Yes, but remember when you and *Tía* 'Nica found me at McDonald's?"

"Yes, I remember."

"I was alone then. There was a police lady, but I didn't know her."

"You must have been frightened," Edward said. "Your aunt and I were so happy to come and get you."

"My papa left me there."

"I know. I'm sorry."

"Would you ever leave me alone some-where?"

Edward swallowed, took a deep breath. "No, Emilio, I never would."

Emilio smiled and took another bite of his sandwich. "Then I like you better than I like my papa. Is that okay?"

"I'm happy that you like me." Edward had to pause until he was certain his voice would sound normal to this child. Edward had never been close to a child, with the exception of the few he encountered in foster homes. And those were not happy memories. Now he was sharing time with Monica's nephew, and he was about to meet his nieces and nephews in South Carolina. All at once those experiences were beginning to appeal to Edward as he never thought they would. He patted Emilio's hand and said, "I like you, too."

While they finished their meal, Edward thought back to his interview with Miguel. He still believed that Miguel hadn't murdered the judge. But he didn't like thinking that the man might have unsupervised contact with his son again. Maybe there was something he could do about it when he was back to work in Miami. Edward knew what it was like to have frightening moments as a young boy. He didn't want that life for Emilio.

ON MONDAY MORNING, Edward was busy going through more of his father's possessions. As he worked, several questions about the judge's life occurred to him. Why did his father have a gun in his nightstand drawer? Was he afraid for his safety? Why was there an unidentified key ring in his desk with only one key attached? What did that small key unlock? There didn't seem to be a lock in the house that suited that tiny key.

Edward planned to turn the gun into the sheriff's department for appropriate handling. The key, he slipped into his wallet. Most of the numerous trinkets and souvenirs Edward found, he added to the boxes he intended to donate to the Keys Family Center. Perhaps some of the objects he discovered had some value and profits from their sale would help families in need.

As he looked around the large home, which held the minutiae of his father's life, he realized that there were aspects of Judge Smith that had remained unknown to Edward through the nineteen years they had been a family.

"Don't dwell on what you didn't know," Edward said to himself. "The memories you have of your father are enough to sustain you." But what if there were clues that Edward needed to know? What if he discovered a piece of his father's past that might identify his murderer?

By midmorning, he called the Keys Family Center and requested a pickup for Friday morning. "There will be furniture and boxes of small items," he told the coordinator. He then made an appointment with a Realtor to discuss the fate of the house, which was now in Edward's name. In fact, everything the judge owned had been left to Edward. He wasn't surprised. The judge had no other family that Edward knew of. Surprisingly, the judge had very little of monetary significance. A modest bank balance and pension from the state of South Carolina were the main sources of his father's income after he retired from the bench.

Edward wondered at the lack of funds in

his father's estate. He knew that the purchase of the marina must have taken most of his dad's savings. Edward had been happy when his father achieved his dream. Because of his father's generosity in supporting him through school, Edward made a good living and didn't care about inheriting his father's money. Nor did he want the big Florida-pine home that had given the judge solace in his last years.

It used to be a warm and welcoming place, but it had lost its appeal since... Well, Edward would talk to the Realtor about possibilities.

At lunchtime, a car pulled into the marina parking lot. He looked out the window to see if A.J. was around. Not seeing him anywhere nearby, Edward went outside. He thought all the renters had either canceled plans or shown up to lease boats this morning already. He was delighted to see Monica's sedan slow to a stop near the house. Wiping the sweat from his face, Edward went to the porch to greet her.

Monica looked like the official employee she'd appeared to be the first day he saw her. If only he'd known then what he knew now, that while small in stature, her competence was vast and inspiring. Now that he thought back to that day, Edward realized he'd been attracted to her even then. She'd shown compassion for his grief and empathy for his search for answers.

He could see beyond the stiff police uniform and severe hair to the beautiful person she was when she was just herself, a warm and caring woman.

She walked onto the porch. Edward reached for her and bent to kiss her. She smiled and stepped back. "Not now, Edward. I'm on duty."

"I'll take that as a postponement, not a rejection," he teased.

"No, not a rejection." She went to a pair of chairs on the porch. "Can we sit for a moment?"

"Of course." He was puzzled by her demeanor. All official and serious. Did she have news about his father?

"I have something to tell you," she said after they'd sat. "About the case of your father's death."

"I thought as much," he said.

"I have been advised… Hmm, that is not

accurate. I have been *instructed* to move on from this investigation."

He sat back, shocked. "You're quitting? You're not going to look further into this? Who gave you this order?"

"The sheriff," she said. "I can't find fault with his decision. We have limited manpower in the Keys, and while this case is important to you, it simply cannot take up any more time without there being good leads to follow."

"But Monica, so far it's been a pretty limited search. And you have discovered possible suspects."

"Yes, and I've spoken to each one. There's simply not enough evidence to pursue any of these people. The truth is, Edward, none of the people I've talked to has a motive to kill your father. All the facts point to accidental death."

He sat silently for a moment, tempering his shock. He'd known, of course, that the sheriff's department believed the theory of accidental death. But so far Monica had been willing to listen to his side. He hadn't imagined that her office would cancel the investigation less than two weeks after his father died. He'd thought he would have time.

He'd thought Monica would fight to keep the case open.

He faced her squarely. "What do you think? Forget the sheriff and orders from the top for a second. What do you feel in your gut? Do you believe me?"

She sighed. "I want to, Edward. You know that. But I have to agree with the call to close this as an active investigation. We're not quitting the case completely. It will remain on our radar."

He nodded. He knew what that meant— little else would be done.

"But in the meantime, the department won't allocate any time, money or officers to actively look for clues?" he said.

"That's about it." Her eyes were warm and caring when she looked at him, though her lips were rigid. "I'm sorry, Edward. This isn't my decision, but I have to do what the sheriff deems is right."

"And you don't disagree with him?"

She shrugged, keeping her expression unreadable. "I don't. Again, I am sorry."

He stood. "Well, that's it, I guess. Any investigation will have to be on my own and I'm not giving up."

She stood, too, keeping her back straight. "Edward, please, you're not trained to actively pursue a potential criminal. Don't do anything that could put yourself in danger or could cause you to break the law."

"Thank you for your concern," he said, his voice cool. "But I know what my instincts are telling me about my father's death."

She took a deep breath, held it. "I didn't mean to insinuate that you're not experienced in some aspects of criminal investigation, but Edward..."

He frowned. "I know. You don't want to see me hurt."

"That's it exactly," she said. "You should leave the investigation to officers, those of us trained—"

"Excuse me, Monica, but the officers you're talking about have given up."

She didn't respond.

"Let me tell you something, Monica," he continued. "Speaking of hurt, I was hurt when I came out to the dock that morning and saw the man I love and owe my life to, floating in the murky water. That is hurt, Monica. Hurt that doesn't go away."

"I understand, but—"

Whatever she was about to say, he wasn't interested. The words would only reflect more law-enforcement speak about "all they can do," or "in time you will get over this." He didn't want to hear another platitude. "Are you finished?" he asked.

"Yes, I suppose so. Again, I'm so sorry…"

"Me, too."

She descended the steps to the parking lot. Before walking to her car, she turned and said, "Thanks for taking Emilio out yesterday. He hasn't stopped talking about his snorkeling lesson, about you."

Edward almost choked on his next words. "He's a good kid." He wanted to add, "Take care of him," but he knew Monica would do that regardless. After all, family meant more to her than almost anything.

It wasn't too long after Monica's visit that Edward received a phone call from his supervisor in Miami. "How're you doing, Edward?"

"Okay, I guess. Tying up some loose ends."

"I can imagine this has been hard. Sorry I couldn't make it down for your father's service."

"That's okay, Marvin." Edward liked his supervisor. He wasn't a sentimental man, but when he expressed sympathy, it was clear that he meant it.

"There is another reason for my call today," Marvin said. "I don't want to pressure you, but I need an ETA on when you're coming back. You have a number of open case files that we need to clear up."

"I understand," Edward said. "I'm about done here. Meeting with a Realtor on Friday to discuss what happens to the house. I should be back at my desk next Monday."

"That'll work. I'll inform the department and have some counseling sessions set up for you when you return."

Edward was grateful and almost relieved to be thinking about his job again, his own responsibilities. His life was not in the Florida Keys. This had been his father's life, and Edward had merely participated. And now, his father was gone. Maybe it was time for Edward to consider that there was nothing else for him to do in Sweet Pine Key.

"Thanks for the time off," he said.

"Sure. Again, I'm sorry, Edward. If there's anything I can do…"

"I've got it handled," Edward told him. "But thanks." He disconnected. Sure, he had it handled. He'd buried his dad, cleared out his belongings. He'd made donations to local charities. He'd tried to reconcile his gut feeling with the facts the police had gathered and believed were true. Only that gut feeling hadn't gone away.

And most of all, he'd met a woman—a beautiful, kind woman who seemed to understand him. A woman who wore her emotions like a badge of honor, a woman who not only cared about the people she loved, but who also protected and honored them and put their welfare above her own. A woman who kept her promises…or, so he'd thought. Logically, he knew she had to follow the sheriff's orders. But emotionally, he still wanted her to believe in him.

Edward went back to the task at hand. He had to have everything of the judge's sorted by the weekend. There was still so much to do. At closing time, A.J. knocked on the front door. Edward went out on the porch. "I have your pay," he said. "Thanks for taking over so much of the work around here."

The smells of the Gulf floated around them. Fish smells, earthy smells, the pungent odors of saltwater and the myriad creatures that lived in it. "No problem," A.J. said, wiping his hands on his shorts. "All the boats are in and I'm going home now."

Edward recalled that besides an occasional stay in the bait house and, once in a while, a night in a tent, he had no idea where A.J. called home. He knew the man's main mode of transportation was a bicycle. He knew as well that the judge had always paid him a fair wage, but certainly not a lavish one. So, what was A.J.'s life like when he left the marina? Maybe the judge knew about his employee, but Edward was just a bit ashamed that he did not.

Edward walked back into the house and came out with A.J.'s pay. He handed over the customary cash. "See you tomorrow?"

"Sure. I'll be here. But…"

After a short, uncomfortable pause, Edward said, "What is it, A.J.? Do you want to talk to me about something?"

A.J. wiped his brow with a rag from his pocket. "I was just wondering what's going to become of this business, the house, the boats? This place is kind of iconic, you know, a Keys tradition, and well, for a while now, I've sort of been a part of it all."

A.J. had hinted before that he was concerned about the future and that was understandable. He'd been working here for over a year. As far as Edward knew, the judge had been happy with his performance. A.J. deserved answers, and Edward wished he had them.

Edward rubbed his nape. "The truth is, A.J., I'm still thinking about what I'm going to do with the property. I'm talking to a Realtor on Friday…"

"You're going to sell the place? The marina, too?"

"I might. You know that my job's in Miami. I only came down here to see my father. I'm not much into the sport-fishing thing."

"Seems like a shame to me," A.J. said. "This was your father's dream for retirement."

"Yeah, I know. Every decision I make lately seems to come with a boatload of guilt or regret."

A.J. seemed uncomfortable. He switched his weight from one foot to the other. "Just so you know, I'd be happy to stay on until you decide. Might have to hire a helper. And I'd probably want more money to keep this place running. I'd deserve it."

Edward kept a knowing smile from creeping onto his lips. So this was the purpose of the discussion. Giving A.J. managerial power and more money. He couldn't blame the guy. After all, A.J. was looking at having to move on when the property sold, and he was still a young man. But he could find another job. There were opportunities for single guys with no attachments like A.J. all over the Keys.

"I'll think it over," Edward said. "Like I told you, I'm considering options at this point. Nothing has been decided." *Except that I'm going back to Miami this coming weekend. And I can't keep worrying about this place day and night.*

But why not? Won't I be thinking about Monica and Emilio?

Edward said good-night to A.J. and went back inside the house. Yes, maybe it was time to make a complete break from this place, which stirred memories from the past, and, recently, hopes for a future. Bottom line, Edward's life wasn't here in the Keys. He'd said that often enough.

CHAPTER FIFTEEN

ON TUESDAY AFTERNOON, Monica arrived back at the station from a thankfully routine day on patrol. She'd then spent very little time in her office—time she'd expected to use to tie up loose ends from Edward's case. She needed to fill out a final report and send the paperwork to her boss. This was not a task she wanted to do.

Realistically she knew there were no other leads with respect to the judge's death, but she felt terrible about how she'd left Edward the day before. She felt as if she'd betrayed him. She tried to banish those thoughts from her head. She was a professional first. She'd worked hard to get where she was and she couldn't defy a direct order.

But she'd met a man, a wonderful man with principles and a humble gratitude for what life had given him. And he was a man who was suffering from a loss he couldn't understand.

Monica stood outside her inviting home.

The people inside meant everything to her… until Edward. Now he'd become almost as important to her as Rosa and Emilio were. But her responsibilities were tied to her family, not a man who'd invaded her senses with his kisses, his kindness, his ability to feel the same hurt she'd experienced when her own father had died.

Her father… Juan Cortez. Everything she'd done ever since he died five years ago had been to live up to the promise she'd made him. Her job with the sheriff's department allowed her to do this, to keep her family safe and happy. She couldn't jeopardize what they had in this home, certainly not when she believed the department was right about how William Smith had died.

She opened the screen door and was immediately aware of the strong scent of roasting chicken and black beans. She took a deep breath of the Cuban spices. The traditional aromatic flavors would scent the house until another dish was prepared.

"*Tía* 'Nica." Emilio raced from his bedroom.

"Hello, *chico*," she said. "How was your day?"

"It was okay, but not as good as Sunday. Can I see Edward again, puhleeze? He promised to take me in the Gulf soon." He breathed through his mouth, demonstrating the snorkeling skills he had learned. "See how good I am at breathing?"

Monica smiled at him. "I'm sure you are, Emi, but Edward is busy right now. He's sorting through his father's stuff and preparing to send some of it to a charity. You understand that, don't you?"

"Yes, but his father died, right? Isn't he sad doing that? I can make him happy again. We had fun."

Monica sat on the sofa and pulled Emilio onto her lap. "I know. And Edward had fun, too. I'm sure he wishes he could be with you now, but it's just not possible. He has grown-up work to do."

Emilio's pout was replaced with a giggle when Monica ruffled his hair and tickled his ribs. "Maybe this weekend I can take you to the beach, and we can try what you and Edward did. Would that be okay with you, *chico*?"

Emilio jumped down. "And Edward can come, too. Weekends are for fun, okay?"

Rosa stood in the kitchen doorway, wiping her hands on her apron. "Everything okay, 'Nica?" she asked.

"Sure, Mama. Everything is fine."

Emilio ran to the front door. "Can I go outside? Ricardo is in the yard."

"Yes, Emi," Monica said. "But don't leave the yard. It's almost dinnertime."

He ran to join his friend, and Rosa came into the room.

"Something is wrong, Monica. I can feel it. I can see it in your eyes." She sat next to Monica on the sofa. "Did something happen between you and Edward? I know you went to see him yesterday. Did you have a squabble?"

"No, Mama."

Rosa covered Monica's hand with her long fingers. "You know, *chica,* I always thought you would marry a nice Cuban boy with a good job and good family. But you have not found such a man, and I feared you would be unhappy—"

Monica started to interrupt, to tell her mother that her happiness was not dependent upon finding a "nice Cuban boy."

"Let me finish. I have since come to believe that Edward could be the one to walk into the future with you. He is an honorable man, 'Nica. He is courteous and respectful, everything I would want for you." She grinned. "And I am sure your father would approve." She made the sign of the cross on her chest. "Something I never thought would happen. I always believed that Juan would never approve of a match for his baby girl."

Monica considered her mother's words. "Courteous and respectful." And handsome and smart and comforting. A man whose kisses lingered on the mouth and whose embraces felt as if they borrowed the warmth of the sun.

"Mama, you shouldn't think so far into the future," she said. "We don't know what will happen from one day to the next."

"You are right, *chica*. And this is your business, not mine. But sometimes a word from your wise mama can make you think about things in a different way."

Monica chuckled. "That's true, Mama."

Rosa's face grew serious. "There is something I must tell you, 'Nica."

Monica's senses went on alert. "What is it, Mama?"

"Miguel called today."

Monica had to tell herself to breathe. She looked around the room, forgetting for the moment where she'd last seen Emilio. "Where is Emi?"

"He's outside, 'Nica, playing with Ricardo from next door. I can see them through the window. Don't be nervous. I said Miguel called. He's not here."

"But Mama, after what happened—"

"I know, but Miguel is in Miami. That was the first question I asked him."

"Why did he call?" Monica didn't want to point out that her brother never called his mother.

"I think he might be in trouble."

"Mama, you know that I can't have anything to do with Miguel's troubles. I'm a cop. I don't even want to hear about them."

"I know, and I told him that. I told him that you were so angry when he took Emilio without asking. And I told him that I was angry, too."

"So what was the purpose of his call?"

"He wants to come home, *chica*. He sounded afraid and worried."

"No, Mama. I won't discuss it."

"I told him you would not want him here.

He asked me to find him a room to stay in. He said he would not live in the house if you did not want him."

Monica could hardly believe her brother's gall in asking for Rosa's help. "It would be better if Miguel wasn't even in the same town as us, Mama. He can't be trusted with Emi." She took a deep breath. "Do you know how frightened Emi was when Miguel left him in a strange place? I have had to reassure Emi that that will never happen again."

"Yes, I'm aware that you have been extra sensitive to Emilio. But he wasn't hurt."

"Mama, he could have been!"

"But he wasn't." Rosa wiped a tear from her cheek. "I know you love Emilio. But you must realize that Miguel is my son, and I love him. It is a mother's love, a deep, unconditional love that does not go away, just like your love for Emilio will never fade."

Monica was silent, letting her thoughts form into words—words that would not hurt her mother. "Your heart is big, Mama. It's big enough to still have room for Miguel. But I don't want him anywhere near us. You have to promise me that you won't encourage him to come to Sweet Pine Key."

Rosa sobbed, but did not speak.

"Mama, please, promise me."

Slowly, Rosa nodded. "I promise. I know you are doing your best for Emilio and me. I know you gave your father your word. You are protecting Emilio. But I believe in my heart that Miguel is in trouble. I fear that someone will hurt him, and I can't bear to think of that."

Monica loved her mother, but sometimes she became so exasperated with her, like when she allowed her emotions to get in the way of common sense.

"Miguel is a man now, Mama. He makes his own choices, and often those choices are bad ones. But we can't correct his mistakes or magically make him into a better man. He must do that on his own, and he must convince us that he has changed. So far, he hasn't done that.

"You were right when you said I love Emi with all my heart. You and I have raised him since he was an infant, and I will fight with all I have to keep Miguel away from him. To keep him safe and give him a good place to grow and learn."

Monica gulped a lungful of air. She could

not go on and she buried her face in her hands. Rosa put her arms around Monica's shoulders. "I am sorry, *chica*, to have brought such distress to you. I am sorry I told you that Miguel called."

Monica looked up. "No, Mama, you were right to tell me. I can only protect Emi when I know what we're up against. It hurts you when I talk about Miguel as if he were our enemy, but right now, Mama, that's the way it is."

Rosa stroked her hand down Monica's hair. "I understand. We are a family, 'Nica, and we will stick together. If Miguel calls again, I will tell him he is not welcome anywhere near Sweet Pine Key."

Monica rested her head on Rosa's shoulder. "Thank you, Mama."

AMONG HIS MANY TREASURES, William Smith had an extensive book collection. On Wednesday morning, Edward grappled with the serious problem of what to do with the numerous volumes that lined wall-to-wall shelves in his father's library. He called the local library, mentioned some of the editions and discovered that even the library didn't want free donations of the books the judge owned. Many of the volumes were thick law books dealing with subjects that were no longer relevant, especially to the population that lived in Sweet Pine.

Edward's time in the Keys was drawing to a close, and the problem of the books was just another situation he would have to deal with in the next few days. He didn't have an answer for the books any more than he had an answer for repairing his relationship with Monica. Getting rid of a few hundred old books seemed like a cinch in comparison to his more personal dilemma.

He was boxing up a few novels when he heard a vehicle in the parking lot. Hoping it would be Monica, he went to the window and looked out. No. Monica did not drive an old pickup truck with dents in the side and faded paint.

His curiosity aroused, he waited until the passenger door opened and a middle-aged woman stepped down. Not just any woman—Rosa Cortez. She spoke to the driver of the truck, who shut down the noisy engine and proceeded toward the house.

Edward met her on the porch. "Rosa, nice

to see you." He took her hand to help her up the stairs. "What brings you out here? Is everyone okay at home?"

"Yes, Edward. Everyone is fine. Monica is working. Emilio is with his uncle Horatio at the butcher shop. I asked my sister, Lucy, to bring me here."

Of course. Rosa didn't drive. Edward imagined her mission must be serious for her to have asked for a drive. "Please sit, Rosa. Can I get you a cold drink?"

"No, Edward. I will just be a minute. I need to ask a favor of you."

"Anything, Rosa."

"Monica tells me you work with the police in Miami.?"

"Yes, that's right."

"I want to talk to you about my son, Miguel. I know you spoke with him so you could decide if he might have murdered your father."

"I did, yes. And I decided that in my opinion, Miguel didn't have anything to do with my father's death." Edward hoped this was all Rosa wanted to discuss today. He hadn't changed his mind despite the fact that

Miguel had taken Emilio without inform-
ing Monica.

"I know, and I'm grateful you came to that
conclusion," Rosa said, "but now I fear you
should talk to him again."

What? Rosa actually thought her son
could have killed his father? Edward didn't
know what to say.

"You and my daughter seem to have had a
falling-out," Rosa continued. "I don't know
what it is about, and Monica won't tell me."

Edward shook his head. He didn't want to
discuss his relationship with Monica. "Rosa,
any problems Monica and I are having have
nothing to do with Miguel."

"I believe you, but that is not why I've
come today." She paused to take a deep
breath. "I think my son is in trouble—
serious trouble."

"Why do you believe that?"

"He called me yesterday and seemed to be
reaching out for my help. I probably would
help him, but I can't betray my daughter. She
wants nothing to do with him."

"Miguel caused her a lot of grief, Rosa."

"I know, but he is still my son." She went
on to tell Edward about the phone call, the

desperation in Miguel's voice, his plea to come back to Sweet Pine almost as if he needed to hide out in some obscure place.

Edward listened to the story, to the concern and fear in Rosa's retelling of events. Like Rosa, he would never betray Monica, so he didn't know what he could do to help Miguel.

"What exactly do you want me to do, Rosa?" he asked when she'd finished.

"I want you to talk to him again, this time about what is going on with him. You live in Miami. Miguel lives in Miami. You can ask him to come to your office or you can visit him where he works, correct?"

Yes, that was true, but he and Miguel had not established any sort of trust between them. Miguel was aware from the start that Edward suspected him of murder. "I don't know what I can accomplish with Miguel," Edward said. "He probably wouldn't open up to me about what's going on in his life."

"But you can try," Rosa insisted. "I don't have anyone else to turn to. You at least can determine if he is in some kind of trouble."

Edward stated the bold truth to Rosa. "Miguel was in jail for a time, remember?

It isn't impossible to believe that he's in trouble again. Maybe he's trying to escape the law. If so, I can't help him to do that."

"It's not that," Rosa said. "If he was afraid of being caught, he would simply run. He's done it before. This time it's as if he's trying to save his life from harm, not from jail." Her voice grew more desperate. "Someone is going to kill him, Edward. I just know it! I would much rather he was in jail than in a grave."

Edward could find no reason to doubt Rosa's plea. He knew her well enough to believe she would do anything to protect her family. What she requested was entirely possible for Edward to do for her. He could try contacting Miguel and ask him to meet in Miami to talk. He'd done it countless times before with other people who were in trouble. Miguel could agree or not, but Edward had to try. First, he'd need more information.

"Sit down, Rosa, please. I'm going inside to get a pen and my notebook. I need to know more about your son." Edward needed to know where Miguel worked, where he lived, who his friends were. It was likely that Rosa didn't know everything about his life, but anything would help. Besides, since Miguel had been on parole for a time, there would be a paper trail of his addresses at the police department.

Obviously convinced that Edward would help her, Rosa slumped into a chair with what looked like relief. She clasped Edward's hand. "Thank you, Edward. You're a good man."

"I'm not promising I can do anything," he said. "But I will promise to try."

CHAPTER SIXTEEN

ON FRIDAY MORNING Edward called his supervisor and reaffirmed that he would be back to work on Monday. Actually, Edward planned to be in Miami tomorrow. He needed time to tie up loose ends, contact some folks he hadn't seen in a while and think about Monica. Mostly, think about Monica. He hadn't heard from her since Monday, when they'd argued, or sort of argued. Edward wasn't sure if they had argued or merely disagreed. At any rate, their relationship had changed, and he didn't think they would put it right anytime soon.

Monica had to follow the orders of her superiors. Edward would never be convinced that foul play had not been involved in his father's death. Could he point to a suspect? No. Whoever had killed his father had covered his tracks. But Edward was not giving up on his search, and his promise to avenge his father's death. And he'd discovered that it was impossible to think of giving up on Monica.

People from The Keys Family Center arrived in the late morning on Friday and took the items Edward had marked for donation. He decided to keep some of his father's most treasured pieces. There was a sheet-music cabinet that locals swore had been used by Ernest Hemingway to store his manuscripts. Edward also left a large round wall clock in his father's study. Supposedly it had come from a World War II barracks at the naval station in Key West.

What Edward would eventually do with these treasures, he didn't know, but for now, until he decided for certain to sell the property, he would leave them where they had sat for years. For some reason, perhaps sentimentality, Edward called the Realtor and canceled his appointment to discuss the sale. He didn't have to decide the fate of the house and property today.

He also kept several dozen of his father's books—the ones he might read someday, the ones that seemed to hold a light into his dad's thinking, his dreams, his beliefs. Edward had thought he had known every detail of his father's character and life, but being in this house for two weeks had convinced him otherwise. He still wondered why his father had a gun. And what did that miniature key from his father's desk open?

It had been two weeks of grieving, discovery and decisions for Edward. Mostly he'd discovered that a small but determined, and certainly beautiful, police detective had wrapped her capable hands around his heart. If he had any hope of reconnecting with Monica, he had to see her again. He couldn't leave with bad feelings between them. And he couldn't leave with secrets untold, especially the one about her brother, Miguel, not to mention his promise to Rosa.

He reached her at her desk in the sheriff's office. "Hello, Monica. It's Edward."

"Edward… What? Why?" She stopped stammering and sighed. "Edward, how are you?"

"I'm missing you. I'd like to see you before I leave for Miami in the morning."

His announcement was met with a moment of silence. Then she said, "Tomorrow? I thought—"

"Meet me at Tarpon Joe's. We'll have dinner, talk. We don't need to discuss my father's death. We both know where we stand on that issue. But I feel there is so much more to say."

He could practically sense her thinking through his proposition through the phone. He stopped breathing until she said, "That would be all right, I suppose. I get off work at five. Give me time to run home, see Emi. I can meet you at Tarpon Joe's at seven."

"That's perfect." A sweet breath of relief filled his lungs. The meeting would not be perfect however. Tarpon Joe's would be crowded on a Friday night. Most of the locals knew Monica and would stop and talk. He would be close to her, yes, but still miles away.

"I'll see you then," he said and disconnected. How would he fill the hours until seven o'clock? He could pack his car, read a book, give final instructions to A.J., whom he'd decided to let run the marina for a while.

And he could also walk to the bait house, where he'd held Monica in his arms and kissed her and discovered that he was falling in love with her.

EDWARD WAS A few minutes early. He chose a table in the corner, where he could see the door, and ordered a beer. He didn't order for Monica. Sometimes she had a beer. Sometimes she had opted for iced tea.

At seven, she entered Tarpon Joe's. He waved, and she worked her way over to him, stopping to talk to people she knew. She wore a pair of white shorts and a sleeveless top printed with familiar fruits from the state of Florida. She could have been an eighteen-year-old on spring break, she looked so fresh and alive. But to Edward she was every inch the woman who took his breath away and managed her life with maturity and dedication.

He stood. She sat down and he did, as well. He signaled for a waitress. "What would you like to drink?" he asked.

"I think I need a beer," she said with a smile. "For some reason I feel like I'd be more comfortable pulling over a speeding tourist than I am at this very moment."

He touched her hand with his index finger. "It's just me, Monica. A man who is glad to see you for no other reason than because it's you."

Her cheeks flushed a delicate rose color. She reached for her nape and pulled her long hair over one shoulder. "Okay, now I definitely need a beer."

He laughed. "So, tell me how you've been. I know I last saw you on Monday, but it seems like it's been much longer than that. How's your family?"

"Emilio is still pestering me about when you're going to take him snorkeling again. You probably kept him in the shallow water, but to him, he thinks he swam halfway to Texas. I have to keep reminding him that he's still a beginner."

"He'll be a natural someday. He has the enthusiasm and curiosity that he'll need in order to feel at home in the water."

"And I thought he was all about trucks and dinosaurs."

"And you? How has work been?"

"The same. No unexplained deaths that required my investigation skills this week…" She paused. "I'm sorry, Edward. I didn't mean that the way it must have sounded."

"Forget it. I said we wouldn't discuss my father, and I meant it. This is just about you and me."

"In that case, I can tell you that my job has been routine. A few traffic stops, one minor threat of robbery at a convenience store and a lot of paperwork. Mostly that's what being a cop is all about."

"I'm glad you're not a cop in Miami. Your job would probably be much different there."

"For sure. I wouldn't want to work in a large city. Sweet Pine Key is perfect for me." She acknowledged the waitress who brought her beer, and she took a sip. "And what about you? You said you're leaving tomorrow?"

He looked for some sentiment of sadness in her voice. Tomorrow was so close. "My car is mostly packed. The house is empty of many of my dad's furniture and things." He chuckled. "My father had a lot of things."

"And you'll be back to work on Monday?"

"That's right."

She studied the menu for a moment. "I want to talk to you about my mother," she said.

"Your mother? Is she okay?"

"Yes, she's fine, but she told me she came to see you on Wednesday. I didn't know she was coming, and she didn't tell me until I was ready to leave to meet you tonight."

"I was going to tell you myself," Edward

said. "Just waiting for the right time." He wondered if Monica was going to ask him to ignore her mother's request. If so, he would probably do it, but he didn't like disappointing Rosa. "It's really okay, Monica," he said. "I don't mind talking to Miguel if it will ease Rosa's mind. But if you'd rather—"

"No, no, I won't interfere. My mother is upset about Miguel, and I don't like to see her worried. Maybe you can get to the bottom of what's troubling him. I can give you the latest phone number I have for him if it will help." She gave him a piece of paper with Miguel's number on it.

"Thanks. I'll find time to talk to him this week."

"One thing, Edward…please don't give him any indication that I feel the same as Mama does. I don't want Miguel back in Sweet Pine. I'm still upset about him scaring Emi, not to mention me and Mama. I have to think about Emi. We have a good life here, and all that might change if Miguel were suddenly here again. I feel like I would always be looking over my shoulder and worried for Emi."

Edward nodded. "I understand." He

paused a moment, wondering if he should say what was on his mind. He decided to broach the subject that he was sure was often on Monica's. "I'm curious, Monica. Have you ever thought of petitioning for legal custody of Emilio?"

"More than that," she said. "I want to adopt Emilio. But Miguel would have to agree."

"And you don't think he would?"

"No. I think he wants his position as Emi's parent to hold over me." She shook her head. "My brother believes that I had something to do with his arrest years ago. I didn't, but Miguel has never been one to relinquish a card if he thinks he can play it someday. Unfortunately, Emilio's the ace he is holding."

"I'm sorry, Monica. I know how much you love Emilio. You shouldn't have to be dealing with this kind of stress and tension."

"I'm grateful for every day I have with Emi. Unfortunately, each day is one where I fear that Miguel will play that card." She stopped talking, took a breath. "It's not a good way to live," she said. "But it is my life."

Her voice shook. Edward reached for her

hand. "Let's get out of here," he said. "We'll order and I can tell the waitress to box up our food. Will you come back to the house with me?"

She nodded. "I'd like that."

Twenty minutes later she followed Edward into the marina parking lot. Theirs were the only cars. The renters had come back to the dock and taken off, and A.J. had obviously pedaled away on his bicycle. The house was dim in the setting sun except for a porch light shining down on the wicker chairs that faced the water. Edward had decided to leave those pieces behind, as well.

He turned on the ceiling fan and went inside to get two more beers and some silverware. When he came out, Monica was seated on one of the chairs. She had leaned forward, placed her arms around her knees and rocked in slow motion back and forth.

"It's so beautiful here," she said. "Looking out at the water brings a sort of peace. Maybe it's a false peace, but there is a feeling of security about this house, this property. It's been here so long, defying every storm, every plan to tear it down and build something shiny and new."

"It's a strong house, Monica, just like you're a strong woman."

She shook her head. "I don't know about that. Miguel..."

He placed his hand on her back. "It will be okay, Monica. Maybe I can establish a relationship with Miguel. Maybe I can help."

"I don't know," she said. She reached up as if searching for his hand and he freely gave it to her. "Sometimes I feel as if it's all so hopeless. But even so, each day with Emi is a blessing."

He gently pulled her from the chair and wrapped her in an embrace. She buried her face in his shoulder. She wasn't crying, but he felt a tremble go through her body. He stroked her back until she calmed. "I want to help you, Monica."

She looked at him, her eyes clear, reflecting the moonlight in the near darkness. "I know you do. And I wish I could have helped you."

"Shh. You did help me. You listened. You understood. You wanted to believe me."

"But it wasn't enough. And now you're going away without the answers you need." She sighed. "Oh, Edward..."

He lifted her face and bent his head. When their lips met, he felt a connection so strong it was almost cosmic. Yes, it had only been two weeks, but he'd never known anyone better than he knew this woman. He'd never felt this way about anyone before.

She clung to him as though he was a lifeline. He wanted to be that for her. He wanted to be the one she turned to. Her goodness made him want to be better for her, to be better than he'd ever thought he could be. To let her know that she didn't have to be the strong one all the time.

They ended the kiss, but remained standing close. "Let's go inside," he said. "It'll be cooler. We can eat in what's left of the kitchen. At least there's a table and chairs."

He opened the door for her, and she went inside. To his knowledge, she'd only been in his father's house the night of the funeral. Everything about the place was different now. Stark and lonely, with no one to enjoy the fireplace, no one to collect mementos of a life. Boxes were still stacked by the front door. Boxes he would take with him tomorrow.

"It's a beautiful home," she said. She

glanced at the boxes. "These are all your father's books?"

"Not all," he said, chuckling. "Just those I thought I would keep."

She picked one off the top and opened the front cover. "This is a first-edition Hemingway," she said.

"Yes. My father was a fan of Papa's."

She reverently laid it back down and took another. "This one is so unusual. Tooled leather binding, a tiny brass clasp." She held the book up for him to see. "Look, Edward, it's locked. I wonder why. It has no title on the front."

He'd put that particular volume in with the others just for its unusual appearance and quality. He'd never examined the small lock. He took it from her and tried the clasp that would have opened it. But it was locked tight. "I can't imagine," he said and then stopped short. "Oh, no, Monica. I think I know where the key is."

His mind raced to days prior, when he'd taken the mysterious key from a box in his father's desk. He'd wondered about the key, but having no answers to its existence, he'd finally left it in his wallet and forgotten about it. Until now…

His hand shook as he reached for his wallet in his jeans pocket. When he withdrew it, he quickly checked the slits where he had credit cards and identification. He felt the key and pulled it out. "I think this will work," he said.

"Your hand is shaking. May I open it for you?"

He nodded. She took the key from him and opened the clasp. It was not a book at all, but a book-size box. Inside was a single piece of folded paper. Monica took the page from the box and opened it.

"Edward," she said breathlessly. "This is a birth certificate."

CHAPTER SEVENTEEN

EDWARD DIDN'T KNOW what he expected when
Monica had discovered the piece of paper.
Perhaps a love letter, a stock of some sort.
But never a birth certificate. It must be his
father's.

"Let me see it," he said, taking the document from her. He read aloud. "'Ronald
Carl Blaine.' The date of birth is fifty-five
years ago."

"It's not your father's birth certificate,"
Monica said.

"No, it isn't." He continued to read. "Monica, listen to this. The parents of Ronald Carl
are a woman named Sophie Isabel Blaine
and a man named William Russell Smith—
my father."

"How can that be?" she asked. "You said
your father had no other children. When he
adopted you, you were his only family."

"That's what I thought." Edward nearly

dropped the certificate. He stared hard into Monica's eyes. "That's what he told me. He never mentioned a son. But it makes sense. The secrecy, the locked box, the hidden key. He didn't want anyone to know."

Monica sat on one of Edward's boxes and took a breath. "I wonder what happened to this person, this Ronald. And what happened to Sophie? From this certificate it appears that Sophie and your father weren't married."

Edward's mind raced as he tried to recall everything his father had ever told him about his family. "My father was married once," Edward said. "To a woman named Carolyn. He loved her very much and was devastated when she died of cancer. She was young, only thirty-two, I believe. My father never married again."

"And possibly he never married before Carolyn," Monica said. "But he had a child. How old was he when Ronald was born? You said the birth date is fifty-five years ago."

"Right. My father would have been twenty-one years old. He was in the navy then."

"Check the signature," Monica said. "Does it look like your father's handwriting?"

Edward studied the now blurred name at

the bottom of the certificate. "I think so. The signature is old. My father may have changed it over the years, but it looks like the signatures I've seen on some older documents I've discovered in the last two weeks. If I had to say, then yes, I would say my father signed this certificate."

"Wow, Edward. Somewhere out there you have a stepbrother."

Edward couldn't get his mind to focus. How could this be happening? Just days ago, he'd discovered two stepsisters that he never knew he had. And now this. A stepbrother who obviously meant no more to his father than to place his existence in a box and lock it away forever. Why hadn't his father ever mentioned Ronald? Edward had never thought his dad a secretive man. Every question Edward had ever asked him, the judge answered with thought and care. So to hide a son? It didn't make sense.

"We have to find Ronald, Monica," Edward said. "Whoever this man is, he doesn't know that his father has died. He should know."

"I agree we should find him," Monica said. "But we don't know if Ronald ever knew William Smith. He may not know who his father was. Smith is such a common name. Ronald may never have tried to find him."

Frustration knotted in Edward's stomach. "And for the same reason, we may never find Ronald."

"Sophie may still be alive," Monica said. "She might have some answers about this birth." Monica stood, took Edward's hand. "But Edward, there's an even more pressing reason to unlock this mystery."

"What are you talking about?"

"Edward, what if there was an ongoing connection between your father and Ronald? What if your father didn't tell you because the relationship was bitter? What if they hated each other?"

He started to connect the dots in his head. "Then what you're saying is, could Ronald have hated my father enough to kill him?"

Her eyes widened. She shook her head. "I don't know. It's a long shot for sure. But it's worth pursuing, isn't it? I'll be in my office at eight tomorrow morning. I can start investigating these two names…if you want me to."

Edward considered his answer. Was he opening a legacy of hate that he'd rather not know about? Would his impression of the man he loved for nineteen years be altered by what he might find? Why had William Smith hidden the information about his own flesh and blood? Would it be better for everyone, himself included, if he never found Ronald Blaine?

Of course, Edward knew his answer from the start. He had to find out the truth. He'd invested so much of his time, energy and love to someone to not uncover the facts about the person. He couldn't simply ignore what was on this document. It might contain the solution to the judge's death, the one mystery he'd agonized over.

"I want to know, Monica," he said. "Please, do what you can to find these people."

"I'll copy the important facts before I leave tonight. Then I might know something by the time you return to work on Monday. I hope so, at least."

Edward hugged her. "No matter what happens, Monica, it's nice to have you on my team again."

"I was never not on your team, Edward.

Maybe not in the way you wanted, but perhaps in the way it matters most."

He kissed her, not with the same passion he'd shown earlier, but with a warmth and caring and gratitude that warmed his chest and expanded his heart. "I wish I weren't leaving tomorrow," he said. "But I have to."

"It's fine. We'll see each other again."

"You got that right," he teased. "Now let's go warm up those dinners. I'm suddenly very hungry."

MONICA HAD NOTHING pressing on her desk when she went to work the next morning. She could devote the first hours of her day to finding Sophie Blaine. The hospital where Ronald was born was in San Diego, California. That made sense because Edward had said his father was in the navy fifty-five years ago. If he was stationed in San Diego, it was likely he could have met a girl there.

The first thing Monica did was run a standard Google search for Sophie in the San Diego area. The search produced no results. She then called the hospital, which thankfully was still in existence, where the birth occurred. A woman in the records department was of no help. They didn't keep records older than fifty years, even in the hospital's archives.

Tapping her pencil on a notebook where she'd written all the relevant details, Monica considered her next step. She so wanted to help Edward. She'd felt badly when she'd told him that the investigation into his father's death was being relegated to the cold-case files. She'd known that most of these cases were likely never to be resolved. Edward deserved better from the Keys sheriff's department, but she hadn't been able to convince her superior officer to leave the case open.

Maybe the birth certificate they'd discovered last night would lead to answers that would at least allow Edward to move on from this tragedy. Sophie and Ronald were long shots to be the murderers, after all. It was also highly probable that neither had maintained a relationship with the judge. But a deeper insight into the man he'd loved might give Edward some peace of mind. She didn't want Edward to be disappointed with this discovery about his father, though knowing the truth might ease his pain.

Seeing no alternative, Monica looked up the phone number for the San Diego Police Department. It was a large department, so she chose a number for the district nearest the hospital. She was connected to an officer in charge of missing persons. "This is Officer Criswell."

"Hello. Detective Monica Cortez of the Florida Keys Sheriff's Department."

"Hello, Detective," a bright voice responded. "What can I do for you?"

"I'm hoping you can help me locate someone who might have lived in your district more than fifty years ago."

The California officer asked for her badge number, which was standard protocol to eliminate the possibility of a crank or misleading call. "Okay, Detective, give me a name and whatever info you have on this person."

Monica gave him the limited information from the birth certificate.

"This isn't much to go on," the officer said. "But I'll run some standard ID protocols and see what I can come up with. You realize this Sophie person might not even be alive. All I might find is a death notice."

"I'd appreciate anything you can do," Monica said.

"Might take me a couple of days, but I'll get back to you."

"By the way, Sophie had a son. His name is Ronald Carl Blaine, or perhaps Smith. He may have used his mother's maiden name. He would be fifty-five years old now. Locating him would also be helpful."

"Got it. Talk to you the first of the week."

"Thanks, Officer."

She disconnected without feeling confident. The search probably wouldn't produce any helpful information. But it was a start.

"Hey, Monica."

She recognized the voice of the dispatcher in the front office. "What is it, Mack?" she called out to him.

"Someone out here to see you."

"Okay. I'll be right there."

Edward was waiting when she came to the outer office. He appeared in shorts, a T-shirt and sandals, like a man who was ready for a casual drive through the Keys. Yet his expression was serious.

"Edward, I thought you would have been on the road by now," she said.

"I'm leaving as soon as I'm finished here. Can you step outside with me a moment?"

"Yes, of course." She told the dispatcher she would be back in a few minutes. "Is something wrong?" she asked when they were outside of the sheriff's office.

"No. I just had to see you one more time." He looked across the main road that ran through the Keys and took her hand.

"Walk with me a ways," he said.

They crossed to the Gulf shore. The morning breeze still held a hint of coolness, but Monica knew the unforgiving sun would soon be scorching.

He stopped behind a palm tree, one of the few in the area that wasn't part of a hotel or restaurant property. It was private and secluded.

"I suppose you want to know if I've discovered any information about your father's family yet. The answer is no, but I've put some feelers out…"

"I have absolute trust in you, Monica," he said. "But that's not why I stopped. This is." He bent his head and pressed his lips to hers.

She gulped a gasp of surprise and soon was kissing him back with equal intensity.

He held her close after the kiss. "I know we're only going to be a couple of hours away from each other, but now that I'm leaving it seems like half a continent. I won't be able to see you, hold you like this. You have your responsibilities here and I have work to catch up on in Miami. We'll be busy. But I want you to know I'll be thinking of you every day, every hour."

"I feel the same," she said, looking into his eyes. "But we'll talk. I'll contact you with news as I uncover it. I don't know what we'll discover, but whatever it is, I hope it gives you peace with what happened here."

"You have given me peace, Monica," he said. "There are still questions in my mind, but you aren't one of them. In case you haven't noticed, I've become rather crazy about you." He stared at her with such pure longing in his eyes that she trembled. No one had ever looked at her like that before. Edward's eyes held passion, yes, but also honesty and tenderness and a promise so sweet that tears dampened her eyelids.

"I will miss you," she said.

"I'm hoping for that." He smiled and kissed her one more time.

"I should get back."

"I know. One more thing. If you hear from Miguel, call me. I plan to talk to him soon, but I don't want him threatening you or Emilio. I think I can get through to him."

"Be careful around him, Edward. I don't know what kind of trouble he's in or what kind of people he's associating with, but my hunch is that it's probably serious."

He walked her back to the station and then got in his car. Through the open window, he said, "Take care of yourself, Detective. Always call for backup and don't be a hero."

She smiled. "This is Sweet Pine Key, Edward. I appreciate your concern, but if I stop traffic to help a slow turtle cross the road, I'll have had a busy day."

He backed out of the parking lot and drove north. Monica ran her finger over her lips where he had kissed her. She knew her mother worried about her. So did her uncles and aunts and cousins, but never had someone's concern touched her so deeply as Edward's had just now.

She wanted to be here when he came back. She wanted him to hold her again. In short, she wanted to do as he said and be safe…for him.

ON TUESDAY MORNING, Monica got a call from the police officer in San Diego. "Hello, Officer Criswell," she said. "I hope you have news for me."

"I do, but I'm not sure it will be of much help. You never gave me details of the case you're working on, so I wasn't aware of exactly what type of information you need."

He was right. She hadn't told him many specifics and hadn't mentioned the judge's death. And Officer Criswell hadn't asked. Once he'd verified that she was indeed a fellow officer, he was willing to do what he could to help. Monica appreciated such loyalty.

"Anything you can tell me about either person would be helpful," she said.

"Okay. Let's start with Sophie Blaine. I know this much. She's still alive."

That was a great start. Perhaps she and Edward could get the woman to provide missing information about what happened and the rest of the judge's background. "Do you know where she is?"

"Sure do. She's in a nursing home in a small town outside of San Diego. Apparently been there for something like ten years. She's quite elderly, eighty-five years old."

So, Sophie was nine years older than the judge. That wasn't so strange. Age differences like that existed in lots of relationships.

"If you can tell me the name of the nursing home, I'll contact her directly," Monica said.

"Okay. It's Valley View in John's Ridge, California. But you won't have much success in getting information from her."

"Why not?"

"She has advanced dementia. I believe I got as much information as I could."

Another roadblock. Monica dreaded telling Edward. "Is there a chance her condition will improve?" she asked.

"Not likely. The case manager at Valley View said Sophie's memory is gone. She barely speaks. There isn't any more they can do for her unfortunately."

"But she must have family. I told you about a son born to her fifty-five years ago."

"Ronald Blaine. Right," Criswell said.

"Yes. And I'd suggested his last name

might be the same as his mother's, especially if his parents never married."

"Found him. He's the one who signed the papers to have Sophie moved into Valley View."

So Monica still had hope. If she could reach Ronald, she and Edward could fill in the large gap that existed in the judge's life. "Good work, Officer," she said. "Can you give me contact information about Ronald? Where can I find him?"

"Hold on to your hat, Monica. Ronald is in the county crematorium."

"What? He's dead?"

"Yes. He was shot in what was recorded as a random act of violence. No one claimed his body, so his remains were sent to the closest crematorium, and the county picked up the bill. That's what happens to a lot of homeless people."

Homeless? This was horrible news. Two people who had a connection to Judge Smith and neither one of them could help her and Edward.

"Officer Criswell, did the police ever find the person who killed Ronald Blaine?"

"Nope. A thorough investigation was conducted, but there was never enough evidence to charge anyone. The detectives closed the case within weeks of the crime."

"Weeks? How long ago was Ronald murdered?" she asked.

"Five years ago. That's when his mother took a bad turn." Criswell sighed. "Sad case all around," he said.

Monica thanked the man for his work. "If anything else pops up on this family, you'll let me know?"

"Of course. Good luck with your case, Detective Cortez."

Luck—that was all that would help them now. Two leads that couldn't give them any information, other than neither of them were responsible for murdering a judge in Florida over two weeks ago. Monica would tell Edward what she'd discovered tonight when he called. This information wouldn't support his belief that his father was murdered, so she would urge him to move on from the search.

The death of Judge William Smith seemed to embody the phrases that had become commonplace, Monica thought. *Unsolved mystery, cold case, lack of evidence.*

Four days ago, Monica and Edward had found the birth certificate and believed it might prove to be a clue in what had happened to the judge. Now there were no clues and there was nothing more to be done.

CHAPTER EIGHTEEN

ON TUESDAY AFTERNOON, Miguel Cortez came to Edward's office. Edward stood up from behind his desk, came around it and offered his hand to Miguel, who was dressed in dirty jeans and a grease-stained mechanic's shirt. As before, Miguel declined to shake hands.

"What's this about?" Miguel asked, his tone belligerent. His mannerisms were stiff and guarded.

"I could say you missed an appointment with your parole officer," Edward said. He wanted Miguel to know that he had the upper hand from the start. Missing a parole meeting was a punishable offense and Miguel had missed his latest one. He would hit Miguel with the information and then work on getting the man to open up.

"I couldn't help it," Miguel said. "Besides, I called Harry and explained things to him. He was okay with it."

"That's lucky for you, Miguel," Edward said. "But it's important that you not miss another check-in."

Miguel glanced around the room. "So this is your fancy office, Eddie? And your name on the door."

"It is."

"Can't imagine a top guy like you following up on somebody's missed parole appointments."

"I do a lot for the police department," Edward said.

"Well, fine, but if all you called me in for was to scold me for an appointment mishap, I'll go now. I don't need anybody to analyze me. All I did was screw up one schedule."

Edward gestured toward a chair. "Please, sit down, Miguel. I didn't call you in to analyze you. I just want to talk about things, make certain you're not slipping into old habits."

"Monica talked you into this? She's always been one to stick her nose into other people's business."

"She knows I'm talking to you, yes, and maybe you shouldn't say negative things about your sister. She could have had you arrested for child endangerment for that stunt you pulled with Emilio, but she didn't."

Edward didn't really know if that was true, but it was a good enough bluff to get Miguel to listen to him. The truth was, he didn't want Miguel to talk badly of his sister, period. Edward had to stay calm to accomplish what he intended to today.

Miguel reluctantly slumped into a chair. "So talk, Eddie. Some of us are on the clock, and I've got to get back to work."

Edward asked a number of questions to put Miguel at ease. He discovered that Miguel was working six days a week repairing cars at a body shop near the Everglades. He was drawing a decent salary. And he had a chance of moving up in the business, perhaps branching out to a larger, busier location.

"I've never heard of a body shop out on Seminole Trail. What's the name of it?"

"Bobby Ray's Body Shop."

"How does the owner advertise the business?"

"I wouldn't know," Miguel said. He looked at his dirty fingernails. "I'm not exactly in middle management." He shifted his weight in the chair. "If that's all, I'm going to go now."

"No, it's not all, though I'm glad to hear you're showing up for work every day. But there's one more thing, Miguel. I understand you called your mother recently."

"So? She's my mother. Don't you ever call your mother?"

"I don't have a mother," Edward said. Not exactly the truth since he'd heard from Brooke that their biological mother was still alive. But since she'd rejected him and his sisters, she was dead to Edward.

"Well, if you did, you should call her."

"Rosa said you sounded worried. You told her you might be moving back to Sweet Pine Key and you asked her to find you a place to live."

Miguel shrugged. "Looks like Monica isn't the only busybody in my family."

"Did you ever think that maybe your mother is truly worried about you?"

"I suppose she is, so for her sake I'll just tell you that I don't know what I'm going to do. Moving back to Sweet Pine is a thought, that's all."

Edward leaned back in his chair. "I don't

want to beat around the bush, Miguel. Are you in some kind of trouble?"

"Everything in my life is great, Eddie. Isn't a guy allowed to move in this country without cops coming down on him?"

"Sure. But you just told me how well you're doing at your job, and that leads me to believe that you wouldn't want to move right now. Yet you asked your mother about finding you somewhere to live in Sweet Pine." Edward shrugged in turn. "You know, Miguel, I can have that business checked out. All it takes is a few phone calls to see if Bobby Ray's is licensed and bonded. It's easy enough to find reviews to see if there are any complaints about the work, or if Bobby Ray's has legitimate customers. And I can even drive out there myself to inspect the place."

Miguel snickered. "Come on out. All you'll see is a bunch of car parts and old tires."

"I won't see the occasional auto-transport truck taking nicely rebuilt automobiles to the port of Miami?"

Miguel twisted his fingers together. "What are you getting at?"

"I've done some preliminary investigating

of body shops on Seminole Trail, Miguel. And what I've uncovered points to the fact that Bobby Ray's doesn't exist. What does operate out there in the boonies might be a chop shop. I think Bobby's got a gang of car thieves stealing vehicles and bringing them to an undisclosed location to be reconfigured into automobiles that are hot sellers in South America."

Miguel's face flushed, and Edward knew he was right. Basically, it was a lucky guess. The location was perfect for a chop shop. An old run-down warehouse in an area with no neighbors around. No paperwork had ever been filed under the official business name. And the best clue was Edward's own background in stealing cars. Sometimes a checkered past helped to identify another person running afoul of the law. Definitely something crooked was going on at Seminole Trail.

"I don't know anything about that," Miguel said. "I'm just the guy who fixes the cars and paints them after the work is done."

Edward gave him a serious warning look. "If you're involved in a chop shop, Miguel, you're going back to jail, and this time you won't get parole."

Miguel remained silent for a long while. Finally, he said, "If you're so sure about this, why are you telling me? Why not just send the cops out there and raid the place?"

Edward sighed. "Oh, the cops are going to Seminole Trail to have a look around, believe me. But I'd like to save you from yourself, Miguel. I happen to like your family. I'd like to help your mother sleep at night." He stared hard into Miguel's eyes.

"Tell me what's going on out there and what you're so afraid of, and I'll do my best to help you. If you don't, then Bobby Ray and everyone who works for him is likely going down."

Miguel licked his lips. "How can you help me?"

"First *you* have to help *me*. I need information. If someone is threatening you, I have to know it. Then I can protect you."

"Can you keep me out of jail?"

"I'm not a miracle worker. There will still be consequences for what you've done. But I can guarantee you'll be safe if you have to return to jail, though."

Minutes ticked by while Edward waited. He now knew that what he'd suspected was true. Miguel was involved with some bad people. They were threatening him, and he didn't have a way out. All the signs were there. Miguel's nervousness, his body language, his lack of focus. Edward hoped the man would take the offer he'd handed to him.

"There's one more thing, Miguel."

Miguel looked at him. His hand in his lap trembled. "What's that?"

"You should allow Monica to adopt Emilio."

Miguel's eyes widened. "You're asking me to give up my kid?"

"You took that kid and then left him on his own at night. You haven't tried to contact him or contributed a cent to his welfare for five years. What's scarier is that you'll most likely have to go back to prison soon. So, I'm asking you to think of Emilio first, his needs, and make Monica's custody of your son legal. In spite of everything, I think you know that Emilio is in a good place with Monica and your mother. He's happy. Can you make him happy? Can you care for him, given how this may play out?"

The air in Edward's office grew tense. Edward knew he was asking Miguel to give up the last card in his hand. Emilio was the leverage Miguel could use to influence his mother and sister. But Edward was willing to bet that saving himself was more important to Miguel than anything else.

"These are really bad men, Eddie," Miguel said. "Can you keep them away from me?"

"I can and I will."

Miguel Cortez looked defeated. His hands dangled between his knees. His shoulders slumped. "Okay. What do you want to know?"

"Okay to both, Miguel?" Edward asked. "You'll give me information and you'll sign papers so Monica can adopt Emilio?"

"I'll still get to see him sometimes?"

"Monica seems fair to me. I don't think she wants to keep you from your son. It's time you trusted someone, Miguel, and your sister would be a good place to start." Miguel nodded but didn't speak.

"I WISH I had better news, Edward," Monica said on the phone late Tuesday night. "But once I found out that Ronald had been killed, I knew we had no avenue left for us. I realize you're disappointed, but there's not much I can do."

"Disappointed doesn't begin to cover how I feel," he said.

He'd never sounded so disillusioned before, and Monica couldn't help feeling that his bitter emotions were aimed directly at her. She'd failed him again and they were at the end of their investigation.

"How are things going at work?" she asked, trying to change the subject to something current in his life.

"If it weren't for the fact that my father died a short while ago, I might never have believed I'd left my desk. But as it is, I'm having trouble concentrating."

She almost told him that it would get easier, but then she remembered folks saying the same thing to her when her father died. In truth, the pain became less intense, but missing her dad had never become easier.

Edward's simple statement stung. They'd only just met and become close, and yet now he sounded as if nothing in his life had changed. His pain was still great. His determination to uncover the truth wavering. In Monica's life, everything was different, certainly better, until now. Edward was bitter. She couldn't blame him for feeling that way. She just wished she could have helped him. She wished he had something positive in his life to think about.

"Oh, there is one thing," he said.

Hopeful, she asked, "What? Tell me."

"I spoke to your brother this morning."

"And was Mama right? Is he in trouble?"

"Yeah. He's involved in illegal activity at a chop shop. Apparently the owner is coming down hard on him."

"Were you able to make him see sense?" Monica hoped Miguel would change his ways, but that didn't mean she wanted him back in Sweet Pine.

"I think so." Edward explained that Miguel was going to help the police in exchange for a lighter sentence when arrests were made. "He's not in the clear, Monica," Edward said. "But I will do all I can for him."

"I appreciate that, Edward. And Mama will certainly think your halo is shining more brightly."

"Oh, and Monica..." he said, and then stopped.

"What?"

He cleared his throat. "Nothing. I'll tell you later."

"Okay. Talk to you tomorrow?"

"Sure. And if I forgot to say it, thanks for contacting the police in San Diego."

"I wish it had turned out differently," she said.

"So do I."

They disconnected, and Monica went into the kitchen to help her mother with dinner cleanup.

"How is Edward?" Rosa asked.

"He's fine but disappointed that I didn't have promising news for him about what happened around his father's death."

"Can't you keep looking for more people, 'Nica? Edward is our good friend now. Friends help each other. He's going to talk to Miguel for me."

"I know he is, Mama. In fact, he's already spoken to Miguel. I have news for you. We'll talk after Emilio has gone to bed."

"You seem sad, too, *chica*. Are things not well between you and Edward?"

Truthfully, Monica didn't know. Something had been uncomfortable during tonight's phone call. Nothing personal had been said. No sentiments of missing each other. No promises of getting together again soon. The phone call had almost seemed like a discussion between two colleagues. But to her mother, Monica said, "It's okay, Mama. Distance can make things difficult sometimes."

EDWARD THOUGHT ABOUT why he hadn't mentioned the adoption to Monica. He had started to, but something stopped him. He knew she would be thrilled to learn that Miguel had agreed to allow Emilio to finally be hers in terms of the law, but he'd kept the news to himself. Had he been too cautious in not mentioning the arrangements he'd made with Miguel? Did he worry about disappointing her if Miguel changed his mind? Did he want to wait until the papers on Miguel's end were finalized before telling her? All of that was part of his decision to stay silent for now.

Though the real reason he'd kept the news to himself was that he wanted to see her face when he told her. He imagined her bright eyes lighting up, her smile glowing with happiness. Telling her over the phone was not how he wanted to give her the news. And besides, distance made things difficult sometimes. Had she felt the same thing during tonight's conversation?

His phone rang once more before he went to bed. He recognized the number. Brooke.

"Hello, Brooke. How are you?"

"Fine. We're all well, thanks. Cammie and I were hoping you could come to Charleston. Maybe this weekend? Catch a flight up on Friday and stay until Sunday. It'd be great for you to meet everyone since you're family now. What do you think?"

"Now isn't such a good time," he said. "I've just gotten back to work, and I have a backlog of cases to catch up on."

"That's understandable. You've had so much to deal with recently," she said. "If you do decide to visit, I've got some friends I'd like you to meet."

"I'll think about it," he said. He appreciated Brooke's acknowledging his reluctance to come to Charleston right now. Although, maybe a change of scenery would help alleviate the bitterness he was experiencing at another dead end with respect to the judge's death. He hoped Brooke wasn't referring to any single girlfriends when she offered introductions. His thoughts were on one woman only and he wanted to see her again. If he'd made Monica feel as though he blamed her for the dead end with the case, he needed to change that.

He cleared the air with his sister with one question. "You're not thinking of introducing me to a potential girlfriend, are you?"

"What would be the harm?" she asked and smothered a chuckle. "Unless you and Monica have grown closer? You're the best-looking brother I've ever had, and in Charleston, you'd be quite the catch."

He laughed, too. "I'll let you know tomorrow."

His sister obviously hadn't picked up on the fact that he and Monica were already close. He would have to make that clear very soon. Because he hoped Monica was his future.

CHAPTER NINETEEN

MONICA AND EDWARD continued to phone each other the rest of the week, but since Edward had decided to go to Charleston, he couldn't tell Monica that he would see her over the weekend. He had carefully thought about Brooke's invitation and could find no good reason to postpone a trip to meet the rest of his family. Besides, Edward needed a diversion, and connecting with his sisters and nieces and nephews seemed a welcome and necessary break.

He dialed Monica's number on Friday morning as he was preparing to leave for the airport. He hoped she would understand his reason for the trip, and he hoped he could convince her that he would be looking forward to seeing her the following weekend, when he would return to the marina and check with A.J. about how things were going.

Unfortunately, Edward connected with

Monica's voice mail. In as few words as possible, he told her about the trip to see his sisters. "I'll definitely be down next weekend to see you and Emilio. In fact, I can't wait to see you. Maybe we can take Emilio snorkeling if it's not raining. Would you like that? I'll have to look in on A.J., but it shouldn't take up much of my time…" Edward halted in midsentence when his breath caught in his chest. "I've just thought of something, Monica. I'll call you back."

It was a wild thought and probably wouldn't lead to anything, but when A.J. became part of his conversation with Monica, Edward couldn't ignore a possible theory that had taken root in his brain. *If it's not raining…*

Monica said she had talked to A.J. soon after his father's death. A.J. had said he was not in the bait house that night—he only stayed in the shed on rainy nights. Had he been lying? Did he stay in the shed more often than he'd indicated? What had the weather been like on the night of the death? Had A.J seen something, after all? Edward called the weather station in Monroe County and asked what conditions had been like on that fateful night.

When he disconnected, he called the airline and canceled his flight to Charleston. Then he called Brooke to tell her something important had come up. He'd have to reschedule.

FRIDAY MORNING WAS busy at the sheriff's office. Monica had taken several calls, but none more important than the one from Officer Criswell in San Diego. She was speaking to him when she had to ignore a call from Edward.

"I have some interesting news, Detective Cortez," Criswell said. "I had some spare time this week and I followed up on that case we talked about."

"The case about Ronald Blaine?"

"Yes. I pulled the file and looked over the paperwork. Remember I told you Blaine had no family except for his mother in the nursing home?"

"Yes, of course, I remember."

"Well, I cross-referenced Blaine's name with birth certificates, and it turns out

Blaine did have a relative, a son born almost thirty years ago."

"A son?" Monica was stunned. Her hand holding the phone receiver began to shake. "Then Blaine also may have had a wife and—"

"No. He never married the mother, a woman named Karen McGinnis. But McGinnis listed Blaine as the father on the kid's birth certificate. Consequently, the records have cross-matched."

Monica's heart started to beat rapidly. A connection to the judge existed. Maybe Judge Smith never knew about a grandson, but if Criswell was correct, the grandson definitely existed. "Were you able to locate Karen McGinnis?"

"I was. Talked to her late yesterday. She still lives in the area. Found out some details that might help you. She stayed in contact with Blaine for a few years. Blaine and his son had a sketchy relationship. They knew of each other's existence but weren't close. And when Blaine had a streak of bad luck and ended up on the street, that was the end of his contact with the kid, who at this point was in high school."

"Did McGinnis tell you the grandson's name?"

"Sure did. His name is Andrew Jefferson McGinnis. She said he lived with her until a year or so ago and then he took off for Florida. As far as she knows he still lives there in the Keys somewhere. Since your jurisdiction is the Keys, I thought that could be a pretty interesting connection."

Monica had been taking notes as fast as Criswell talked. She wrote the name *Andrew Jefferson McGinnis* on a piece of notepaper. While she was still on the phone with Criswell, the capital letters in McGinnis's name stood out from the other letters. A.J. Andrew Jefferson.

"I hope this helps you, Detective," Criswell said. "Like I told you, I was just fishing around for anything that might prove significant…"

"You have helped more than you can know, Officer. I can't thank you enough."

"In this business we never know when

some little detail might make a difference," he said. "I remember one case when—"

"I've got to go, Officer. We'll talk again sometime soon. Thanks so much."

She hung up and immediately called Edward.

"Monica, I'm so glad you called," he said. "I've just found out something about the night my father died. I'd like to follow up on it."

Breathless, she said, "Edward, I heard your message. Don't go to Charleston."

"I'm not. I need to tell you—"

"I want to interview A.J.," she said. "I know I talked to him before, but I just got news that changes everything."

"That's what I was going to tell you," he said. "Remember when I told you that A.J. stays in the bait house on rainy nights? I don't know why I didn't realize the importance of that. I called the weather service in the Keys. Monica, it had rained that night, only about an hour or so after I went up to bed, but enough so that A.J. might have been there the night my father died. He might have seen something. He might not have remembered it when he talked to you.

Maybe he'd had too much to drink. Maybe his memory was foggy. But if he was there, then he very likely must have seen something or heard something."

Monica took a deep breath. "Edward, listen to me. A.J. is more than an employee of the marina."

"What are you talking about?"

"I just heard from the officer in San Diego. He discovered a record that proves A.J. is your father's grandson. Ronald Blaine was his father."

Silence. "Are you there, Edward? The cop in San Diego is sending me verification right now. I probably already have it in my email. This is serious, Edward. I'm going to the marina now to talk to A.J."

"Hang on, Monica. I should be there in a few hours."

"Oh, Edward," Monica murmured. "This could prove you were right all along."

"I know I was right about one thing, Monica. You are the best detective I could have had on my team. In fact, you're the best thing in my life."

For the second time in maybe fifteen minutes, Monica was breathless.

"See you soon," Edward said. "And Monica? Remember what I told you. Don't be a hero. If A.J. is our man, he's a dangerous guy."

"I'll be careful. Promise."

After Monica disconnected, she considered her options. From what Edward said, she assumed he wanted her to wait until he arrived so the two of them could confront A.J. together. That plan made sense because Edward was a criminal psychologist and could read the cues in A.J.'s answers—cues that Monica may have missed during her first interview with him. But waiting would waste too much time. Officer Criswell had talked to A.J.'s mother. Monica knew how mothers were, the instinctive protectiveness they felt toward their children. A.J.'s mother could be contacting her son right now and warning him about what she had told Criswell.

She couldn't wait; she had to follow this lead immediately, stop A.J. from leaving the Keys and heading somewhere they would never find him. She remembered Edward's words. *Don't be a hero.* He was right. A.J., if he knew he was a suspect, could be dangerous. She called a fellow officer she trusted in the department.

"Lincoln, this is Monica. Are you busy right now?"

"Not too much, Monica, and never too busy for you. What's up?"

"I'd like you to go with me to follow up on an important lead. Short trip, just a few miles away. Do you have time?"

"Sure. I'll come to your office right away."

Grateful for the backup, Monica strapped on her holster and waited for Lincoln.

Monica felt a sense of satisfaction at wrapping up loose ends. This was what she was paid for. But even more than that, she felt a sense of completion that Edward would now surely have. He'd never put the tragedy of losing his father behind him, but knowing he was right about how the judge met his end, and that the guilty party would go to jail would do a lot to help Edward move on. And perhaps his moving on would include her.

AN HOUR AFTER talking to Monica, Edward was ready to leave his office. He had contacted his patients and rescheduled appointments for later the following week. He wouldn't even stop at his condo to pick up anything. He simply got into his car and drove south through heavy midafternoon Miami traffic. As he headed toward the Keys, the traffic thinned, and he made better time. When he was an hour away from Sweet Pine Key, he called Monica to tell her he would arrive soon.

"Detective Cortez," he said to the dispatcher who answered the call.

"One moment." The dispatcher came back on the line. "I'm sorry, but Detective Cortez isn't in her office. Can I give you her voice mail?"

Where was she? Edward had told her he would leave as soon as possible. "No, thank you," he said. "I'll try her cell phone."

The call to Monica's cell went right to voice mail. The first hint of anxiety raised the hairs on the back of his neck. Why was her phone off? Had she gone in search of A.J. without waiting for him? Surely she wasn't facing A.J. alone. No, she was an experienced investigator. She wouldn't do that. Nevertheless, he ignored speed-limit signs and headed with urgency into the Keys.

MONICA HAD TURNED off her cell phone when she approached the marina. If A.J. was attempting to run, she didn't want to alert him to her presence. Experience had taught her that surprise often provided the best results.

She asked Lincoln to check the dock area. Most of the boats were moored. Obviously, it wasn't a busy day at Smitty's. "Just do a quick search," she said. She showed Lincoln a picture of A.J., one she had taken when she first interviewed him. "We're looking for this guy or anything that seems suspicious around the boats. Anything that might indicate that someone is planning to take one of the boats for an extended trip."

Lincoln understood the seriousness of this investigation. Monica had filled him in on the details on the way to the marina. And he knew Monica had a personal interest in the outcome of the case.

"Where will you be, Monica?" Lincoln asked her.

"I'm going to the bait house. Sometimes A.J. hangs out there. I'll radio you if I find him." Both officers had quieted their phones, but they still had means to communicate with their shoulder radios. Lincoln was a big man and a competent officer. Monica knew he could handle himself. While Lincoln headed off toward the boats, Monica walked to the bait house.

She waited, but heard nothing. She knocked on the door. When no one answered, she looked through the windows, to where customers stood to wait for their bait orders to be filled. No one appeared to be inside. She went back to the door and slowly turned the knob.

All was quiet inside the shack except for the hum of the air and filtration systems that kept the bait alive. The usual paraphernalia was stacked against the walls and on a table. Different-sized nets, cans of feed, boxes and canisters for the captured bait. The smell was usual for the Florida Keys—fishy, salty, the rotting smell of decaying seaweed. Monica felt slightly nauseous. She wiped sweat from her brow.

She began a preliminary search of the small hut since A.J. was obviously not here. She didn't know what she was looking for, perhaps a slip of paper that would prove as beneficial as the birth certificate she'd found in the judge's fake book. She halted when a low, hoarse voice interrupted her thoughts.

"Can I help you with something, Detective Cortez?"

She turned to face A.J. and swallowed. "I was just looking for Edward," she said, delivering her rehearsed line with confidence.

"He's not coming this weekend," A.J. said. "I would have thought you'd know that. You two are kind of cozy, aren't you?"

The thought flashed through her mind that A.J. had been watching them, perhaps seen them kissing or exchanging a private moment. She squelched a shiver of disgust.

"He changed his plans," she said. "He's supposed to arrive today." Her hand itched to reach for her radio. A.J. hadn't done anything to prompt suspicion yet, but his presence was somehow different today, threatening. She kept her hand at her side and decided not to call Lincoln. She didn't want to alert A.J. to her anxiety.

"Change of plans or not," A.J. said, "the boss doesn't come to the bait house often. He just orders what I tell him to and lets me run things here." A.J. delivered a sly smile. "He doesn't like to be around much."

The comment made Monica pause. "Oh, because he doesn't care for fishing?"

"Yeah, right." A.J.'s grin broadened. "I don't think he fishes much from his fancy condo in Miami."

Monica tried to smile. Keeping A.J. at ease was important. Her impulse was to lure A.J. from the bait house and into the open. Then Lincoln would have a chance to see them. She tried to step around the man to be nearer the door. He blocked her path.

"Let's go outside to wait," she suggested. "It's hot and stuffy in here."

"Guess that's why the other officer you brought along was poking around the boats instead of sweating in here."

A.J. knew about Lincoln. Two thoughts collided in Monica's brain. One, had A.J. hurt Lincoln? Two, was she alone with this man with no backup? She tried again to side-step her way to the door. "I'd almost forgotten about him," she said. "He rode along with me this morning on an investigation. It's time we left here, anyway."

A.J. situated himself in the doorway. "You've got time," he said. "Your officer is taking a nap out by the last boat. I can't see him waking up anytime soon."

What had A.J. done? Was Lincoln injured

or possibly dead? Monica tried to calm her escalating fear. Lincoln was a family man with two kids. Monica was friends with his wife. His son sometimes played with Emilio. She straightened her spine. "Please step aside, A.J., I need to check on Officer Quinton. Perhaps he suddenly fell ill."

"It's true," A.J. said. "He's not feeling too well right now."

Monica resisted the urge to draw her weapon. A.J. had not threatened her. At this point he seemed to be playing a cat-and-mouse game. Officers had been trained not to use a weapon unless a life was being threatened. She didn't know if A.J. was even telling her the truth. She couldn't assume he'd done anything to Lincoln.

She took a forceful step forward, tried to dip under A.J.'s arm. He stopped her by grabbing her upper arm, the one nearest her pistol. He twisted her arm until she felt her shoulder pop. Pain shot up to her neck. Already her right hand could be useless.

"Let me go, A.J.," she said through gritted teeth. "You are attacking a police officer. I'm arresting you."

A.J. shoved her to the rear of the bait

house. She collided with a wall. Her right shoulder burned with pain. With one swift movement, A.J. unsnapped her holster and removed her weapon.

Despite the pain, a thought from her training days coursed through Monica's brain. Never let a suspect get to your weapon. So many bad stories had been drummed into rookies' heads about criminals who had gotten hold of a pistol.

A.J. pushed Monica toward a bench and grabbed a length of mooring rope. She knew that now was her last chance to get away. She stood up and kicked furiously with one foot while maintaining her balance with the other. A.J. hollered and clutched his abdomen, but didn't go down. Instead, she felt the sharp, brutal force of one swift punch to her cheek. A dark fog clouded her brain and she felt herself being shoved onto the bench, sensed the rope going around her arms and legs. She might have passed out except a bucket of murky, foul-smelling water was doused on her face.

Her eyes snapped open and she gasped. She drew in an agonizing breath and stared into A.J.'s eyes, brilliant with the lust of victory.

"Okay now, Monica…" He said her name with the lilting mockery of one who has conquered. "Why don't you tell me exactly why you came out here today?"

"I think you know that already, A.J.," she replied.

EDWARD TRIED MONICA'S cell phone several times before he reached Sweet Pine Key. He only got her voice mail; his heart raced. There had to be a reason for her phone silence, and Edward feared the worst. When he got to Sweet Pine, he called the sheriff's department and requested that officers be sent to the marina. Without specific details and no word from Monica, the dispatcher was reluctant to send out a patrol, but she promised she would pass along the request.

Monica's gray sedan was the first thing Edward saw when he got to the marina parking lot. He sped across the gravel and slammed his car into Park. Why hadn't she waited for him to arrive? And knowing he was coming, why had she turned off her phone?

There would be time to sort out the details later. Right now, Edward's first thought was to get to Monica. He ran toward the dock, and, seeing nothing out of the ordinary, he turned back toward the house. He stopped midway across the lawn when he heard a low moan that seemed to float on the breeze. He stopped and listened, then determined the sound had come from the pier and ran back again.

He darted across the wooden planks to the end of the dock. Praying he wouldn't find Monica injured, he was shocked to find a male officer bound to a dock piling, with rope wrapped around an oily rag stuck in his mouth. The officer was groggy but trying to return to alertness. Edward crouched beside him, loosened the rope around his mouth and removed the filthy rag.

The officer shook his head and spit saliva from his lips. "What happened?" he asked. "Who are you?"

"I'm Edward. I own the marina." He began trying to free the ropes from the man's hands and legs.

"Never mind that," the officer said. "Find Monica. She asked me to come with her.

Said she had to interview A.J. And then, I don't know, I was hit on the head."

After a quick glance around the dock, Edward noticed a wooden oar floating in the water. The tip was stained with blood. "I'll call for an ambulance," Edward said. "Where is Monica?"

"Never mind the ambulance. I'm okay. Just find her."

Edward's sharp gaze searched the property. "Is she in the house?"

The officer's eyes started to close. Edward shook him back to consciousness. "Where is Monica?" he shouted.

"Bait house. She said she was going there."

"Have you got a weapon?" Edward asked. He'd never fired a gun at anything other than a target, but now might be the time he fired for real.

"Locked in my desk back at the station," the officer muttered. "Didn't think… Go. I'll be fine."

Edward knew the poor guy wasn't fine, but he also knew backup help might arrive at any time. "Hang in there, buddy," he said, then stood and ran toward shore.

The bait house was in view about a hundred yards away.

Edward slowed when he got close. He didn't know what he would find if he opened the door. Would the building be empty? Would Monica be inside, injured or worse? Would A.J. have escaped?

His heart pounded in his ears. His lungs burned from running in the extreme heat. He felt as if his world was about to collapse.

"Please be safe in there, Monica," he whispered to himself. Nothing mattered now except for Monica. He didn't care if he solved the mystery of his father's death. He didn't care if he ever saw this land, this marina, this house ever again. All he cared about was Monica. He prayed that she was alive with an urgency he'd never experienced before.

He wasn't a trained investigator, not a cop who faced danger every day. Not a man who risked his life charging into situations that held uncertain outcomes. But today he wanted to do the right thing in the right way. Today his purpose was clear. For their sake—his and Monica's—and their future.

Their lives depended on his clear thinking and ability to make the right choices.

He stopped at the door, took a deep breath and leaned in. He heard her voice, garbled, as if she was having trouble talking. But it was Monica's voice. She was alive.

"You're in a lot of trouble," she said. "What did you do to Officer Quinton?"

"You haven't answered my question." A.J.'s voice rose in anger. "Why did you come here today?"

"Okay, A.J.," she said. "But if you need it spelled out, I came here to talk to you about the death of Judge Smith."

He made a sound like a growl deep in his throat. Footsteps, ones too loud to be Monica's, sounded on the wood-plank floor of the bait house. He was pacing, as if he was nervous. "You think I did it. You think I killed the judge."

"I think you know more than you told me. If you didn't kill the judge, then you know who did." Her words were slurred and weak. "If you tell me now, there is still a chance to save your life. If you hurt me or Officer Quinton, there is nothing I can do to help you."

"You can't help me now, you stupid—"

"I can." Monica coughed, seemingly struggling with every breath. "But if you kill me…"

Edward couldn't wait any longer. A.J. obviously had the upper hand, and Monica was running out of time and energy. With no weapon, no means of protection, he slowly opened the door. A.J. spun around. He had a gun. Edward's body tensed as he prepared to take a bullet.

He focused on the pistol aimed at his chest, saw A.J.'s hand shake. A.J. didn't speak. The room was eerily, threateningly quiet.

"Put the gun down, A.J.," Edward said in a voice much calmer than he'd expected. His years of education and experience with criminals flashed through his head. One mistake and they could all be dead. "Please put the gun down, A.J. We'll talk. You're not going to get away. Cops are probably right now pulling into the marina. I called them."

A.J.'s hand shook more violently. There was a good chance if he fired he would only hit the wall behind Edward. But Edward couldn't charge him and take that chance.

His eyes darted behind A.J. and he saw Monica strapped to a bench with mooring line. Her head lolled to one side, but her eyes were open. The side of her face was bruised. Edward had never known hatred like he felt in that instant, but hatred for A.J. wouldn't keep Monica alive. Only clear thinking and calm action would.

"We know who you are, A.J.," he said. "We know the judge was your grandfather."

"Then you know what a rotten man he was. He had everything, and we had nothing. My father, who died in the streets, my mother who lives in a one-room apartment in San Diego—the judge didn't do anything for any of us. He didn't care if we starved."

A.J. raised his free hand and placed it under the elbow of the hand that held the gun. The pistol steadied, making a shot more accurate now. "And the judge took you in, a stranger without a drop of his blood. The judge gave you everything."

Edward raised his arms as if surrendering, a gesture to hopefully calm him. "I want to hear about that, A.J. I want to know everything about you and your family. This is all a mystery to me, and only you can clear it up. But you can't tell me with that gun pointed at my face. Put the gun down, A.J., and talk to me."

A.J. cleared his throat. His voice rose to a high pitch. "I'd been waiting for the right time to talk to Smitty," he said. "I worked here for over a year, did everything the old guy told me to. He couldn't have run this place without me."

"I'm sure that's true," Edward said. "I know how much my father depended on you."

"Don't call him your father! You've got no right."

Edward didn't argue. "Go on with your story, A.J. What happened the night my fa— the judge died?"

"I waited up until the judge came out of the house. I just wanted to ask him for what was rightfully mine, what I deserved, what my dad had deserved before me. I figured he'd be in a mood to hear it."

"Sure, I understand," Edward said.

"I showed him proof of who I am. I told him I wanted part of his marina, not all of it, just some, enough to help me through a tough time."

"And he didn't agree to give you any of the marina?" Edward said. "That must have made you angry."

"He laughed," A.J. said. "The man you think is so caring, so fair—he laughed in my face." A.J.'s voice cracked. He seemed to have trouble continuing.

Edward was stunned by the thought of the judge behaving that way, but he had to stay focused. "Go on, A.J.," Edward encouraged.

"All I did was shove him. But I was mad, you know. Anybody would've been."

"And then what happened?"

"I didn't mean to kill him. He fell off the dock, and when he came up for air, I don't know what happened. I just saw his face. I knew then I wasn't going to get anything from him. So I pushed him down, held him with my feet on his shoulders."

Edward's stomach roiled. The image of his father's last moments, his struggle to break free of A.J.'s hold on him, his eyes open in the murky water. Edward pictured the pocketknife he took from his pants, the desperate carving in the piling which Edward now suspected was his attempt to carve the letter *A*.

A.J.'s words dissolved into gasps for air. He squeezed his eyes shut. "I just wanted… what should have been mine." He slowly lowered the gun until the barrel was pointing at the floor.

Edward took three steps, carefully reached out and slipped the gun from A.J.'s hand. "Sit down, A.J.," he said in a soothing but commanding voice. Once A.J. did that, Edward quickly untied Monica.

"What's going to happen to me?" A.J. asked.

"I don't know, but you'll have to face what you've done. A court will decide," Edward told him.

Tears ran down Monica's face. But in spite of the bruise on her cheek and the sweat running down her brow, she looked absolutely beautiful in Edward's eyes. She managed to smile at him.

"The police will be here soon," Edward said. He took his phone from his pocket and called for two ambulances.

A.J. sat quietly, not speaking. His head was bowed, his eyes closed. Edward recognized he was no longer a threat.

Edward leaned toward Monica. "Hang in

there, baby," he whispered. "Help is on the way."

"Edward, I was so afraid for you. I knew you were out there. I wanted to tell you to run from the bait house."

"Shh, Mon. I wasn't about to run anywhere. Not without you."

"I let him get my gun," she said. "That's the worst thing an officer can do…"

"It's okay. The worst thing would have been if you had died, but you kept that from happening."

Edward wrapped her in a tight hug. She flinched, cried out in pain. He released her immediately. "What is it, Monica?" Edward asked. "Your shoulder?"

"I think I bruised it."

Edward gently probed the affected shoulder. "Monica, you didn't bruise it. You dislocated it." He stared at A.J., his fists closing. He had the urge to punch the man.

"How do you know that?" Monica asked.

"I know two things, Mon. I know that you have a dislocated shoulder because I've had one. But don't worry, you're going to be fine."

"What's the other thing you know?"

"That I'm in love with you," he said. "And I know that because I realized that finding you alive meant that I would be fine." He knelt down in front of her, put his hands on her knees. "It's over, Mon. A day or two in the hospital and you'll be back with Emilio, and I'm not going anywhere."

She gave him a genuine smile then. Edward heard the crunch of gravel in the parking lot. Help had arrived.

Soon Monica and the wounded officer would be in the hospital. A.J. would be in jail. And Edward would have kept his promise to his father.

CHAPTER TWENTY

MONICA HOPED TO BE RELEASED from the hospital soon. Once A.J. was taken to the station and put in a holding cell, the police came to the hospital and interviewed Monica and Edward. One of the officers was Officer Patterson, who had interviewed Edward the morning his father's body was found in the bay.

"Wow, Mr. Smith, I sure never suspected that your dad was murdered," Patterson said during the interview.

"Sometimes hunches pay off," Edward said. "This time it did."

Patterson shifted his attention to Monica. "Good detective work on your part."

She adjusted her arm in the newly applied sling and smiled at Edward. "I wish I had believed more in Edward's theory from the beginning."

"You believed enough," Edward said.

"How is Lincoln?" she asked.

"He'll be okay," Patterson reported. "He's got to stay in the hospital overnight. He had stitches and they want to keep an eye on him, since it's a head injury."

"Thank goodness he's going to recover. I feel terrible about what happened to him," Monica said.

The two officers asked questions, gathering the details they needed to make a case. Since A.J. had confessed and both Monica and Edward had heard it, there wouldn't be a problem in proving A.J.'s guilt. Monica figured his lawyer would simply plead for a lighter sentence due to emotional distress and temporary insanity.

When the officers had gone to file their report, Monica's cell phone rang. She answered immediately. "Hi, Emilio. How was camp today?" She was always glad to hear her nephew's voice, but today his phone call nearly brought her to tears.

"I'll be home soon," she said, answering his question. "Edward is coming with me."

"Oh, good. I want to see him," Emilio said.

Monica was pleased that her mother hadn't told the boy about her encounter with

A.J. and the extent of her injuries. She would have to explain the sling and the bruise on her face, which had swelled her upper lip and cheek. She would tell Emilio that she was fine and make up a little white lie to cover the complete truth. He didn't need to know that she had been in such danger. It was enough that Rosa had called her hospital room in tears.

A discharge nurse came in the room with papers for Monica to sign. "You can go home now, Monica. Do you have a ride? The doctor doesn't want you to drive until the shoulder is healed."

"She has a ride," Edward said. "And I guarantee she won't be driving anytime soon."

Monica met Edward in front of the hospital entrance. She got out of the required wheelchair and sat in the passenger seat. Soon they were on their way to Lantana Lane. Edward stopped in a shady spot, kept the air conditioner running and turned to look at Monica. Her mind flashed to the words he had spoken at the bait house, when he'd said he loved her. Had he said those words in the context of the moment or had he meant them? They had only known each other for three weeks. Would he have said he loved her if she hadn't been in danger?

He spread his arm over the back of the passenger seat. "I can't begin to tell you how terrified I was when I saw you in that bait house," he said.

"But you kept your cool. You talked to A.J. in a calm manner. I really admire your ability to connect with such troubled people."

"This was the worst time I've ever had doing that," he said. "There was my grief in losing my father and knowing A.J. was responsible. And then there was my fear that I would lose you, too, and in that moment, I realized that losing you would be even worse."

Monica's heart began to pound. Never before had a man said he loved her. Many men had tried to be with her, and she had pushed them away because they had been wrong for her. But this man she didn't want to push away. Edward was the man she believed she had been waiting for. "Edward, I—"

"I need to tell you this, Monica," he said in a hoarse whisper. "I didn't expect to fall in love with you so soon and so completely, but it happened. I have never loved anyone in any way except for my father in my entire life. I didn't know the meaning of the word. But you've taught me the true definition. Love is a feeling in your heart, a glorious mixture of pain, and pleasure and passion. A feeling I never want to lose, and I know I won't with you."

She blinked to erase the moisture gathering in her eyes. She didn't want to miss a second of this moment. She didn't want Edward's face, his beautiful eyes, to be a blur in her memory. "Edward," she said. "I'm pretty sure I love you, too."

He smiled. "Then let me try to convince you that 'pretty sure' can be 'absolutely sure.'" Taking care not to touch her injuries, he placed his hand on her good shoulder and gently pulled her close. He kissed her in a way he never had before. His lips were tender and yet strong. He was right. Love was all the things he'd said. Pain when she had feared for Emilio and when she had seen Edward in the path of A.J.'s gun. Pleasure when she had been reunited with her nephew and pleasure every moment as she got to know Edward. Passion? Oh, yes, passion, the way she felt now, the way she knew she would always feel with Edward.

"Edward," she murmured when they ended the kiss.

"Yes?"

"I'm absolutely sure, both about loving you and one other thing."

He smiled, kissed her again with the utmost care and gentleness. "What's that?"

"I need a shower. I stink."

He laughed. "That can be arranged. Let's get that lip healed so we can do more of this kissing."

He started the car, pulled away from the trees and headed for Lantana Lane. "I have something else to tell you," he said.

BEFORE THE CALL from Monica that morning, Edward had received the paperwork from the social worker in Miami. The woman worked in the Miami-Dade County family services department, and Edward had asked her to visit Miguel, who was currently in isolation for his own safety at the county jail. The social worker had rushed the paperwork through and finalized the adoption procedure for Emilio. Miguel had signed his approval. Now all that remained was for Monica to sign and accept legal custody of her nephew.

"What do you have to tell me?" she asked as they drove toward her home.

Edward took an envelope from his pocket and handed it to her.

"What's this?"

"Open it and see."

She took out the official document and unfolded it. "This is from the family court," she said.

Edward smiled.

She read on, her breath coming in shorter gasps as she followed the words. "Edward, does this mean what I think it means?"

"If you think it means that Miguel has given his consent to legally let you raise Emilio, then yes. You never have to worry again about Miguel or anyone else taking him from you."

She looked over at Edward, her eyes bright with tears that were about to spill onto her cheeks. "Miguel signed this," she said, her voice almost reverent, as if a true miracle was more than she dared believe.

"Now all that remains is for you to sign your part at the bottom, have a short interview with the social worker, see a judge in family court and it's official." He reached over and squeezed her hand. "Congratulations, Monica. I know one little boy who is about to be the luckiest kid on earth."

"But—but…how did you get Miguel to agree?"

"He knew how well you've cared for Emilio. And he realized that he wouldn't be in any position to take as good care of Emilio for a long time."

Monica frowned. "You're making him sound like a generous person. I can't take that step."

"Maybe in time you will, Monica. There's a chance Miguel could change. We don't know what will happen in the future, but for now Emilio can have the life you always wanted and provided for him."

"Edward, I hope you're right. I want to believe that Miguel can change."

"It's time to trust that he can," Edward said. "He was in a bad place and wanted a way out, and I was able to help him with that. He should get some credit. In the end he did what was right for his son. Emilio should be going to school, having fun with his friends, and not be faced with the possibility of getting swept up in Miguel's world."

A smile broke across her face. "So this is really happening?"

"Really and truly."

"If we weren't driving right now, I would—"

"Hold that thought," Edward said. "I won't be driving forever."

"Wait 'til I tell Mama. Not only do we get to raise Emilio forever, but Miguel is safe, too."

Edward nodded. "This is probably the best that Miguel could hope for. He was involved with some pretty unsavory guys."

Edward pulled into the Cortezes' driveway. Monica reached for the car door handle before he'd come to a complete stop. "Hold on there, Detective. Slow down. You still have a dislocated shoulder and a bruised lip." He smiled. "And a fella who wants you in tip-top shape sooner rather than later."

She laughed. "I want that, too."

Rosa came out of the house, her arms spread to take Monica into a hug. "Come here, *chica*. I've been so worried."

"I'm fine, Mama," Monica said as she

stepped out of the car. "All I need is a cup of tea and a shower and I'll be good as new."

"Don't believe her," Edward said. "She needs lots of rest and time to heal."

"She will get the best care," Rosa said. "Lucy is on her way over now, and Horatio is bringing soup soon. You stay, Edward. I want to hear everything that happened."

Monica slipped her hand in his. "Yes, Edward, please stay." She looked at her mother. "I have the best news, Mama. Let's go inside and Edward and I will fill you in. After I have that shower."

Edward followed the women inside and prepared himself for the onslaught of Rosa's family. He didn't know how much rest Monica could get once the Cortezes and their relatives arrived, but he knew Rosa was right. Her daughter would be well cared for.

He told Monica that he would only stay a short while. He wanted some time alone to return to the house by the marina and think about how he would take care of Monica for the rest of her life.

THAT NIGHT EDWARD called Brooke.

"How wonderful to hear from you," she

said. "We were so disappointed when you canceled your trip, but at least we can plan for another time."

"I'm sorry I couldn't make it," Edward told her. "But it couldn't be helped. Some additional clues regarding my father's death surfaced and Monica and I wanted to follow up on them right away."

"Well, of course," Brooke said. "Did these clues prove that your father was murdered?"

"Yes. In the span of a few hours today, we caught the guy that did it, and he's been arrested."

"That's good news. Gives you the closure you were looking for." She asked questions about the clues and how the guilty man was apprehended. Like a typical newsperson, she seemed to marvel at how mysteries can unravel with determination and a bit of luck. "Now there's nothing to keep you from coming to Charleston."

"That's not exactly true," Edward said. "Monica was injured during the apprehension."

"How horrible," Brooke said. "How bad was it? You weren't hurt, were you?"

He explained the events of the afternoon

in as few words as possible. "So you can see, Brooke, that even though Monica's injuries weren't terribly serious, I don't want to leave her right now."

"It's reassuring that she has that whole big family, isn't it?" Brooke pointed out. "I could tell that her family is close-knit. She should have plenty of care."

"That's true," Edward said, truly believing that a large, caring family was a blessing, one he'd never known. "But I'd like to stay around at least through the weekend."

"Sure. You two are close, too."

Obviously, Brooke didn't understand the full picture. "Uh, there's something I need to tell you, Brooke. Monica is becoming more than just close."

There was a pause before Brooke said, "Edward, you're in love with her."

"Yes. I'm planning to ask Monica to marry me."

Brooke whooped with joy. "You know the old saying, Edward. You don't just marry a person. You marry their whole family. I can't get over this—our small clan has now, what, quadrupled in size?"

Edward took a long, calming breath. His

sister had reacted perfectly, with such excitement.

"Here I'm marrying a man who has two children, and Camryn's married a guy with children. If anyone should understand about marrying an entire family, it should be us."

Brooke's words mirrored his own thoughts. Edward was used to his family being just himself and the judge. Now look what had happened.

"That's for sure," he said. "But I'm probably never going to turn into Uncle Horatio. I can't see myself roasting a whole pig. But I will try to be the best fiancé for the woman who has turned my life around." He smiled at that and added, "As a matter of fact, make that three women who have turned my life around."

"I'll take that as a compliment," Brooke said. "If Monica says yes—and why wouldn't she?—don't forget to invite us to the wedding."

"You'll be at the top of the guest list."

They disconnected. Edward settled into a chair on his front porch and thought about his future, one that would be exciting and filled with love and compromise, a wonderful woman and a boy who loved snorkeling. He looked up at the sky. He had learned a lot about his father in the last weeks. Some good and some bad. But one thing he would always keep first in his heart. William Smith saved him and gave him a chance, and Edward was thankful to have kept the promise he made at the funeral home. "I think you would be pleased with this day, Dad."

ON SUNDAY NIGHT Edward took Monica to dinner at the Harborage in Key Largo. He picked the best restaurant in town, one on the fourth floor of a luxury resort hotel. An important event deserved the finest venue. He hadn't yet purchased a ring, but he and Monica could pick one out later. He would enjoy having her come to Miami, where the choices would be great and the glittering town would smile upon their future.

Despite the sling still on her arm and the remaining puffiness in her cheek and lip, Monica looked lovely in a coral dress with a matching sweater. The dress fit her perfectly and showed off the magnificent curves that were all hers, whether she was in a dress or a police uniform.

He ordered a bottle of wine, and they enjoyed a glass while looking out over the water on a beautiful, star-streaked night. Edward told her that he had come to terms with losing his father, and she said she might be ready to make amends with her brother. And they talked of Emilio and Rosa and Edward's sisters. It seemed the perfect night to suggest a joining of their families.

Edward poured a second glass of wine when their entrées arrived. He smiled to himself when he admitted he had a rare attack of nerves preceding what he was just about to do. This was the first time he had ever considered proposing marriage. He had no doubts about his decision, and accepted the small tremors of fear were all part of the excitement of the moment. What man's hands hadn't shaken when he was so close to taking the hand of the woman he loved?

"This is just the right night, the right place," he said. "And you are the right woman."

She smiled. "What are you talking about?"

"I love you, Monica. I think I loved you even when I was grieving, even when you and I differed on how my father might have died."

"It was so difficult for me to tell you that the investigation could go no further. I wanted to help you, to make your father's death easier to handle. I'm sorry how it all unfolded, that we found out the way that we did."

"It's over. It's time to move forward. I've donated most of my dad's possessions. And made up my mind about the marina. As of tomorrow, it's officially closed. I'll list the property with a Realtor soon."

"Are you sure that's what you want to do?" she asked him.

"The marina was my father's dream, not mine."

"Of course. You have to do what you think is right."

"You are what's right," he said. "You are my dream. You and Emilio and a life together." He rubbed his thumb over her knuckles, smiled at her. "Will you marry me, Monica? I want you and Emilio to live with me in Miami. Rosa, too, of course. We can buy a house and she'll live with us or have a place of her own." He squeezed her hand. "It's the future I want, Monica, and I hope it's the future you want also."

She swallowed, stared down at their joined hands. When she looked up after a full minute, her eyes were misty. Her voice cracked as she said, "My feelings for you are as strong, Edward. I do love you, and I wish I could say yes."

He felt his mouth quirk up at the corner, as if he wanted to smile but couldn't. "You wish?"

CHAPTER TWENTY-ONE

MONICA DIDN'T TRUST herself to speak. Edward's words were the ones she had longed to hear since that fateful day she'd met him. In the weeks that followed, she had sympathized with him, admired his determination, appreciated all his kindnesses and fallen in love with a man who loved her for who she was. And now he had asked her to marry him and share his dream. Only his dream was not the one she had committed to when her father died.

She withdrew her hand from his. She knew her future was not the one he hoped for. She could not share his dream or his vision for their life. The look she gave him was one of regret and sorrow and acceptance. "Edward..." she began. "I can't marry you and live in Miami."

His eyes widened, making it much easier to see the hurt, the shock in their deep blue depths. "Why not? You just said you love me."

"I do, so much, but I have to stay here in Sweet Pine."

"Is it your job?" he asked. "Because I understand that. Obviously, I support your wanting to stay in the police force. I know how hard you've worked. There must be openings in Miami."

"I do love my job," she said. "Being a police officer is important to me. I like helping people, coming to their assistance. I'd probably find the same satisfaction in Miami, though the job would involve some getting used to after working in Sweet Pine Key."

"Then what is it? Is it your house? It's a loving home, but any place you lived would be like that." He blinked hard. "I will do whatever I can to make you happy, Monica."

Once again she was disappointing him, once again her heart was breaking. "I have come to love my little house on Lantana Lane, but that's not the issue. I can't leave Sweet Pine Key because of a promise I made to my father."

He leaned across the table, his gaze

searching hers, trying to understand. "What promise?"

"Before my father died, my mother was quite ill. Papa nursed her back to health, and she recovered. But she was never the confident woman she'd been before. When she came to America, she was brave and full of hope for a life here. After the illness she was frightened and unsure. For a long time, she didn't go out. She stayed home and looked after all of us. Eventually, she became content again, even happy, but she was happy within the context of the life she knew. Her life here is simple, her love for her family strong.

"She likes it in the Keys. Her roots are deep. I would never want to unsettle or undo what she and my father built for us, our family. It would feel, I don't know, disrespectful somehow. Mama isn't interested in living anywhere else, especially a big city."

Edward rubbed his nape, shook his head slowly. "I had no idea," he said. "I've always moved around quite a lot. Started over for good when the judge took me in. I guess I just didn't think... What you're telling me is that moving to Miami would be a difficult adjustment for her."

"Yes, I'm telling you that, but it's even more than what you think. Mama thinks Miguel would still be with us if he hadn't gone to Miami, gotten in with the wrong crowd. I understand if you don't believe that, but Mama does. She sees Sweet Pine as a haven."

"But we can find a community in Miami where she'd feel comfortable and fit in."

Monica frowned. How to make him understand that the promise she made to her father was a covenant, a solemn pledge to the man who counted on her to hold them all together. She had already failed Papa with Miguel. She would not fail him by taking Rosa from her home, her family, her security.

"Edward, I am so sorry." Those words did not express her sadness, her grief. "As Papa lay dying, he made me promise to take care of Mama, to keep her safe, to understand her and make sure she was happy in Sweet Pine with her family. I pledged I would always do that."

"But we could come back often to see Lucy and Horatio."

He said the words as if he knew they were only a salve to the confusion between them. They were not a cure. Monica's honor was at stake here, and her word was important. Edward knew that, and Monica hoped that this was one of the reasons he loved her.

"I will not go back on my word," she said, the ache in her chest proof of the difficulty of this decision.

Edward remained silent, then said, "Would she stay here with Lucy or another family member? And you and I and Emilio would come often—"

"You still don't understand," Monica said. "Emilio and I are her sense of belonging to a family. Miguel has broken her heart. Perhaps his latest decision has helped the healing process. We'll see, but I can't do the same thing to her."

Again, Edward did not speak for a long time. His eyes were cast down as if he couldn't bear to look at her.

"Edward, please say something," she urged. "I can't stand this silence. I have to know what you're thinking."

He gave her a straightforward look, holding her gaze. "Monica, do you love me?" he asked.

Her answer came out as a choked whisper. "I do. You know I do."

"I'm trying to figure this out," he said. "I really am. But I'm struggling here. These ties you all have... I've never experienced anything like them exactly. You're all connected in ways I haven't experienced in my lifetime. I...can't believe there isn't a solution for this somehow."

One tear fell to her cheek. "Not if I have to take Mama from Sweet Pine." She grasped his hand, holding it tightly. "Remember your father's service when you thought you were alone with him at the funeral home?"

He nodded. "Yes."

"I was there, standing in the doorway. You were saying private words to your father, and I felt like a trespasser, but I heard your promise to him."

He swallowed. "I promised to avenge his death. Then you know I kept that promise."

"I do. You promised you wouldn't stop until you found the truth about what happened to him. Even when I couldn't go on believing your theory, you persevered. You kept looking, searching for clues. I'm ashamed to say that I abandoned you for a time."

"But you didn't, Monica. You were the one who finally tracked down the clue that brought us to the guilty party. I couldn't have done it without you."

"Perhaps that's true," she said. "But the important thing to know is that I never stopped believing in you, in your determination, your loyalty to your father. I never thought you would give up on your promise. And now…" She wiped the tear from her cheek. "Our situations are not so different. I have a promise I must keep."

"I wish the consequences of what you're saying were different, Monica. But I have to accept your loyalty to your father."

She released a deep breath. "Thank you, Edward."

"But Monica, a life apart, living hours from each other. My job is in Miami. Yours is almost three hours away. I don't know that I could do that. I miss you even when we're apart for a day. What kind of a marriage would that be?"

"I don't have an answer," she said. "We'll have to think about it. It wouldn't be easy, but Edward, don't you think that now is the time for us both to believe in something together? Maybe this is the thing."

The waiter came to their table and delivered the check. Edward pulled a credit card from his wallet and placed it on top. Until the waiter returned with the card, neither Edward nor Monica spoke. They were lost in their own thoughts, their own priorities.

Monica knew that Edward needed time to sort this out. How much time, she didn't know. What his decision would be, she could only speculate. But his answer could break her heart.

EDWARD SPOKE VERY little on the drive back to Lantana Lane. When he pulled onto the gravel entrance, he viewed the house in a different way. It was a fortress for Rosa, a place of calm and acceptance. To Edward, it was an obstacle to the life he wanted.

But he couldn't deny what Monica had said in the restaurant. They had both made promises to their fathers. They both believed that a promise made should be a promise kept. But perhaps Monica's was the deepest, most profound of the two. She made her father's dying moments comforting because he heard her words and believed her.

Edward made a promise to a man who was already gone. He could have gone back on his word, and his father would have never even known about the pledge. He didn't. He wouldn't. But Monica had made a solemn promise to a man who took her words into the afterlife knowing his daughter would make everything okay when he was gone. How could Edward tell her now that she should forget the moments when her father was dying and think only of herself now? He wouldn't. He couldn't.

And the truly sad thing was what would Edward think of her if she did that? He and Monica were from two different worlds. They lived different lives—hers full of family and togetherness. His was, even now with Cammie and Brooke, mostly a solitary life Or it had been, until he'd met Monica. Yes, he loved her. He'd never loved anyone as much as he loved her. But could they make it work? Could they be weekend partners and sometime lovers?

Edward reached across the console of his car, drew Monica close. "I love you," he said. "And since I can't stop loving you, we will find a way."

CHAPTER TWENTY-TWO

THE NEXT DAY Edward rescheduled an appointment with the Realtor. At the time his father died, he wasn't ready to sell the house that had meant so much to his dad, but now he was. His life wasn't about this old Keys place. Nor was it about the marina his father had purchased.

For Edward, the property only brought sad memories. This was where his father had died. It was where Monica had almost died. It was where Edward spent many lonely nights mourning what he had lost and what he might still lose. It was the place that had housed the many mementos of his dad's life—mementos that Edward had given away, mementos that proved his father had a life Edward had never known about.

Yes, it was time to let go of the past, to look to the future—a future that he hoped included him and Monica and Emilio. And maybe more children. If he could just figure out a plan.

The Realtor arrived at noon. Edward showed her around the home, with special emphasis on the large living room, the "parlor," as his father had called it, where Edward and he had spent many nights in front of the stone fireplace. He showed the Realtor the library, which had housed so much of his father's past, the ample kitchen with its many cupboards and large pantry. They toured the five bedrooms, including the master, where the judge had slept, and the light and airy room with a wonderful view of the ocean and large open windows, where Edward slept.

The Realtor commented on the endurance of the rich pine with which the house had been constructed and that had withstood hurricanes and punishing salt air. "You don't find homes of this quality and character any longer," the Realtor said. "Now all new construction is made of cinder block and brick. But nothing will outlast this structure."

When they walked onto the porch to examine the hardy wood planks and newly refinished roof, Edward drew a long, deep breath. "Is there always a breeze like this?" the Realtor asked.

Edward thought a moment. "Yes, I suppose there is, especially on this porch. Even in the hottest temperatures, one can still experience fresh Gulf air."

They sat. The Realtor took paperwork from her briefcase. "I really don't have any comparables to show you," she said. "This home is unique. I'm sure I can sell it quickly. With that in mind, we should look for a cash buyer. Once we find a buyer you can close immediately and get the payment right away."

She told him the price she had in mind.

Edward inhaled a gulp of air. "You're not serious?"

The Realtor smiled. "Obviously you're not aware of home values in the Keys these days. And this house, with its unique history, is highly desirable. I get calls every day from people wanting a home with a unique Keys perspective. I don't doubt we can get this price and perhaps even have a bidding war." She handed him a pen and a contract. "I can have this listed by tomorrow, and as I said, I believe it will be a quick sale."

He stared at the amount on the contract,

double what his dad had paid for the place. A small fortune. And as he read the details of the contract, his hand began to shake. He tightened his grip on the pen.

"Is something wrong?" the Realtor asked.

"I don't know," he said. "Suddenly I'm not so sure…"

In his mind, he replayed the last half hour of his life. The rooms he had visited on the second floor, the ones on the first, the parlor, the kitchen, the library. And he remembered the words he had uttered as he showed the Realtor around. They had been words of affection, of fond remembrances, of connection. They had not been words of grieving and sadness. All at once, sitting on the porch with the Gulf breeze fanning his face, he realized what he had overlooked until now. This house was not a problem. It was a solution.

He handed the contract and pen to the Realtor. "I'm sorry, Belinda. I think I've changed my mind about selling at this time."

"What do you mean?" she asked. "I thought you were sure."

"I was. Or at least I thought I was. But now I'm going to keep the house."

Her expression went from one of triumph to

confusion and disappointment. "The time is right for listing this home, Edward," she said.

"I realize that, but I need to talk to someone first. Again, I'm sorry, but I don't think I'll list the house now. If things change, I'll let you know."

Belinda packed up her papers and stood. "I hope I hear from you. You're making a mistake to wait." She went down the steps and to her car.

Edward took his cell phone from his pocket and called Monica's number. "Are you busy?" he asked when she answered. "I'd like to talk to you."

"No. Is something wrong?"

"Something might be very right. I'll be at your house in a few minutes."

WHEN EDWARD PULLED into Monica's drive, she was waiting for him on the front steps. His heart swelled with love. She was beautiful in a yellow sleeveless blouse with tiny ruffles on the shoulders and a pair of plaid yellow shorts. She was always beautiful, and she was Edward's heart and soul.

She came to his car. "Do you want to come

in?" she asked. "Mama is grocery shopping with Aunt Lucy, and Emilio is at camp."

He reached over and opened the door from the inside. "Take a short ride with me."

She climbed in. "You have me worried. I know you said nothing was wrong, but your voice sounded anxious."

He reversed onto the street and drove the same way he'd just come. "Hang on to that thought," he said. "If, in a moment, you still think something is wrong, then we'll start over with another plan."

She remained silent for a minute, her gaze on his profile as he drove. "We're at your father's house," she said. "Did you meet with the Realtor this morning?"

He got out of the car and came around to open her door. "I did meet with Belinda, and I have decided that this is no longer my father's house."

Monica stepped out of the car. "Belinda gave you good news about the price then."

Edward reached for her hand and walked her to the edge of the water. The sun had started to heat up the air and the sand, but that breeze, that wonderful breeze that Belinda had noticed and Edward had always taken for granted, was still cool and fresh.

"Actually, I won't make any money on this house," he said. "At least not for a long time."

"What do you mean?"

"There are people I need to talk to, blessings I need to ask for."

"Blessings? Whose blessing do you need?"

"Emilio's, Rosa's, Uncle Horatio's, Aunt Lucy's—many others, including my two sisters'." He turned her to face him. "But mostly yours."

Her eyes grew wide and especially brilliant in the early afternoon sun. "I don't understand."

He took both of her hands in his. "I'm not selling, Monica. I'm going to live here, as often as I can, anyway."

Her hands began to tremble in his. "Live here?"

"Yes. With Rosa and Emilio and with you. Most importantly with you, if you'll have me. It won't be perfect all the time. I'll split my workdays between Miami and Sweet Pine. Temporarily, at least. I'm sure there are inmates at Keys Correctional who need my help, and I intend to put my name in to be the counselor in this area as soon as a spot opens up."

The smile she gave him warmed his heart and made him all the more certain that his decision was the right one. He grinned at her. "Of course, you have to agree to marry me."

She dropped his hands and threw her arms around his neck. "Edward, I love this house. I always have. And I have waited for you my whole life. I knew you were out there someplace, and I knew you would come. I will marry you. You're the kindest, most understanding man."

He whispered into her hair. "My pleasure, Detective. I plan to spend my life making you happy."

She stepped back, looked into his eyes. "We will be a wonderful, huge, loving family," she said, chuckling. "And I can persuade Uncle Horatio to keep his pigs and spits away. Mostly." She took a deep breath. "Plus, Emilio will have more cousins!" She stood on her toes and kissed Edward soundly. "Thank you for making my dreams come true."

Edward put his arm around her and looked up into the clear blue sky. "And thank you, Dad. Somehow you knew that your dream would eventually be mine."

EPILOGUE

FALL IN THE Florida Keys was a beautiful time of year, and even more so this year because Edward and Monica were planning a wedding. The date was set for the third week of November, a few days away, and most of the details were in place. Only one major consideration needed to be addressed.

Monica, Edward and Emilio walked up the sidewalk of the Miami-Dade Correctional Institution. Edward held Monica's hand. She held Emilio's. "Are you ready, honey?" Edward asked as he opened the door to follow her inside.

"Yes. I talked to Miguel this morning. He knows I'm bringing Emilio."

Edward showed his identification to the guard at the desk. "Oh, yes," the guard said. "I heard you were coming in today. Miguel Cortez is one of your patients. He's doing very well."

"I'm aware he's made significant strides, but it's always good to hear," Edward said. "This is his sister, Monica Cortez. She's a police detective."

"I'll call and have Miguel brought to the visitors' room."

Edward led the way. Monica had been to see her brother twice before this visit, but Emilio never had. But he was ready. Perhaps his birthday two months ago had convinced the boy that he was willing to accept his father's role in his life. Emilio had also made the decision that Edward would be his "second papa."

The three entered the visitors' room, where Miguel was seated, waiting at a metal table. He stood when they came in. "Hi, sis," he said, giving Monica a hug. "And look at this guy, will you?" He ruffled Emilio's dark hair and smiled at him. "You're more handsome than when I saw you in Sweet Pine, buddy."

Emilio blushed and lowered his head. "Thanks."

"How's everything with *Tía* 'Nica?" Miguel asked him. "Are you ready for the wedding?"

"I'm going to carry the wedding rings," Emilio said proudly.

"And you'll do a great job." Miguel turned to his sister. "Just a few more days, Mon, and you'll be married. I'm happy for you."

Monica smiled. Edward shook Miguel's hand. He believed Miguel's words. The guy had made a lot of progress while working with Edward.

"Sorry you can't be there, Miguel," Edward said.

"Me, too. I'd like to give the bride away, but I suppose Uncle Horatio will do a good job."

They all sat down at the table. Miguel took a package wrapped in plain brown paper from his pocket. "I have something for you, buddy," he said to Emilio. "I guess you could say I've taken up a hobby."

"What is it?" Emilio asked, keeping his hands in his lap.

"Let's call it a late birthday present. I remember you telling me that you like the ocean."

Emilio nodded, then tentatively reached for the package. He carefully opened it, revealing two carved wooden dolphins, one slightly larger than the other.

"I think they could be a papa and a boy," Miguel said. "But you can imagine them to be whatever you want."

Emilio smiled. "I like them to be a papa and boy."

Monica smiled over the top of Emilio's head and gave Miguel a thumbs-up sign. "They are beautiful," she said.

While Emilio played with his gift, the adults talked mostly about how Miguel was doing, if he'd been attending his high-school-equivalency classes, if he was thinking about what he'd like to do when he was released in a few months.

"I think I'd like to come back to Sweet Pine," he said. "I'll get my own place, and at least look forward to Mama's great meals on Sunday." He settled back in his chair. "Time to start thinking about a job."

"I have an idea about that," Edward said. "I'd like to start the marina up again. Now that I'm in Sweet Pine four days a week, seems like something to consider. If things work out for you, Miguel, there'd be a job for you running Smitty's."

Edward carefully studied Miguel's reaction to the suggestion. Would old grudges resurface? Would Miguel adamantly refuse the offer? But Miguel merely smiled. "I'd like to give it a try," he said. "Thanks, Edward."

"And there's still the matter of the twenty percent of the marina my father wanted to give to Juan," Edward said. "In time, I can make good on that promise."

Miguel reached across the table and shook Edward's hand again. "I don't know what to say."

Edward shrugged. "No need to say anything."

"Thanks for coming, you guys," Miguel said. He sent a fond look in Emilio's direction. "Great to see you, Emi."

"Yeah, thanks," Emilio said.

Edward noted that the tension in Emilio's voice had eased. Soon his relationship with his papa would improve.

"Mama will be here to visit after the wedding," Monica said. "Her first trip to Miami in a long time, and I can't keep her away."

"I'm ready to see her," he said. "I think that now she'll be able to see that I've changed for the better."

Monica gave him a parting hug. "Anyone can see it," she said. "I'm very proud of you."

"That means a lot. Have a great wedding and an even greater life."

As Monica, Edward and Emilio walked back to Edward's car, Edward looked from one to the other. "Are we ready for the drive back to Sweet Pine and a big celebration?" he asked. "By the time we get there my sisters and their families should have arrived at the house."

Monica laughed. "I told Horatio not to bring a pig on a spit," she said, once they were all in the car.

"I don't care if he brings a pig in tennis shoes," Edward said. From the back seat, Emilio hooted. "So has this been a good day?"

"The best," Monica answered. "Only to be surpassed by the most fantastic wedding in a few days."

Edward leaned over and kissed her cheek. "We both have started to put some stock in dreams."

"Thank you for giving me back my brother."

Edward put his hand in hers and nodded

toward the back seat. "Thank you for giving me a share in one super kid."

Emilio stared up at both of them. "What are you guys talking about?"

"Happiness, Emi," Edward said. "The absolute best kind, the kind that lasts a lifetime." He smiled at Monica before turning his attention back to Emilio. "You'll see, kid. If you believe in dreams, you'll see."

* * * * *

For more romances from acclaimed author Cynthia Thomason, visit www.Harlequin.com today!

Catching Midnight

"*Catching Midnight* is a marvelous paranormal novel . . . There are powerful erotic romance overtones, as well as a few kinky moments that will fulfill readers' desires for Holly's signature erotic love stories. Overall, this is a highly imaginative, creative romance of mortals and immortals, à la Donna Boyd and Alice Borchardt."

—*Romantic Times*

"Emma Holly has outdone herself in this erotic tale of supernatural beings living and interacting in the human world." —*Affaire de Coeur*

"Ms. Holly has written a thrilling paranormal romance . . . She's created a world filled with fascinating characters . . . and added elements of mystery, intrigue, and sensuality that will keep readers eagerly turning the pages."

—*Old Book Barn Gazette*

Fantasy: An Anthology

"Emma Holly's Luisa del Fiore takes sexual allure to new heights . . . A five-star winner . . . Will keep you reading under those covers late into the night."

— *Affaire de Coeur*

Beyond Seduction

"This erotic Victorian romance . . . [brings] the era to life . . . Emma Holly, known for her torrid tales, treats her readers to an equatorial heated romance." — *BookBrowser*

continued . . .

"Holly brings a level of sensuality to her storytelling that may shock the uninitiated . . . Fans of Robin Schone and Thea Devine will adore the steamy love scenes here, which go beyond the usual set pieces. [A] combination of heady sexuality and intriguing characterization."
— *Publishers Weekly*

"Emma Holly once again pens an unforgettably erotic love story . . . A wonderful tale of creative genius and unbridled passion."
— *Affaire de Coeur*

"Ms. Holly is a rising star who creates tantalizing tales . . . Delicious."
— *Rendezvous*

"Steamy sex, interesting characters, and a story that offers a couple of twists . . . A page-turning read."
— *The Romance Reader*

"This book deserves its place in the top line of romances. Titillating, erotic, and fun."
— *The Best Reviews*

"Unique mix of intense sensuality, well-crafted characters, and romantic plot."
— www.Erotica-Readers.com

Beyond Innocence

"A superb erotic Victorian romance. The exciting story line allows the three key cast players to fully develop before sex scenes are introduced, which are refreshingly later in the tale than usual."
— *BookBrowser*

"The love scenes were an excellent mixture of eroticism and romance and they are some of the best ones I have read this year."
— *All About Romance*

"A complex plot, a dark and brooding hero, and [a] charming heroine . . . a winner in every way. Go out and grab a copy—it's a fabulous read . . . A treat."
— *Romance Reviews Today*

"Truly beautiful."
— *Sensual Romance*

Hunting
Midnight

EMMA HOLLY

BERKLEY SENSATION, NEW YORK

HUNTING MIDNIGHT

A Berkley Sensation Book / published by arrangement with the author

PRINTING HISTORY
Berkley Sensation edition / November 2003

ISBN: 0-425-19303-9

A BERKLEY SENSATION™ BOOK
Berkley Sensation Books are published by The Berkley Publishing Group, a division of Penguin Group (USA) Inc.,
375 Hudson Street, New York, New York 10014.
BERKLEY SENSATION and the "B" design
are trademarks belonging to Penguin Group (USA) Inc.

PRINTED IN THE UNITED STATES OF AMERICA

10 9 8 7 6 5 4 3 2 1

This book is dedicated to the many wonderful authors who keep my love for vampires alive . . . so to speak.

In the Beginning

<hr>

CALAIS, 1370

Not a soul saw the pair of immortal beings who hid among the wine casks piled on the quay. A wooden crane, with a chain and winch for offloading cargo, explained the barrels' presence—not that either immortal cared. Known to their own kind as *upyr*, they were beautiful male creatures, white as snow and perfectly formed in each detail: from their long black hair to their graceful limbs to the arrangement of the lashes around their jewel-bright eyes. A hint of red, like garnets glinting in shadow, shone from their locks.

It would have entranced any human who saw it.

So similar was the pair's appearance, they might have been brothers, a coincidence that had drawn Emile and Bastien together many years before. Even their wolf shapes resembled kin. Complementary natures had done the rest; to them, "friends for life" was no empty phrase.

Now there were differences between them. Emile had smudges of dirt on his raiment, in particular on his hose.

Bastien was as clean as if he had been polished as well as scrubbed. His eyes mimicked the pale, clear green of a peridot. Despite their lightness, they burned with a flame of determination any priest would have called demonic.

Possible diabolic nature aside, night cloaked the fugitives as mercifully as if they were saints, helped in its task by a thick gray mist from the surrounding marshes. Both darkness and fog were welcome. Though the hour was well advanced, a number of watchmen still strolled the docks. Had their hiding place been discovered, the *upyr* could not have passed as ordinary beings. They were too drained from their long flight to hide their natural glow—dim though that was now.

Bastien, the stronger of the two—though that wasn't saying much—inhaled deeply in an attempt to marshal his flagging power. One of the ships had recently taken on a cargo of spices. In addition to human effluvia and brine, the lapping waves carried the scent of Indian cinnamon. Bastien had never been to India, nor to Spain or even the Low Countries. His branch of the immortal tree was not encouraged to roam. Maybe one day, when this was over, he would make a journey.

He promised himself he would get the chance. Freedom was too sweet a prize to give up.

"You should leave me," Emile said, his eyes a near lifeless brown. To any but his companion, his words would have been too soft to hear. "You could escape more easily alone."

Bastien offered a weary smile. "I succeeded in conveying you all the way from Burgundy, most of it over my shoulder. It would be the height of folly to leave you now."

He turned away before he could see the hopelessness in Emile's face, peering instead at the half-dozen vessels that swayed and creaked on their anchors out in the harbor. The ships were all old-fashioned, single-masted merchant's cogs: English to a one. The English had held Calais for more than a decade now, using it as a staging point for further incursions into France as well as a thriving commercial port. Normally, this would not have mattered to the *upyr;* like most of his kind, Bastien held himself aloof from human conflicts. Tonight, though, he was glad. He wanted an English ship, one that could carry him and his companion far from French soil.

If they failed, Bastien did not think much of their chances. Their enemy would do anything to drag them back. Hugo would have to, to demonstrate to the others what would happen if they rebelled.

"As soon as the docks seem quiet enough," Bastien said, "I shall steal one of those rowboats and take us out to a ship." He rubbed his jaw in regret, his skin smooth and stubble-free. "I wish these cogs were larger. I doubt any hold more than a hundred men. Thankfully, once I have fed a few times, I will be able to hide us with my glamour. God grant the crossing will be short."

"For the crew's sake, if nothing else," said the other with a crooked smile.

Bastien squeezed his wasted shoulder, thinking of the days when Emile had been robust. He wished he dared share his blood, but he would need all his remaining strength for slipping them onboard.

"We will make it," he said, reassuring himself as well. "Mortals sail with compasses these days, and far better channel maps. And there will be rats to feed upon, if preying on people seems too dangerous."

Emile shook his head over all the rules they had broken to get this far. They were not supposed to drink from humans at all, only from the natural quarry of their beast halves. Bastien did not care. He would have broken all the laws there were to keep the other safe.

Eternity was too long to face without a friend.

"We will make it," he repeated. "We will find allies

among the English packs. We will petition their king and return with a force so mighty, Hugo will regret ever hearing the word *magic*. We shall cure you, Emile. Never fear."

"But if the English refuse to help . . ."

"They will agree," Bastien said, his fangs lengthening startlingly with his passion. "We will not give them a choice."

Chapter 1

❦

"Thou art a sexy bastard," the woman purred, her finger trailing lightly down Ulric's jaw.

He dragged his cock from her body even though he was still hard, still vibrating with the lust his kind could never completely slake. He had spilled, but the lingering excitement kept him long and thick. With hungry eyes, the woman watched him tuck himself into his codpiece. Her cheeks bore spots of red within their English cream.

He had bitten her at the end.

That, as much as anything else, accounted for her enjoyment.

"Yes," he agreed to her accolade, "I am the sexiest bastard you shall ever meet."

They stood in the alley behind a tavern, one of seven in this human town. He had taken the woman against the wall without preliminaries: easy—nay, eager—prey.

To be fair, Ulric was no ordinary seducer. He was a member of the *upyr,* a race of shapeshifting immortal beings who lived by drinking blood. As strong as they were beautiful, they had few vulnerabilities. Most who died did so by their own hand, out of sadness or ennui. The touch of iron was a danger, but far worse was the sun. To his kind the sun was death, a slow, honeyed poison that addled their minds as surely as liquor addled a human's. If they stayed in it long enough, they would burn. At night their powers of attraction were at their height. With the superior force of their minds, they could thrall their victims into their arms, then make them forget they had ever seen them. If they chose, they could use an illusion called "glamour" to assume a human façade.

They were shadows in the mortal world, among but not of the crowd.

The line of *upyr* Ulric belonged to, the children of Auriclus, were forbidden to interact with mortals. His sire would have been shocked to know Ulric was here, much less that he was drinking human blood.

Ulric did not require it, after all. He could take his wolf form and feed as a beast. He had learned, however, in the nights during which he had haunted these winding streets, that human blood was the sweetest dram. For a while at least, it filled his heart with human passions and human joys. It strengthened him as no other creature's could.

Even if it had not, Ulric would not have cared a whit for Auriclus's rules. Not today. Not tomorrow. Not until he understood why the only woman he ever loved, the queen to his king wolf, had chosen a human lover over him. The man Gillian selected did not even have a title. He was a mere second son. Ulric was handsomer. Ulric was better in bed. Ulric could make his pack members quail with a single glare. Ulric had everything Aimery lacked. And still Gillian had left.

She had loved Ulric, but not enough.

It passed beyond understanding. Ulric could not fathom it. In fact, he positively refused to.

Sensing the loss of his attention, the woman was murmuring to him and pawing his chest, obviously greedy for more of the pleasures she could already but half recall. Her hands found the bulge between his thighs, stroking it high and hard. Her touch went no deeper than his skin.

"Leave me," he ordered, pushing her away.

When she stumbled and caught her weight against the wall, he felt a twinge of guilt. It was not her fault their coupling had left him empty. No human could give him what he needed, and no *upyr* could except for Gillian. He was broken, and cruel with it, but this female was not to blame.

"Go home," he said more gently, putting the force of his mind behind the words. "Sleep well and wake easy of mind. You did not meet me tonight. I was simply a sweet daydream."

She blinked at him with glazing eyes, far more susceptible to his thrall than one of his own kind would have been. He was strong in this human world, as powerful as a god. He might have thought that was the lure for Gillian, but she had made her lover her equal. She had made him *upyr*.

Ulric himself could not transform a human. Only the oldest and most powerful *upyr* could do that. When Gillian had discovered the ability, young as she was, that had seemed a betrayal, too. Ulric was supposed to be her protector . . . her superior, in point of fact.

"Go," he ordered the woman before his anger could rise to lash out at her.

She went, halting and reluctant, her slippers dragging in the dirt. Her head turned back over her shoulder, her veil and wimple fallen, her hair like a bird's nest straggling down. Ulric watched her gaze at him with longing, but he did not really see—no more than she had seen him.

One more night, he thought. One more night survived without Gillian. Though he knew his face remained impassive, his chest ached as if the wound were fresh. He wondered if this heartbreak would be immortal, if he would ever feel whole again. The prospect seemed intolerable, but he decided to wait and see.

～

"Bastards," said Henry Buxton. "Think they are too high and mighty to marry a son of theirs to a girl of mine."

Juliana Buxton, his daughter, tucked a blanket around him in his chair. She had already stoked the fire, just enough, and set the leather flagon next to the hearth.

Her father seldom drank, but when he did it made him fractious. He could mutter for hours about every slight anyone had ever done him. This particular rant was an old one, involving the refusal of Edmund Fitz Clare, the local baron, to affiance his eldest son to her.

"I have more money than the lot of them put together," her father said, jabbing his thumb at his sunken chest. "Was his wife's idea to turn the offer down. Too proud by far, that Claris. *She* had merchants in her family. I know for a fact her grandfather was a brigand. Stole a silver chamber pot once, from a big castle in France. Said every time he pissed in it he felt like a king."

He chuckled at this, darkly, his head pulled into the quilted velvet of his robe. Henry Buxton was a cloth merchant, and thus the material was very fine. Nonetheless, he resembled a broody owl with his heavy eyes and his feathery white hair. He was old, Juliana realized, though she could not remember him young. Her mother, God rest her soul, had been a child compared to him.

Squeezed by sudden sympathy, she knelt by his chair and pressed her cheek to his knee. Whatever his faults, he had loved Juliana's mother, and he missed her now that she was gone.

Touched by the gesture, her father's long, gnarled fingers smoothed her hair. "Look at you," he said with teary fondness. "My Juliana. Beautiful and good. Those Fitz Clares would have been blessed to have you."

Tenderness forgotten at the reminder of the slight, his hand clenched over her winding braid.

Carefully, Juliana disentangled it. "It matters not," she said, hoping to calm him. "I did not want to marry Thomas Fitz Clare."

It would have been ridiculous, for one thing. The boy was just fifteen.

"I should think not," her father huffed, "not when I have found a far better mate for my clever dove."

Though Juliana closed her eyes, she could not shut out the words. His ambitions thwarted for a noble match, her father had promised her to an associate, a rich London tradesman by the name of Gideon Drake. His financial empire—for naught else could she call it—was ten times the size of Henry Buxton's. Juliana had met Drake once and judged him no monster, only old and set in his ways—ways that were far more hidebound than her sire's.

Gideon Drake would make a trophy of her. She had seen that the moment his eyes drifted down her twenty-two-year-old curves. A smile of satisfaction had curled his lips. Her beauty pleased him. Her intelligence he deigned to ignore. Unlike her father, he had more assistants than he could use. She could easily foresee her future in his home, restricted to a suite of luxurious private rooms, her every need seen to by silent staff, her person trotted out now and then for admiring guests.

My bride, Juliana, Drake would say in his cool and mocking voice. *Is she not a model of wifely grace?*

Juliana doubted she would rebel once she was married. She would be who she was to her father, dutiful and quiet, without the warmth of affection to ease the burden of doing what she ought, without the sense that she had any purpose beyond her looks. A child to love was the best reward for which she could hope. Drake had two

grown sons by a previous wife, and Juliana had met them
as well.

Milton and Milo were . . . well, peculiar was the kindest word she could use, with pale, slightly bulging eyes
and impassive faces. Drake might be cold, but his sons
regarded her as if she were a bug. Certainly, no joy would
come to her life from them. If Gideon Drake were capable of begetting other sons with her, she suspected the
cocoon that swaddled her would become a prison.

She would be the proof that her husband was virile yet.

Admittedly, this was not the worst fate a woman could
endure. She would want for nothing, and her future
would be secure. Juliana believed she was strong enough
to fulfill her obligations. She merely wished the thought
of it did not make her feel as if she were choking on her
own heart.

Her father was so gleeful about the match he had not
complained about having to find a servant to take her
place. The contracts had been drawn up, and the betrothal
was days away. Once formal vows were exchanged in
front of a priest, backing out would be awkward, to say
the least.

She had one choice, really, if she wished to escape the
destiny her father had planned. She had to run away—
before she put on Drake's ring. No matter that she dreaded leaving, not to mention her father's hurt, she could not
delay any longer.

"I must go out," she said from the door of their dim,
sparsely furnished parlor.

Startled, her father turned his eyes to the window, to
the leaded glass and the faint pink light. "It is dark."

"Not quite, Father." Her voice was gentleness itself. "I
want to see if the shoemaker has mended your favorite
boots."

Though her father could buy new ones, he liked the old
for their well-worn ease. Juliana knew she had him when

he stretched his stockinged toes against the dark-brown tiles. "You will keep to the high street?"

"Yes, Father."

"No dilly-dallying at the church or old Tom the Harper's?"

"No, Father. I shall conduct my business directly."

"Well," he said, hemming a little, "take your cloak. It is cold out."

It was nearly summer, comfortably mild, but her father could not feel the warmth anymore.

"I must leave," she said, "else the light will be gone."

He waved her on, then began to nod off. To her relief, he did not suggest she take a servant. He would sleep soon over his wine. It might be hours before he noticed she had not returned.

Into the covered basket she used for shopping, she tucked her folded cloak, a sack of coin she had been saving from the household accounts by dickering over every penny, a loaf of bread, and a hunk of cheese wrapped in cloth. A good, sharp knife seemed a wise addition.

After a brief debate over frivolity, she added her prized possession: a volume of stories she had been collecting since she was a girl. They ranged from tales of high adventure in the world of knights to those of simple folk. Juliana had copied every one onto the parchment pages in her own crisp hand. The earlier ones included pictures her mother had drawn before her death five years before. Monsters, for the most part. Her dam had dearly loved tales of terror. Smiling, Juliana caressed the tooled leather binding, then snapped the basket lid shut.

Keenly aware that she might be doing this for the final time, she descended the narrow stairs, stepped over the threshold, and shut the door.

Their house rose four tall stories, with a shop on the lowest level and sturdy half-timbered eaves that overhung the street. She called a greeting to her father's apprentice, who was preparing to close for the night. As the shutters rattled together, top and bottom, she drew her first deep breath. Within her plain blue gown, her shoulders relaxed.

Juliana did not mind being good. There was a kind of contentment in knowing precisely what was expected, in knowing she was able to do her duty well. But she also needed moments like this, incandescent bubbles in the regimen of her life. Tonight she was neither daughter nor future bride, just a woman whose thoughts and feelings were her own.

Turning from her home with the faintest of palpitations, she headed for Bridesmere's high street. Her final promise she would keep. After that, she would guide her life for herself.

"You have taken leave of your senses," Bridesmere's single tanner sputtered to Juliana.

Behind her tall and sweating form, two muscular females scraped hair from a pair of skins that were draped on a wooden beam. The tannery yard emitted an unearthly reek, a product of the concoctions in which the hides were cured. Many of the women—because all who labored for Mistress Melisent were of that sex—had tied linen cloths across their noses and mouths.

If Juliana had been employed here, she would have covered her eyes as well. Blinking against the heavy fumes, she tried to look strong and stout.

Mistress Melisent's own travails had taught her to value stoutness. Her husband had beat her daily when he was alive, but now that he was dead and she had taken control of his business, she was acclaimed the stubbornest woman in town.

"I assure you, Mistress Melisent," Juliana said, "I am in full possession of my wits. Your tannery transports leather all over this part of England. No one would think of searching your carts for hidden passengers."

"That is hardly the point. What would you do if I helped you run away? How would you live?"

"I could work in the fields or as a laundress. I have a skill for it, you know. No one's linen is as white as mine. If I am careful, I will have money enough to open a shop."

The tanner snorted. "If you had asked me for a position, I might have agreed, even if you are a scrawny piece of work. But you will never survive on your own."

"I will," Juliana insisted. "I am not afraid of hardship, only of being trapped."

Mistress Melisent sighed. "I almost believe you, but I would not like your 'hardship' to be on my hands. The men of this town rail at me enough as it is. Your father would have me in the pillory if you came to grief."

"He need never know!"

"I cannot help you," said Mistress Melisent, going back to stirring her steaming vat with a long, wood pole. "Go home, Juliana. Live the life you were born to."

It was a dismissal Juliana lacked the nerve to ignore, despite the fact that Mistress Melisent was her only remaining hope. Out of caution, she had compiled a limited list of prospects to approach: people who, while fond of her, were not overly indebted to her father. Mistress Melisent had been the last of the three. The first two had refused her out of hand, no matter what she offered to pay. They did this not from fear of her father, but because they felt too much care for her. Incapable of believing she could succeed, they did not want to see her hurt.

She had thought it to her advantage that most of Bridesmere liked her. Plainly, it was not.

She contemplated accepting the tanner's lukewarm offer of a job. Sadly, if she remained within her father's reach, he would be certain to drag her home. Worse, she would have destroyed his trust. Once his faith was squandered, Henry Buxton did not give it again. Chances were, neither would Juliana's intended. She would end up more a prisoner than she was now.

She plodded from the tannery, scarcely noticing where she went. She should have been heading home in the hope that she could slip inside before her father woke. She should have been praying no one she had spoken to tonight would give him word of what she had done. While she had put no gossips on her list, prayers like that seemed unlikely to be answered. Clearly, she could have used more practice at rebellion. If only she had tried subterfuge, rather than seeking aid . . .

I have cast the die already, she thought. It is too late to turn back.

Overwhelmed by the realization, she stopped dead in the street and dropped her basket. She stared at the patterns in the dirt, cloven hoofmarks from a herd of pigs who had been driven back to their stable after a day of foraging. She might never see sights like this again. She might be locked in her room for good.

She laughed at the idea of getting misty-eyed over pigprints, then covered her face and sobbed.

She allowed herself one tearing rasp. When it was done, she lowered her hands to fist them at her sides. She had tried and she had failed, but she would live with whatever consequences came. She was Juliana Buxton. If nothing else, she had fortitude.

Retrieving her belongings, she started walking toward the light and noise of the Dancing Cat. Maybe she would find someone she knew at the tavern. Maybe they would see her home. Shaky as she was, she would not have minded the company.

This decided, she pulled herself from her thoughts.

She saw a minstrel had gathered a group of watchers outside the tavern, most of them female. The clink of their coins as they tossed them caught her ear. A pile of them lay at the minstrel's feet.

"No stinting now," he said in a teasing voice. "It will take more than a few farthings to prime my pipes."

Juliana suspected something other than his pipes had drawn this crowd. He was taller than average, by at least half a head, and his rich gold hair hung to his shoulders in a shining mane. From his jaunty chaperon to his pointed shoes, he was dressed in crimson velvet, product no doubt of the famous *Arte*—or guilds—of Tuscany. Even more eye-catching, his tunic was scarcely long enough to obscure his loins. From the well-packed appearance of his codpiece, he had a great deal to hide.

"I would be happy to prime your pipe," offered one of the women, no doubt as sharp-eyed as Juliana. "I would not even demand you sing!"

Her companions laughed bawdily, while Juliana restricted herself to a smile. Their enthusiasm might be unseemly, but the minstrel was worth admiring—and not merely for the obvious. The belt that cinched his tunic's pleats showed off a narrow waist. His thighs were solid, and his calves quite nicely curved. He held no instrument to accompany his song, but his hands were music in and of themselves. White as snow and seemingly as light, their tapered fingers held a fascination Juliana could not explain.

"Very well," he said, spreading them in surrender. "I shall let you have me cheaply just this once."

From the first note he uttered she was lost.

To call his voice a pleasant tenor was to be cruel. Each note was clear but mysteriously complex, hinting at barely heard harmonies, like a howl forced to obey the laws of time and tune. Her hair stood up as if her skin were being brushed all over by butterflies. What he sang did not matter: some romantic nonsense such as high-born ladies liked to hear. It was the sound itself that nailed her to the earth with bliss. She closed her eyes and let his voice roll through her, the troubles of the evening melting away.

So powerful was the effect, she found herself swaying. When she opened her eyes, she was actually walking toward the man. To her surprise, the street was empty but for her and him. She had not heard the other women leave.

Even more surprisingly, he was staring directly at her. His gaze was gold and fiery, as penetrating as his voice. A tingle centered between her legs. She would have been embarrassed except that what was happening seemed like a dream. She felt tugged by the intensity of his expression, chosen for something she could not name.

What are you doing? she demanded of herself. You do not know this stranger.

Her feet did not listen. She came to a halt a foot away from him. He smelled delicious, like a wild thing from the woods. When she inhaled a second time, he smiled at her, a lazy upcurve of perfect lips. Amazingly, she had not noticed when his singing stopped.

"You need a player," she blurted out before she could guard her tongue. "A voice like yours deserves accompaniment."

"Does it?" His hand was in her hair, pulling the pins from her braid and spreading it across her shoulders. A wave of heat coursed through her limbs.

"Yes," she gasped, striving not to tremble. "I play the harp, as it happens, passably well. If you wished, I could come with you when you leave town."

Mistress Melisent was right, she thought, astonished by her own boldness. Juliana must have gone mad. On the other hand, what did she have to lose? Everyone else had refused her. And she still had her knife if it came to that.

The stranger continued to smile at her like a teacher humoring a child. His face was so beautiful it seemed unreal. Flawless as a pearl, his skin glowed in the darkness, even brighter than the torches of the Dancing Cat. His lashes looked as if a jeweler had attached them to the lids—pure gold spread out in multi-layered fans.

He is alone, she thought out of the blue. Magnificent though he was, he had been abandoned.

She swayed again, dizzy, knowing her musings made little sense. The man caught her elbows with cool, firm hands.

"Why not come with me now?" he said. "I would adore your accompaniment."

She did not agree so much as not know how to resist. He half-carried, half-led her to a nearby alley, past people who suddenly seemed to find them invisible. The shadows of the buildings covered everything but his face.

She gasped as his body crowded hers into the wall. She was small and helpless, trapped beyond breaking free. Her basket, and the knife she had tucked inside, fell with a thunk from her nerveless fingers. She could not remember why she should care. Her heart beat like a cornered rabbit, but fear was not what drove it.

Oh, yes, said something she had not known she had inside her. *Oh, yes, keep me right here.*

The bulge of his codpiece pressed her mound as fiercely as if her desires had instructed it where to go.

"Yes," she might have whispered out loud. "Yes, please, keep doing that."

He rolled the hardness against her, his head dropping to her neck. Slowly, savoringly, he dragged his tongue up one tendon to her ear. She would not have thought this could arouse her, but it did. Him, as well, apparently. His breathing came shallower.

"What are you doing?" she forced herself to ask.

"I am getting ready to swive you," he said, "unless you have some objection."

He said this as if he knew she would not, as if seducing

a perfect stranger were the most natural thing in the world. She felt his shaft pulse eagerly against her mound.

"I—" she said, surprised it was so difficult to turn him down.

"You?" he teasingly responded.

Before she could speak, he covered her mouth with his.

Oh, that kiss—! His lips were silk, his arms a wonderful pressure around her back. They tightened the moment she wished they would and lifted her off the ground. Juliana was not such a goose that she had not been wooed a time or two, but this kiss was a different beast, not merely skilled but enchanting. Her head spun with pleasure as she kissed him back, clutching his shoulders and opening to his forays.

He drew on her as if she were a piece of honeyed fruit.

"Like that, do you?" he chuckled against her lips, but *like* was not the word. This was what she had been missing all her life, this marvelous freedom.

When he kissed her again, his tongue stabbed inside. His aggression affected her even more strongly than being pressed to the wall, making her quiver and go weak. She could not hold back a moan, but he seemed to like the reaction. One of his hands was lifting her skirt and chemise, freeing her legs to move. She raised her thighs to his narrow hips without thinking twice. The warm spring air swirled around her bareness. Behind the cloth of his codpiece, against her most private parts, his erection throbbed.

"The people from the tavern . . ." she murmured, still hearing them in the distance.

He kissed her hard enough to bruise. "They cannot hear," he said. "And they cannot see. In all the world, you and I are alone."

She did not know why she believed him. What he said made no sense. But when his hand slipped between them to free his member, she could not protest. Completely unashamed, he stroked it leisurely with his fist.

For you, his gesture seemed to say. *Look at what I have for you.*

With each manipulation, his knuckles brushed her woman's hair. She gasped for air and he let go, using the selfsame hand to cup her quim. His prick pressed her belly beside his forearm. He had stretched even more with his own caress. Liquid heat flooded her body. She tried to tighten the place it filled, but the moisture trickled onto his palm.

"You need this," he growled against her mouth. "You cannot live without it."

Surprise widened her eyes. "You are right," she said. "I feel as if I shall die unless you take me soon."

He pulled back to peer at her. "I almost believe you know what you are saying."

She reached for his mouth and kissed him of her own free will. The hand that supported her bottom clenched painfully.

"Now," he said. "No more waiting."

He shifted her until her folds met his thrusting hardness. The tip of his penis was broad and smooth. For one moment, as he eased it inward, its skin felt cool. A heartbeat later, it blazed.

No pain, said a voice that seemed to come from within her head. *It is easy for you to take me.*

He pushed, determined, steady. The sense of being stretched would have alarmed her had she not been eager to have him inside. With a brief and painless flash of heat, her barrier rent.

He swore, at himself perhaps, then murmured praise: how tight she was, how wonderfully warm and wet, how he loved the feel of her around him. Reluctant to disappoint him, Juliana did her best to hold on.

He seemed immense as he worked his shaft incrementally in and out, reaching a little deeper with each effort. The push and pull was delicious, tugging every inch of

her sexual flesh. She widened her hips and received a
grunt of thanks. His hair spilled over her arms where they
twined behind his neck. Unable to resist, she ran her fingers through its silken thickness, her head falling helplessly back.

"Do not tempt me," he panted against her throat. "I am
close enough to losing control."

She neither knew nor cared what he meant. With a final
shove, he achieved full penetration, his weapon contained
but not conquered.

"Hold tight," he warned. "I am about to give you the
ride of your life."

She would have laughed, but he did not lie. Nothing
she had ever done for herself prepared her for this. The
first slamming thrust made her cry out with excitement,
impossible to think of as anything but an assault—on her
body, on her nerves, on her understanding of what coupling was supposed to be. And this was only the beginning. Pulling her arms from behind his neck, he trapped
them against the wall and stretched them out by the wrist.
The stone was hard, but not as hard as his fingers. His
body coiled, drew out, and then he began to drive in a
swift and steady rhythm.

"Open to me," he demanded. "Take it all."

She was taking it all, every inch of his length and girth.
She shook like she had a fever. She groaned like she
wanted more.

"You need this," he rasped, sweat dripping down his
beautiful face. "You were born to be ravished."

She moaned because her mouth would not work well
enough to say yes. Waves of red-hot sensation spread out
from her pummeled loins. The pleasure suffused her
thighs, her breasts, the tips of her tingling fingers. She
was almost there, almost over the edge.

As if he knew, he switched angles, pounding some
unsuspected sweet spot. One hand released her wrist to

grip her hip, to position her just so, to hold her where he could slide his bulbous tip against that aching place.

"Yes," he said, "I can feel how much you want it."

She gasped for air, the ecstasy so intense it approached pain. Desperate to touch him, she wrapped her free hand behind his neck. He was trembling, tight in every muscle. She could feel him shake even as he drove inside her with all his might.

"Come," he snarled in her ear, his lips pulled back, his teeth gleaming strangely sharp. "Die . . . with . . . me."

When he sucked in a breath of shock, she knew his crisis was upon him. She had a moment to feel him drive to his deepest limit and then her body convulsed, a head-to-toe squeeze of genuinely startling bliss. Her flesh could barely comprehend such pleasure. It sparked and flared like pinecones thrown in a fire.

A glow followed the conflagration, wonderfully warm and sweet. The sigh she released seemed to belong to a different woman.

But she was a different woman. Maid no more, she had seen the carnal world.

She smiled into the stranger's hair. She had both arms wrapped around him—and both legs. Despite their mutual accomplishment of delight, his hold on her was tight. Barely diminished, his member remained inside her. Occasionally it jerked, small, unpredictable surges that reminded her just how much she had enjoyed its more energetic activity.

At the memory, a fresh rush of moisture slid from inside her.

Feeling it, he ground himself a little closer. "I must get you somewhere more private. I cannot swive you like this and keep up my glamour."

How lovely, she thought, indifferent to the mystery of his words. He was going to ravish her again.

Chapter 2

❧

Ulric had just begun to sing when he noticed the woman watching dumbstruck from behind the crowd. Women often did this, but rarely without him first turning his attention to them. Left to themselves, they were circumspect.

She was pretty enough to catch his jaded eye: slim, a bit above average height, with a pair of breasts that cried out to be cupped—more than a handful but not by much. A braid of perfectly ordinary brown hair was coiled up neatly and pinned to her head. Her gown, while plain, seemed to fit her better than the others'. Or perhaps she stood inside it differently. With her shoulders straight and her head erect, she seemed capable and unafraid. He suspected she had been born in Bridesmere and knew her surroundings well. The roses in her cheeks and the sweetness of her scent spoke of good health.

She looked a doughty daughter of England, with a roof over her head and an unshaken faith in her next meal—same as he had seen a hundred times before.

Only her eyes told a different story. Huge and sable dark, they held the emotions the rest of her hid. Vulnerability. Imagination. A hunger for more from life than Fate seemed likely to offer. Something in those eyes set Ulric's heart beating harder in his chest. He was not the strongest reader of minds. Emotions he could sense, but seldom specific thoughts. He was more adept at putting thoughts *into* other people's heads.

He had not, however, put that lust for experience into hers.

Intrigued, he dispersed the crowd and called her to him. She obeyed the silent order without resistance, seeming as drawn by his voice as by his power. When she spoke, he barely listened to what she said, something about playing the harp and wanting to leave town. Her words could not have mattered less. What mattered was that she interested him more than anything had since Gillian left, more than blood, more than rest, certainly more than the woman he had coupled with earlier.

He did not know why this should be, nor did he care. He wanted her, and he would have her without delay.

When she kissed him, apparently of her own volition, he was surprised—not because no woman would wish to, but because he had thought her more deeply under his thrall.

Whatever the cause for her initiative, the pleasure of touching her, of knowing he would have her frayed his concentration. He barely managed to hide the two of them with his glamour as he took her that first time.

Her maiden state surprised him; she had not seemed that young. It pleased him, too, though he could not have said why. That it did he could not doubt. His climax was all-consuming, as if for one mindless moment he knew the pleasure of completely being his wolf. He wanted, he took, he got—until he should have been incapable of wanting more.

But he desired her again as soon as it ended. More kisses. More sighs. More gentle touches from her human hands.

Maybe, he thought, I should seek a virgin every time.

"I must get you somewhere more private," he said half to himself. "I cannot swive you like this and keep up my glamour."

Completely pliant, she put her head on his shoulder. He carried her, her little basket over his elbow, into the stable for a hostelry. Her hair was a cape of silk hanging down his back. Up the wooden ladder, he hefted her to the loft. Then, behind a wall of bundled hay, he laid her down.

She smiled up at him from the blanket of his crimson cloak, sprawled but somehow still innocent. Her hand reached out to caress the side of his knee. "Thank you for bringing my things. They might not have been safe left in the alley."

He set the basket down. He had picked it up without thinking. He hoped she did not interpret this as implying he would take her away from Bridesmere. He vaguely recalled her asking him to do that. Judging it best not to speak, he knelt beside her and cupped her gown against her mound.

He had held back with her earlier, as he had learned to do with human women. All the same, he knew he had been rough.

"Are you sore?" he asked.

"Yes," she answered, then smiled quite blindingly. "I loved it: the feel of you inside me, the way you went so fast and hard I could barely move."

She seemed clearheaded, virtually unthralled apart from the lessening of inhibitions. Hardening furiously at her words, Ulric cleared his throat. His body was eager for hers again.

With an eye toward seeing if she was, too, he tightened

his hold until the fine wool of her gown pushed between her folds. She was damp there, and she dampened more as he massaged her, despite the layer of linen beneath her gown. Her hips squirmed up at him in a small, involuntary motion. When he looked at her face, her teeth had caught her lower lip, red now from his kisses. At the sight, his fangs shot out against his will. He wanted to put his teeth where hers were; he craved it as if he were starved.

He was not certain what held him back. Maybe fear of losing what control he had, or perhaps of liking her taste too much. It was rare to kill a human simply by feeding. His kind required no more blood than a healthy mortal could spare. On the other hand, he did not want this woman to be his first mishap.

He knew it was possible. Nim Wei, his sire's rival, had few rules for her children beyond not getting caught. Before Ulric had agreed to oversee the packs, he had met a few of her broods. They cared even less for humans than he did, less than his wolf did for a rabbit. His wolf never made the rabbit fall in love.

Uncomfortable with his thoughts, he rubbed his thumb along her labia. "I could kiss you here," he offered. "It might help to ease your soreness."

She pushed up at him, this time deliberately. "Is that what you really want?"

He thought of her secret parts, of how hot they would be and how tender against his skin. All *upyr* had some ability to heal injuries in human beings. Ulric had no doubt he could soothe hers. But then her hand slid up his thigh to his tarse, exploring it with a boldness he did not expect.

"Is that what you really want?" she repeated.

Something flickered through him that felt like fear. Women never asked him this. They did not have to. What he wanted, he took. Rather than answer, he bent to drag his cheek along her breast.

"Shall I guess?" she whispered. "Is that what I am supposed to do?"

He groaned as her fingers worked inside his codpiece to find bare skin. The touch of mortal hands, so warm compared to their own, was especially pleasurable to *upyr*, a magic as potent as a thrall. Her fingers skated up his length, delicate yet strong. His swollen rim fit the curve formed by her palm and thumb. She looked at what she held, then up at him, wonder clear in her eyes. When her fingers tightened around him, his last scrap of consideration fled.

"I want you," he growled, crawling over her and caging her in his arms.

Her breath caught with excitement. She pulled up her skirt and urged him in.

The first sultry, slippery contact set his instincts free. He took her as wildly as before, plunging instantly to the hilt, completely selfish in his quest for satisfaction. He was aware that she was with him, and grateful for it, though he was not certain he could have stopped. He lost count of her orgasmic cries, knowing only that every peak had him shuddering with shared echoes.

"How do you do that?" she asked after a particularly pleasant spasm, breathing hard and stroking his face. Beneath his thrusts, her body gave with delicious ease, a cushion fit for a king.

"How do I pleasure you?" he asked, "or how do I keep wanting more?"

"How do you know exactly what I want?"

He could only answer her with a kiss. He had not known what she wanted. He had been taking what he desired. That she wanted it as well was simply luck.

Fisting his hands in her hair, he began to stroke for a final peak, a sweet to top what had been a sensual feast. His thrusts were slower but still deep. *Upyr* nerves were more sensitive than humans' and recovered almost immediately from surfeit. Now her every fold and quiver registered against his shaft. If this had been their first coupling, he might have embarrassed himself by finishing too fast. Instead, he relaxed into his pleasure, relishing the dreamy sensation of peace.

His urgency was sated. He could take his time.

When the woman stretched her back and hummed, he knew she felt it, too.

"Last one," he warned softly.

"You need not rush," she answered back.

He laughed, delighted with her understanding, as euphoric as if he were drunk. The gods had been smiling on him tonight. This whole encounter had been an unexpected gift.

The woman's scent, warmer now and rich, mingled with that of the hay and the horses stamping in their stalls below. The wolf in him enjoyed all the smells immensely. The man in him sent his senses out to survey the sleeping town. Their dreams were quiet, even complacent. The people of Bridesmere did not care that they were not lords, or that their lives were the merest blink. Their little dramas were more than big enough for them.

For once, that did not annoy him.

Instead, he was endeared. These people, these humans, lived with a courage they were unaware they had. They struggled for achievement, knowing it would not last. Ulric could almost understand why Gillian admired them.

Not that he wanted to think of her. He felt too good, too comfortable in his skin. He smiled at the woman and she smiled back, her eyes shining in his glow like stars. In his enthusiasm for coupling with her, he had dropped his glamour. But what matter? He could thrall her later. She would forget everything. For now, she had caught his rhythm and was lifting her hips in perfect synchrony with his thrusts, her enchanting human hands smoothing lazily along his back. When she cupped the rounds of his buttocks, her grip made his penis jolt.

Amazingly, he was almost too tired to spend. She sent him over with a broken sigh.

"Oh," she said, pulsing around him. "Oh, that feels so sweet."

Savoring the last burst of pleasure, Ulric felt almost fond as he gazed at her love-flushed face. The woman looked as relaxed as he. Her lashes fanned against her cheeks and her breasts gently rose and fell in her gown. With a start, he realized she was asleep. She had dozed off with him still inside her.

Taken aback but also amused, he rolled onto his back and pulled her atop him, wrapping them both in the half of his cloak that they were not lying on. He could do with a nap himself, a short one, with plenty of time to slip away before she woke.

Yawning hugely, he closed his eyes and gave in.

It did not occur to him to check if the hayloft had a window. Even if it had, he might not have bothered. Ulric had never, in all his life, failed to secure himself for the dawn.

                                  ⌐∞⌐

Lying on her back in perfect comfort, Juliana stretched beneath the soft velvet cloak, curling her toes and cracking her spine. The bed of hay rustled at her movements, crisp and fragrant in the morning warmth. Her body felt wonderful, every ache mysteriously turned pleasurable. Best of all, she was free. No fires to rekindle. No breakfast to prepare. No floors to sweep or linens to wash. All because the stranger had agreed to take her away.

The stranger. Her smile curled deeper into her cheeks. Obviously, traveling with him would have benefits.

She opened her eyes a slit to check the height of the sun. Alive with dust, beams shot through the chinks in the stable walls, as well as through the single window near the peaking roof. The workers in this hostelry must be lazy. Well past dawn, she heard no grooms moving below.

She did hear a long, weak moan. To her confusion, the stranger lay on his face a short distance away, as if he had been trying to crawl somewhere but had not made it. His hands, which moved feebly in the hay, were marked by angry welts. His beautiful golden hair, spilled across his heaving back, seemed to be issuing a wisp of smoke.

Had someone attacked him? Was he hurt? Juliana rushed to him, looking for the source of whatever had burned his hands. As she reached him, a tiny flame sprang to life in his hair.

"Dark," he pleaded weakly as she beat it out. "Drag me into the dark."

Juliana's mind instantly shut out everything but action. Grabbing the stranger beneath his arms and digging in with her heels, she dragged his heavy body into a cul de sac of bales. He was able to sit up then, but he lifted his hand to shield his face from a ray of sun. As he did, his palm turned pink. Juliana ran back for his cloak, tossing it over the hay bales to form a tent. The door she blocked with her body.

Then she let herself think.

She knew what he was. The knowledge snapped into place like one of the counters on her father's abacus. Merchants and their employees journeyed around the world. Along with silk and spices, they brought back tales, some witnessed for themselves, others merely gossip, and many very strange indeed. Juliana had heard them all as she played hostess to her father's friends. This tale would have been too strange to credit had she not seen it for herself, had she not experienced the stranger's thrall. No wonder she had acceded to his demands. He was *upyr,* an impossibly handsome, impossibly powerful drinker of blood.

Oh, how mortifying it was! Everything considered, she supposed she could live without her maidenhead. Drake would have expected her to possess it, but the chance that she would end up with another man of his station seemed remote. What troubled her were the things she had said and done . . . Why, she practically begged this creature to bed her. In fact, if you put a fine enough point on it, she had.

Her cheeks flamed hot as coal beneath her hands. Yes, she distinctly remembered urging him on.

"You are *upyr*," she accused, furious with herself for having been gulled. "One of those French monsters."

"French!" His laugh was hoarse. "No doubt in France they claim we are English."

"Fine. You are not French. You are still a monster."

"You did not think I was a monster last night."

Juliana ignored the reminder. "I suppose you never had any intention of helping me run away."

"No," he admitted without remorse. "You convinced yourself I had promised."

Juliana ground her teeth. Because of him, she had delayed her departure beyond any chance of success. By now her father had surely raised the alarm. Soon every soul in Bridesmere would join the search. She did not ride well enough to steal a horse, even if she had been willing to turn to crime. Certainly, no townsman in his right mind would let her buy one.

It was hopeless. She had no choice but to throw herself on her father's mercy.

But how could she bear to do that when she had tasted how sweet freedom could be? When turning back meant living under the cold, old thumb of Gideon Drake?

"Now, now," crooned the *upyr*. "What could be so bad that you believe you must run away?"

"Would *you* want to live in a cage?"

When he flinched, she felt a flash of satisfaction that she

could make him react. How could he understand what it was to live without what you truly wanted, to not even dare admit to yourself what that was? She felt a monster herself in her frustration, wanting to roar to the heavens in impotent rage.

Then, as if it had been in her mind all along, the idea came. She was not powerless. She had something to bargain with. While she might be biddable at home, if anyone knew how to ruthlessly press an advantage, it was the daughter of Henry Buxton. She must think of this as no different than haggling over a roast.

Girding herself, she crossed her arms beneath her breasts. "I will expose you," she said, "if you do not agree to help. One moment in the sun and everyone will believe. What is more, I shall tell the townspeople you abducted me and that is why I did not go home."

The *upyr* gaped at her. "You would not dare."

"But I would."

To prove it, she stepped aside from the door to his makeshift shelter. His breath hissed through his teeth as a beam of light struck the side of his face. Juliana felt sick to watch the burn that was there begin to blister. Nonetheless, she held her ground.

"All right," the *upyr* surrendered, fruitlessly shrinking back. "I will help you."

"I want you to make me what you are," she added. "I want to have your powers."

The demand astounded her even as she spoke it, though it made a kind of sense. Whatever skills she might have to sell, as a woman alone she was vulnerable. Only with an *upyr's* strength could she be positive of thriving. The need to drink blood did not appeal, but she had faced unpleasant necessities in the past.

If her stomach clenched with anxiety, that was because she had no experience in making decisions of this scope. She had never had the liberty before. But better to bite

someone than to live with Gideon Drake and his fish-
eyed sons.

Assuming, of course, that she was not shoved off in
disgrace on someone worse.

"You know," said the *upyr* as he tried to pull his tunic
over his face, "most people run from monsters. They do
not attempt blackmail."

"You are the one who is about to go up in smoke."

"I take your point. Could you—?" As hunched as he
could get, he gestured toward the entering light. "I will
agree to escort you to safety."

"That is not all I asked."

"And I will agree to see that you share my powers if
you still want them by summer's end."

Juliana wished her response to this delay did not include so much relief. She would have preferred to trod
her path with unswerving courage. That aside, his suggestion seemed reasonable. Being a monster was not a
choice one should rush.

"Done," she said and stepped in front of the sun.
Exhilaration swept her from scalp to boot. Unswerving or
not, she had outbargained a powerful immortal being.
Surely that bode well for her destiny.

"Glad to have made you happy," said the *upyr,* noting
her bounce. "Do you think you could stack a few more
hay bales across that door?"

"Your word is good?" she asked, suddenly unsure.

The *upyr* sighed. "Yes. Sadly. Monster though I am,
my word is good."

Elated once more, Juliana hurried to find the necessary
bales. She heaved the last one into place with an undeniably common grunt.

"You are lucky I am strong," she panted, plunking
down to sit beside him.

"I assure you, I feel positively blessed."

Pricked by his sarcasm, Juliana bit the side of her thumb. "I am sorry I had to threaten you."

He snorted. "That 'had to' undercuts your apology just a bit."

"My father wanted me to marry an old man. I saw no other way to escape."

"You could not have told your father you did not like his choice?"

"No," she said. "He loves me, but he believes he always knows what is best. He would not have heard."

The *upyr* held her eyes as if measuring hers for sureness. Being looked at that way felt strange, as if she were a person whose judgment might be worthwhile.

After a moment, he blew out a breath. "Ah, well. No doubt, in your shoes, I would have done the same." She could barely see him in the dimness, but she heard him shift on the straw. "If we are to travel together, I suppose I should know your name."

Juliana laughed, the outrageousness of their situation striking her all at once. "My name is Juliana," she said, "and I am very pleased to make your acquaintance."

~⊗~

He winced at the similarity of the names. Gillian. Juliana. But it did not matter. This woman was nothing like the woman he loved. In any event, he doubted he would have her on his hands for long. As soon as she saw what *upyr* life entailed, this pampered town girl would beg him to let her go.

He would never have to admit he lacked the power to make her *upyr*.

"My name is Ulric," he said. With no room to bow, he settled for inclining his head. "It means 'wolf king.' I am a shapechanger."

"A shapechanger?"

"The wolf is my animal. Because I took one as my familiar, his soul exists within my own. If I wish, I can assume his form. But I am not surprised you have not heard of my kind. Shapechangers are different from the line of *upyr* who most often cross paths with humans. We live apart from the mortal realm."

She took this in, turning on her hip to face him. "Do you look like a real wolf when you change, or are you in between beast and man?"

"I resemble a wolf—a very large, very dangerous wolf."

"Good," she said.

Amusement lifted his brows. This woman was the most audacious mortal he had ever met. "Good?"

"I meant no offense . . . Ulric, but the other option sounds rather—"

Exhaustion overwhelmed him without warning. His head nodded down before she finished, bumping her shoulder as it fell.

"Oh!" she exclaimed as he jerked back. "You are weary. You should sleep."

The concern in her voice was strangely touching, but he knew better than to succumb. "I need to keep my glamour in place, to ensure our hiding place is not discovered."

Juliana glanced upward. "I was thinking your cloak is bright enough to call attention, but I can slip out, get my basket, and put my own up there instead. Mine is gray. I can scatter some hay atop it like a hunter's blind."

Before he could stop her, she put her words into action. Such was his fatigue that she woke him again when she returned. He had not even noticed her make the change.

"You rest," she said firmly. "I will keep watch and alert you if anyone approaches."

"You need sleep yourself," he objected, thinking of their long amorous discourse.

A smile ghosted around her lips. "I feel as if I have been sleeping all my life."

The smile told him she, too, was speaking of last night. To have her first experience be that exciting must have shocked her. However much she might have heard older matrons talk, their stories would not have prepared her for him. Under other circumstances, he would have teased her into saying more. Regrettably, at the moment, he could barely keep his eyes open.

"Sleep," she said, her hand curling firmly behind his neck. He listed irresistibly at the pressure, then found his cheek lying on her thigh. The contact stung where he had been burned, but more compelling than pain was his need to rest.

"I will watch," she promised, her fingers combing through his hair, making him feel even heavier.

"Th—" was all the thank you he could get out.

A change came over Ulric as he slept, one that fascinated Juliana even as it unsettled her. His breathing slowed, then appeared to stop. His skin grew cooler, and his pulse was too weak to count. If she had not known a bit about his kind, she would have worried. As it was, he lay against her leg like a corpse. The gradual fading of his burns was all that told her he was alive.

He is helpless, she thought. *Without me to protect him he could be slain.*

The recognition that she had almost murdered him made her break into a sweat. Part of her thought maybe she should have. She had no sensible reason to trust him. The fact that he had not hurt her, that he had—truth be told—shown her nothing but pleasure, guaranteed nothing at all. All the traders she had spoken to claimed *upyr* were ravening demons. Just because Ulric seemed more

rational than ravening did not mean he would not kill if it
became convenient.

But was Juliana any better? She had nearly killed him
to get her way. She stroked his thick golden hair behind
his ear. The strands had a marvelous texture beneath her
hands, a cross between human hair and a pelt. Truly, to
kill such a handsome beast without better reason than
some vague fear would be a shame. She would judge him
for herself, she decided, as she had done all her life.

Men's tales could be unreliable. Well traveled they
might be, but sometimes they made monsters of things
that threatened their sense of mastery. Juliana could hardly imagine anything more threatening to the average
human male than a paragon like Ulric.

Smiling to herself, she rubbed his back through his
tunic. She was glad it was in her interest to give him a
chance.

Chapter 3

❦

"*You are not going home to get your harp,*" Ulric said as though he begrudged the time it took to contradict her. "You have already almost killed me once."

"But I can help you earn money with it," Juliana said, "when we are traveling. You can hide me with your glamour while I sneak in."

They were having this argument, or Juliana was, in the shadows beside the public bathhouse. With night's arrival, Ulric's vitality—and his arrogance—had returned. He cupped her cheek in his big, cool palm. Despite its strength, his hand was smooth as satin. Every sign of his burns was gone.

She was glad for that, though she would not say so. He seemed unimpressed enough with her supposed murderous tendencies. If he concluded she had been bluffing, he might leave her behind.

"First," he said. "My glamour can only hide you if we are touching. Second, God only knows how many men your father might have gathered to search for you. If they are at your house, there is no guarantee I could thrall them all. Finally, never have I sung because I needed coin. That is simply a part of passing as human. Half the time I do not even pick it up." When she opened her mouth to ask why, he pressed his finger to her lips. "Think, Juliana. Does a man like me have to pay for what he wants?"

The smugness of his smile underscored his meaning. Of course he did not sing for money. He sang to draw women to him, so he could feed from them or whatever else struck his fancy. That, after all, was what he had done to her.

Embarrassment smoldered in her cheeks. Naturally, Ulric saw it.

"Do not worry," he teased, bending to kiss the warmth, to touch it with the very tip of his tongue. "I have other ways you can *contribute* to our trip."

Juliana wanted to say something barbed; she truly did. Unfortunately, when he spoke to her in that fashion, his voice gone husky, her insides began to melt.

She knew she would betray herself if she spoke. Wiping his lick mark from her cheek was all the riposte she could afford.

Ulric's knowing chuckle rumbled in her ear. "Ah, Juliana, if you knew how good you smell to me at this moment, you would run screaming into the night. I cannot decide whether to bite you or lift your skirts."

"Neither," she huffed, ignoring her breathless tone. "I refuse to spend another day inside Bridesmere's walls."

"Then you will not balk if I insist we leave immediately."

He did not wait for an answer—most likely he did not care if she had one—but took her hand and led her to the empty street. A candle or two burned in the windows of the buildings along the way, casting a gentle, domestic glow. At this hour, most residents were at home. Juliana did not need to fear many eyes—though there was little enough to see. If she squinted, she could just make out Ulric's glamour around them both, like a ripple of heat on a summer day. The illusion dimmed his glow but not his beauty. Now and then an admiring head turned their way.

"They cannot recognize you," he assured her in an undertone. "With my glamour to shield your looks, you are too plain to merit a second glance."

"I notice you have not made yourself look plain."

He laughed at that. "You are not plain to me, my dear. You are a feast for mouth and eyes."

"Wonderful. Now I feel like a fresh-baked pie."

Though the friendly way he squeezed her fingers eased the offense, her nervousness remained. Her heart beat harder as Bridesmere's two-towered gate rose up ahead. Every night at sunset the great wooden doors were barred. Getting the guards to let them out would be a true test of Ulric's power.

To her dismay, a knot of armored men stood in the street before the gate. They were dressed for riding and had swords buckled at their hips. When Juliana saw whose colors covered their mail, she pulled up short and spat a curse no well-mannered female should have known.

"Do you recognize them?" Ulric asked.

"No, but that is Gideon Drake's livery, the man I am supposed to marry. He must have had men in town."

"He does not live in Bridesmere?"

"His firm is based in London, but my father and he have frequent dealings. Drake has been looking into establishing a local branch." She clutched Ulric's arm in a sudden panic. "Please, they must not find out who I am."

Ulric patted her hand, but the muscles of his face were tight. "Leave this to me," he said distractedly.

Juliana bit her lip and tried to let him think in peace.

She knew he was handsome and had who-knew-what exotic powers, but was he clever enough to get them through this? She was considered clever and, at the moment, she could barely recall her name.

"Maybe we could climb the wall somewhere else," she said. "You could toss me over with your *upyr* strength or, um, maybe we could rig a ladder so I would not break every bone in my body when I came down."

He grinned at her, the first full-out amusement she had seen him wear. He looked wonderfully boyish with those lines crinkling his eyes.

"I have a better idea," he said. "Sometimes a glamour needs a bit of help."

He took off his cloak and handed it to her.

"What?" she said, wondering confusedly if he meant for her to put it over her head.

"Ball it up and stick it under your gown. You are my pregnant wife and you have been having early labor pains. You insist on seeing your mother, who lives in a cottage outside the walls. I tried to stop you, but you are scared and determined."

He stood in front of her while she hurriedly obeyed. The effect was not terribly convincing. Juliana had to hold the lump of cloth in place to keep it from falling. Looking scared was not going to be hard.

"Leave the talking to me," Ulric said as he once again took her hand. "The more they hear my voice and meet my gaze, the deeper I can thrall them. Whatever you do, keep your hold on my hand. The contact will help me make your condition look genuine."

The gatekeeper, whose watch post was a chamber built into the wide stone arch, had come down to speak to Drake's soldiers. Ulric approached him sheepishly.

"Sorry to put you out," he said, his cap to his breast. "My wife here has been having early pains. Wants to see her mother in case the babe is on the way."

He shrugged as if to say *what can you do when a woman makes up her mind?*

The gatekeeper peered at Juliana, then back at him. "Her mother works at the castle?"

"Nay," said Ulric. "She is a shepherd's wife."

"'Tis a bad night to be roaming out," one of Drake's men put in. Beneath his bright mail coif, he had the same cold gaze Juliana had noticed on Drake's sons. His stance was wide, as if he were prepared to fight. Perhaps by chance or perhaps not, he gripped the pommel of his sword.

"Really?" Ulric turned his face to the sky. "The weather looks clear enough."

"Wolves," said the soldier, and even Ulric flinched at that.

"Wolves?" he said once he recovered.

"Or things that act like wolves but are not. A woman was attacked outside a tavern the other night. Said a wolf seduced her and drank her blood."

Ulric laughed, but Juliana could feel the sweat on his palm. "Sounds like she might have got a bad batch of ale."

"Maybe," said the soldier. He seemed neither amused nor convinced. He barely blinked as he faced Ulric. Hopefully, this meant Ulric's thrall would succeed. Juliana prayed the soldier could not hear her heart thumping in her breast. If he turned to her, she knew she would wear a look of guilty terror.

"Well, I have my dagger," Ulric said, patting his belt. Juliana saw a flash as if an old baselard hung there, but then it disappeared. For whatever reason, Ulric's illusion did not work perfectly on her. "To tell the truth, gentlemen, I would rather face a wolf than my wife's mother when her back is up. You would think a child had never been born before this one."

"I remember that," said the gatekeeper with a laugh. "That first one is always the end of the world."

Ulric shifted his gaze to him, a natural enough thing to do, though she felt him tense in preparation. *Control your fear,* he said to her in her head. *Otherwise, you will distract me.* Juliana blew out a breath and silently said a prayer. As soon as she calmed, she felt a prickling whoosh. Ulric was exerting the fullest potency of his thrall. The gatekeeper blinked at the assault.

"Thank you," Ulric said. "It is kind of you to let us out."

To Juliana's ears, his voice sounded strange, as if another, darker voice were layered beneath it. The gatekeeper's eyes went a little crossed. A heartbeat later, he shook his head. "It is no trouble," he said. "Just take care if you leave the road."

Juliana expected Gideon Drake's men to stop them, but they remained where they were, silent and watchful, as the guard unbarred the heavy doors.

"Godspeed," he called as they exited the outer arch.

Ulric returned the hail by touching his forelock.

By silent agreement, neither of them spoke until they had crossed the open fields and reached Bridesmere's woods. Juliana returned his cloak. Even as he put it on, she could not bring herself to drop her comforting hold on his hand.

She thought it rather nice of him not to complain.

"They knew you had been in Bridesmere," she said, "even if they did not know you were you. They knew an *upyr* had been in town."

"It appears that way," Ulric said. "I suppose I owe you my life for bullying me to leave."

"This is serious. Did you— Were you in your wolf form when you seduced those other women?"

"Of course not." Clearly, he found the suggestion humorous. "I did as I always do. I told them the encounter was a pleasant dream and that nothing unusual had happened. One of them must have sensed the wolf inside me and spun that into her fantasy."

"But she remembered you had drunk her blood."

"I cannot dictate what women dream."

His nonchalance spurred her temper. "That is precisely what you do. I would not put it past you to leave them a bit of a memory out of pride, to allow them to compare every other lover with you."

"Why, Juliana, are you suggesting that I am vain?" When he grinned, his eyeteeth were sharp as knives. Brief experience had taught her what this meant. Their brush with danger must have aroused him. A sound broke in her throat that was not fear.

Hearing it, he pulled her to him with a single tug, his mouth dropping ruthlessly to cover hers. His chest was hard, his hands locking her to him at head and waist. His body warmed as he rubbed against her like a cat. Being close to her seemed to raise his temperature. Warm or not, the ridge of his loins was firm. His tongue slid between her lips, slowly this time, stroking and sucking hers, making the kiss a true persuasion.

"Hold me," he said. "Wrap me in your human arms."

She held him because she could not help it. She did not sense him trying to thrall her, but his lure without it was just as strong.

"Yes," he urged, lifting her off the ground. "Yes, I need your hands."

She put them on whatever skin she could reach: the hollows of his cheeks, his jaw, behind his neck where his hair fell free. Every inch of him was perfect, every plane and curve a tactile delight. Her hands were humming, her own skin hot. Obviously craving more, he ripped off his belt and coaxed her arms beneath his shirt. The muscles of his back felt like silk-wrapped granite, rippling everywhere she touched.

When she traced the furrow of his spine, he quivered like a horse.

"Juliana," he gasped as if she had hurt him.

She knew she had not. He kissed her over and over, each penetration hungrier than the last. Pulling down the bodice of her gown, he bared her breasts and caressed them, then buried his face between. She shivered to feel his teeth scrape gently across her skin, especially her hardened peaks. She expected him to bite her. She feared it a little, but was prepared. To her surprise, he only teased her. Or perhaps he teased them both.

"Just a kiss," he whispered before he took one reddened nipple into his mouth. When he pulled it deeper, her pleasure swelled.

He must have heard her groan of longing, but all he did was move to the other breast.

The act of holding his desires in check seemed to excite him. By the time he lowered her onto a bed of crackling leaves, he was half-crazed. Wrenching her thighs up and apart, he rocked forward on his knees and took her quickly—deep, smooth strokes that drove her to moans of enjoyment almost at once. When he slid his hand between their bodies to touch her, she could not contain a sob.

He came as she did, a gasping, jerking peak that looked just as hard as hers. He rolled off her immediately after.

"There," he said, slightly breathless. "Now I can think straight enough to hunt."

His words raised a knot of hurt she told herself to disregard; they were, after all, hardly sweethearts. She wondered, though: If he intended their coupling to be a matter of mere convenience—as his words implied—why care that she was pleasured? Why refrain from biting her as he wished? Did he think she would not taste good?

Juliana shook her head, bemused by her own concerns. What a thing to worry about! Apparently, this business of taking lovers was more complicated than she guessed.

Ulric stood above her, offering his hand, feeling stupid and hoping she could not see. To have stopped this close to pursuit, and for such a reason, was insane.

"Did I hurt you?" he asked as she gripped his fingers and pulled to her feet.

"No," she said. "You just surprised me."

Unconvinced, he watched her closely as she tried to smooth her hair. She seemed flustered, withdrawn into herself. That he did not like. Admittedly, his apology came a little late, but he had no wish to cause her harm.

"I am all right," she insisted, then: "Will you hunt as your wolf?"

"Yes," he said, letting her change the subject. "But not here."

If those soldiers were on the watch for *upyr*, every wolf they spotted would be suspect.

He regretted bringing the danger. Juliana had called his behavior pride. In principle, she was right. In his anger and grief over Gillian's betrayal, he might not have been as careful as he should. If any real wolves had to pay for that, their deaths would be on his hands.

"We must walk," he said, chafing Juliana's fingers between his own. "There is better hunting farther on."

She nodded as if she could guess the reasons for herself. To his relief, she did not argue or ask why he had taken her as he did. Ulric was not sure he could answer that. He only knew, when he heard her moan of arousal, he had been unable to wait another instant to pull her close.

That being the case, he appreciated her restraint. Human women could be contentious, even though—unlike female *upyr*—most could not hope to best their mates in a fight. Of course, in talking a thing to death, he had observed that human females could hold their own.

Happily, Juliana was showing better sense—apart from running away. That could only be viewed as reckless, though he understood the impulse behind it. Freedom was the heart of who *upyr* were.

He swept his thumb across the back of her hand. "You handled yourself well," he said, judging she deserved the praise. "You did not panic back at the gate."

"I felt like I was panicking."

When her eyes met his, twinkling wryly, something warm and unexpected slid through his chest. At that moment, they were so attuned she could have been pack.

"What you do," he said, "is more important than what you feel."

She smiled to herself as if she knew a secret he did not. But that was to be expected. She was a woman. Pack or human, women thought their feelings mattered most of all.

"Ulric," she said, "have you decided where we are going?"

His step faltered as he realized how thoroughly she had put her fate in his hands. "To my home," he said, "across the border—unless you see a settlement you like better along the way. I have a cave in the Highlands where we will be safe."

She thought about this for a dozen steps. "You live with others of your kind?"

"Yes. I am leader to a pack of *upyr*, to all this realm's packs, though we rarely gather."

"Meeting your pack would probably help me decide if I want to become like you."

Unless I scare you off before then, he thought but did not say.

They walked in silence until they neared the northern edge of the woods. The open land beyond, where their progress would be exposed, would take hours to cover. Juliana was growing weary and, unlike some of his kind,

Ulric was unable to share much of his vitality without first biting its recipient. Only a blood-bond could forge a strong enough link. Given his recent loss of control, he was loathe to form one. For all he knew, a single taste might be dangerous.

He had not intended to take her under his protection, but now that he had, he could not do it halfway. Their safety depended on him keeping his head.

Given his thoughts, he was happy to spy a hollow beneath the roots of a large oak tree. The space looked big enough to shelter them both.

"You wait here while I hunt," he said. "I will bring something back for you."

Juliana wrinkled her nose at the shadowed hole. "Can I not come with you?"

"No," he said. "You would only get in the way."

"But what if there are bugs?"

"There are bugs in town, Juliana, and those bugs have no fear of humans." Once again he handed her his cloak. "Spread this beneath you. The cloth has absorbed my power. It will keep vermin away, at least for a couple hours."

"Will it?" Juliana examined the garment with new interest. "How convenient!"

Ulric left her pressing the velvet curiously to her face. Let her try to sniff out its secrets. He was glad to have her distracted.

Then again, if he wanted to discourage her ambition to become *upyr,* he ought to let her watch him hunt, ought to rub her nose in the gore. He knew why he did not. He was enjoying the trust with which she accepted almost everything he did. He did not have to fight or thrall her. She wanted what he did. When they made love, he did not gaze into her eyes as the last sigh faded and know he had made her sad. When she looked at him, she did not see a jailer.

That, he thought, had been the worst thing Gillian did.

If he revealed the beast who lived inside him, Juliana's acceptance might be destroyed.

He decided he could show her later, once he had burned this attraction out. Human that she was, surely it would not take long. With luck, he would have many nights to dissuade her from her goal.

The matter settled, at least in his mind, he stripped off his clothes before he changed. Though this was a more natural state for him than being dressed, he felt odd preparing by himself. If he had been with his pack, they would have had a communal howl. Sharing their excitement helped them work as a team. He shrugged off a homesick twinge. His wolf was strong enough to hunt alone.

Shaking his arms, he cleared his mind to summon his familiar. His beast was too much a part of him to need a name, their thoughts woven together like a single being. After centuries of exchanging forms, a simple wish was enough to pull the other out.

He pictured the forest rushing by him as he ran, the scent of prey, the feel of soft, spring earth under pounding paws.

Come, he thought, and his world broke into glittering pieces. It hurt, but only for an instant. As his edges shattered, the wind of the nothing-place filled his soul. There, where no one could hear, his wolf howled to the brothers it could not join.

Now, thought Ulric and fell onto four strong limbs.

⊸

Juliana willingly followed orders when they made sense, or even when they did not if she had no choice. She failed to see, however, why she should follow orders now. Clearly she was safer in Ulric's presence than huddling under a tree. She had a right to see him in his wolf form.

How else could she decide if his existence would suit her?

So thinking, she wrapped his cloak around her shoulders, retrieved her knife from her basket, and trailed him to a clearing, being as careful as she could to make no noise. Perhaps the power that clung to his cloak helped her achieve this. When he began to pull off his clothes, he showed no sign he knew she was near.

Heavens, Juliana thought, her breath catching in her throat as she watched the various parts of him appear. He had been garbed in all their encounters thus far. Now she saw him as God—or perhaps His opposite—had made him. Whoever his maker had been, he was exceedingly well put together. Lean without being thin. Muscular but not big. His arms were lovely, his hind parts quite the nicest she had ever seen. Biteable, she thought, her mouth watering unexpectedly. When he shook out his limbs and rolled his head around his shoulders, he looked the way she pictured Adam in the Garden.

This was where he belonged, in the wild places and the woods, getting ready to seek his prey.

Her hands had steepled before her mouth in a kind of prayer when he broke into a million sparks. She cried out, but it did not matter. He had no ears to hear, only a whirl of power and light. A heartbeat later, he hit the ground as a wolf, the biggest she had ever heard of. Long of leg and sleek of pelt, his shoulders came to her waist. He lifted his muzzle to scent the air. She expected him to smell her then, but he did not. Perhaps his cloak shielded that as well. Chills swept her skin as he took off with a silent, four-footed leap.

Oh, she thought. Oh, my, he is marvelous.

She hesitated a moment too long to follow. By the time she recovered, he was gone. To her relief, the ground was soft enough to take tracks. Each print was huge and amazingly far apart. Fortunately for her human sight, the depressions glowed like fireflies around their edges—at least until they dissolved. She had to be quick to catch them before they vanished. They moved in as straight a line as the trees allowed. Whatever Ulric smelled, he was heading directly for it.

A crashing noise alerted her to activity up ahead. She shrank behind a tree in time for a large gray hare to burst through the undergrowth. It quartered from side to side, but Ulric was right behind it. With a final pounce, he caught its long hind leg. The hare barely had time to squeal before Ulric tossed it up in the air. When it fell, he broke its neck with his jaws.

It was a clean kill; merciful, she supposed. He ate every bit of it, down to its final, furry foot. As he did, his eyes glowed gold and his throat vibrated with muffled growls, growls that sounded very much like enjoyment. When the hare was gone, his tongue swept out to clean his bloodied teeth. Juliana could hardly breathe. It was the single, rawest act she had ever seen.

Evidently, it was not over. As soon as he finished panting, the wolf-Ulric turned, his nose lowered to snuffle back along the hare's zig-zagging tracks.

Juliana could not have put a word to her feelings as she trailed behind him. Dread mingled with excitement, while pity and horror formed a turmoil behind her ribs. She could not do what he had done. She knew that with all her heart . . . or wanted to believe she knew. Maybe what he had done was no different from wringing a chicken's neck. And maybe it was better. For all the wolf-Ulric's swiftness, that hare *did* have a chance to escape.

The wolf-Ulric stopped at a snarl of bracken, then nosed at the soil beneath. He must have found the mother hare's burrow, because three small leverets tumbled out of the ground. Two escaped in different directions. The third ran straight at him.

Juliana covered her mouth. "No," she said, the tiniest whisper of sound.

This was too much for his cloak's magic to conceal.

Ulric whirled around with the baby squirming in his teeth. His gaze was bright, intent, and terribly familiar. Whatever his shape, this was the man she had slept with. The same intelligence filled those golden eyes.

She could not begin to guess what was passing through his mind. He padded toward her, paw by paw, his tail high but not wagging. His ears pointed slightly toward her, and the hair on his neck looked puffed. His wolf eyes watched her as he laid the leveret at her feet, gently, like a dog leaving a gift. Juliana had never wanted a present less. The leveret did not move except to tremble.

I told you, his husky voice said in her head. *I told you I would catch something for you to cook.*

She was shaking her head before she realized she had done it. That helpless bundle . . . That quivering baby thing . . .

It will not live without its mother. If you do not eat it, some other animal will.

Like a woman in a dream, Juliana bent to pick up the baby, cuddling it against her chest as she rose. Its fur was soft and warm.

This is food, she thought, trying to convince herself. Like a lamb or a side of beef. Just because someone else kills those creatures does not mean I take no part in their end.

The wolf-Ulric cocked his head at her as if trying to hear her thoughts.

Kill it with respect, he said. *Quickly, so it does not feel pain or fear.*

She was already holding the knife. She set the leveret down again and slit its throat in a single stroke.

The wolf's eyes flashed at the blood, a hint of green

touching the gold. It licked the side of its mouth. *Take it,* he said, sounding angry. *Take it away.*

She retreated a step with her burden, but farther than that she would not go. Nor would she look away from Ulric's wolfish glower. She sensed he was waiting for her to flee, that part of him wished she would.

"It *is* food," she said defiantly. "I was not happy to kill it, but I understood."

He must have changed when she blinked. Suddenly he stood before her in his own form. His hands, warm now from feeding, brushed away the tears she had not known she shed.

"I am sorry," he said. "I did not want you to see that."

"Why not?" She sniffed and tossed her head. "This is who you are."

"Who *you* will be if you hold me to my promise."

"Do you think this is worse than what humans do to eat? You were not cruel, Ulric. I saw you. You enjoyed the chase, but you were not cruel." She wiped the back of her hand across her cheek. Ulric's gaze lingered on her blood-ied fingers. She forced herself not to hide them. "You should find the other two and catch them. They should not go to waste."

With a muffled laugh, he kissed her forehead. "Now you are pretending to be harder than you are. Let the foxes catch them if they can. You have faced enough for one night."

She did not argue, more relieved than she wanted him to suspect. "I will dress this one," she said briskly, "when we get back to your tree."

⁓

Usually, after a hunt, Ulric liked nothing better than a good, hard tumble with a willing lass. Tonight he felt as if his body belonged to someone else, as if it were more foreign to him than his wolf's. He could not fall on

Juliana as he had before. His mind was too busy making sense of the night's events.

Juliana claimed to have found him by following his glowing tracks, but they should have been impossible for her to see. Most *upyr* did not have the skill to trace energy. Juliana was human, and unbitten. Ulric could imagine no reason for the two of them to be manifesting that strong a bond. Good or not, two nights of carnal acquaintance was insufficient cause.

But perhaps she had a bit of the Sight and did not know it. Perhaps that accounted for her resistance to his thrall.

Not that Ulric had been trying very hard to thrall her recently.

He could have expunged her memory of his hunt, could have spared her the horror before it sank in. Instead, he had dropped that leveret at her feet, knowing it would appall her tender woman's heart. Every female he knew got teary over baby creatures. Hares, squirrels, even baby turtles could make them coo. And he had dared her to kill one.

He did not understand his own intent. Had he wished to shock her? Or did he want to see if she could accept his most brutal self? Neither answer made much sense. This human's opinion ought to have meant nothing to him.

Unable to sort it out, he curled around her in the space beneath the old oak's roots. In spite of his confusion, the closeness was comforting. The hollow was tall enough for her to sit but not him. Her cloak and a heap of branches blocked the door. With the exit shielded, the sound of her breathing filled the earthen walls, a soothing music he did not know if he had heard before. He had been young when he fell in battle, no more than seventeen. He could not remember if he had bedded a woman before that. Being saved by Auriclus and learning to live as an immortal had dimmed those memories.

Juliana called him back by wriggling slightly in his arms.

"Ulric?" she said into the intimacy of the dark. "When you changed out of your wolf form, how did you finish digesting that hare?"

He nosed a lock of her hair from his face. "Even in my wolf form, I am *upyr*. We process sustenance very quickly. By the time I changed, it was gone."

"Even the bones?"

He smiled against her ear. Her tone was barely squeamish. He should have known her horror would fade. If nothing else, the neat efficiency with which she had prepared her own meal told him that.

"Even the bones," he confirmed. "All the substance of its life became mine."

She hesitated, a tiny inhalation before she spoke. "Is drinking from humans more exciting?"

Abruptly, her scent was everywhere in his head, his body stirring with telltale force. All too easily could he imagine her on his tongue.

"Yes," he said and no more after that.

⤛⤜

He would not bite her. He wanted to. She had known that from the start. But every time he came close to it, he pulled back. He would kiss her throat as he drove inside her, would caress it with his mouth and hands and groan as if he were dying. He would drag his fangs across her breasts and lick the bending of her arm. When he came, he sometimes sucked her skin so hard bruises would bloom.

He kissed them later and made them heal, but now and then she would hide one for the pleasure of touching it privately. The marks told her the hold she had on him was real, more real than he might have cared to admit.

Sometimes she caught him staring at her veins as if he were transfixed. A simple flash of her wrist could make him stumble. He would swallow then, and lick his sharpening teeth, but he never pierced her skin and drank.

She knew he could not make her *upyr* simply by feeding. On that the merchants' tales agreed—though the actual secret of the transformation was a mystery.

No, the significance of being bitten was that it made *upyr* coupling complete. Reputedly, humans liked it as well, but—from what she had seen—it was the thing Ulric's kind most wanted when they reached climax. Unfortunately for her, the more he refrained from claiming this pleasure, the more she desired to give it.

She feared she was dangerously close to falling in love. It seemed impossible, briefly as she had known him, but Juliana was not in the habit of hiding from her heart.

He was all she thought about, all she wanted to think about. His praise, his amusement were prizes she wished to win. When he looked sad, she wanted to soothe him. When he was kind, he seemed to her a knight. Even his flaws, which she was not blind to, seemed charming.

If these were not love's warning signs, she wished someone would tell her what were.

"Why?" she asked the third night in succession that he had torn his lips from her throat. "Why will you not bite me?"

His pupils dilated at the word. "It is too enjoyable," he said, turning away as he dragged his hand across his mouth. "Biting you would not be safe."

"It did not harm those women in Bridesmere."

"That was different."

She laid her cheek against the tension of his shoulder. "Because I am different?"

He slipped from her hold so swiftly her arms tingled at the loss. He stood over her, feet spread wide on the forest floor. His muscles bunched as he crossed his arms.

"Biting you would give me more power to control you. Is that really what you want?"

"You have the power to control me now. You have not used it since we left."

The reminder seemed to incense him. "You should not trust me," he said, his features gone faintly pink. "I could kill you!"

"I could kill you as well, every day when the sun comes up. Instead, I lie between you and the light."

"Because you want something from me. You are glamoured by the idea of being *upyr*." He dropped his arms, his anger faded to peevishness.

"That is not all I am glamoured by," she said with a suggestive smile.

Her teasing did not amuse him. "I will not bite you," he said, "and that is that."

She inclined her head, implying agreement without offering a promise. Life had taught Juliana there was more than one way to get around a stubborn man.

Chapter 4

⮜❧⮞

"You are getting better at that," Ulric said as she polished off a piece of roasted ptarmigan. Juliana had stuffed the bird with wild garlic, and the smell was heavenly—not too burned and not too raw, but crackling with juice and fat. At home she mostly sent their meat to a cookshop. Happily, along with many other things, her cooking skills had improved since joining Ulric.

Well into Scotland now, they lazed beside a campfire in a hollow between two hills, open but empty country. Her gown and chemise, newly washed in a stream, were drying on a rock. She had scrubbed herself as well, with Ulric's cloak to warm her when she got out.

Ulric had simply peeled off his clothes and set them aside. Like his person, they required no cleaning. His sigh of relief told her how much he preferred wearing naught but skin.

More modest than he, she could still appreciate the sense of freedom. Her existence could not have been more different than her life back home. No bed of feathers awaited her rest, no brazier or heated wine. A pit Ulric had dug in a nearby copse would serve as tomorrow's shelter. For tonight they lounged at ease beneath a star-filled sky. If she closed her eyes, Juliana could imagine the world was theirs.

For a week they had been traveling, making steady progress north—through forest when they could, but also unsettled land. Forced to do everything for themselves, Juliana had grown fitter and Ulric more relaxed. He seemed to take her presence for granted, as if bringing her with him had been his idea. She wondered if this was the effect of his wolf soul, to accept life as it came.

In other ways, he was very much like any man. His moods she could not predict. Sometimes he told her what he knew of the country around them. Sometimes he did not speak for hours. Luckily, since the incident with the hare, he had shown her whatever she wished to see. Sometimes he gave her orders, but for the most part, he left her to her own good sense.

They fell into a pattern, each choosing whichever chores suited them.

In all their travels, they had seen no sign of pursuit.

Juliana had a feeling she was seeing Ulric as he ruled his pack, a leader who was at his most benevolent when he got his way, but also one who kept his inner nature to himself. Even at their most intimate, she never breached his reserve.

Most likely, Ulric would have said there was nothing to breach.

This night, her full stomach made her feel expansive. On the chance that Ulric's recent hunt might have had the same effect, she licked her greasy thumb and gestured to the dripping spit. "Would you like some?" she offered. "There is plenty."

Ulric leaned back on his elbows and shook his head,

one leg lolling out to touch hers. "I would have to change to consume it, and I am too comfortable as I am. I like the smell, though. It reminds me of when I was a boy. My mother used to spoil me terribly."

"My mother treated me like a partner, as if I were important to our house."

"You probably were, from what I have observed. I, on the other hand, was a wastrel. I might not remember much of my mortal life, but I remember that. We raised goats, I believe. I liked to lie on my back in the pasture and dream as I watched the clouds. I was the youngest. Everyone protected me."

She could see his eyes reaching for the memories, wistful, unable to catch what he had lost. She put her cheek on her bent knee, doubting she would ever tire of watching him. "Now you are the protector."

"Yes," he said with a glimmer of a smile. "Auriclus made me that. In some ways, my sire was more unreliable than I was. He needed someone to keep order among his children, once he had taught them what secrets he had the patience to impart. I found I liked being responsible when I learned how."

"You said he changed you after you fell in battle?"

"My fellow foot soldiers left me for dead on the field at Hastings. I never got to see William conquer the day, though I doubt I would have enjoyed it, as I was fighting for King Harold. Auriclus found me round about my last breath. He claimed the way I fought to live made him decide to save me. I remember . . . I remember lying there in the dark on the cold and broken ground, squeezing the dirt between my fingers because that was all I could move. I was cursing in my head, I think, and crying with anger at the unfairness of dying young."

She touched the leg that bumped hers, picturing the boy he had been. "Are you glad he made you *upyr?*"

Ulric tweaked a lock of her hair. "I should lie to you,

but no, I was never sorry. He found a boy that night and turned him into a man. I never would have been what I am now if I had remained a mortal. You, however, could make a good life. I could find you a husband, you know, in any village along the way. A bit of a thrall to hook him and the rest would be up to you. I am sure you could handle anyone you chose."

She stared at him, taken aback. Could he really hand her over that easily? But perhaps she should not have been surprised. When he could have any woman he wanted, it must have been difficult to esteem any one more than the rest. Especially when he had only known her a week.

Hurt, but wishing to hide it, she turned her gaze to the fire. "I do not want to marry. I like living free like this."

"It is true you have proved more adaptable than I expected, but surely—in time—you will miss the luxuries you left behind."

He sounded like her father. *I know what is best for you and the devil take what you want for yourself.*

"You promised me," she said, struggling not to grind her teeth. "I have the summer to make up my mind."

She could hear her own defensiveness and feared he knew what lay behind it—not so much a love for freedom as a growing tenderness for him.

"There is more to life," she said, "than luxuries."

His shrug was cool. "As you please. Your decision makes no difference to me."

It was difficult to convince herself he was lying. She might think of herself as special, but that did not mean he would.

He rose then and stretched, his beautiful, naked body limned by the flames. She ached inside to see him, and even more when he turned to face her. His shaft was thickening and rising, as if he could will it upward with his mind. His thatch was honey-gold, the same bright color that furred his muscular thighs. The evidence of his maleness struck something deep inside her, something beyond her control. Her body tightened and grew wet. She knew when he caught her scent, for his nostrils flared. He smiled at her with hooded eyes, not speaking, merely letting her watch him grow.

He did not have to thrall her. Without a single instruction, she found herself on her knees. His cloak dropped to the ground behind her and the cool night air caressed her breasts. When he gripped her hair in a single fist, she uttered a longing cry. With a force she could not resist, he pushed her mouth toward the reddened crown.

"I do not know how to do this," she said, even as her body shook with excitement.

He brushed her lips with the silken skin, with the tiny, dampening slit. "It does not matter," he said. "It is impossible for you to hurt me."

Something in his voice made her look up.

"Did someone hurt you, Ulric? Is that why you hold a part of yourself aloof?"

"Do it," he said in his harshest growl. "Take me in your mouth."

She took him, as gentle as he was rough. He trembled when her lips enclosed his swollen crest.

"Ah," he sighed, rich and throaty, "you burn like fire."

She had learned, in the nights since they had met, that her touch had power. He tried not to betray how much he loved it, but she knew. To him, her human warmth was as magical as his thrall. With it, she could make him almost as weak as he made her.

"I burn because I want you," she whispered against his tip. "I burn because my desire for you fills my blood."

"I will not—"

She drew him in before he could repeat his vow to leave her unbitten. He used his words to guide her then, and his hands, surprisingly careful not to overwhelm her.

She loved the feel of him, the way he pulsed when her lips tightened around him, the way he shivered and grew hot.

"Do not come," she whispered, knowing it would make him wild. Though their first lovemaking of the night pushed him the hardest to release, if he put his will to it, he could hold off his peak. She wanted him to be desperate by the time he drove inside her, wanted him to forget everything but taking what he wished. She stroked his scrotum as he groaned, then ran her palms up and down the back of his legs. His buttocks clenched as she moved her caresses there. He swore at her but did not order her to stop. In fact, he widened his stance to better brace his weight.

"Squeeze me again," he said, the order hushed. "I like it when you cup my stones."

His toes curled strongly into the grass as she not only obeyed him but also pulled him deeper into her mouth. She took him at his word that she could not hurt him, using both force and the barest edge of her teeth. He began to pant and lengthen even more, until his swollen size was too much to take. Holding the base of him in one fist, she sucked strongly at the rest.

"Lord," he cursed, his fingers clenching in her hair. "Juliana, yes."

He was fast approaching his edge, but he held on. His hips began to push at her: tight forward jerks he seemed unable to restrain. She teased the tip of her tongue into the little slit and kneaded his drawn up sack. This he tolerated for a heartbeat, then thrust greedily past her lips again.

"Harder," he growled, his thickness pulsing against her tongue. "Wetter."

When he could stand the torment no longer, he pulled free and dropped to his knees. With hands like heated steel, he swung her splay-legged onto his lap.

His anxiously throbbing crown homed immediately on her gate.

"Now," he said, breathing hard around the words, "let us see if you can handle what you have wrought."

The answer was not in doubt. Ulric knew she had been ready since he turned and let her watch him rise. Whatever the differences between them, their bodies were in harmony.

He entered her clinging warmth as if he were buttered, barely needing to push until the final inch. Her growl as she accepted it could have been his own. At his coaxing, she rose on her knees to ride. His hands on her bottom guided her untutored movements, adding to the pleasure of touching her the undeniably stronger one of telling her what to do.

He urged her as fast as he could bear without going over the crest of climax. For once, he intended to take his fill of anticipation.

There was, after all, so much of it to enjoy. He loved seeing Juliana naked, loved watching the light play over her human flesh. No *upyr* could jiggle this delightfully, nor give so readily before his thrust. How many levels of melting softness could there be? How many shades of pink and cream?

Her nipples were a blend of plum and rose, swollen at their base and hard at their tips. The threads of blue that ran beneath the silken surface of her breasts called irresistibly to his hands. He palmed one soft weight and lifted it, watching the peak grow dark. Brushing his fingertip back and forth made it even sharper.

Kiss it, he imagined he heard her say, though he was not trying to read her thoughts. Real or not, the exhortation spurred him. He bent her backward over his arm, then fastened his mouth to the peak. She trembled as he drew on her, her hair swinging to the grass. While its brown might be ordinary, its satiny sheen was not. Its shining length no longer bore the ripples of her braids. It was as free as the rest of her.

"Ulric," she sighed as he played on her with his tongue.

His fangs were fully extended, and he had to draw carefully. It would have been all too easy to cut her, to take a sweet, accidental taste. His body burned with frustration, despite the movement of her hips. As if she wanted to soothe him, her fingers stroked the knotted tendons behind his neck, then slid apart to massage his shoulders.

"You are a cat," she teased. "You would let me pet you all night."

He groaned as her nails dragged up and down his spine, fearing the words were true. The way she touched him, the way she sighed his name and melted beneath his kiss, was different from any woman in his past. Her tenderness reached inside him to twist and tug the strings of his heart. As it did, the bruises Gillian had left there ached.

He knew Juliana believed she loved him.

The irony should have made him laugh. Part of him welcomed her feelings, if only to salve his pride. How long had he chased Gillian, only to end up rebuffed? In one week, this woman had shown him more true attraction, more faith in his good intentions, than Gillian had in years. He felt taller when he held Juliana, the king he was supposed to be.

But all of it, every scrap, was based on an illusion. His outward perfection had tricked Juliana into thinking his insides were perfect, too. Any *upyr,* whether he thralled her or not, might have had the same effect. Juliana was dazzled, and that meant he could trust her emotions no more than she should have been trusting his.

Pleasure was no substitute for love.

He steeled himself as he felt his orgasm rise, always the lowest ebb of control. It was like trying to stop a flood. The siren song of release had him in its spell. His hips took over from her rhythm, driving faster, growing more frenzied with his desire. His fangs were like stakes driven in his gums.

But he would not bite her. He would not bind them in that way, even if every fiber of his being urged him on.

Wrenching his mouth from her breast, he hid his face in her shoulder, but that flesh was tempting, too: salty and smooth, with a good, firm muscle to take his teeth. Her hands seemed to coax him to it, combing through his hair to press his scalp. She found the spot behind his ears that always made him shiver. Groaning, he tipped his head to the stars.

Juliana clasped his jaw.

"Ulric," she said, exasperation mixing with pity. "For God's sake, take what you want."

Her eagerness was too much. Crying out, he tore himself from her body, sprawling backward, so close to spending and so in need of it that he could not keep from finishing with his hand—hard, fisting pumps that had him spitting against her belly like a callow boy. The fluid came in spurting arcs, as if his body meant to spill everything at once.

Juliana gaped at him as he finished, her palm covering the mess.

Angry and embarrassed, Ulric did not know what to say. What could he say? He would not let himself be sorry. He had done what he knew was right for them both. If she was unsatisfied with their exchange, she could damn well follow his example.

The thought of her doing so made his member twitch.

"I am going to the stream," he announced, rising stiffly to his feet. "I feel in need of cooling off."

"You feel in need," she said, the most sarcastic he had ever heard her. She shook her head and turned away, leaving him to his hollow victory.

~⁓~

Even though she was furious—with herself as well as with him—Juliana spread her body on top of his when they squirmed into their carefully camouflaged pit. If anything knocked off the woven branches that formed the roof, she did not want to see him burn.

"You do not have to do that," he said, already sounding drowsy.

"Of course I do. What if you accidentally set fire to me?"

He snorted into the darkness, but it was no carefree laugh. Beneath his tunic, his muscles felt like boards. His arms lay at his sides rather than hold her.

Juliana sighed. More than anything in the world, she hated having to apologize. She minded it especially when she was in the wrong. She, after all, was the one who almost always did what was right.

"Ulric," she said against his velvet-covered chest. "I am sorry for pushing you to bite me earlier. Even though I know you wanted to, and even though I fail to understand your reasons, I should have respected your wishes."

"Yes," he agreed. "You should have."

She coughed in disbelief. This was how he accepted her apology?

"You should have," he repeated. "Or do you think your words will have more meaning if I say you did nothing wrong?"

"You could apologize back."

"I do not feel the need."

"Of all the—"

"Juliana." His hand came up to cover her mouth.

"There is something you should know. Seven days before I met you, the woman I loved for the last two decades left me for another man. These feelings you have are wasted on me. From the first time I saw Gillian, when my sire abandoned her on my doorstep, I knew she would be important to my life. I spent years coaxing her to trust me, watching her grow into her powers. I taught her the pleasures of flesh and hunt. I could never love anyone after her."

Juliana's skin felt as if he had plunged her into an icy stream. He loved someone else. Ulric loved someone else. She could hear the depth of his devotion in the gentleness of his tone. What was worse, she could tell he knew that she possibly loved him. As swiftly as it had chilled, her face blazed hot. The clenching of her jaw made it hard to speak.

"I shall keep that in mind," she said with all the dignity she could muster.

"Good," he said. "That will make everything easier."

Then he fell asleep, effectively giving himself the final word.

Juliana, naturally, lay awake most of the day. A mist had settled over the surrounding wood shortly after dawn. Damp and cool, it collected around the needles of the pines to roll off in intermittent drops. Though Ulric's gift kept their refuge dry, the unpredictable *plip plop plip* of water to the forest floor formed a background to her circling thoughts.

Who was this Gillian? A human? Another wolf-*upyr?* That seemed likeliest if, as he said, his sire had abandoned her on his doorstep. Twenty years was a long time to be pining after a woman, but why was Ulric so certain he could never love again? And why was he so insistent that Juliana know? Maybe his telling her meant he was afraid he *could* love her, and to avoid the risk he pushed her away.

Though that idea was appealing, it reeked of self-flattery. Most likely the thought of Juliana wanting him for anything but bed play was just annoying.

And he might have wished to be kind by warning her. He did seem to like her at least a bit.

Her cape and the pine-bough roof screened out most but not all the light. Pushing up on her arms, Juliana stared at Ulric's sleeping face. He looked an enchanted prince as she curtained him with her hair. His brow was noble, his feature white and pure. Sadly, his still, marble visage told her nothing of his secret thoughts.

You have fallen for a statue, she thought, but she could not make herself believe it. He was arrogant and controlling and probably too powerful for his own good, but under that handsome immortal exterior, he was definitely flesh and blood. She flounced back on his chest with a sigh. For one tempting moment, she thought of beating him with her fist. Either he would wake and argue with her, or he would not feel it at all. Neither outcome seemed very useful.

"It must be love," she grumbled to herself. No other man had ever made her act like a child.

Chapter 5

❦

She was still angry at him when she awoke. Ulric
knew this because she was making little faces to herself
as she helped erase the signs of their camp. Despite her
pique, he noticed she wore his cloak to walk to the
stream.

"Yours is warmer," she said, spying his raised eyebrows.

"Be my guest, Juliana. Just remember if you do not let
me don it now and then, the good of it will wear off."

"You slept on top of it all day," she said, caught
between annoyance and interest.

"True, but I have more power for it to soak up after
dark."

Even with that, she did not return his garment. As Ulric
suspected, its magical properties were not its greatest
attraction—and probably not its warmth, either. Gri-
macing, he shook Juliana's cloak free of leaves and
tucked it into her basket. He knew he had been right to

tell her about Gillian. Unlike some *upyr,* he found no entertainment in breaking hearts.

"There is a town just east of here," he said when she returned from washing. "As we have seen no pursuit, I think it is safe to purchase supplies. I expect you are weary of eating meat."

She had been untangling her hair with her fingers. Now she glared at him through the strands. "I am not picking out a husband."

"No one said you were."

"You did not have to say it. I can guess what is in your thoughts. I am not a puppy to be left on the first convenient doorstep. If you wish to break your promise, you will have to do it without my cooperation."

She cursed as her fingers refused to go through a knot, her brown eyes glittering ominously close to tears. Ulric put his hand over hers. "I will help you if you promise you will not cry."

At that, she dropped her hands and said something truly nasty.

Ulric grinned and worked through the snarl, using a pulse of power to encourage the locks to lie straight.

"There." He smoothed the silken mass over her shoulders. "That should stay mannerly for a while."

She did not smile or thank him, but removed his cloak and handed it back. "I am warm enough. You can put your power inside the cloth again."

He had wanted her to distance herself from him. That being so, he could not account for the sting of insult he felt.

~≈~

The "town" Ulric spoke of was more of a crofter's village, an assemblage of crooked stone buildings built low to the ground. Moss grew up the sides of the houses and over the weathered thatch, which was secured by nets of rope. A square, four-storied tower—also crumbling but somewhat repaired—overlooked the village from the north. Juliana surmised this was the dwelling of the local laird.

The still-thick mist lent the humble scene an air of romance—at least until they got close. As she and Ulric entered the single, rutted street, they found a litter of piglets rooting in the dirt.

Before she could worry that they might look tasty to her companion, a boy in a ragged linen shift came running out of a cottage, calling what she assumed was the Scottish version of "Here, piggy." It being Gaelic, Juliana understood not a word.

"Hm," said Ulric as the boy shooed his charges back inside. "I am not sure these people can spare what I could charm out of them."

Juliana handed him her sack of coin. "You can pay them with this if they will take money."

"Oh, people have use for coin even out here. We are not that far from the markets of Dundee."

"I thought your kind of *upyr* stayed away from humans."

"We have to know which places to avoid, do we not? In any case, I thought you"—he jingled the sack—"had no money but what you were going to earn with your harp."

"I was saving that to open a little shop."

"Very practical," he said, beginning to walk toward what looked like the busier end of the village, where lanterns hung outside doors. "Even I, however, would not suggest you try to start a business here."

If she had not known he was teasing, she would have bristled. Unfortunately, it was hard to stay angry when he assumed that affable expression, as if he were delighted with all the world. He had spun just a touch of glamour, enough to dim his glow and color his complexion. When a dog began to bark wildly at their approach and Ulric growled it to silence, the pleasant set of his features did not change. He looked a too-handsome human, a rake to be reckoned with. A housewife stared as she came outside to empty a bucket of slops. Ulric tipped his cap at her, and her hand fluttered to her breast.

Juliana rolled her eyes. If he was not vain, she was the queen of England.

She had to admit his manner got them what they wanted. Before much time had passed, he had coaxed a few blushing wives out of a round of cheese, two loaves of bread, a crock of dried figs, an ivory comb, and, best of all, a tiny collection of spices. Ulric had insisted on smelling each packet before she decided which ones to buy. The price was dear, of course, but she had not been able to resist the pleasure on his face.

"We should get you a little cauldron," he said, taking her loaded basket over his arm. "Then you will have a choice as to how you cook."

Turning back, he spoke to the woman who had just parted with her larder's prize. She answered shyly and pointed in the direction from whence they came.

"Blacksmith," Ulric explained to Juliana. "She thinks he might still be working at his forge."

As if there were no reason for him to refrain, he hooked his elbow around hers. Juliana's arm tingled strongly at the contact, but if he could be casual, so could she.

"How is it that you speak Gaelic?" she asked. "I thought you came from England."

"Most *upyr* have a knack for picking up what they need, and we travel occasionally amongst ourselves. Lucius came to us that way." A single crease appeared on his forehead. "Lucius was . . . is a member of my pack. I never did learn where he came from originally. He simply showed up one night and asked permission to join a hunt. But as I was saying, there are five packs in Scotland. One in Skye, one in Orkney, and two in the Grampian Mountains. My pack lives a day or so west of Inverness. Because there is only one English group, had I not learned the Scottish tongue, it would have been difficult to rule them all."

Juliana smiled to herself. *Difficult,* he said, but not impossible.

Despite her averted head, Ulric caught her amusement. "Come, Juliana. Do you really doubt I could have prevailed?"

"No, no," she began to laughingly deny. He cut her off by pulling her without warning into a building's lee. If he had been in his wolf form, she would have said his ears were pricked. She began to ask what was wrong.

"Hush," he said, touching her cheek. "I hear English voices."

Juliana heard nothing, but could not doubt his wolf-*upyr* ears. With Ulric holding her hand, they crept to the window of what had to be the village forge. A glow like hell itself filled the single room. Crouched beneath the unglazed window, Ulric set her basket silently on the dirt. Glad it had not occurred to him to leave her behind, she tried to stick her nose over the ledge.

Before she made it, Ulric put his hand on her head and shoved her down.

She would have argued had she not suspected one was easier than two to cloak with a glamour. He, of course, could look all he pleased.

Whoever the other Englishmen were, their reception was not as warm as Ulric's.

"Nay," said a rumbling Scottish baritone, thankfully speaking English. "I am not interested in yer coin."

"How about our swords? Are you interested in them?"

The cool, drawling tones turned her blood to icicles. This voice belonged to Milo Drake, Gideon's younger son. Ulric covered her mouth as soon as she drew breath to warn him. For once, she cursed his lack of skill in reading her actual thoughts.

The blacksmith made a sound that said Milo's sword was prodding a sensitive body part.

"We only want to know," Milo went on, "if you have seen the woman in this locket. Her name is Juliana Buxton. She is English just like us. She might be traveling with a man, a very handsome, very pale, gold-haired man. We think they are pretending to be man and wife."

"Oh, give it up," said a voice Juliana recognized as Milo's older brother, Milton. "We have ridden to every chicken-scratch bunghole on the map. Good riddance, I say. Father can find himself another broodmare to disrupt our home. No one has seen them. They have not come this way."

"They would go north," insisted another man. "His kind live in the wilderness."

" 'His kind,' " Milton sneered. "What a steaming heap of twaddle. Did you ever think they might have had the good sense to avoid stopping in towns?"

"He has partaken of human blood," said the voice she could not place. "Once they get a taste of the prime elixir, they lose their appetite for beasts."

"Christ on a pitchfork," Milton swore. "I am weary to death of this nonsense."

The smith cried out as someone scuffled through the dirt. Juliana guessed the someone was Milton and that he had poked the smith with his sword.

"If you know anything," Milton snapped, "tell us now, or you can watch your favorite member roast in your fire."

"I ken nothing," said the smith and loudly spat.

Juliana winced. The Milton she knew would kill the

blacksmith out of pride alone. Gideon's heir would not care that he was innocent. She straightened beside the window, out of sight but trembling in every limb. "I must stop him," she whispered to Ulric.

He opened his mouth, but to her astonishment did not protest. She had to admit, a shameful part of her wished he would.

Give me your wrist, he said instead. *I am going to drink from you and loan you my power to thrall. They will not expect you to have it, and that will give you an advantage, but the transfer will not last long. You must lure them out here, all of them if you can, where I can bite them. Once I do that, I will be able to change their beliefs in a lasting way. I can make them forget they ever wanted to find us—at least long enough for us to disappear. Nod to me now if you understand.*

She nodded, her teeth beginning to chatter.

Sh, he hushed her. *This will not hurt at all.*

He kissed her wrist, then the center of her sweating palm. The unexpected tenderness closed her throat. Despite the situation, his breathing sped up. She felt his fangs start to lengthen against her skin. The sensation was peculiar in the extreme.

"I am sorry," she mouthed, the barest brush of sound. "I know you did not want to do this."

His lashes rose, his gaze reluctantly leaving the veins that marked the base of her arm. He was paler than she had ever seen him, a pure blue-white. His glow was so bright it was leaking out from beneath his glamour. With his pupils nearly swallowing his golden eyes, his tongue curled between his teeth.

Juliana's body tightened deep inside.

I will enjoy this, he admitted, *no matter what we might regret afterward.*

He lowered his head, licking her wrist as he closed his eyes. His mind-voice murmured her name as reverently as a prayer. Her heart hammered as he set his teeth. Then he bit down.

His tiny moan of pleasure, soft but eloquent, drowned out the quick stab of pain. For a heartbeat, she was in his head, sucking hungrily at her wrist, feeling the sweet, hot fluid run down her throat. Her body resonated with his delight, a languorous orgasm of the mouth.

Lost in his pleasure, in his longing, she had the most astonishing urge to surrender everything she was. *Here I am,* she thought. *Take what you wish.* She tasted spice and wildness. Smelled a forest after a rain. Time folded back on itself and spun. A memory swallowed her in light.

It could have been happening that very moment. She was small, only four or five, and she was sitting on her mother's lap in their home in Bridesmere. They were at the battered kitchen table, the scent of flour heavy in the air. Her mother's long, work-hardened hands covered her short ones. Under both lay a ball of dough.

"Here is how we knead the bread," sing-songed her mother, kissing her wispy hair. "Knead it up, knead it down, knead it all around the town. Yes, Juliana, look how clever you are!"

She was young enough to take her mother's love for granted, but she sensed it all around her like a wonderful, soothing hum, her favorite music in the world. Her mother's voice, her smell, the touch of her gentle hands had faded in the five years since her death, but now Juliana had them back.

She would not let the chance slip away.

"I love you," she said, squirming around to see her mother's face.

"I love you, too, sweetheart," said her mother.

No time would have been enough to savor her smile, and no time was what she had. With a snap like a fresh-washed shirt flapping on a line, Juliana was in the street again, behind the smithy, with Ulric kneeling at her feet. His forehead rested on her hip as if he were too weak to hold it up.

His fingers pressed the place he had bitten. The wound tingled and itched, and she thought it must be healing. Whether it was hardly signified. Ulric had given her a gift greater than his power. Her cheeks were wet with tears she did not trouble to wipe away.

"Thank you," she mouthed when his head came up.

He looked away as if he were embarrassed. *Be careful,* he said, his mind-voice much clearer than it had been before. *Try to catch their eyes, but do not be obvious. You want to convince them just as you would if you had no power. The thrall is merely to help you be more persuasive.*

She could not feel where inside her his thrall might be, but she was calmer now, her shakiness nearly gone. She squeezed his hand and he squeezed back, the grip comfortingly firm. If he believed she could do this, she imagined she had a chance.

She bent to retrieve her knife from her basket, feeling slightly woozy as she changed position. Then she walked around the building to the door. The smoke from the furnace, or some of it, fed through a hole in the roof. The room was hot. Even standing on the threshold, she broke into a sweat.

To her dismay, six men—rather than the three she had expected—ranged around the fire-lit room. She discovered she knew them all.

The four soldiers who accompanied Milton and Milo were the same who had gathered at Bridesmere's gate the night she and Ulric escaped. The captain, the only one who had spoken then, wore a silver cross on a chain around his neck. She did not recall seeing it before. Holding it in one hand, he rubbed it absently with his thumb as he watched the burly, soot-streaked man who had fallen to one knee on the bare dirt floor.

Juliana knew this man must be the smith. His arm and
chest bore bloody slashes, and the top of his leather apron
hung in strips. So far Drake's sons seemed to have
administered nothing but shallow cuts. As she watched,
the smith clutched the large stone block on which his
anvil sat, trying to regain his feet. Seeing his opponent
had no intention of giving up, Milton laughed and
caressed his sword.

"You must stop this," Juliana said, turning all eyes to
her. "I am the one you want."

This was not the wisest statement to utter when in possession of a borrowed thrall. Every man but the smith
took a step toward her.

"Well, well," said Milo, "look who turns up at our
heels when we least expect her." He leered at her, his face
for once showing an expression, though that particular
expression was small improvement. He rubbed his hand
up and down his mail-covered thigh. "You cannot imagine how happy I am to get this chance to put you in your
place."

Juliana did not think she wanted to know what this
meant. "I am sorry," she said, resisting her inclination to
bow her head. Ulric had told her she must hold their eyes.
"I panicked at the thought of marrying your father, but I
am over it. I am ready to go home. Running away was
harder than I thought."

Her beaten tone was precisely what Milo expected.
Still smirking, he closed the distance between them and
clamped his hand on her jaw. At the instant of contact, a
glaze entered his eyes. For the first time, Juliana was sure
the thrall was at work.

"You do not want to hurt this man," she said softly. "He
has nothing to do with me."

Milo's eyes narrowed, but he jerked his head toward
his brother. "Release him, Milton. We have what we
want."

"Ask her where the *upyr* is," the captain of the men insisted. "We want him as well."

Juliana considered denying Ulric's presence, but feared that lie was too big to sell. "He is outside," she said, careful to meet the captain's gaze. "I wounded him when I got away—rather badly, I believe."

She held up the knife to show them how. To her amazement, the blade was redder than could be accounted for by the fire.

"I will handle him," Milo sneered, but the captain grabbed his arm.

"Do not repeat the mistake I made in Bridesmere. We must take this beast seriously. The *upyr* will heal quickly. We need to catch him before he runs."

"You must all go," Juliana said, trying to look at each face in turn. Even Milton shivered when she did. "I fear his power is too great for any less."

As the six men piled through the door, she prayed she was making the right decision. Strong though Ulric was, she was not certain he could overcome them all. But he had peered in the window. He must have known how many there were.

She directed them around the building where Ulric, bless his quickness, lay in the dirt with his feigned wound. His pretense was so lifelike, she could see blood.

"Do not kill him," Milo said. "He has secrets we might be able to use."

The captain rushed ahead. "Stay back," he ordered. "Whatever you do, do not meet his eyes. I will stun him with my crucifix."

For an instant, the cross did seem to flare with holy fire, but when Juliana blinked, the effect was gone. Maybe the silver had caught a reflection. Whatever the source of the flash, the captain would have been better off leading with his sword. As soon as he was close enough, Ulric's hand shot out to grab the chain, which he used to yank the soldier to his mouth. Thrusting back the aventails of his coif, Ulric bit his neck.

He swallowed once before shoving the man away.

"Be still," he said with a wolflike growl.

The captain collapsed to his knees, two lines of red trickling down his throat. He did not even lift his hand to check the wounds.

Ulric had not lied about a bite giving him more power.

At the sight of their companion, empty-eyed and open-mouthed, the others cried out and ran.

"Stop," Ulric ordered, but only two of them did.

Juliana managed to stick her leg in Milo's way, but not to rob him of breath when he tripped. He grabbed her ankle and pulled her down beside him, immediately climbing on top of her and shaking her by the neck. As she struggled to wrench off his choking hold, she saw the blacksmith clout the other two with a pan. Milo's brother, Milton, dropped with a broken moan.

He was lucky the smith had not grabbed his hammer. His skull would have been split.

Not that her own was in such good shape.

"Release me," she ordered, but Milo ignored her, her power to thrall plainly spent. Milo was grinning like a wolf himself. If he did not mean to kill her, he certainly meant to make her swoon—and who knew what he would do then?

To her dismay, she barely had strength to fight. Ulric's feeding had sapped her. Unable to knee her attacker with any force, she attempted to rake his eyes. More annoyed than hurt, he buffeted her ear hard enough to ring. Both hands, apparently, were not required to hold down her neck.

"Help," she gasped, not knowing what else to do.

Milo was swinging his fist again when Ulric grabbed his hauberk from the back and half-yanked, half-hoisted him away. In case she could be of aid, Juliana fought off a fit of coughing. She might as well have indulged. In a blur of motion, and with one hand, Ulric drew Milo's sword from its scabbard and tossed it into the dark. Milo fumbled for his dagger, but Ulric already had it. He threw it hard enough to whistle as it whirled end over end. Juliana heard it stick in the ground with a distant thunk.

Her heart pounded with more than relief. The sight of Ulric coming to the rescue was really quite wonderful— a thrill she would have sworn she was too practical to appreciate. He seemed ten feet tall as he spun Milo around and lifted him by the neck.

If she had not been in love already, this would have sealed her fate.

"You dare," Ulric said in the fiercest voice she had ever heard, his features twisted with rage. "You dare to touch my mate?"

"Ack," said Milo, his feet dangling a foot off the ground. Ulric's left fist held him firmly beneath the jaw, a more impressive echo of what Milo had done to her. Juliana understood Milo's fear. The *upyr's* eyes were practically spitting fire.

"Please, your worthiness," Milo pleaded, "I meant no harm. I did not know she was yours."

The groveling won him no quarter. Ulric tossed him against the wall with rattling force. "You are almost too disgusting to bite."

He did bite him, though, then yanked the portrait locket Gideon Drake had commissioned off Milo's sword belt. That taken care of, Milo sank under Ulric's thrall as easily as the captain had.

Ulric moved to the others one by one. Even the unconscious men felt his teeth. The instructions Ulric gave them were mind to mind and, whatever they were, they struck each man like physical blows. After the twitch of reaction, their eyes went glassy, the muscles of their faces slack. The effect was eerie, as if they were losing part of themselves. Finally, only the smith remained.

The Scotsman lifted his work-scarred hands to show he was harmless but did not back away. Breathing hard, he looked as if he had thought the brawl good fun. Perhaps a big man like him refused to fear anyone.

"I helped ye fight," he said. "Ye doona have to mess with me."

"I must erase your memory," Ulric said.

The blacksmith grinned and shook his head. "Ye canna," he said. "We follow the old ways here." He pulled aside what Milton had left of his leather apron to bare a blue tattoo in the center of his hairy chest. The simple figure was a warrior with a shield and spear. His feet stood on a spiral, and above his head shone the sun. "Ye see. The wolf-men are no enemies to me and mine. Leave us be, and our races can live in peace." He chuckled as if he were remembering a good joke. "Always thought me granddad was lying when he told those tales."

"No," said Ulric. "He did not lie."

The blacksmith slapped his knee. "Nearly laughed meself silly when that fellow ran at ye with his cross."

Juliana wondered if she were the only one who had seen it flash.

"That is human nature," Ulric said with a shrug. "People like to think their God wipes out the ones who came before."

"Not here." The smith gestured to the cross carved roughly above his door. "In Dunburn we honor them all."

Though Ulric's expression was serene, Juliana sensed his discomfort with this exchange. She stepped forward to catch the Scotsman's eye.

"Master smith," she addressed him politely, "now that these men pose no danger, do you suppose you could sell us a small cauldron?"

This, to her, did not seem a humorous request, but the smith roared out a laugh. "Aye," he said. "Never lose sight of business and ye'll go far."

He fetched what she wanted from his sweltering workroom, then accepted Juliana's coin with an approving nod. Juliana took the cauldron herself, knowing Ulric could not touch the iron.

"Ye're a smart, braw lass," the blacksmith said, adding to Ulric, "Ye take care of her."

They were dismissed, it seemed, a treatment Ulric took in unexpected stride. Once again collecting her basket, he left the smith to deal with the fallen Englishmen as he pleased.

As soon as the village was well behind their backs, Juliana spoke. "What was that picture on his chest?"

"Honestly, I do not know. A Pictish spell drawing is my best guess. The packs use similar designs to mark their territory, but my sire never said much about their origin."

From tales her mother told her as a girl, Juliana knew the Picts were early inhabitants of Scotland. They lived in tribes at first, later uniting under a king. Hunters and warriors, they liked to run around naked except for their blue tattoos. It was said they were small of stature but as swift as their fighting steeds. Good seamen, they worshiped the sun, and their priests were called Druids. Their successors, the Scots, adopted many Pictish practices as their own, later blending them with Christian rite.

This was the sum of Juliana's knowledge and yet, from what Ulric was saying, she knew more than he.

"Could the smith's tattoo have prevented you from thralling him?"

"Possibly. He did seem to have strong guards."

"But why would a Pictish spell work and not a cross?"

"Because, supposedly, Pictish magic was inspired by the magic of the first *upyr*. Whatever essence makes us immortal understands and does homage to those symbols."

"Are you certain a cross has no power? I thought I saw a flash when the captain first held it up."

"I see no reason for Christian objects to work on us, but, as I said, I cannot tell you more than that."

"Forgive me for being blunt, Ulric, but had I been in your shoes, I would have insisted my sire explain."

"You and Gillian both," Ulric said dryly. "She always wanted to know the reason for everything."

The reminder of her rival—if Juliana did not flatter herself with the term—quashed any thought of further conversation. How fortunate she was to possess none of his previous lover's good points, yet still have room for the bad!

But bitterness would gain her nothing. She comforted herself that he had called her his mate and had reclaimed her locket. Ulric might not have meant much by these deeds, but both suggested attachment.

Assuming, of course, that she was not grasping at straws.

She began to shiver as the night's events caught up with her nerves. Seeing Milton and Milo again, witnessing the violence she had not known they were capable of, made her aware of how fragile her freedom was. Certainly, she need no longer feel a shred of remorse for running away. Her decision had been wiser than she suspected.

Seeing her shudder in earnest, Ulric swung off his cloak and wrapped it around her. "Take it," he ordered, though she had not thought to resist.

That his arm would have been more welcome she kept to herself.

In silence, they labored up a slope on which the grass had been cropped by cattle. When she glanced over her shoulder to see if she could spot the herd, the village had been engulfed by the mist. She wondered if the smith would tell his children of the encounter, and if they, too, would roll their eyes.

However far-fetched, the tale would make a perfect addition to her collection, just the sort her mother had preferred. Nothing pleased her more than drawing scenes of fantastic combat. Demons with lots of teeth had been her favorite, followed closely by dragons.

And maybe, Juliana thought, that preference went a way toward explaining her daughter's affinity for Ulric. She had cut her teeth, so to speak, on tales of monsters.

She had this revelation as they reached the top of the hill. Beyond it lay another even higher, dotted with clumps of trees and cut in two by a silvery stream, the same that she had washed in earlier. As if they stood within the edges of a cloud, here the mist thinned to a veil. She could just make out a line of mountains behind the hills. Their bulk stretched like a wall across the horizon, remnants of the winter's snow snaking at their peaks.

For a moment, she was frightened. This country was too big, too remote. It would swallow her like an ogre in a tale. But then the shiver of fear was chased away by exhilaration. Juliana broke into a grin. The wild, strange beauty of the land sang to some newly awakened corner of her soul. She wanted to paint it, or perhaps hold it in her arms.

To her surprise, Ulric did not pause.

"I want to thank you," she said, knowing she owed him that.

"I need no thanks. You are the one who risked the most rescuing that smith."

"I meant for the memory of my mother. I had almost forgotten what she was like. When you bit me, you gave her back."

Ulric stopped and rubbed his face with both hands. When he dropped them, he met her eyes. His held an emotion she could not read, though it might have been wariness.

"That was your doing," he said. "Your heart called her up. And I am the one who should be thanking you."

He strode ahead of her, almost too quickly for her to keep up—not what she considered the actions of a grateful man. She drew breath to question him, then let it out. In his current mood, she was not certain she wanted him to explain.

He might start in again about how he could never love her.

"We will reach the Grampians tonight," he said, nodding toward the mountains' spectacular silhouette. "It will not be much longer till we are home."

Till *you* are home, she thought, biting her lower lip. Where she would find hers seemed much less clear.

<hr />

She wanted to thank him. *She* wanted to thank *him*.

Ulric watched the early summer grasses flatten beneath his boots, his mind refusing to stop reeling. He had barely been able to control his thoughts since he bit her, shoving back his shock from necessity. Now that the danger had passed, his extremely unwise feelings whirled to the fore.

She had opened her soul without hesitation. Never had he connected with anyone so deeply, not even Gillian. He had been there with Juliana, held in her mother's arms, the love they shared jabbing his heart as if he, too, were cherished. This memory was the key to who she was. Her bravery, her warmth, her confidence in herself, even her natural sensuality, all grew out of her mother's love.

Juliana was real to him now, as real as he was to himself. Because of this, he was forced to admit the very last thing he wanted to. Less than a fortnight after meeting her, less than a month after Gillian broke his heart, he had fallen in love with this human girl.

His stupidity would have been comical had it involved anyone but him. Only hours before, he had been congratulating himself on driving her to arm's length—an accomplishment that now seemed especially idiotic. Even worse, Juliana was more like Gillian than he had guessed, with the same curiosity, the same craving for independence, the same attachment to the creations of the human world. Never would she be content living with his pack, taking his orders, isolated in a cave.

He would lose her, just as he had lost Gillian.

Unless he changed.

The thought pulled him up short. Could he change? He had been who and what he was for two hundred years. But maybe, if he put his heart into the effort . . . He rubbed the ball of his chin and finally noticed Juliana panting in his wake.

"Phew," she said, drawing her sleeve across her forehead. "That is a little too fast for me."

"Forgive me, Juliana. I should have kept to your normal pace."

"No matter." She waved her hand in dismissal. "Now that we have left the danger behind us, I feel more vigorous than usual. All that excitement must have done me good."

Her grin caused his chest to tighten in the most ludicrous way. What spirit she had! What a wonderful *upyr* she would be! And, oh, what nonsense men in love could spout.

"That is the effect of my bite," he said gruffly. "After a brief period of weakness, it endows a human with extra strength."

"I see. Maybe if you keep biting me, we can reach your home in record time."

Your home as well, he thought but did not presume to say.

"We can rest if you require it," he offered, determined to make a start on his reformation.

"No, no." She drew a bracing breath of sweet Highland air. "I am ready to push on."

Despite her declaration, he proceeded more moderately. He felt awkward, unable to think of what he ought to say. She was quiet, too, matching him stride for stride. Because they often walked without speaking, the atmosphere should have been more comfortable than it was.

Without the distraction of conversation, his mind returned to what she had said. The thought of biting her again caused him to fist his hands and swallow hard.

He could keep biting her. The damage was already done.

He wanted to that very instant, wanted to push her over the nearest boulder, face down, skirts shoved to her waist, to take her in every way an *upyr* could. He did not want to ask permission or be polite. He just wanted to do it—hard, fast, deep—until she cried out in complete surrender.

He shook his head in disgust. He was a beast, an unrepentant marauder of maidens. The mere thought of changing his ways made him want to ravish her even more.

"Ulric?" Juliana said, reduced to trotting again to keep up.

He cursed himself under his breath.

"I was wondering," she said, seeming more hesitant than upset. "I am not doubting you, only asking. Are you certain Gideon Drake's men will not trouble us again?"

"Yes," he said, then debated whether to explain. Gillian would have wanted him to. Most likely, so would Juliana. "I was not . . . delicate with them. When they return to normal awareness, they might not recall their names. Most of the effect should wear off within a season, but a full memory of what happened might never come back. Hopefully, the people of Dunburn will point them back toward England."

Juliana's eyes were wide. "You have that much power?"

"Actually, the extent of the damage is evidence that my

power is not as practiced as it might be. Greater skill than mine is required to remove precisely what is desired. With my victims in Bridesmere, I was careful to do no harm. That might be why they were left with vague memories."

Concern flickered across Juliana's face an instant before she hid it.

With a fair idea of what she was thinking, Ulric clasped her shoulder to make her stop. "Juliana, I shall never thrall you against your will."

He felt better as soon as he said it, as if the promise lifted a burden of doubt. Whatever his faults, Ulric never broke his word.

She stared at him for a moment and then blinked. "Thank you, Ulric. I would appreciate that very much."

"It is nothing," he said, beginning to walk again. "Besides, I am not certain I could coerce you as I did those men. I suspect you have a partial resistance."

"I do?" Her voice was as pleased as if he had given her a gift. "I thought I might but I was not sure. Of course, I have no idea why that would be. Until I met you I never had the least bit of sensitivity to otherworldly things. Never saw a ghost or had a vision—though I knew some who did. Maybe I understand human nature better than others, but that is only because I listen to what people say."

Her words burbled over him, a definite spring entering her step. He wished she were not this elated. More than anything, her reaction convinced him that she wanted to rule herself. He could not conceive how that would work when his nature drove him to conquer everything he saw.

Hell, he thought as she lifted her skirts to scramble over a fallen pine. Keeping Juliana happy would be the biggest challenge of his life.

Chapter 6

Appropriately enough, they took shelter for the day in the weedy ruins of an ancient Pict's tower. Built as two concentric shells of dry stone, the broch's thick walls still held between them a few sound rooms. In one of these Ulric and Juliana curled up together, front to back, truly safe for once from entry by the sun. They did not build a fire, but Ulric's closeness and his cloak were enough to keep Juliana cozy in the chamber of cool, damp stone.

She had never been anywhere this quiet. No bird sound penetrated the massive walls, no wind, no rustle and snap of squirrels through leaves. The only noises were those she and Ulric made themselves. From the manner in which he held her, with his fingers idly fanning her hip, she could tell he was still awake.

She would not have minded making love, but his mood had been so strange since they left Dunburn, she lacked the nerve to suggest it. Instead, she squirmed a little deeper into his hold. Lifting his arm to let her move, he grunted as the front of his knee hit the back of hers. Happily, the grunt did not seem annoyed.

"I wonder how your kind first crossed paths with the Picts," she mused aloud. "Do you suppose some of the early Druid priests were *upyr?* Maybe their position as kings' advisors ensured that the people of this region would view you in a friendly light. Perhaps it was considered an honor to give a blood sacrifice."

She blushed to remember how she had enjoyed it, but Ulric's response was another noncommittal noise. The arm he resettled around her waist seemed tense. Maybe she should not have mentioned blood. Just because he had finally bitten her did not mean he was reconciled to the idea. Obviously, it was a very personal act.

"Do you suppose the Picts hid in these towers when they were attacked?" she asked, trying to choose a safer topic. "I think they must have had other dwellings for day to day. Living without windows would get dreary."

Ulric released his breath, a wearier sound than she expected. "I cannot answer these questions. I was not here."

"You really are not curious?"

"I do not think about the past. The present has interest enough." He shifted behind her as if he could not get comfortable, despite Juliana having fit them together perfectly. "Possibly I could learn to be curious."

He sounded like a child offering to eat a turnip as the price of some better treat. Juliana did not try to hide her amusement. "Do not strain yourself," she laughed. "I think people are either born curious or they are not. Of course, you might be saving your curiosity for things like wolves and deer."

"I like wine," he said, oddly defensive. "When I was in Bridesmere, I enjoyed it—though it did not make me drunk. And velvet. If one has to wear clothes, velvet is acceptable. It is almost as soft as skin."

"Silk velvet," she said with a merchant's daughter's sigh. "The Italians make the best. And their brocades! Though they cost the moon, they are worth every penny. Of course, much can be said for English wool. If it is well woven and fulled, you could drag it behind a donkey and it would not shred—as I am proving on this trip. Then again, the survival of my gown might be due to you lending your magic to preserve it."

"I would happily preserve whatever you wish."

His arm tightened around her, his chest moving close enough to support her back. She suspected she felt more comforted than was wise.

Never mind, she told herself stubbornly. I will enjoy this for as long as it lasts. Bodily, at least, she was safe. If he had ever wanted to hurt her, he would have done so by now.

As if he also enjoyed their closeness, Ulric nuzzled closer to her neck. The growing heaviness of his hold told her he would soon rest.

"Ulric?" she said, determined to overcome her earlier cowardice.

"Mm?"

"The woman you loved—was she an *upyr?*"

"Yes." The acknowledgment sighed out against her ear. "Gillian was *upyr.*"

"And the man she . . . left you for?"

"He was human. She made him immortal after she fell in love."

"I cannot imagine any woman turning away from you."

She meant the words to reassure him, but his answer was strangely dour. "It is true we *upyr* possess a powerful draw."

"You are irresistible," she said, trying to tease.

All she got for her efforts was a grunt. Behind her, Ulric's chest felt more rocklike than usual.

"You do not want to talk about her."

"No, but if you insist, I will."

This response was quite enough to shut her up.

❦

Ulric roused before Juliana, the arrival of dusk bringing him fully awake. Not so for his companion. Either Juliana was growing accustomed to days turned on their heads, or she needed to see the sun to know the hour. Ulric could feel its departure, a cool and quiet tingling beneath his skin. His eyes snapped open, the world once again safe for his kind.

In the distance a fox yipped to her kits—a scold, he thought, for wandering from the den.

Ulric was tempted to answer with a howl. He and Juliana lay on their sides as before, but she had turned in her sleep until her face was buried in his tunic. One arm hugged him to her, while the other was caught between their bellies. Her upper leg was slung over his, completely lax, the roundness of her calf pressed softly behind his own.

Observing how deeply she slept made him realize she was usually on guard, watching over him when he could not.

Would she really do this for any *upyr,* or was a portion of her protectiveness just for him?

At a loss to answer, Ulric eased away from her and straightened his clothes, ignoring the nagging heaviness of his loins. He knew how to test his theory easily enough. As soon as they joined up with his pack, she would be confronted with one of the most flirtatious immortals ever created. Though Ulric would stop him if he went too far, Stephen could be relied upon to try to seduce her. For that matter, Lucius had been known to attract female eyes. By the time they returned, his most senior pack member should have gotten back from his self-appointed mission as Gillian's mentor.

The memory of Lucius's defection further darkened

Ulric's mood. Lucius had supported Gillian's efforts to run away, then helped her learn how to change her human lover into *upyr*. Ulric would have disciplined any other subordinate, but Lucius followed him strictly by choice. Had he ever challenged Ulric, Ulric could not say who would have won. In the end, Lucius turned out to have more power than anyone suspected—including Lucius himself. He was, so he claimed, one of their kind's few elders. Until Gillian prodded his memories with her endless questions, Lucius had forgotten how much he knew.

The discovery had startled them all, but no one more than Ulric. The man he had known for ages, the man he had considered a sort of friend despite his reserve, had turned out to be an utter stranger. Ulric had to wonder if it were possible to know anyone. What he would say to Lucius when they met again he could not conceive.

Ulric shook his head. He would cross that bridge when he got home.

To that, he was looking forward. Once he returned to familiar surroundings, once he had people to lead, he was certain he would feel more himself, more able to lay siege to Juliana's heart. He would be glad to see even Gytha, who never missed an opportunity to be a thorn in his side.

He doubted she would be pleased to meet Juliana. As the pack's dominant female, Gytha had hoped to replace Gillian as his queen. That he had not invited her to do so stuck in her craw. If he showed up with a human . . . Well, he would have to move swiftly to put Gytha in her place—before she chewed Juliana to pieces and spit her out.

Juliana drew him from the thought of that daunting prospect by mumbling in her sleep. His gaze drifted to the pulse beating in her throat. If he were sensible, he would feed from her when she woke. By the time she finished her ablutions, her lassitude would have faded. She would be ready for hard travel.

Or maybe it would be better to abstain. If he bit her now, with his nature urging him to claim her, they might not end up traveling at all.

She was strong for a human. They could manage as they had before.

⁓

Juliana heard the river before she saw it, neither roar nor splash, but a ceaseless ripple where waves met air.

"The Spey," Ulric said, tipping his head toward the sound. "We have reached the crossing."

They had been tramping up and down forested slopes most of the night. Now they emerged from a final line of trees onto a gravel shingle. As they did, a twisted pine branch, silvered by the crescent moon, swept down the current. The speed of its passage stopped her breath. To her horror, by "crossing" Ulric did not mean over a bridge.

"Er," she said, "would now be a good time to mention I cannot swim?"

Ulric's laugh rumbled in his chest. This, of all things, restored his mood. "We can wade much of the way. The bed is shallow along the banks. Where it is too deep, I will carry you on my back. My wolf is an excellent swimmer."

"Your wolf! Ulric, I do not think—"

He hooked his arm behind her neck and kissed her, a cheery smacking of lips. "We will tie you on if you like. Believe me, your head is likelier to stay above water that way than if I took you in my human form."

She swallowed back further protest. Bridges meant humans, and she would not soon forget the pursuit they had faced in Dunburn. One memory in particular haunted her thoughts. While trying to prevent his men-at-arms from killing Ulric, Milo had claimed Ulric had secrets they might be able to use. To her, that suggested they were as interested as she was in Ulric's power. Many humans wanted to cheat death or gain advantages over their peers. Could a desire that seductive be erased from their minds? Until she was certain, she did not want to risk meeting Milo and Milton again—or anyone else who might share their aims.

She began to see why Ulric's sire wanted his children to live apart from her kind. Juliana herself could not claim her desire to become *upyr* had brought out her best.

Ulric had been chosen. Juliana tried to demand.

Ulric read the consternation on her face, if not its cause. "I will not let the river have you," he assured her, gently stroking her cheek. "You are in my care."

After tucking his clothes into her basket, he changed into his wolf form at the river's edge. For once, she was too distracted to enjoy the show. Though the water was icy and the gravel slick with moss, she forged ahead until the current rose to her hips. At that point she could not keep her footing except by clinging to his ruff. Her skirts felt ten times as heavy wet.

Her hands were shaking far too badly to tie herself to his back.

Give me the basket, he instructed, his eyes dancing as if this were a game of fetch. *I will carry it in my teeth. If you lock your hands around my ribs, you will not interfere with my stroke.*

His back was broad, thank goodness, and a far less slippery platform than the riverbed. Gritting her teeth, Juliana wrapped her arms around him and gripped each of her wrists with the opposite hand. His fur did not smell the least bit doggy even wet, but more like the forest they had just left. In the hope that the danger she could not see would not upset her, she screwed her eyes shut and buried her face behind his ear.

Here we go, he said, his voice laughing in her head.

She would have cursed him if she had not wanted to keep her mouth firmly shut.

As soon as he began to swim, they started lurching up and down. Waves broke over her shoulders, soaking even her hair. Sputtering, she opened her eyes.

"You are not going straight!" she exclaimed, to which Ulric's wolf gave a wet snort.

Even I cannot fight a current this strong. We will land downstream at that other spit where the river bends.

She kept quiet after that because he actually seemed to be laboring. Beneath her chest, his heart was beating as fast as hers. The farther shore seemed leagues away.

Oh, God, she thought. I should have insisted he feed from me when we woke. That pine marten he caught could not have been satisfying. Maybe he is too weak.

He was puffing through his nose by the time his paws hit gravel again. Completely numb, Juliana rolled off his back. Had he not changed quickly enough to grab her, the current would have washed her away.

"Only knee-high here," he panted. "We can walk the rest."

Stumble was more like it. No longer able to feel her feet, Juliana fell face first onto the bank.

"I cannot move," she mumbled into the flattened reeds.

"Fine," he said. "You wait here."

To her surprise, she heard a whoosh of air as he changed into his wolf form and then, even more amazingly, a splash.

Juliana was so stunned she managed to sit up. If she had not seen it for herself, she would not have believed it. He had gone back into the river and was performing a peculiar dance, pouncing left, then right, then disappearing altogether beneath the waves. Though the logical part of her knew he would be all right, the part that had just been dragged across an icy deluge began to cry.

When she saw what he had dived under the water for, her tears turned into sobs. He had no consideration—none!—risking that river a second time for a stupid fish.

He, naturally, had no idea she was angry. Ears erect and tail waving proudly, he was prancing as he trotted toward her. He dropped the fish, a fat Scottish salmon, at her feet. He was laughing already as he whirled into his human form.

"There," he said. "Something for dinner. I thought I would give my wolf the chance to sample your cookery."

At that moment, she regretted she was too well brought up to slap him.

"Hey," he said, kneeling down as he saw her tears. "Did something happen while I was gone?"

"What happened was that you left!" she spat. "You went back into that terrible river."

"No, no." He dried her cheeks with his palms. "It is a good river, Juliana. See, it gave us a fish."

"I suppose you expect me to gut it."

His faint, pink flush gave her a satisfaction she was almost ashamed to feel. "It *is* your knife. And you do have more practice at that than I."

"I am all wet," she said. "And I am freezing. And you frightened me very much!"

"Very well." He pulled her into his naked chest. He, she noticed, was completely dry. "I suppose you are entitled to have a cry. God knows, you have been through enough in the last few days."

"Do not humor me. I am not being childish!"

"No, no," he agreed against her hair. "The thought never crossed my mind."

She knew it had and, what is more, she knew it might be justified. He had, to be fair, carried her across that river at some effort to himself. Indeed, he had been a good sport for this whole journey, considering she had forced him to bring her along. Most likely she did owe his wolf a meal.

Pulling her dignity together, she stuck out her hand. "I will take the fish now."

"No," he said more firmly. "Sit for a bit and get warm."

Without waiting for permission, he lifted her into his lap, running his hands over her clothes and skin. His *upyr* magic dried her quickly, but then she did not want to move. She could not say which was more mortifying: her earlier loss of control or this boneless compliancy. She supposed it did not matter. She intended to remain as she was either way.

She could not be blamed if Ulric put her humors out of sort.

"We should have stripped you," he said. "That English wool weighs a ton."

Another woman might have been insulted. Juliana sighed and pressed her nose to his neck. She knew it must be cold if his skin felt warm.

Ulric squeezed her upper arm. "Better get up," he warned, "before you fall asleep. We would not want the fish that struck such terror to go to waste."

She had recovered enough to smile.

He pressed his own smile lightly onto her lips.

He cares for me, she thought, whatever he may tell himself. For now, that was enough to get her on her feet.

"Ulric?" she said, glancing at her sodden and increasingly battered basket. "Do you think you could dry my spices, too?"

"I live to serve," he said with a grin.

Watching him turn on his knees to rescue her belongings, she wished he would as easily agree to serve her in bed. As he propped himself on one arm, the muscles of his back fanned out from his spine in lovely patterns. The single dimple at the top of his narrow buttocks put her in mind of his waving tail. Beneath that flawless skin, his wolf still dwelled, a creature of impulse and dark hungers. If nothing else, she thought she could count on those traits to drive him back to her arms.

She needed every chance she could get to win him from the memory of Gillian.

～

As it turned out, Juliana's cooking tasted as good as it smelled. Ulric's enjoyment was marred only by his efforts to eat it delicately. Though he had to change form to consume it, it seemed inconsiderate to wolf her creation down.

"Ulric?" she said as he swallowed the last smoky pink bite.

The sound of her voice saying his name made a shiver run through his pelt. It felt odd that she was beginning to treat his beast and him as one—not bad, but slightly unnerving.

He wagged his tail in answer, wondering if he should change.

"Could I pet you a bit?" she asked. "If that would not be impolite?"

A whine slipped from his throat over which he had no control, the sound of a puppy pleading for a cuddle. He snapped his teeth on the noise, hoping she could not guess what it meant.

He had not known his wolf could fall in love, as well.

Aware that she was waiting, he rose from the place where he had laid down to eat, stretched his legs, and padded to her side. As soon as he sat, she buried both face and hands in his fur.

"You are so soft!" she exclaimed, then fought a laugh. "I am sorry, Ulric. I will try not to coo again."

He was not certain he would have cared. Her gently thorough scratching sent him straight into wolfish bliss.

Behind the ears, he said, giving in to his longing to lay his muzzle on her feet.

Tomorrow night would be soon enough to put her wishes first.

~

Juliana did not know why, but Ulric was politeness itself during the next stretch of their journey, consulting her on more decisions than she felt any need to be consulted on. She had no idea if it was easier to hike down a valley or over a pass, nor if hunting geese was better than hunting deer.

"Do as you wish," she said. "You know these lands and, I trust, the preferences of your stomach."

"But I want to do what you would most like."

"Do I have some strange transforming substance in my blood? You have not been yourself since you bit me."

His chest inflated with offense. "I am myself. Who else would I be? This is precisely who I am. I treat my companions as equals."

Juliana paused to shake a pebble out of her shoe. "Maybe it was biting Milo that caused the problem. If anyone's blood contained something sickening, it would be his."

"There is nothing sick about my wanting you to enjoy this trip!"

Juliana stared at him, taken aback by his display of temper. She could actually hear him grinding his teeth. "I am enjoying this trip. This country is beautiful. But because I know nothing of what you are asking me to choose between, I cannot predict which I would like more. Truly, I did not mean to upset you."

"I . . . am . . . not . . . upset."

The words were so close to a growl, she had to grin.

"Go ahead," he said, throwing up his hands. "Laugh at the foolish wolf king. God knows, I would laugh if I could."

Still confused as to what was bothering him, she slipped her hand under his hair to cup the back of his neck. The smoothness and strength of the tendons that lay beneath gave her pleasure all by themselves. She tried to encourage them to relax by kneading them with her fingers.

"Devil take it," he surrendered, rolling his head around with a sigh. "We will follow the route that leads by Loch Ness. Maybe we will get lucky and see the monster."

"Good," she said, lowering her hand to lightly scratch his back. "Monsters are my favorite things."

Even a week ago, he would have preened at this obvious compliment. Now, he pulled a face and pressed on. Her only consolation was that he did not avoid her touch.

Loch Ness was huge and deep and long, its waters black from the peat-soaked rivers that flowed in from the surrounding hills. Though Ulric and Juliana watched for some time, they were not fortunate enough to encounter the famous monster, merely a herd of tall red deer. Ulric's wolf self was just as pleased with that, nearly driving him to change before he noticed what was happening and forced a stop. The slip filled him with unease. The more Ulric suppressed his hungers, the stronger his wolf's became.

Juliana could claim to love monsters all she liked; if Ulric was not careful, he would never convince her he could be more.

And he did, after all, prefer that she love one monster above the rest.

"Go," she said, misreading his hesitation. "I will be fine right here."

Their camp being nowhere near habitation, Ulric expected she was right. Eager to be off, his wolf gave him just enough time to remove his clothes.

More control than he had ever exerted was required to keep from gutting the first deer he brought down. The scent of the creature's fear, the excitement of the chase, and the warmth of its russet hide went to his head, leaving him with urges and instincts and precious little rational thought. The merest shred remained to remind him Juliana watched. If a hare had shocked her, she would faint at the sight of him tearing into a deer's viscera.

With a whimpering growl, he wrenched his muzzle away, changing into his man form so he could drink from the young stag's neck. His instincts calmed at the first few swallows. He was able to leave the animal alive.

Two more deer succumbed to his chase before he was sated, the hunt leading him far from Juliana's camp. He returned near dawn, weary, but at peace. He waded into the loch to cool the last of his hunter's heat.

When he emerged, temporarily dripping and raking his hair back with his hands, the way her eyes slid over his body made him break into a sweat again.

"You did not kill that first deer," she said, looking away too soon to see his member swell.

For some reason, Ulric was embarrassed to admit he had refrained from killing because of her. "It would have been wasteful," he said. "Without the pack to help me, I could not have eaten all that meat."

"Ah," she said, her hands smoothing her skirt.

She sat on a boulder near the shallow cave where they would sleep, their doorstep further sheltered by the drooping branches of a pine. Needles carpeted the ground around the circle of stones in which she had built her cook fire. Only embers remained, but they lit her face enough for an *upyr* like him to see.

When she tucked her hair behind her ears, her down-turned profile entranced his eyes. Her nose was straight, her cheeks childishly soft, her lips both wide and full. The slight squareness of her jaw was all that intimated stubbornness. Ulric tried to imagine her as an *upyr* but could pick no feature in need of improvement. Even the tiny pock that marked one temple had won a place in his heart. She was Juliana. She was perfect just as she was.

"I suppose you are weary after your hunt," she said, her eyes sliding to his.

Through the heavy perfume of pine he thought he caught a hint of arousal, suggesting that she, too, was tired of him holding back. The possibility made his body throb hard and hot.

Say the words, he thought, without pushing into her mind. Ask me to take you, and I will have proved that I can wait, that I can put a woman's desires above my own.

But perhaps she was remembering his earlier rebuffs. She pointed toward the outcropping of rock behind her. "I have woven some branches together as a barrier for the opening."

"Good," he said. "Thank you."

Despite his recent feeding, his mouth went dry at the graceful turn of her neck. He wanted to kiss that firelit column, wanted to drag his teeth and lips over every inch of her skin.

Then he wanted to repeat the process with his cock.

"I will—" He stopped to clear the roughness from his voice. "I will come in with you in a moment. I think I would like to take one last swim."

She did not offer to join him. He had a feeling she guessed why he needed to cool off and was—to judge by the pursing of her lips—insulted by his restraint. Ulric cursed himself in his head.

He had backed them into a corner he could not fathom how to escape.

Chapter 7

❧

Almost lost among the oak and ash, two upright slabs of granite marked the southern edge of Ulric's territory. Like winter frost, the moon reflected off the tiny crystals that made up the stones. As if uncertain what she was seeing, Juliana squinted and rubbed her eyes.

"What are those things?" she asked in a stymied voice.

"Menhirs," he said. "Standing stones." He laid his hand on her shoulder, the urge to touch her too strong to defy. She belonged beside him when he crossed this final barrier to his home.

"Why do they look so blurry?"

Ulric glanced back at the stones. To him, the menhirs seemed bright and clear, almost white under the rising moon. "Perhaps they carry a touch of glamour, to hide them from human eyes. Take my hand and I will lead you through them."

The bracken was thick here, the path the merest shadow of clearer ground. Juliana shivered as they passed between the sentinels, but her fingers remained warm. By unspoken accord, they turned once they were through. The stones were twice Ulric's height and wider than his arms could reach. Unlike the roughness of their backs, their fronts were clearly worked. Chisels had planed them flat and marked them with carvings.

"Those are the symbols you spoke of," Juliana said, her voice hushed with respect. "The ones that guard the boundaries of your lands."

"Yes." He carried her knuckles upward for a kiss that she was too caught up to notice. "These glyphs have probably been here for thousands of years. I am sorry I cannot translate them, but at least you are seeing them for yourself."

"They are amazing. And so simple! I feel as if I ought to know what they mean, as if all I needed was the patience to stare at them long enough and they would speak."

Ulric smiled at her fancy. "I cannot promise that method would lead to success, but if you like, you can come back some time and try."

"There is a fish," she said, pointing at the obvious. "And, look, that must be the sun!"

Ulric tried to see the marks as she did. They were spirals for the most part, crudely drawn and interspersed with signs for the sun and moon. Seemingly at random, they grouped themselves around a centaurlike version of a wolf, half-person and half-beast. On the right stone, the wolf had a man's torso, and on the left it bore a woman's, both worn to faintness by wind and rain.

They did not strike him as particularly interesting depictions, but when Juliana tentatively traced the outline of the female wolf, hairs bristled on his arms. Dimly, perhaps only visible to Ulric's eyes, the lines bore a tinge of rust.

"I should feed them," he said, remembering a long-ago lesson from his sire.

"Feed them?"

"My sire, Auriclus, once told me that a blood offering is supposed to renew their magic. They must still have some if they are hiding themselves from you."

"And maybe humans who had not been traveling in your company would see nothing at all. Maybe they would walk right past this place and keep going."

"Maybe," he agreed. They met each other's gaze and smiled, the moon-bright stones reflected small in Juliana's eyes.

"I will leave if the ritual is too private," she said, but Ulric shook his head. Whatever magic lived in the stones, he sensed it had accepted her.

Not one to fuss, he cut his wrist with a quick slash of his teeth, dabbed his fingertip in the blood, and dragged it around the man-wolf's outline. The cut had healed by the time he moved to the second stone.

"Wait." Juliana stopped him as he lifted his wrist to his mouth again. Her manner was hesitant. "I would like to make an offering—if you think the stone would not mind." She nodded toward the drawing in front of her. "I know I am not *upyr,* but this one *is* a girl."

"So she is."

He did not suggest she prick herself with her knife— even he did not have that much self-denial—but brought her hand slowly to his lips. She could have stopped him any time she wished. As he had behind the forge in Dunburn, he kissed her palm, then drew her middle finger into his mouth. Rather than bite her wrist, he nipped her finger's pad. She gasped in surprise, her gaze widening on his own. He sucked at the wound, once, to start the flow. Even at this small taste, his body thrummed. She was as sweet and potent as he recalled.

The bite affected her as well. He felt the change in her vibration like a caress.

With obvious reluctance, she pulled her finger free.

She stared at the welling crimson as if entranced. When he tried to speak, his voice was hoarse.

"Less blood from a finger," he explained. "You bleed more easily than I."

She shook herself, then turned to press the cut to the stone.

The instant she touched it the air seemed to quake, as if the stone were shaking itself, too. If Juliana felt it, she gave no sign. Biting her lip and careful not to miss a spot, she drew her blood around the glyph. He would have laughed at her concentration if he had been able to keep his lungs filled with breath. His veins were throbbing, his skin itchy and warm.

He desired her, but more than that, he wanted her to complete the rite. Her act fed something deep inside him, as much as it fed the stone. It was a gift a queen would give, a gift a queen should have been giving for centuries.

Guide me, he thought, a spontaneous prayer to the old gods. *Help me make her mine. I know she will always treat you with respect.*

Light flared as she closed the outline, not flame but hot blue glow. Abruptly, every spell-picture on the menhirs sprang to life—suns, moons, spirals, as well as carvings that had been invisible before. Ulric spotted a serpent and a tree and an odd, pointy cylinder, which two stick figures rode like witches on a broom. He could not imagine what they represented. No *upyr* he knew had the power to fly. Without warning, the desire to solve the mystery swelled inside him. This was what Juliana experienced every day. This was curiosity.

He turned to her, watching her hands draw back to cover her mouth.

"Oh," she breathed. "Look how marvelous."

Ulric could not look. Ulric only had eyes for her.

She was glowing in the reflection of the stones, flushed with wonder and delight, the biggest mystery of all. What did she feel, truly? What did love and loyalty mean to her? What drove her to embrace the world so completely? He had seen a hint of the answer in her mother's memory, but it was not nearly enough.

He wanted to spend his life discovering her secrets.

"Juliana," he said, his voice more wolf than man.

When she turned to him, joy thumped in his chest.

"Did you see?" she said with a gasping laugh. "I did a little bit of magic."

"Not just a little." Throat tight, he tugged her into his arms. "You used your magic to steal my heart."

Her lips moved on his name. He could see the war in her: to believe or to guard her heart. His tone had been deliberately light. Was he teasing, she must wonder, or did he mean what he said?

The words she needed for reassurance were too big, too soon; he could not admit to them yet. Instead, he lowered his head to kiss her. It seemed an eternity since he had held her without restraint. In truth, he was not certain he ever had.

"I missed you," she said when he finally let her break for air. She cradled his face between her hands, her beautiful, dark eyes on the edge of tears. Seeing them shimmer, his own felt hot.

The depth of her emotion was humbling. One wrong step, one wrong sigh, seemed as if it would shatter all.

I cannot do this, cried the part of him that remembered being devastated by Gillian. *I cannot fall from this height.*

"Juliana," he murmured helplessly. "Oh, Juliana."

She gathered her hair and pulled the mass of it to one side, the invitation obvious. Less clear was whether she knew the symbolism of her act. His wolf knew and exulted in victory. To bare the vulnerability of one's throat was to admit who was one's king.

Unable to check his reaction, Ulric's breathing turned rough.

"I offer you what you want," she said, her breast rising and falling in time with his. "How long do you intend to wait to accept?"

Her challenge snapped the last thin thread of his control. Desire blazed through his body, blinding him to everything but her blood. Gripping her upper arms, he lifted her neck to his mouth until her feet dangled off the ground. Her skin was smooth and warm, her pulse an unbearably exciting patter. He licked the salt from her, felt the throbbing ache of his teeth.

When he clamped down on her skin, the taste sent him to his knees.

Their moans tangled together, her arms wrapping his back, his cinched beneath her bottom and behind her neck. His body was almost more aroused than he could bear. He rubbed his hardness against her belly as she rode his thigh. His prick sang at the friction, his ballocks aching for release. He wanted more than to feed from her but could not tear himself from her throat.

This was the elixir of which the fables spoke, not simply blood, but the blood of a woman loved.

Slowly he drew on her, taking her essence in tiny pulls to make it last. Sparks of color danced in the air around them. Lemon. Rose. The blue of the autumn sky. Each color had a scent, each a unique sensation against his skin. Like gentle fingers they plucked his loins, tugging and teasing until, without him realizing it was near, the pleasure grew so intense his climax broke. He spilled before he could stop it, a gasp the only remnant of his lost control. When she shuddered against him, he knew the release was shared.

At her sigh, he drew his teeth from her skin.

"Lick it," she whispered, her head fallen languidly back.

Neither order nor plea, the words caused him to shudder with renewing lust. He curled his tongue across the wounds, healing them even as he drew one final shiver of ecstasy.

Like a woman waking from a dream, Juliana lifted her head. "I saw lights," she slurred drunkenly, "and colors like dancing flowers."

He coaxed her forward until her cheek rested on his chest. He was aware of the two menhirs behind them, still glowing faintly, still exuding a sense of presence—as if they held something alive. If they did, Juliana had woken it. He had never seen them burn like that before.

He suspected they did not mind this impromptu erotic rite.

Beginning to come down from it, he stroked her hair. "I saw the colors, too," he said. "They are not usual, but feeding is our closest connection. Even those who cannot normally share thoughts can do so then."

"Mm," she hummed. "A woman could get used to that."

A woman could grow addicted, he thought as he rubbed the small of her back.

The possibility should not have troubled him. It would have bound her to him as nothing else. But he was too proud. He wanted her to love him for him, rather than for something any *upyr* worth his salt could do.

"Jus' lemme rest for a bit," she mumbled against his neck. "Then I shall be ready to go."

But he did not intend them to go any farther. He wanted to slide inside her and join their bodies in the human way. He wanted to make the act they had shared complete.

For one last night, they would savor their privacy.

Emile

❧

"I promise," Bastien said to his friend Emile, "once I am certain I have Ulric's pack under my thumb, I will get you out of this hole. Without their leader, they are ripe for plucking. In no time, we shall have them battling for our cause."

The hole Bastien spoke of was a burrow, previously home to badgers, and now Emile's hiding place. Emile should have been accustomed to his confinement, but every night his fears gained ground, driving his heart a little faster, draining his small reserves of energy. Buttressed by a net of roots, the actual hollow of the den gave him room enough to sit up. Thankfully, he still possessed the strength to do so. Thus far, the weakness that crept like ice from his feet had only reached mid-thigh. In the beginning his toes had tingled. Tonight they were empty space, as if they had been not just paralyzed but erased.

Emile did not share this new development with Bastien. He had worries enough.

"It shall be soon," Bastien insisted, helping him lie down. "I promise. No more than another sennight."

Though Emile nodded as if he believed, he had grown to dread the words. Doubt dwelled like a canker beneath the forced cheer of Bastien's gaze; fear, too, that the lengths to which he went to protect his pack mate would damn his soul. If Emile had been braver, he would have insisted he be let go.

Sadly, he was not brave. As the days and weeks drew out with nothing to do but lie here fighting panic, he had discovered in himself a terrible wish: that he and Bastien had never stood against their pack leader, that they had let Hugo's villainy stand. Shamed, Emile turned his face to the earthen wall.

Bastien gave his elbow one last squeeze. "I shall return tomorrow to share my blood," he said. "Right before dawn just as always. Trust me, Emile. I know it is hard, but we shall prevail."

As his friend squirmed out of the burrow, Emile swallowed back his pleas for more assurances. Even if Bastien's chances were better on his own, even if Emile had become no better than a leech, he knew his friend could be counted on.

"Tomorrow," he rasped, but Bastien was already heading for the absent pack leader's cave in his need to outrace the sun.

Without him there, the whispers were impossible to drown out. What if some disaster prevented Bastien's reappearance? What if Emile were left in this hole alone?

He would starve, without even the strength to drag himself into the sun. He did not know how long his kind were capable of living without sustenance. Conceivably, he might languish here for years.

When he closed his eyes, a tear trickled out one corner.

The tear disgusted him enough to stop. Wallowing in misery would accomplish nothing.

Forcing his breath to slow, he let his senses reach beyond the burrow. The forest surrounded his little hill, sweet and spacious and quiet, sinking its roots deep into the earth. The wind blew, the streams clattered over stones, and the land hummed with the magic of the growing things.

Without warning, fear grabbed his heart and shook it. More than earth magic hummed outside. The magic of the *upyr* rode the midnight air.

Hugo must have come for him after all.

Except . . . the magic did not feel like Hugo's, not built from fury and theft. No, this was a gift given for a gift, a wall of warm safety. Feeling it, the *upyr's* eyes welled with hope. Up from the soil the good magic rose, stretching through the woods like two golden, embracing arms until the ends met and closed.

As they did, his hackles rippled in alarm.

No, he thought, the cry locked in his throat.

Whoever had raised that sheltering wall had shut him outside.

Chapter 8

❦

The next night's wind gave Ulric no warning. The pack was almost on them before he sensed their energy in the air: not wolf, not human, but a dangerous mingling of both.

He stood, helping Juliana to her feet as well.

"They come," he said as she laid one hand inquiringly on his arm.

Knowing her reception might be ticklish, he was already on guard. His nostrils flared as he caught an unfamiliar scent, a male he did not recognize. Immediately, every muscle in his body coiled. What *upyr* would dare intrude upon his lands when he was not here to give leave?

"What is wrong?" Juliana asked.

"Hush," he said, the sound coming out a growl. "I shall handle this."

He was glad he could trust her to be quiet. She stilled as the others galloped in wolf form through the trees, her hold thankfully calm. He felt her stand even straighter as he frowned at his approaching pack.

They should have been howling a welcome, should have been groveling on their forelegs and waving their tails. Instead, only Stephen gave an uncertain yip. His tail was curled between his legs. As if afraid to come closer, he sat a body length away. The two subordinate females, Ingrith and Helewis, came to a quivering halt on either side of him, but whether to protect or be protected Ulric could not say. They did not sit, but leaned their shoulders into Stephen's flanks.

Gytha and the stranger were the first to shimmer into human form. Her usual defiant self, Gytha slung her arm around the male *upyr's* shoulders and tossed her head.

She was a handsome woman, tall and taut, with flashing eyes and blue-black hair as rough as a horse's tail. Helewis was larger, but what Gytha lacked in bulk she made up for in combativeness. She never walked but strutted, never stood except with feet planted wide. She did not merely meet others' eyes, she dared them to take her down. The thrust of her nose was an insult to lesser beings, the swing of her hips a mockery. No man took Gytha without invitation, and no man had refused her before Ulric.

Ulric knew the stranger's presence was meant to challenge him.

I welcomed him, said Gytha's stance. *To my bed and to this pack. Make of it what you will.*

Ulric lifted his brows and was pleased to see her bravado falter, though not for long. "I see we have a guest."

"A new pack member," Gytha contradicted.

"That," Ulric said mildly, "remains to be seen."

The stranger stepped forward at the cue. He was as tall as Gytha, and as strongly built. His hair was berry-black, not coarse, but satiny smooth. It fell over his shoulders in shining waves, nearly reaching his waist. His eyes, a pale, clear green, were tilted with an amusement that invited

Ulric to smile along. What lay beneath the amusement Ulric suspected the stranger did not wish him to see.

Behind the façade of sardonic humor, this man walked a desperate, knife-sharp edge. Wherever he had lived before, Ulric did not think he had left of his own accord. This, far more than Gytha's backing, made him dangerous. An *upyr* without a home, who felt his survival in question, would fight tooth and nail to be safe.

Ulric was grateful for the handspan of height being made *upyr* had added to his human frame. He had inches on this man and likely a couple stone. The stranger's power Ulric could not judge without more study. He thought it less than his own but not by much. This was no follower wolf. A second perhaps, one with the potential to be first. Though it did not show, Ulric sensed that he was weary to his bones, the sort of weariness that has nothing to do with lack of sleep.

"My name is Bastien," said the stranger with a hooded smile and a French accent. "Gytha was kind enough to offer the hospitality of your pack."

He extended his hand in the human way, the picture of bonhomie. Ulric stared at the pale appendage, then into Bastien's green eyes.

"Offer your throat," he said just as pleasantly, "and perhaps I shall extend Gytha's kindness."

The stranger flinched, obviously not expecting the demand. Before he could speak, Gytha lost her control.

"Have your whore offer her throat!" she cried. "No one invited her!"

"No one but me," Ulric responded with a coolness that should have warned her to hold her tongue.

"She is *human*," Gytha hissed. "And you have bitten her. I can smell her stench on your breath."

Ulric moved before Gytha could blink, twisting her arm behind her back so that she had to go on her toes to prevent him from popping it out of its socket. With his second hand, he yanked her head back by the hair. Her throat was bared to him then, her pulse beating with a wildness *upyr* seldom showed. Though she snarled her defiance, a bead of fear-sweat rolled down her neck.

"I do not answer to you," he said, putting his power into the words until the air pulsed with his will and the leaves shivered delicately on the trees. "And though it is not your concern, I will tell you this: You should be so fortunate to know a fount as sweet as my Juliana."

"I imagine she is sweet," Gytha scoffed. "You could not master Gillian and thus you try again with this paltry human."

"Human now," Ulric said, "but not for long, and perhaps not as paltry as you think. Juliana woke the old menhirs. Their power protects us because she gave her blood."

"We felt them wake while we were hunting," Helewis put in. He had not noticed her change, but she wore human form, as sturdy and diffident as ever. As befitted the lowest member of the pack, she spoke through the fox-red curtain of her hair. "We wondered what had happened."

"Idiot," Gytha snapped, ignoring the fact that Ulric held her. "You are too stupid to speak. Bastien will put you in your place when he leads the pack."

Using her bent arm for leverage, Ulric forced Gytha down until her nose touched the ground. Though she tried to evade the humiliation and cursed him most passionately, she could not counteract his strength.

"Do you not think," he said, "that you are being premature?"

Through the whole exchange, the newcomer, her supposed ally, simply watched. Ulric did not assume this meant Gytha's dreams of grandeur were all her own. He had no doubt the stranger hoped to take his pack. He had sense enough, however, to wait until he judged the moment ripe.

Wait as long as you please, Ulric thought. This pack will always be mine.

Because Gytha was crying now—angrily, he presumed—he let her up. Wisely, Juliana stepped to his side, but Gytha's fit of temper had run its course. He squeezed Juliana's hand. To his surprise, she was only shaking a little.

"We will discuss this back at the cave," he said to his pack in a tone that demanded obedience. He was careful to hide his relief when they complied. For Juliana's sake if not his own, this was altercation enough for one night. By the same reasoning, he did not ask why Ingrith and Stephen still walked as wolves. Whatever their justification, he would handle them in good time.

<hr />

Of all the ways Juliana had imagined meeting Ulric's pack, none had come close to this.

Being greeted by beautiful naked people was disconcerting enough—as was Gytha's immediate hostility. The way she said "human" made it sound like a pestilence. The Frenchman, Bastien, seemed to want Ulric's place, the two who remained in wolf form cowered like beaten dogs, and the solidly built redhead refused to meet anybody's eye.

What really troubled her, though, was watching Ulric make a woman cry.

She could see Gytha was rebellious, but using violence to subdue her seemed as natural to her lover as catching hares. Though he did not appear to act out of anger, he also did not turn a hair at her tears. Was this how he led his pack? Was this how he would lead her?

Gytha had accused him of not being able to "master" Gillian. Was he hoping to master her?

Juliana's legs felt numb as she plodded through the trees beside him, her fingers stiff and chilly within his hand. Ulric was too distracted to notice, or perhaps too watchful for more trouble.

She was surprised when the big redhead, the one who had seemed so shy, fell back from the others to keep pace with her.

"I am Helewis," she said softly, as if she did not wish to disturb Ulric. Her gaze slid briefly toward him before returning to Juliana.

Apparently, humans were lowly enough that staring at them was allowed. Juliana felt her shoulders stiffen, then told herself to be tolerant. She was a stranger here. Neither of them knew each other's ways.

"I am Juliana," she responded, equally soft.

Helewis smiled and nodded. "A pretty name for a pretty woman. I can see why Ulric brought you back."

Even as she bristled at the assumption that she was some sort of souvenir, Juliana thought how odd it was to be called pretty by this glowing creature. Helewis might be big, but her muscles were fluid, her movements graceful and strong. Watching her made Juliana feel too scrawny by far. Whatever her inadequacy, however, she would not be taken for a toy.

"I tricked him into bringing me," she said.

Helewis's smile widened to a grin. "He would not have let you trick him unless he liked the idea."

"I am right here," Ulric reminded them, "and have not gone deaf."

Despite the treatment her sister wolf had received at his hands, Helewis dared to laugh. Skipping ahead of them backward, she took Ulric's hand—with Juliana's still in it—and pressed its back to her cheek. It was a gesture Juliana might have made to her father.

"I am happy you have returned," she said, "and glad you have found a mate."

Juliana's eyes went round. *This* was what Helewis assumed?

"Helewis," Ulric said, but if he meant to contradict her, he got no chance. Quick as a wink, Helewis changed and bounded away in wolf form, curving off into the trees to give Gytha and the Frenchman a nice, wide berth.

They did not see her again until they arrived at the cliff.

In Juliana's horrified opinion, the path that led up the sheer granite wall would not support a goat. Indeed, the few saplings that had taken root on its ledges looked in danger of toppling off.

Apparently, *upyr* had no trouble with steep ascents. The other four had gone up already. Only Helewis awaited them.

"I can carry her," she offered. "You know I am the best at climbing."

Unsure what she thought of this, Juliana was relieved when Ulric turned to her. "You are probably strong enough to manage by yourself, unless the height bothers you too much."

Juliana squinted at the towering rock, noting how the moon made long, jagged shadows of even small projections in the stone. She was not aware if she were afraid of heights, though it struck her any reasonable person would be. "Your cave is up there?"

Ulric put his hands on her shoulders, his thumbs stroking her neck. "It is two-thirds up the face. You need not attempt it unless you wish, but you will have more freedom if you can scale it on your own—at least until you decide what you want to do at summer's end."

This was the first time in a while that he had mentioned the deadline to their agreement. She wondered what it meant that he was bringing it up now.

"I will try," she said, "if you stay close."

He patted her cheeks as if he approved, but also as if he thought her a child. "We will tie you to my waist as a precaution. I did not bring you this far just to let you fall."

Without waiting to be asked, Helewis scurried up the cliff to find a rope. Juliana grew dizzy watching her clamber quickly up and down. The *upyr* jumped the last few meters when she returned, landing lightly on broad bare feet. The rope was coiled around her shoulder.

"Shall I help?" she asked, handing Ulric the twisted hemp. "I could follow behind her."

Ulric thanked her but refused. As unquestioning as before, Helewis disappeared the way she had come. Fortunately, the climb was within Juliana's power, at least with the added strength Ulric's bite had lent her. After she had tucked up her skirts, she followed his instructions, putting her feet where he stepped, trusting her fingers to the crevices that held his. The only order she disobeyed was his injunction against looking down. That did make her head swim, but she thought she ought to face it once.

"Good," he said when she reached the midpoint. "You are doing better than I hoped."

She took more pleasure than annoyance in his surprise.

Despite the shocks she was facing, she reveled in her success, a tiny taste of what life would be as an *upyr*. *Is it really so bad?* a voice whispered in her head. *Can you not forgive him his roughness against Gytha? Look what you would get in return.*

Finally, they reached the entry to the cave, a low, vine-shrouded opening lipped by a solid ledge. Ulric made no complaint when she tottered to the nearest wall and collapsed. Lowering himself beside her, he laid his palm atop her now banged-up knee.

"Very well," she admitted, "that was really hard."

Ulric laughed and kissed her bruises. A tingle of sensation told her he was working to make them heal.

She found it difficult to reconcile his care with the man who had rubbed his inferior's nose in the dirt.

"We do not always fight," he said as if he had read her

mind. "We hunt, we sleep, we play. Our life is simple. Once this . . . situation with Gytha and Bastien is settled, you are more likely to be bored than afraid." He wrinkled his brows as if he disliked the thought. "Maybe we will begin to do new things. Times seem to be changing whether I wish it or not."

He sounded lost when he said this, and Juliana did not know how to comfort him. From what she had seen, a change or two might be just the thing.

⤞

Ulric could not say when being with Juliana had become his idea of peace. He only knew he did not want to face his pack. He wanted to sit here with his shoulder pressed to hers, with his hand on her bruised knee and his power flowing gently out.

Instead, he released his breath and stood. Nothing would be gained by avoiding what lay ahead.

Juliana reached up for the hand he was holding out, groaning with human tiredness as he pulled her up.

"Let me settle you in my room," he said. "I am sure you would like to rest."

"Where will you be?"

He wondered if any *upyr* had ever had eyes that wide. "Speaking with my pack. I must decide if it is safe to let the stranger stay, and I must make clear how everyone is to treat you."

"Are you going to hurt them?" Her voice was low.

"Only if they force my hand."

She opened her mouth, then closed it and shook her head. Without a word, she gestured him to lead the way.

The cave was a warren of tunnels and chambers honeycombed into the rock. Some were in use, and some were neglected to the point of filling up with rubble. Though many stretches were rough—whatever wind and water had carved—elsewhere the hand of man was obvious.

Walls would be finished to glassy smoothness, or passages marble-tiled. One room boasted a temple's worth of columns, while another was decorated in mosaics so intricate they resembled paint.

Someone—Helewis, no doubt—had hung their path with small oil lamps. Without them, a human like Juliana would have been blind.

"How old is this place?" Juliana breathed.

"No one knows. My sire once told me it was a home other elders built, elders who walked into the sun before he was born."

"But why would they—"

Her voice stopped as he halted before his chamber. He did not mean to hesitate, but suddenly he felt odd. The last time he had shut these heavy planks behind him, he had expected to be returning with Gillian. He had vowed he would, had promised himself she only needed to be reminded of what she had been missing and she would come back.

How can I trust my judgment, he thought, *when I have given my heart again?*

Gritting his teeth, he forced his hand to the door.

To his shock, his chamber was occupied.

Upyr *hands, or perhaps unknown* upyr *devices,* had hollowed Ulric's chamber from the rock. Square in shape, its only structural adornments were the marks left by the chisel and the natural striations in the hard gray stone. A sleeping niche, large enough for two, had been carved into the rightward wall. Two wooden stools, a tapestry of men hunting stags, and a strange glass lamp in which the oil never burned away—all collected by Gillian from forgotten caches and given to Ulric as gifts—comprised its furnishings. No window brightened the gloom, no hearth, no shelf on which to display prized possessions.

It seemed very plain when Ulric pictured Juliana stepping inside.

At the moment, he barely had room to step inside himself. Everyone was there except Lucius, whom Ulric had not yet seen. He was uneasy to think that the pack's third male, the one with the steadiest nature, might not have come back. Of course, he had known it was a possibility—maybe even a likelihood. If Ulric had discovered he were an elder, he would not have wanted to bow to anyone else. The admission did not make Lucius's absence palatable. Changes enough had come into Ulric's life since Gillian left.

To judge by Gytha's smug expression, this invasion of his chamber had been her idea.

Making themselves at home, the pack had dragged Ulric's furs from his sleeping niche to the floor, where they spread them for sitting in comfort. Bastien was the sole exception. He lounged on the first of Ulric's stools with his feet propped on the second. His hands were folded across the muscles of his belly, and his shoulders rested on the wall. His hair hung over them like a cape. Interestingly, he had not invited Gytha to sit on his level. Gillian's rescued lamp he also kept to himself. It stood on the floor beside him, bathing his lean and perfect body in a golden glow.

The pose presented quite the image of a king.

"Would you prefer I moved?" he asked with the same faint smile he had shown before.

Ulric shook off his annoyance. He would look weak if he argued over a stool. "Sit where you please," he said and turned to the rest.

To his amazement, Stephen and Ingrith still held wolf form.

"Enough," he said, losing patience. "You know better to stay in beast form during a discussion. Both of you change at once."

Stephen whimpered a wordless plea.

"Now," Ulric insisted.

Stephen heaved a human-sounding sigh before he obeyed, coming into man form on his knees. His soft brown curls hung around his beautiful face. His neck was bowed and his fists opened and closed on his thighs.

A moment later Ingrith appeared. Ulric stiffened in shock. Though she buried her face behind Stephen's shoulder almost at once, she had too many bruises to hide, bruises no *upyr* should have been able to inflict. They covered her from head to toe, blotching her skin in shades of brown and green.

"Ingrith," he gasped and immediately crouched beside her. She was trembling violently. Gingerly, he tilted her face away from Stephen. Her lower lip was split and scabbed, and one of her eyes was swollen shut. Between the blackened lids it was leaking tears.

"Who did this to you?" he asked, torn between the need to be gentle and mindless rage. "Was it Gytha's friend?"

Ingrith choked out something too garbled to understand.

"I did it," Gytha said, bringing him around and to his feet. Her arms were crossed beneath her breasts, her expression a mix of stubbornness and shame.

The shame he suspected she would rather die than admit.

"You did this?" he repeated. "You beat a sister wolf?"

"She did not want Bastien to stay. She said he 'frightened' her."

Gytha's scorn was obvious in her mimicry. She had never had much use for Ingrith. The pretty blonde was too docile to earn Gytha's respect: a rival for males' attentions without being a true match. Nor was Ingrith as useful as Helewis, who at least had a stout arm. This, however, was beyond what Ulric would have guessed she would do.

He turned back to Stephen. "Why did you not fight?"

"You left us!" he said, a cry of accusing pain. "We did not know when you would be back from chasing after Gillian. Gytha was too strong. Especially with Bastien helping her."

"But there are three of you," Ulric protested. "Together you could have held them off."

Even as he said the words, he knew the solution was not that simple. Without Lucius to bolster their nerve, none of them had the aggressiveness to be lead wolf. When Gytha pushed her will on them, their instincts would have driven them to submit. The effect was subtler than a thrall, but it was strong.

Though he must have known this, Stephen's head sank even lower, his chin nudging his chest. "Helewis tried to fight," he admitted, "but Ingrith and I were scared."

Ulric looked at Helewis, mildly surprised. Of them all, she was the most submissive.

"They were stronger than us," she said in defense of Stephen, her eyes briefly meeting his. "And the Frenchman was using magic. That is how he made Ingrith's bruises stay." She pointed to a glyph painted in blood on Ingrith's arm, almost lost among the discoloration. Ulric did not know many letters, but it looked like a curving M with an arrow on the final tail.

He licked his thumb and tried to remove it to no avail. The glyph would not come off. He felt nothing when he touched it—which did not mean no magic was there. Clearly, Ingrith was not recovering as she should.

"I assume you tried to heal her," he said to Helewis.

She nodded emphatically. "Nothing we could think of helped. Gytha told Stephen if he even thought of standing against them, Bastien would never erase the mark. We feared Ingrith would end up scarred."

"She would not let us bow, though," Stephen said, touching his lover's averted cheek. "You are still our king."

"Yes," Helewis agreed. "Our vows still belong to you."

Ulric supposed he should be grateful for this favor. Indeed, Ingrith's stubbornness surprised him a bit.

Gytha had chosen her victim well. Stephen and Helewis could each bear pain on their own, but Ingrith was a gentler soul, made for loveplay not fighting. She was, without question, the most innocent of them all. Even among *upyr,* her angelic loveliness was rare. Ingrith was not overly vain herself, but Ulric understood why the prospect of seeing her beauty ruined would disturb the others. Her looks were a matter of pride for the pack.

He closed his eyes to fight a surge of fury. Justice, he had always thought, was best meted out cold.

Before he could calm, Gytha's temper exploded.

"Interfering bitch," she snarled, leaping forward to claw her accuser. Luckily for Gytha, the Frenchman held her back by the arms. A more trusting soul might have concluded he was less violent than she. Ulric thought Bastien had simply realized the tide was shifting against them.

"Bastien," he said, calling his gaze.

The stranger's eyes showed none of Gytha's awareness of guilt. Instead, they looked so resigned they were almost dead. His humor of before might have been a dream.

"I needed shelter," he explained without inflection. "Gytha offered it in return for my cooperation. For the price of a home, I would have done anything short of letting her kill Ingrith."

It was a stupefying admission, and one Ulric hardly knew how to address. But whatever sympathy he might feel for Bastien's situation, whatever his understanding of Gytha's desire to seize her chance to rule, he could not let their behavior stand. In the end, the decision came swifter than thought. Long before the stranger could read his intention, long before Gytha could move to help, Ulric changed and leapt for Bastien's throat.

He knocked both conspirators over when he hit. A stool splintered beneath them and a female shrieked. Gytha's head struck the wall with a solid crack. Bastien tried to wrestle Ulric off but was too slow—stunned perhaps by his fall. Even as his hands grabbed Ulric's ruff, Ulric's fangs sank home. He tore the flesh they held, determinedly overcoming the resistance of *upyr* skin. Cool red blood flew into his face. More screams. More hands. He shook them off and backed away from Bastien.

The Frenchman lay on his side, his eyes white all

around, his muscles twitching as his blood pooled beneath his head. Even to Ulric, who had made it, the gash in his neck came as a shock. For any other creature, this would have been a mortal wound. In truth, his wolf believed it should be. Battling back the urge to finish the kill was no small feat. Breathing hard, Ulric returned to his human form.

"No," he barked as Gytha tried to crawl to her lover.

He knelt beside Bastien himself, his hand closing on Bastien's wounded throat. Beneath his palm, the muscle and cartilage squirmed like living things, already trying to knit. Ulric's power could help or hinder that process as he desired. The stranger's eyes said he knew this, but weakened by loss of blood, he could not escape.

"Please," he rasped. "Please let me live. I will do anything you want."

The agony in his voice sounded utterly sincere, taking Ulric aback. Defiance he expected, not a plea.

"I do not intend to kill you," he said, "only make you understand that in my pack we are more than our wolves. Perhaps matters are different in France, but here we protect those who need protecting. We do not maim them with magic."

The stranger closed his eyes. "If that is true, I will serve you with all my heart."

At a loss for words, Ulric turned to Gytha. She had shrunk back against the wall, her arms straight at her sides, her fingers digging into the stone. Her reaction he understood. She knew she was in trouble, and he had shown just how easily he could defeat her sole ally.

"This wound should have been yours," he said to her, "for yours was the greater sin. You betrayed your pack to an outsider, choosing to fight not the strongest, but to harm the weak by unfair means. I would be within my rights to do far worse to you than I did to him."

"Then do it," she snapped, one last burst of rebellion.

"Go to your chamber," he said. "I will give you my decision before sunrise."

"Go," Bastien seconded from the floor. "He is justified in what he says."

Though Ulric resented the implication that he needed help controlling Gytha, he held his tongue. After all, she was glaring at Bastien as furiously as she glared at him.

"I will go," she huffed, "but I am not in the wrong. No matter what you try to tell yourself, I deserve to be queen."

As she stumped from the room, everyone heaved a sigh—everyone, that is, except Juliana.

Gripped by a sudden panic, Ulric searched the shadows of the passage outside the door. He could not see her, could not smell her, could not feel her essence in the air.

She was gone.

He cursed but could not blame her. If she had seen even a portion of what he had done, she must think him worse than a monster.

"I must find Juliana," he said, knowing where his first duty lay but for once unable to do it. "I want that mark removed from Ingrith before I return."

Thus saying, he left the others with their mouths agape.

⟜

Juliana swore she was not going to weep or scream or flee in terror. Never mind that her pulse beat so hard in her throat she feared she might be sick. Never mind that her knees had turned to water and she had to steady her wrist with her second hand to keep the lamp she had grabbed from spilling its oil.

She was calm. She merely needed to walk and think.

Her strides were jerky, taking her deeper into the cliff. She knew this because the air grew cooler and more quiet, until the silence seemed to have weight. She passed smooth tunnels and rough ones, cluttered ones and clean. They smelled of the pack, like rain-soaked earth and

ferns, like mossy rocks and leaves slowly turning brown
while wildflowers poked between.

You will be lost, she thought, but did not slow. She had
no doubt Ulric could track her anywhere she went.

The image of her lover ripping the Frenchman's throat
came bright as day. Bastien's blood was as red as the doublet and hose Ulric's change had left on the floor. When
Ulric appeared again as a man, the red still painted his
face and chest. She was reasonably certain he could have
thrown off the stain. Instead, she watched him lick it from
sharpened teeth, watched him pant with the same excitement he showed on his hunts.

His body had been aroused.

Everything inside her had rebelled at the evidence of
his bloodlust, but there was no thought in her reaction, no
judgment she could put in words. She only knew she had
to get away.

She came to the end of the passage she was in, not
blank rock but a small octagonal room with carved stone
benches ringing its walls. It had the look of an abandoned
chapel, dusty and lost in time.

A flutter of warm, night-scented air made her lift the
lamp. Above her, a natural chimney pierced the cavernous ceiling, wide enough to admit a glimmer of stars.

She sat beneath the opening, legs crossed, neck tilted
back. The smoothness of the floor told her countless others had done this before.

I am out of my depth, she thought. This *upyr* life is
much stranger than I could foresee.

She had to laugh, ruefully, at Ulric's claim that she
would be bored.

~

With a surge of relief strong enough to leave him weak,
Ulric found her in the solar. She had not run. He had a
chance to win her back. Aware she had not yet seen him, he

watched her as he waited for his hammering pulse to slow. She sat with her plain blue gown spread around her, her head hanging back until her hair pooled on the floor. As if to hold herself together, her hands clutched white-knuckled at her knees.

Despite his fears, he wanted her with an intensity that stole his breath.

"I see you have found our drunkard's chamber," he said, striving for flippancy.

Her head jerked up and her eyes widened. He waved at the star-filled opening in the roof. "We come here when we wish to forget our troubles or celebrate. Just enough sun comes through to blur our thoughts."

She said nothing, her expression wary, seemingly waiting for something more. Ulric hoped he could provide it.

He took a few steps closer and hunkered down. She flinched when he reached out to touch her knee. Not knowing what else to do, he spoke from the heart. "We are not just people, Juliana. We are wolves. What you saw me do to Bastien, that is the language we understand."

"The language of violence? Of might makes right?"

"Unless I seriously misspent my time in the human world, your kind speaks that language, too."

Though his response was gentle, she looked away, fussing with a crease in her skirt. "What will happen to Gytha?"

He began to answer, then stopped, some intuition checking his response. "What do you think should happen to her?"

"Me?"

He had her eyes again, round and shining. "Yes, you."

"I . . . I do not know. You could . . . banish her."

"Gytha has been a part of this pack from the beginning. It is true she has more will than wisdom, but will is part of what allows our kind to survive. If I banish her, the other packs might refuse to take her in. I think she would be unhappy on her own."

"She deserves to be unhappy. She beat Ingrith black and blue!"

He stroked her shining hair around her shoulder. This time she was too caught up in anger to pull away. "Perhaps I should banish Stephen as well. He failed to defend her. True, expecting a subordinate wolf to do battle against a superior might be unfair. Perhaps I should banish myself for leaving them without a responsible leader."

"There must be consequences for her actions!"

"I agree. I am asking you what they should be."

She frowned at him. "You are trying to show me it is easier to criticize a choice than to make one."

He was, but he knew enough not to admit it. "Make a suggestion, Juliana. Maybe it will be one I could not devise on my own."

"If I thought you really believed that . . ." She shook her head. "All right. Reward Helewis. Move her up in the pack."

He was unprepared for her decisiveness. "I cannot do that. Helewis has to earn her rank. She cannot move up unless she fights the female wolves above her: either Ingrith, which she will not do, or Gytha, whom she cannot defeat."

"Those rules are for wolves. You said yourself that you are more. If you treat Helewis with extra respect, the others will as well. And," she added, warming up, "I think no one in the pack should speak to Gytha until Ingrith ceases to be afraid of her. Because you can smell fear, I assume you will know when that occurs. For as long as Gytha terrorizes Ingrith, she should be shunned."

Ulric rubbed his chin, then released an ironic laugh. "I suspect Gytha would rather I beat her senseless."

"Which is precisely why you should not." Her hand almost touched his arm. He felt the heat shadow it left. "Just consider my idea. If it does not change Gytha's behavior, you can do whatever you would have before."

Ulric mulled over her words. He had asked her opinion on impulse, not realizing she might expect him to take it. He was king here, after all. His way had worked for centuries.

"And another thing," she went on with an earnestness that made his shoulders tense. "You must ask more questions."

"Questions?"

"Yes. You should demand to know what that magic symbol was and how it kept Ingrith from healing."

"I demanded that Bastien take it off."

"Well, yes, that was the most important thing, but you need to know how it worked in case he tries to do it again."

"I will order him not to."

To his amazement, she looked dubious, as if she doubted his orders would suffice. "Oh, never mind. I can ask him myself."

"You shall do nothing of the kind!" he exclaimed. The thought of her nosing around the Frenchman made him want to gnash his teeth. The men of Bastien's country had a reputation for seducing women. Unlike Stephen, Bastien was not an *upyr* Ulric could govern with a look. "I do not want you near him!"

"If you think he is dangerous, why let him stay?"

Her tone was challenging enough to make his hands ball into fists. With an effort, he forced them to relax. "We are all dangerous, Juliana. I let him stay, for now, because our kind are few. He deserves a chance to earn a home. And, in case you had any doubt, I shall judge his worthiness by observing what he does, not by peppering him with intrusive questions."

"I should have known you did not really want my opinion."

"I did," he said, stung by her bitter tone. "I do. But you cannot be with my pack for an evening and think you know how to run it."

"You are right," she said, letting her shoulders slump. "I do not know anything."

Her surrender should have made him happy, but it did not. Filled with a vague unease, he stroked her arm. "It is not safe for you to be alone here. You should return to my room."

She shook her head. "I need to think. I need to make sense of what I am doing."

He did not like the sound of that any more than he liked the thought of leaving her on her own. If nothing else, tonight had proved his pack was unpredictable. If one of them slipped his control, she would have no defense. The desire to order her—nay, to compel her—to be sensible burned in his throat. His promise not to thrall her against her will chafed like a chain.

"As you wish," he said, his reluctance roughening his voice. "Return when you are ready. Just promise it shall be soon."

"Soon," she agreed, without sharing her understanding of what that meant.

He ran into Helewis at the tunnel's end.

"Stephen is still with Ingrith," she reported before he could ask. "Bastien is removing the mark and Ingrith was nervous to be alone with him. Did you find Juliana?"

"Yes." He glanced back over his shoulder. "She is fine, just . . . sorting her feelings out."

Helewis nodded as if she could not imagine this posing a problem, then scuffed her feet. "Ulric, where is Lucius? We thought he would return with you."

Ulric blew out his breath. "I do not think he is coming back."

"Not coming back! But—"

"He discovered he is an elder."

Helewis's brows shot up in surprise. "An elder! You mean he can—"

"Yes, he can make a mortal one of us. He taught Gillian how to change the man with whom she fell in love."

"I did not know that secret could be taught. And Gillian is so young. But I upset you. Forgive me for treading on painful ground."

Ulric waved his hand, knowing his frustration showed on his face. He was not certain why Lucius's absence bothered him this much. What was Lucius to him? A friend? A brother? Someone whose presence he had taken for granted but apparently never understood? Though the pack was more than a comforting huddle of bodies, that was part of its appeal. Take one member away, and its very fabric came in to doubt.

"I am not angry at you," he said to reassure Helewis. "You did well. You stood against the danger."

"I knew you would have wanted me to," she said shyly. "I am only sorry I did not succeed." Without warning she touched his wrist. "Ulric, you should forget Gillian. You have this Juliana now. Maybe she—"

He cut her off. "I do not 'have' her any more than I had Gillian. After tonight, I suspect my hold on her is even shakier." He rubbed Helewis's hand to take the bite from his tone. As usual, she ventured only a glance at his eyes. He remembered what Juliana had said about her rank. "Helewis, you could help me now if you would. I would like you to guard Juliana when I cannot, or when she would rather I stay away."

"You would trust me to do that?"

"No one more."

As if his words held a spell, she pulled her shoulders back. "I will do it," she declared, immediately moving to position herself before the tunnel where Juliana had flown. It was the only entrance to the solar. No one would get past her without a fight.

In spite of his worries, Ulric had to suppress a smile. He had done what Juliana advised; he had shown Helewis more respect. Now they would see how Juliana liked the results.

—⟨⟨⟨⟩⟩⟩—

A hand shook Juliana from her doze on the solar floor. It was Helewis, the big *upyr* who had spoken to her before.

"It is nearly sunrise," she said. "Ulric will worry if you do not join him."

Juliana pushed herself stiffly up, knowing there was little point in proclaiming she did not care what Ulric felt. She did care after all; she simply did not know what she ought to do.

Just as muddled as before, she shoved her hair back from her face. "Is Ingrith all right?"

Helewis seemed happy to speak to someone she did not have to be afraid of. "Oh, yes. As soon as Bastien's throat closed up, he said a chant to take off the mark. It was Latin, which I do not speak, but Stephen told me he was saying something like 'remove the force of my stars.' After a few minutes, the symbol disappeared."

"'Remove the force of my stars'? As in, the stars he was born under?"

"I do not know," Helewis answered. "I have never seen anyone use that kind of magic. I am sure it is not allowed."

"I would like to know where he learned it," Juliana mused, allowing Helewis to help her up. Sadly, Helewis did not have the same effect on her clothes as Ulric. Juliana supposed she had less magical force to share. As a result, her skirts stayed dusty.

"I could never dare to ask," the *upyr* declared. "Such things are dangerous to know."

"Or not to know, in this case."

Helewis pursed her lips in disapproval, but Juliana had no intention of giving up. If no one would help her, she would find a way to ask the Frenchman herself.

They walked in silence to Ulric's door, with Juliana doing her best to memorize the landmarks along the way, especially the bathing chamber with the hot spring. From the looks of the room's appointments, humans had been guests in this cave before. She knew the facilities would make her residence more comfortable.

"Well," she said, turning to thank Helewis.

"Do not fight him," Helewis blurted in an undertone. "Gillian always had to get her way, but it is good to have a strong leader. When the leader is strong, everyone feels safe."

Juliana thought it was more important to be safe than to feel safe but did not say this aloud. Rather, she dipped her head in a bow. "Thank you," she said. "I am grateful for the escort."

Her thanks seemed to put Helewis off balance. The *upyr* nearly tripped as she backed away.

With a sigh for all the dilemmas she had not solved, Juliana opened the door.

Inside, Ulric perched on the edge of his sleeping niche, his hands braced beside his hips as if deciding whether to leap up. His nakedness seemed different here, both more natural and more erotic—perhaps because this was the place where his beast ran free.

Ill-at-ease with the change, she turned her glance from the curves and shadows of his sex. The lamp she had noticed before sat on the floor beside his feet. It was a strange creation, an opaque, gold-white glass tube that did not smoke or flicker or have an opening for oil. She meant to greet Ulric, to say something to assure him that she had calmed, but the conundrum of the lamp distracted her completely.

"I do not know how it works," he said even as she opened her mouth to ask. "I do not know where it came from or what it burns. Someone found it in one of the older tunnels and gave it to me. We think the elders lived here in ancient times and they are the ones who made it."

"Oh," she said and rubbed her finger across the tip of her nose.

His lips twitched with a smile that was half grimace. "If I knew, believe me I would tell you."

"I have no doubt you would," she answered politely.

"Juliana," he said with a little laugh, then patted his furs. "Lie down, Juliana, where I know you will not come to harm."

She felt awkward, but did not remotely want to leave. She climbed into the bed behind him, guessing he would want to lie between her and the door, to protect her from whatever threat might come in. The niche was cozy, the furs cloud-soft. She settled into them with a shiver of pure enjoyment. When Ulric stretched out in front of her, she curled herself around his back. She did not try to distance herself but snuggled close. The other distance, the one in her head and heart, he needed no reminder of. His movements were too cautious to be unaware.

He held her arm against his chest as if he had missed its warmth.

"I am sorry I worried you," she said.

"And I am sorry I frightened you. It was my fault you had to see me discipline the Frenchman. I left my pack alone too long. I was too angry, too proud to return from Bridesmere without her."

Juliana knew very well who he meant by "her." She strove not to let her tone grow terse. "Your pack members are not children, Ulric. They should have been able to behave themselves."

"They are unused to being on their own. I should have prepared them."

"Maybe, but even if you had, you cannot control their every thought and deed. If you could, they would be puppets. I suspect you would take no pleasure in ruling that."

He was quiet while he considered what she had said. Though he did not agree in words, she sensed a slight unwinding of the tension in his back. His hip and shoulder shifted into more relaxed positions. "I only left them once before," he said. "If we met with other packs, we traveled together."

"Where did you go the other time?" she asked, more to keep him talking than anything else. His answer made her sit up.

"I went to visit my mother before she died. She never had a body to bury after the battle. I wanted her to know that I had survived."

He rolled onto his back while Juliana blinked down at his face. His hair gleamed like spun gold in the strange lamplight. He seemed to relish having surprised her.

"Were you afraid?" she asked once she had found her voice.

His laugh was a rush of air. "Terrified. I worried that she would think I was a demon, that she would wonder why I only came to talk to her at night. I even feared she would not know me. Instead, I almost did not recognize her. She had aged—and I had forgotten much of my human life."

"But she remembered you?"

"Yes. She said she always knew I would return. She prattled at me for a week, cooked meals I could not eat, and never once asked why I looked half the age I should."

"I imagine she was happy to see her son alive."

He shrugged as Juliana laid her hand on the golden hair that dusted his chest. "Maybe. But she did not argue when I told her I had to leave. I sometimes wonder if she suspected what I was and did not want to know for sure."

Juliana thought of her father. She could not imagine

Henry Buxton being that tolerant. His merchant's view of the world had no room for mysteries.

No doubt he was thoroughly annoyed with her by now, having lost not just her services but the right to crow about her match. Oh, he would miss her, but fury was more likely to be the emotion he would acknowledge. She pitied whoever he hired to replace her. Their ears would be ringing constantly with his plaints.

"What makes you frown?" Ulric asked, reaching up to run his finger along her cheek.

"I was thinking my father would not believe what has happened to me if I told him. He would insist I had lost my mind. Probably lock me in my room."

"What about your mother? What would she have thought?"

Juliana's eyes pricked as she laughed. "She would have loved this. Even the gory bits. *Especially* the gory bits."

"Then we must pray more of her blood runs in your veins." His smile was wistful as he ran his palm down her now-clean sleeve. "You are the first person I have told about visiting my mother. I never shared that story before."

"Not even with—" She stopped and bit back the name.

"No," he said, even graver. "Not even with Gillian."

Chapter 10

Given the ordeal his beloved had been through, Ulric knew he ought to leave her alone. His need to be close, to reassert his sensual supremacy, overrode his good sense. And perhaps if he proved he could love her gently as well as rough, that he was in truth more than his wolf, she would forget her horror. For her, he was willing to change his ways. For her, he would risk heartache.

She was leaning over him in his sleeping niche, her hair falling forward in shining waves. Hoping for the best, he reached to cup the side of her neck. She must have sensed what he meant the caress to lead to. Her body went very still.

"Tell me," he said, watching his thumb slide up and down the front of her throat. "Could you bear to let me touch you, or have I grown too hideous?"

"Never," she said and covered his hand.

He knew the gesture was meant to comfort, but the warmth of contact sluiced straight through his body to his loins, bringing him swiftly to readiness. "I wish I had the fortitude to let you rest," he said, "instead of wanting to tear you out of these clothes."

She smiled at his admission. "I want that, too—no matter what else I feel."

That "else" was the problem, but the part of him that yearned to touch her could not care. His skin thrummed with anticipation, his fangs beginning to lengthen despite his wish to conceal his inhuman side. He had no hope of turning back the response. He was *upyr* and wolf, and she aroused every desire he had: for sex, for blood, and most of all for control.

Clenching his jaw so firmly its muscles ached, he tugged her to the furs and shifted position until he straddled her hips. He could see his actions had amused her.

"You cannot reach my laces from there," she pointed out. "I think you will have to let me up."

"Clothes are evil," he growled. "Humans never should have invented them."

"Humans get cold," she said reasonably.

He backed off just enough to let her sit up. Though his cock felt as heavy as iron, he was careful not to tear the material when he loosened the snugging laces behind her gown. Easing off her bodice and sleeves, he left her breasts to rise and fall beneath her chemise.

"You see," she said, her eyes sparkling, "it is like unwrapping a present. The delay increases the delight."

"You think I cannot do this. You think I am going to lose control."

"Oh, no, Ulric, I have faith you can do whatever you set your mind to." Still laughing silently, she wriggled onto her back. Her curves were lush, her nipples pushing tight and dark against the linen of her undergown. The temptation to rip and plunder pounded inside him like an extra heart.

"I can," he said, but he had forgotten what they were

debating. The fact that she was here, in his chamber, in his home, in a place where other wolves might approach her, pushed him to claim her as never before. A slave collar would not have been too extreme a measure for his wolf. She could not have stopped him. As a human, she was totally vulnerable.

"I want to touch you," he confessed, his throat almost too thick for sound. "I want to rub you with my penis, to feel every inch of you through my skin."

Her hands feathered across his chest and down his belly, making his skin twitch like a horse. Oh, yes, he thought, touch me all you wish. He sucked in a breath as she reached his erection, caressing it shyly from root to crown, pulling it subtly longer, increasing its heat and girth. His tension mounted at her gentleness until he could have howled.

Instead, he dragged her clothes down her legs.

They were beautiful legs, long and shapely and even stronger now than when they first met. The lamplight brought out a hint of red in the triangle of curls at her abdomen, sign of the fire he knew awaited inside.

"You are going to touch every inch," she reminded. "I am holding you to your word."

His smile barely supplanted his need to moan. "You may hold me to anything you like." He shifted down the length of his bed, sat back on his heels, and lifted her ankle. Despite their wordplay, this surprised her.

He pressed the sole of her foot against his hardness."You mean it," she said, curling her toes.

"Yes, Juliana. Your wish is my command."

More cat than wolf, he rubbed his shaft against her. The arches of her feet, the roundness of her calves, even her knees felt his swollen length. He propped his weight on his arms to stroke along the silken softness of her inner thighs. She seemed to like the intimacy of the touch. Wriggling with pleasure, she stretched her arms high above her head, her fingertips brushing the niche's wall.

His teeth pulsed to full length.

Her posture was that of a slave waiting to be bound.

With a fierceness that stole his breath, he wanted to shackle her wrists and hold them captive. In Bridesmere he had done that when he took her against the tavern wall. Then, the only limits he had accepted were those of human tolerance. Regretting his good intentions more than he could express, he ran his cock across her belly instead. The curve trembled beneath him, his reward for restraint.

She lifted her knee to caress his hip. "I love the way your skin goes from cool to hot."

"You make me hot." He swallowed hard at the flush that had risen to stain her skin. "Take me in your hand again. Put the tip of me against your breast."

Without his meaning to, his request came out as an order.

"Please," he added and saw her smile knowingly.

"Like this?" She curled her slender fingers around his shaft, then scooted down between his straddled legs, stopping when his crown bumped the underside of one breast. Her flesh was warm and soft, but not precisely what he wished. Even as he told himself to hold his tongue, his preference came bursting out.

"Higher," he gasped.

She pressed the very tip of him against the bead of her nipple. "There?"

"Yes."

"Rub it?"

"Oh, yes." He shivered at the feel of her hard little peak brushing his member, at the sight of her ruddy color against his pink. A tiny bead of moisture welled from his slit. His nerves were practically shooting stars. "All around," he rasped. "Rub the head . . . all around."

She obeyed with the faintest curving of her lips. Her gaze dropped admiringly to his cock.

"You are still pale," she murmured, "but very hard." One of her fingers circled his rim, then tapped the sensitive dome. The touch made him lurch a fraction longer. "I can feel your pulse beating fast right here."

He was struggling not to gasp for air. His eyes slid closed as the nails of her second hand combed up the hair on his thigh. She shifted between his legs again, holding him, turning her face back and forth across his shaft. Her cheeks were soft, her mouth mobile and damp. She kissed the throbbing river of a vein.

"Ulric," she whispered. "I think I would like you inside me."

He groaned because, no matter what he intended, he knew he could not resist.

He dragged her upward along the bed, his hands planting in her outspread hair, his mouth sinking onto hers. Her tongue met his in slow, wet turns. Greedily, he sucked it into his mouth.

Though he longed to nip her lower lip, he did not dare. If he drew blood, he would be lost.

"Now," she said. "Take me now."

He clasped his shaft to guide himself inside her, then felt her hand settle over his to help.

His arousal was almost too much to bear. Everything about her seemed to accept him. Her thighs were spread, her entrance sleek and wet. He pressed easily inward, smooth, hot, holding at the furthest reach, then pulling carefully out. His stroke was steady: not too fast, not too forceful, gliding all the way in and almost all the way out. She pushed upward with a little moan each time he sank home. Her knees rose higher along his sides, and her hands slid down his back. They clenched his buttocks, but her nails did not prick his skin.

Clasped in living silk, he groaned her name and hid his

face in her hair. He could do this. He could stay this gentle. It was good. It was heaven. But, Lord, it was killing him to hold back.

He tried pushing one of her legs over his shoulder, tried kissing her deep and hard. She grew warmer, wetter, while his cock screamed at him to pound in.

When he turned his head to kiss her ankle, he found himself sucking it against his teeth. His fingers dug into her haunches, his hipbones grinding hers hard enough to bruise.

"Ul-ric," she said, a catch in the middle of his name.

To his lust-addled mind, she sounded as though she wanted him to be rough.

Cursing the need to rein his urges, he eased free of her body's hold, hushing her when she whimpered, murmuring soothing sounds.

This was as much for him as it was for her. His cock throbbed with impatience as he coaxed her onto her belly and then up on her knees. Her bottom bumped his loins with unerring aim. The position was nearly perfect but not quite. He lifted her arms until her weight was propped on the niche's wall.

"Knees apart," he said, nudging them with his own, trying not to grow too aroused from telling her what to do. He did not want to spill before he satisfied her. "Brace your palms on the stone."

A shiver ran down her spine. Unable to stop himself, he dragged his tongue up the knobs of her vertebrae. Her shoulders shook again.

"Bottom up," he whispered, fighting shivers himself. "I want to take you from behind."

He spread his hand on her belly to support her, to tilt her mount of Venus just as he liked. Her scent was heady, her secret places glistening wet. He let his tip find its own way into her sweetness, pulsing wildly as he eased in. When she moaned, he withdrew and did it again.

He could tell she was happy to have him back. Her body rippled around him as hot as fire. A sound far too close to a snarl issued from his throat. He had misjudged how enjoyable this would be.

He had thought it would be easier if he could not watch her heat-flushed face. Instead, he found the new position almost too exciting, just what his wolf most craved. Even as he thrust, he could run his hands over her breasts, could tease her nipples, could let his lips curl back over aching fangs without fear of being frightening. Though he kept his movements slow, the pressure hit him exactly right, under the head where he felt it most. Considering his *upyr* sensitivity, that meant he felt it quite a bit. Wanting her to experience their lovemaking as intensely, he cupped her pubis and used his fingers to press the bud of her pleasure against his shaft.

She arched to him, opening her body to each intrusion, pushing back against it cooperatively.

Her eagerness was too much. Already frayed, the remains of his discipline fell in tatters. The only thing that saved him was knowing they both would be spending soon. Juliana's breath was coming harder, her movements losing their grace. His stones felt full enough to explode.

Her head dropped as she braced herself on the wall. Though he longed to cuff her wrists, he merely spread one of his hands beside hers. Seeing it, she gripped his forearm with surprising strength.

"That," she panted as the head of him glided over something she liked, something at the front of her tight passage. "Oh, *there*."

"Harder?" he suggested, or maybe pleaded, already increasing his speed.

Her answer was lost in a pleasured moan. His member swelled at the sudden clutching of her sheath. He mouthed her nape, her shoulder, his instincts urging him to bite, if only to hold her in place for his final drive. He moaned at the longing he could not fulfill. He had a feeling he was pressing her far too hard.

"Ulric," she said. "Yes."

He did not know what she was saying yes to, but he bit and drank as his ecstasy began to peak, half blind with pleasure, clamping down on her neck to suck. As he felt her shudder around him, an unexpected tingle swept his scalp.

The sun was breaching the horizon.

He was so close to complete release, so desperate for it, he could have cried. To his supreme relief, dawn slowed his orgasm but did not dim it. The vessels of his sex contracted, ripples of bliss so singular and so lengthy they felt like tight, oiled hands squeezing down his cock. His spine bowed hard 'as he groaned against her neck, wrapping her in his arms, emptying himself in languorous, heated spurts, filling her with the *upyr's* infertile ejaculate.

He was barely aware of falling into the softness of his furs, of tumbling weakly to the side. Opening heavy eyes, he found her leaning over him as before, as if their loveplay had been a dream. Her expression held a shadow that he misliked.

"Sorry," he mumbled, trying to stroke her cheek with his hand but succeeding only in batting her hip. "Forgot . . . sunrise."

She combed his hair out of his face. "Sleep," she said. "You gave me everything I needed."

He sensed this was not the truth, or not completely, but had neither the wakefulness nor the nerve to ask. When he fumbled to pull her beside him, she slipped away.

❧

Knowing how leaden his arm could get when he fell asleep, Juliana eased away before it could trap her. She was too restless to lie with him all day, even more restless than before. Feeling the need for a shield, she drew on her chemise.

For all her horror at Ulric's violence, she had no objection to roughness in bed. She had discovered already that she enjoyed it, but to find that she *needed* it, that the experience was not complete unless he took her forcefully, disturbed her more than a bit.

His verbal orders had been a tease. The control she longed for was physical. For her, being left a little too tender was as necessary for satisfaction as a drink of blood was to him.

Helewis said when the leader was strong, everyone felt safe. Outwardly dutiful, Juliana had always prided herself on her independence. Could it be that, in her heart, she agreed with Helewis?

Halfway to the door, she hugged herself, shivering in her linen shift. As if of its own will, her hand slid up to find the place Ulric's fangs had pierced, where the muscle of her shoulder met her neck. The bite was healing, a mark a tomcat might have left. She wondered what it said about her that she found this exciting. Certainly, she could not deny she did. Tiny flickers of arousal moved deep inside her as she probed the spot. If Ulric had been awake, she would have climbed on him then and there.

But she could not solve the riddle now. Shaking it off, she pulled Ulric's door open.

Her heart jumped as her foot almost struck a body. For some reason, Helewis was sleeping on the threshold. Juliana wondered if Ulric knew: surely this was taking subservience too far! Holding her breath for silence, she stepped over the slumbering woman and into the corridor. Though the darkness was not as thick as before, she lifted a small bronze lantern from its hook.

She would have to learn to move through these tunnels blind, at least until she decided if she was going to be *upyr*. That she had not ruled this out troubled her anew.

Maybe the difference between her and Ulric—and never
mind between her and Helewis—was not so great.

She padded barefoot down the passage, this time
toward the entry ledge. She had a longing to see the sun.
Even if she was sleeping with a creature of darkness, she
did not have to live like a mole.

To her relief, she recalled the route. As she walked, she
began to see shadows without the lamp. The sound of
ravens cawing in the trees was humorously sweet.

The cave faced west—better for viewing sunset than
sunrise, though there were signs of the dawning day. A
thin line of clouds, their edges fired with reflected pink,
flew like feathers above the trees. Last night, Juliana had
not realized how high Ulric's cave was, or how isolated.
The forest was immense, a sea of pine and oak that followed the rise and dip of the land in every direction she
could see. An eagle circled to the north, riding the warming air.

No wonder Ulric acted like the king of the world. This
was quite a holding. Here, surrounded by this forest, one
could forget the human realm existed, much less that it
posed a threat.

It is up to me to remember, Juliana thought, touched by
an unexpected sense of guardianship.

She was testing the weight of this new emotion when
she noticed something moving along the base of the cliff.
Startled, she drew back behind the opening and peered
out. One of the male *upyr,* cloaked and gloved and boot-
ed in black, was scaling the rock. The clothes foiled her
for a moment, but the height and an errant wisp of black
hair told her the climber was Bastien.

Before she could decide whether to leave, he was there,
his hair smoking faintly as he heaved himself over the
edge. When he threw back his hood, she saw a half-healed
bite mark on his neck. The edges were bruised, as if someone had drawn on it very hard. Gytha, she supposed, and

blushed at the other activities the bruise implied. The mark had to be recent. Evidently, the failure of Gytha's coup had not quenched their mutual attraction.

Knowing he might spot her at any moment, and not wanting him to take her for a spy, Juliana cleared her throat.

Bastien spun around, as startled to see her as she had been to see him. His eyes bore circles as purple as his bruise. His alarm shored up her confidence.

"Step into the shadow," she suggested. "You will blister if you stand and gape."

He shuffled back to the wall, comfortingly out of reach. She hoped the strip of light between them would be as good as a wall.

"I was taking the sun," he explained, then laughed sheepishly. "Getting drunk, you would say. I am afraid it is a personal vice."

"A discreet vice, as few will ever be awake to see you indulge."

"Yes," he agreed, and ran his tongue along his lower lip.

Her father had taught her such nervous gestures were giveaways, signs that it was time to call a rival's bluff. Bastien had lied about his reason for being out. When he spoke again, she was even surer her guess was right.

"If you would keep this to yourself, I would be grateful. The others would think less of me if they knew."

"Tell me what stars were rising when you were born and I shall consider remaining quiet."

He hesitated, though he seemed more interested than angry. "The sign of the scorpion," he said, then: "You are curious about the mark I put on Ingrith."

"It gave you power over her." She made it a statement rather than a query. "I was under the impression that you had to be very strong to have that much influence on each other."

"We do." His smile was filled with genuine amusement. "Mortals, of course, are easier to thrall."

"They are unless they have been bitten by another *upyr* first. Then they have protection."

"Know about that, do you?"

She said nothing of the merchant's stories that held this lore, trusting in silence to serve her ends. The more he thought she knew, the less secretive he would be. Bending one leg, he braced his weight against the rock. Unlike Ulric, who preferred going naked, Bastien seemed comfortable in his clothes. Perhaps he had grown used to them while traveling from France. He was different from Ulric in other ways as well: not as still as the pack leader, nor as self-assured.

She met Bastien's half-smile with one of her own. He might be immortal, but if he thought she was going to run out of patience and speak first, he was deceived. Finally, with a grimace to cede the victory, he answered the question she had been hinting at all along.

"The mark I put on Ingrith is called a *point de convergence*. It draws on the power of my personal stars to concentrate my will, thus allowing me to thrall my fellow *upyr*."

"So you convinced her she could not heal."

"Yes," he said and pushed his long, wine-black hair back from his face.

His answer hinted at a host of possibilities. The power of astrology she was not qualified to judge. A thrall she had seen in action for herself. From what she had witnessed, that was the same as persuasion with an extra boost. She wondered if Ingrith failed to heal because she believed Bastien's claims. If this was the case, was his power responsible or her own? Had Ingrith, in essence, thralled herself? Could another *upyr* have removed the mark if they were as charismatic? Finally, was this the same mechanism by which the blacksmith's tattoo worked?

For the time being, she felt more comfortable keeping these questions to herself. She turned her gaze back to

Bastien. Beneath his sardonic smirk, and despite his story of getting sundrunk, she judged him quite sober. He was wary of her, she concluded, not only because she was Ulric's lover, but because she had the kind of mind that loved a mystery.

"I hear using magic is forbidden," she said, hoping to coax him to reveal who had taught him what he knew. "At least among the children of Auriclus."

This time her feint did not bear fruit. With one gloved hand, Bastien reached out from his pool of shadow to touch her neck. The tip of his index finger traced a vein. "Feeding from humans is forbidden, too, and nonetheless there are those among us who cannot resist."

When she shivered and flinched away, his smile lifted the weariness from his face. She could not help noting that his fangs had partially emerged.

"If Ulric tires of you," he said so softly it was barely speech, "I would be happy to taste you myself."

⟡

Deciding it was unsafe to wander the cave until the sun was higher, Juliana returned to Ulric's chamber, once again clambering carefully over Helewis. Ulric mumbled something as she slipped back in. He, apparently, was a lighter sleeper than his junior wolf, though he was not disturbed enough to rouse.

She lay awake on her back, her fingers laced beneath her breasts as she stared at the niche's ceiling, thinking about magic and the things it might be used for now that she knew it was real.

If her experience with the standing stones was any indication, magic was not a power for *upyr* alone. Not only could renegades like Bastien wield it to their advantage, but so could humans—maybe even humans like the soldier who had rushed at Ulric with his cross.

Ulric said he saw no reason why a Christian symbol

should have power over *upyr*. Juliana was not as sure, but if he was right, the soldiers believing a lie could be providential. The less truth humans knew, the safer *upyr* would be. It might even be worthwhile to spread a few misleading stories: say, that silver weakened them instead of iron, or that immortals had a dread of scallions. Juliana smiled to imagine villagers running around with long green stalks strung on their necks. She knew precisely how such falsehoods could be spread through the merchant network. If she drew on her familiarity with the biggest gossips, fooling them would not even take much time.

Abruptly shocked by her ruminations, Juliana's hands flew up to her cheeks. She was thinking of humans as "them." In her mind, she had begun to side with *upyr*.

I have not yet made my choice, she insisted to herself as she rolled toward the wall to sleep. Regardless of her conflict, rest came easily.

She was not as bothered by her disloyalty as she should have been.

Chapter 11

Ulric woke later than usual, at least an hour past dusk. Juliana was gone, as was Helewis. Disconcerted but not alarmed, he raked his fingers through his hair, smoothing it absently as he turned in a circle to check the room.

Metal flashed in his pile of clothes, folded and left in the corner since his return. He bent to see what the gleam belonged to and found Juliana's portrait locket, the one he had rescued from the sons of Gideon Drake. No more than half aware of what he was doing, he bounced the chain in his hand.

Juliana would not have run again, not without telling him. He had, so far as he knew, done nothing to upset her. More to the point, if Helewis was gone as well, she had a guard.

Knowing Helewis's strict adherence to duty, Juliana might welcome a change of company.

Decision made, he dropped the locket over his head and began his search. Luckily, she and Helewis had moved slowly enough to track. Ulric rolled his shoulders and shook his arms as he followed them deeper into the cliff. Already, Juliana's scent was twining with his pack's. That pleased him, even if Bastien's contribution to the perfume made his hackles rise.

His nose informed him that Juliana had washed in the chamber of the hot spring, with Helewis standing outside. The chamber of the cold spring, where the old mosaics ringed the walls, provided her a drink. Then she and Helewis took the opposite turning from the one that led to the solar. The hall of columns held her attention long enough that Stephen and Ingrith had a chance to join her. From there, the group proceeded down a tiled corridor. This was a seldom-traveled tunnel, low of ceiling and awkwardly round. Ulric moved through it slightly crouched, easily following their footprints in the dust. Because his power tended to repel any kind of soil, he had to be careful not to scatter the trail.

He caught up with their voices in a square storeroom. With a tightening behind his neck, he realized it was the room where Gillian stashed her best finds. Many was the night Ulric had pulled her from her treasures, urging her to join the pack. *Time to hunt,* he would say. *You will learn nothing from this rubbish.*

Four sets of eyes turned to his entry as he stepped inside. Covered in dust and cobwebs, Juliana lit up like the sun. Against her breasts, she cradled a leather volume as carefully as if it were a child.

"Look!" She bounded to her feet. "We found all these beautiful things!"

"I see," he said, happy for her enjoyment but unable to imitate her smile.

"I tried to stop her," Helewis said, her arms hugging her waist. "I told her reading was forbidden."

Stephen clucked in the manner of one who has uttered

a rebuke before. "The rules are changing," he said. "Surely this one can, too."

He turned to Ulric, a plea in his eyes. To Ulric's amazement, the pack's least inhibited member, the one who loved to show off his masculine charms, was wearing what looked like a blanket wrapped around his shoulder and waist.

"It is a plaid," Stephen informed him. "We found it in a chest. I grew tired of her"—he tipped his head at Juliana—"refusing to stare."

"I did not ask him to wear it," Juliana said. "It was entirely his idea. He claimed a woman not looking at him seemed wrong."

"I th-think it is sexy," Ingrith put in so softly Ulric had to strain to hear. "You have to imagine the dangly bits."

Overwhelmed by the chorus, Ulric rubbed the center of his forehead. Of them all, Ingrith seemed the safest to address. He noticed she had a length of sea-green silk bundled to her chest. "Your bruises are nearly gone," he observed. "Do you feel better as well?"

Her head was bowed too low for him to see her eyes. "Yes," she whispered through the flaxen curtain of her hair. "Thank you for asking."

Stephen put his arm around her shoulder, as she was clearly uncomfortable with Ulric. Before Ulric could demand to know why, Juliana spoke.

"Ingrith was wondering," she began cautiously, "would you take it amiss if she wore the dress we found?"

"Because I remembered," Ingrith explained. "When I was human, I liked to wear pretty things."

"She would not wear it all the time," Stephen assured him. "Just now and then."

"Mary in heaven," Ulric swore, "why are you all acting as if I were an ogre? Ingrith can wear whatever she pleases. Gillian——" He caught his breath at the name. "Gillian used to dress all the time."

A silence fell that none save Helewis tried to break. "I do not care what they do. *I* am not wearing clothes."

"Good." Ulric rubbed his brow again. "I would hate to think we were turning into Eden after the fall."

"I know that story!" Ingrith exclaimed with a little gasp. "The nuns taught me about that."

"Nuns." Stephen wagged his brows. "I remember nuns."

Ulric closed his eyes and struggled to keep his temper under control. Juliana had been here one blessed day and she was well on her way to infecting them all with her human habits. Stephen wearing clothes . . . Ingrith recalling her mortal life . . . Ulric dared not contemplate what she might accomplish by summer's end.

Seeing his reaction, Juliana set down the book and came to his side. Like magic, his frustration faded. One of her hands nestled in his while the other stroked the length of his arm.

"It might be useful," she said, "to know your history. You would not want to be caught unawares a second time."

"But how can this help?" He waved at the jumble of chests and furniture. In one corner, a golden throne with wings for arms rested upside down on a bronze table. In the opposite corner, marble statues tumbled together like fallen knights. A collection of red and black pottery lay strewn across the floor, fighting for space with a chess set, a silver harp, and a long, rolled tapestry. This was not history; this was a mess. "These are just the belongings of dead *upyr*."

"Maybe," Juliana conceded. "But maybe they are clues. I found books underneath the piles. Nothing terribly useful as yet: a *Book of Hours,* a few of philosophy, and something that looks like a medical treatise in

French. Alas"—she shook her head mournfully—"I cannot read that tongue."

When her lashes rose again, her big, brown eyes were a little too innocent.

"No," he said firmly before she could ask. "You may dress everyone in feathers and explore to your heart's content but, by all that is holy, you are going to stay away from that Frenchman."

"But—" said Juliana, then shut her mouth. The stubborn set of her jaw told him her silence did not mean she was giving up. She must not have realized how big his concession was.

He put his hand on her shoulder and dropped his voice. "Juliana, if you will not do this out of respect for my authority, then do it for Ingrith. She feels comfortable with you now. Could that continue if you cozied up to the man who helped Gytha attack her?"

"I have no intention of cozying up to him." She jabbed her finger at his chest. "You are not fighting fair to bring Ingrith into this."

Though he knew she had the right of it, he felt no remorse. She was too apt to get herself into trouble, poking her nose where it did not belong. "Promise you will keep your distance from Bastien."

A flush he found distractingly attractive washed her cheeks. "I will not make a promise I am not positive I can keep."

"Damn it—"

"You do not give your word lightly. Why should I?"

"I never asked you to give it lightly. I simply want you to give it."

His voice had risen sharply enough that he knew the others could hear. Of course, with ears such as his kind possessed, they had probably heard it all. When Juliana splayed her hand gently across his chest, he tried to resist its soothing allure. In just this manner, he imagined her trying to get around her father.

"I am not flirting with him," she said calmly. "I am trying to ferret out his secrets."

"You are trying?" he spluttered. "As in, you already have begun?"

She was toe to toe with him, her conciliatory pose forgotten. He noticed she did not deny his claim.

"You will not do what needs to be done," she said. "You think all you have to do is issue a decree, and everyone will comply."

Her defiance sent a flash of blinding red across his vision. She dared to take him to task. In front of his pack. As if she were a fishwife and he her child. All the days of holding back dissolved in one instant. He clenched his hands and felt the hair on his body prick up with rage.

To hell with his promise. He could not allow this. For her own good, he would make her behave. The air thickened and his face grew unnaturally hot. He was dimly aware of the others drawing back at his swelling power.

Let them, he thought. Let them remember who is their king.

"I will show you an order," he said with a warning growl.

"As you please," Juliana snapped back, "but if you thrall me against my will, you will prove your word is worthless."

She was trembling hard, but she was not backing down. He damned the fact that he could not hit her, a human and a female. Then he damned the fact that she was counting on his restraint. His arm muscle was so cramped, he almost could not relax it.

He blew out a long, slow breath before hearing Ingrith whimper. He turned to find her curled into a ball at Stephen's feet. Stephen looked as if he longed to join her. By the skin of his teeth, the younger wolf managed to crouch beside his lover and pat her back. Ulric cursed the picture they made. Was everyone convinced he had lost all control?

With an effort, he swallowed back his vexation.

"I am not angry at you," he said, kneeling down to put his hand behind Ingrith's neck. To his relief, she did not flinch.

"You m-must not hurt Juliana," Ingrith said through chattering teeth. "She is only a human."

Ulric's brows rose at this response, but he found himself oddly touched. He rubbed the knots in Ingrith's back. "I shall not hurt her," he said, then added dryly, "as Juliana knows very well."

"It is true." Juliana stepped to his side. "Ulric would never hurt anyone who could not fight back."

Ingrith lifted her beautiful, tearstained face. The tinge of pink to her whiteness made her look even more lovely. With one slender hand she dashed a last tear away. "I am sorry, Ulric. I did not mean to be a goose. It is just, I am not used to seeing you as you were last night. Oh, I know you had to do it. Violence was the only way B-Bastien would back down. If you had not acted swiftly, there would have been more bloodshed."

"I am glad someone knows that," Ulric said.

"We all know it." Stephen met his eyes head-on, the gratitude in them raw. "Your coming back put things right."

Ulric wished he believed that. Too tired to argue, he rose and put out his arms.

"Give me the books," he said to Juliana, who responded by biting her lip. "I am not going to destroy them, merely carry them to my room. If you are going to read these texts, at least you will not have to sneak away."

She piled them reluctantly into his hold, as if afraid he would change his mind. In truth, Ulric was tempted. This, after all, was how matters first went awry with Gillian. In the end, she had chosen her love of learning over her love of him.

I must not make the same mistakes, he told himself. I must not make Juliana choose. He had to have faith that if he let her sate her curiosity, she would not run away.

❦

The sight of Gytha blocking the tunnel up ahead stopped Juliana in her tracks.

"Well, well," the haughty *upyr* said. "Look who has turned packhorse."

The others had stopped when Juliana did, but Gytha's scorn was directed toward Helewis. Deeply offended by the sight of her pack leader carrying Juliana's books, she had begged him to let her take them, thus earning Gytha's contempt. With her hands on her hips and her lip curled in a sneer, Gytha's wolf nature shone bright. Even in human form, her rough black hair and lean physique were those of a huntress. From the arrogance of her pose, Juliana inferred that Ulric had not imposed her punishment yet.

Gytha seemed to have no idea that her present behavior might be deciding how it was announced.

"I am glad you are here," Ulric said in his coolest manner. "You have saved me a trip to inform you of your penance."

"We should leave," said Stephen, edging away nervously.

Ulric stopped him by lifting a finger. "Stay where you are, Stephen. This concerns everyone." He circled Gytha until he stood behind her, a position that must have made her feel vulnerable. Though she refused to turn, she grew noticeably tense. Ulric waited until a muscle ticked in her neck.

"Gytha is to be shunned," he said to the others. "For a fortnight, none of us shall speak to her or communicate in any way. When the fortnight ends, so does her punishment—on one condition. Ingrith must have gotten over her fear. If she has not, the sentence will continue. So you see, Gytha, you should endeavor not to intimidate your sister wolf."

"Oh!" said Ingrith, a soft, involuntary sound.

When she heard it, Gytha's gape of astonishment turned to mockery. "Poor wittle Ingrith. Is she afraid?"

As threats went, it was not much to speak of, but Ingrith shrank back against Stephen.

"Leave her alone," said Bastien, coming up the tunnel behind Ulric. "Nothing can be gained by terrorizing Ingrith."

"Fine," said Gytha, lashing out to grab Helewis by the hair. "Maybe I should terrorize this idiot instead."

The books Helewis had fought to carry tumbled to the floor just as Ulric caught her attacker around the neck. Gytha screamed with fury and kicked backward at Ulric's shins. They fell and wrestled with Gytha still clutching Helewis's thick red hair. Back and forth the two of them rolled with Helewis trying fruitlessly to escape.

Fight, Juliana mouthed, but for her own sake Helewis would not.

"Hey!" was all she said as Ulric smashed Gytha against the wall.

Gytha swung Helewis between her and Ulric's next rush. He snarled and checked and turned into a blur of motion. Juliana presumed he was changing, but he was simply moving too fast for her human eyes. He grabbed Gytha's ankles, yanked both out from under her, then pinned her neck to the floor.

Gytha's face filled with the faint rose-pink that served the *upyr* as flush. Ulric's forearm and weight were cutting off her air.

"Ow," said Helewis, her head having hit the stone.

Realizing Gytha would rather choke to death than let

go of Helewis's hair, Bastien forcibly unclenched her fingers to set the other female free. This defection drove Gytha so wild she thrashed and wailed like one possessed. Finally, Ulric slapped her to silence.

The imprint of his hand remained on her cheek.

"I will beat you if I must," he said, "but it will not exempt you from my decree."

"I believe I will save the pleasure of being beaten for another day," Gytha rasped from her breathless sprawl. "I know how much you like it rough."

Ulric pushed away in disgust, but Juliana perceived her barb had struck home. "Take your punishment like a wolf," he said, looking down at her where she lay, "not like a coward."

He walked by her without a word, and Juliana knew the shunning had begun. They all filed past her one by one, with Bastien standing as a shield between his lover and the line. Ingrith followed Juliana closely enough that she risked trodding on her heels.

"Traitor," Gytha hissed when Bastien turned to go.

Juliana's ears must have been sharper than she thought because she heard his apology.

"I am sorry," he said under his breath. "I need this haven more than you know."

Gytha's reaction posed no challenge to anyone's ears. Her curses followed them down the passageway. "Take heed, king," she shouted to Ulric. "Bastien is more than ready to rule through a queen. If you choose another, he will steal yours!"

Ulric's jaw was tight, his golden brows glowering. They did not lighten when Juliana reached for his hand.

~

"There must be a desk you can read on," Ulric said, "somewhere in that pile of castaways."

Having little furniture had obliged him to set her books

on his one unbroken stool. They looked odd there, like a tower about to fall.

"You need a wall hanging, too," he added, "one you select yourself. Humans like those, do they not? It will give you something to rest your eyes upon when they are tired."

Juliana came up behind him, sliding her arms around his waist and kissing his nape above her locket's chain. Ulric closed his eyes, his fingers resting lightly on the leather binding of the topmost book. Jewels were set into its cover, as smooth as river stones.

"I am not interested in Bastien," she said, her mouth brushing his skin through his hair, "except as an object of inquiry. You are the one I care about."

For now, he thought, dismayed that his jealousy was this transparent. But any *upyr* might attract her with time. If that were true, he needed to know—little though he would enjoy it.

"What about you?" she said, her breath finding a ticklish spot beneath his ear.

"Me?"

"And Gytha."

"There is no me and Gytha. She has never shared my bed."

Juliana snorted softly in disbelief.

"It is true. I know she is beautiful and wild, but she is far too troublesome."

"Well." Juliana's chuckle warmed his back. "It is good to know I am less trouble than someone."

Ulric turned and took her in his arms. "You are good trouble, the kind of trouble I desire."

"I am glad. I like your kind of trouble, too."

Ulric did not think he was trouble but held his tongue. He enjoyed the way she leaned back trustingly in his hold, the way her eyes caught the light as she clasped his neck. For one sweet moment, they simply smiled in accord.

"Will you hunt tonight?" she asked.

"We should. Working together will help heal what happened in my absence. Gytha will have to be excluded. Hunting without being able to communicate would not work."

"You can watch how Bastien behaves."

"Yes." Ulric scratched the side of his jaw. "That had occurred to me. It is difficult to hide one's nature when in wolf form. Cowards show, and bullies, and those who have no patience."

"You have patience," she said, "even if you lose it now and then."

He did not know what to make of her compliment. It pleased him, but also caused him to feel exposed. She had seen something inside him he had not expected. Unable to answer, he spread his hands behind her shoulder blades.

"Bar the door while I am gone. I do not expect problems, but just in case."

"I will," she promised and kissed his chin where Gytha's elbow had left a bruise. "Ulric?"

"Yes, Juliana?"

"I was wondering . . . Do you read at all?"

He sighed. "I can pick out a few letters, but no more. I do not believe I learned as a mortal."

"But if I showed you a word, you would remember it. *Upyr* are quick-witted, yes? You could learn to read that way."

"I suppose I could—if it means that much to you."

"I was thinking it would be useful if all of you could read a prayer or two. In a pinch, it might convince a human you are not ungodly."

Her suggestion took him by surprise. He opened his mouth to explain that they did not mingle with mortal kind, but that was not as true as it had once been. He had found a reason to break Auriclus's rules, and up till then he had been more dutiful than most. He could not guarantee no other *upyr* would disobey.

As to that, if Ulric had known more of mortals and their ways, perhaps he would not have left signs of himself in Bridesmere.

Mulling this over, he rubbed a lock of Juliana's hair between his finger and thumb. She had recognized what he was without being told, proof that stories of his kind were circulating. If she had taught him anything, it was that humans loved unearthing secrets. Even if every *upyr* in the isles stayed where they were, mortals like those sons of Gideon Drake might decide to pursue them. Capable though Ulric was, he could not subdue them all.

Maybe what she proposed was wise.

"I will think on it," he said finally.

"Good," she answered with a brilliant smile. "I want you and your pack to stay safe."

She seemed to believe his promise to consider her request was the same as him saying "yes."

Chapter 12

⮞⮜

Over the course of the next sennight, Juliana found many books hidden in the cave. Fascinating though they were, none contained what she was seeking. Without exception, they were about and by humans, from religious texts to pagan philosophers she would never have been exposed to as a respectable merchant's daughter—even if she had been able to read Greek. Juliana had been taught only those languages that were useful: the Latin and English required to help her father in his trade. The scholars of her world would have given their eyeteeth to peruse these pages for a single day. Sadly, Juliana mainly felt irked.

She wanted to know the origins of the *upyr* or, failing that, the secret of their power.

"There is nothing there," Helewis sighed gustily as Juliana opened yet another text.

Along with Stephen and Ingrith, Juliana's usual companions, they sat in a cavernous hall of red porphyry columns. The scale of the construction dwarfed them, as if this room had been designed for giants—the how and why of it another mystery for her list.

In the murky shadows of the coffered ceiling, gold and crystal chandeliers glinted like leviathans. The two near the dais still functioned, operating—apparently—on the same principles as Ulric's lamp. No candles were needed to create the soft golden glow. One simply palmed the crystal sphere that perched in the sconce beside the doorway and they sprang to life.

They did not, however, provide enough light for reading. For that, Juliana relied on a collection of ordinary oil lamps. Though rendered easier to keep lit by the *upyr's* influence, their illumination stretched no more than halfway up the forest of smooth red stone.

She was not certain what she would do when the oil they had found ran out. Regardless of Ulric's concessions, she could not imagine him granting permission to purchase more.

Untroubled by such concerns, Stephen, who had gallantly provided the women with cushions, was looking smug because he had found a cache of books in a hollow beneath a floor tile.

Prying it up had allowed him to show off his muscles.

As always, Ingrith snuggled beside him, dressed like a Roman maiden in her reclaimed gown. She was laboriously puzzling through the prayers in a *Book of Hours*. Ever since Ulric had given his consent, she had thrown herself into trying to read. She, it seemed, had learned the skill as a mortal, taught by the nuns with whom she had resided as a young widow.

Less enthused by the lifting of Auriclus's ban, Stephen entertained himself by playing with Ingrith's hair. Helewis refused to consider reading at all, devoting herself instead to her new position as Juliana's guard. Though Juliana could scarcely wash her hands without Helewis's attendance, she did not object. In his own devious way, Ulric had done what she asked.

"What I want to know," Juliana said into the echoing space, "is who collected these books in the first place."

Ingrith's lips stopped sounding out words. "That is easy. They were brought here by Lucius."

Her fellow *upyr* stared at her, causing her to shrink back.

"Well, it stands to reason," she said defensively. "Lucius was always going off without warning, whether Ulric approved or not. Plus, these books smell like him."

"Lucius does not have a smell," Stephen declared with great assurance.

"Yes, he does. He smells like snow, or something like snow, but I am certain he has a scent."

Ingrith was so offended by her lover's contradiction that she forgot to hide behind her hair. Juliana smiled to see it. Ingrith was getting stronger.

"Maybe Stephen's nose is only good for sniffing women," Helewis said in a rare jest.

"Did *you* smell him?" Stephen demanded.

Helewis shrugged her strong shoulders. "I am willing to admit Ingrith's nose is better than mine."

Before the pair could get into a scuffle, Juliana spoke. "Lucius is the *upyr* who turned out to be an elder?"

"Yes," Ingrith confirmed, "though I would not have guessed it. While he was living with us, he never did anything elder-ly."

"He was a good tracker," Stephen put in, scratching his chest where it was draped by the woollen plaid.

"Yes," Ingrith said, "but he did not have special powers. We never saw him turn into a mist, or order an *upyr* to stop breathing with just his mind. If he were old enough to be an elder, he ought to have had those gifts or others like them. Most of all, he did not know the secret of the change."

"You have no proof of that," said Helewis.

"But he never made any children."

"Maybe he made them and forgot, just like you forgot how to read." Helewis nodded to herself as if she liked this theory. It was the first time Juliana could remember hearing her think for herself.

"What I cannot believe," Stephen said, stretching out his legs the better to let the women admire them, "is that Gillian was an elder. She definitely was a young *upyr*."

Ingrith gave her partner a jab.

"What?" said Stephen, looking at her stupidly.

"It is all right," Juliana said. "I know Ulric was in love with her."

"Crazy in love." Stephen nodded emphatically. "Obsessed. Besotted. From the moment she joined the pack. Sometimes I thought if she did not return his feelings, he would go mad."

"Stephen!" Ingrith hissed under her breath.

"The pack leader is much calmer with you," Stephen said to Juliana as if that would undo the harm. "Barely crazy at all."

This time Ingrith responded by whacking him behind the head. Though Juliana laughed, her eyes were dangerously hot. She dared not blink for fear they would spill over. Knowing the man she loved had once loved another was different from hearing he had been "crazier" about Gillian.

As luck would have it, Ulric chose that moment to appear. Juliana pretended the text she held in her lap was infinitely engrossing. Better that than to have him know how close she was to tears.

He wears my locket, she told herself. That has to mean something.

"So," said Ulric, rubbing his hands together, "the deer are grazing at Loch Monar. Who is ready for a hunt?"

"Not tonight," Stephen groaned. "It was raining when we woke and Juliana promised us a story."

"A real one," Ingrith said, "with fighting and blood:"

Juliana could not help herself. She looked up to see Ulric's reaction.

"A story," he repeated, dragging his thick gold hair back along his head. Though the gesture did lovely things to his chest, she could tell the pack's reluctance took him aback.

As usual, Helewis disapproved of anything their leader misliked. "You can hear a story *after* you hunt," she said to Stephen repressively.

"Oh," said Stephen, abruptly realizing how he had just behaved. "After we hunt. Of course that would be best. We would not want to hear about blood until we have had some."

"No," Ulric wryly agreed. "That would be most distracting." His humor mended if not restored, he bent to kiss Juliana's cheek. "Will you be all right on your own? I thought we would try taking Gytha with us tonight. She is getting a little too malcontent for my taste."

Juliana concurred with that. Ever since the pack had stopped talking to her, Gytha had been stumping around like a baited bear. Given her surly mood, Juliana was virtually certain she and Bastien no longer shared a bed—though, come to think of it, she had spotted more bite marks on his neck.

But what the pair were or were not doing was their concern. She merely hoped the punishment she had suggested was not ill-conceived. Maybe Ulric did know his people best. Maybe she had blundered. The only promising sign was that Gytha had not attacked anyone in days.

"I will be fine," she said to Ulric. "I shall take these new books to your room."

"Meet us later," he suggested, his voice gentle and warm. "If the rain lets up, you can cook your own meal outside."

"I would like that," she said and received a second kiss as reward.

"Woo-woo," Stephen hooted, making her blush.

It was after the foursome left that something Ingrith said finally sank in. According to her, only elders could change humans into *upyr*. Because Ulric was not an elder, that meant he could not change her. Juliana thought back to his original oath. *I will see that you share my powers,* was what he said: misleading, but not a lie. A matter of pride, she suspected, especially if his precious Gillian had mastered that gift.

What mattered to her was not his dissembling. Ulric had more than enough strength for her. What bothered Juliana was that, if she became *upyr,* she would have to trust her transformation to a stranger.

Possibly even a stranger like Gillian.

Juliana should have guessed none of the pack would carry clothes to a hunt—whatever their recent habits. Once again, she was surrounded by stunning, naked *upyr*. Obviously pleased by their successful chase, the six immortals sprawled about the fire Ulric had built in a clearing not too far from the foot of the cliff. The light the *upyr* gave off was brighter than both fire and moon, the result—she assumed—of being well fed. Childish though it might be, she took pride in the fact that Ulric was the most luminous. Even Bastien's shine could not compare.

Still being shunned, Gytha lay on her back, staring at the stars with her head pillowed on her hands, slightly outside the others' circle. She had given up on talking, no doubt tired of being ignored, though being included in the hunt had clearly calmed her. To her left, but not close, was Bastien. He had positioned himself among the rest, a move the others undercut by leaving extra space between him and them. Ulric and Helewis sat on either side of Juliana, after which came Stephen and Ingrith. They lay on their bellies, their chins on their forearms, their fingers playing idly—and identically—with the grass. Because Gytha and Bastien were present, Ingrith occasionally hid her face on Stephen's smoothly muscled back. Aside from this, she seemed well.

Stephen, Juliana noticed, had taken to wearing the front of his long curly hair in braids, like a Celtic warrior of old. She wondered if a beaver sporran was likely to be next.

Smiling to herself, she leaned back against a tree, her stomach full, her mood content. An enclosure of pines rose around them, as majestic in their way as the columns in Ulric's hall. Despite the varied tensions in the pack, despite their very foreign appearance, she experienced an unexpected and unfamiliar sense of family. In her home, they had never been more than three.

The emotion was a delicate bubble. How miraculous that she sat among these strange and wondrous people, a race so mysterious that they had barely entered into myth! With her, they shared their natural selves. With her, they shared their squabbles.

She could not deny that felt like a privilege.

"You are an excellent cook," Bastien said, his back resting on a rock, his tongue dragging savoringly across his teeth. Like the rest—excepting Gytha—he had changed into his beast form to taste her roast venison. Though his fellow wolves had snapped back the treat with apparent enjoyment, Bastien was the only one to compliment her skill.

Something about his tone, or mayhap his accent, made the words sound more like a seduction than a compliment.

Lounging there in the firelight, with his sly green eyes and his half-curled smile, Juliana could believe Gytha's accusations. Bastien's nakedness seemed different, too, as if it were a challenge rather than a lack of clothes. Though one upbent knee covered what Ingrith had called his dangly bits, Juliana found it impossible to look directly his way.

Sensitive to her discomfort, Ulric laid his palm on her leg. His hand was pale and strong, his fingers curled protectively around her thigh. The warmth they sent sliding through her put her even less at ease. How could it do otherwise, when every nose in the place would know the instant she grew aroused?

At the very thought of it, her ears turned hot.

"That deer you caught was fat and tender," she said in hope of furnishing a distraction. "A child could not have ruined it."

"Not true," Helewis protested. "My . . . my father was cook to a Norman lord. I never saw him serve a better roast—fancier, but not better."

Juliana suspected this was an exaggeration. Even with the spices she and Ulric had acquired in Dunburn, her skills were only average. Apparently, Helewis felt compelled to defend her charge even from herself.

Bastien found a different significance in Helewis's words. "Interesting," he said, switching the leg he had raised. "A human comes among you and you all begin recalling your mortal past."

"Unl-like you," Ingrith stammered, her face tucked close to Stephen's back, "who do not speak of your past at all."

"Ha!" barked Gytha, but everyone had grown so used to paying her no mind, they did not jump.

Equally unmoved, Bastien leaned forward to rest his chin on his knee. His fingers fanned up and down his shin. "If you asked me, sweet Ingrith, I would bare all."

This time there could be no doubt of the Frenchman's suggestive intent. Juliana wondered if he hoped to sway the pack one female at a time. Possibly thinking along the same lines, Stephen bristled and bared his teeth. Oddly enough, Ingrith seemed unruffled.

"No fighting," Juliana ordered, "or I will not tell my story."

"He is frightening her," Stephen accused in a rumble considerably lower than his normal tone.

"Not as much as you would like," Helewis muttered beneath her breath.

Bastien laughed and lifted his hands. "Forgive me," he said with a beguiling smile. "Your Ingrith is so charming I could not resist. But, please, Mistress Juliana, do commence your tale. I confess I await it with bated breath."

At this, Ulric moved his hand from Juliana's leg to drape her back. The hold pulled her gently against his side.

She was both flattered and bemused. Meeting other *upyr,* the plainest of whom were impossibly lovely, made her realize her appeal for Ulric could not be her looks. *I taste better than they do,* she mused with a mental eye roll. Even as she had the thought, she knew the reasons ran deeper. Ulric might not love her the way he loved Gillian, but he cared for her very much.

Possessiveness aside, the pack leader seemed content to leave his supposed rival in one piece. "Yes," he said somewhat grimly, "we all are panting to hear."

⟨≈⟩

Ulric's words were not a lie. Though the changes his pack had been going through strained his patience, he, too, enjoyed a sensation of shrugging off rusty chains. Gillian and Lucius's discovery of their gifts had disrupted more than his existence. With four elders instead of two, the balance of power among the *upyr* was turned on its head. No one of them could dictate to his or her inferiors as before. Few might know it yet, but tonight the elders' children had a choice of allegiances.

If the world was ripe for changes, Ulric saw no reason why some of them could not be pleasurable.

Pushing off a lingering scrap of guilt for ignoring the edicts of his sire, he stroked Juliana's softly waving hair. She was pulling her much-treasured volume of stories into her lap, opening its parchment pages to a green ribbon. As if reaching through the ink to touch her mother, her fingertips stroked a picture of a huge green giant on a huge green horse, every fearsome detail lovingly drawn. Ulric wished he could kiss away the yearning he saw in her face.

Juliana's mother had indeed liked monsters.

Looking at her daughter, he was struck by what a dear and serious person his love could be, studying his pack with her wide, brown eyes, adding up their foibles like a merchant with a sack of coin. Apart from a moment or two of shock, she had never once turned away, requiting what must have seemed like eccentricities with fondness.

Ulric's sole regret was that fondness would never be enough for him.

But Juliana was ready to begin. He knew that when she cleared the wistfulness from her throat.

"This story," she said, "which I heard from a wandering bard, is the tale of Sir Gawain and the dread Green Knight, the most ferocious, most underhanded, most deathly foe King Arthur's court had ever seen."

This was enough to make Ingrith gasp.

"No, no," she said when Juliana paused. "Please go on. I can tell it will be exciting."

"Yes," Stephen insisted. "Ingrith is fine."

"Goodness," Juliana laughed. "I see I shall not have cause to complain about my audience."

In truth she did not. For good or ill, the pack had been deprived of human stories for centuries. Hunting and eating, fighting and making love had comprised their lives. As a result, not a one of them could resist drawing closer. Bastien's sophistication, Gytha's resentment, even Helewis's love of rules were swept away. Like children,

they listened with open mouths and shining eyes as
Juliana described the giant's uninvited entrance into King
Arthur's New Year's feast.

"The knight who rode into the hall was green," she said,
"from head to toe, as was his charger. Together they were
so much larger than normal beings that the knight had to
duck his head to keep his helm from bumping the roof
beams. The axe he carried stretched the length of a tall
man's arm along its hairsplitting blade. Arthur's famous
knights, who had gathered for the celebration, knew at
once that the stranger was magical. Though they had
fought enchanted creatures before, I would be lying if I
claimed none of them quailed.

" 'Good eve, stranger,' said Arthur, for the king was gracious no matter what. 'How may we serve you this blessed
day?'

" 'I have heard tales of your court,' said the big green
knight, 'that those who follow you are the bravest men in
the land. I admit I cannot credit it myself, but because I
love nothing better than a knock-down, bloody fight, I
thought I would come to you to issue my challenge.
Perhaps, for once, I shall meet my match.'

" 'What challenge would that be?' Arthur politely asked,
clenching his teeth just a bit at the Green Knight's cheek.
Giant or not, the knights at his table were all heroes!

" 'The challenge is this,' said the Green Knight.
'Whichever of your men has the stones to accept shall
take this axe I carry and strike a single blow to my neck.
Should I survive, one year from hence I will smite him
once, and only once, in return.'

"Arthur's men exchanged glances across the remnants
of the feast. One blow from this giant would mean their
deaths. Ashamed of his followers' silence, Arthur leapt
up from his seat beside Guenevere.

" 'I accept your challenge,' he declared, though he was
not a young and beardless champion anymore.

"With a mocking smile, the giant handed him the axe. The haft alone was so weighty, Arthur could barely lift the blade from the floor. To make matters worse, the Green Knight refused to bend. In his attempts to reach the spot prescribed for the blow, Arthur was forced to jump and huff and swing himself clear off his feet.

"Sad as I am to say it, the great King Arthur appeared a fool.

" 'My liege!' exclaimed Gawain, who was Arthur's favorite nephew. "You must not risk yourself in this manner. Allow me, who will not be as sorely missed, to accept the challenge in your stead.'

"To everyone's surprise, the Green Knight agreed to the substitution. Indeed, there were those who said he seemed secretly pleased. Still tottering, the winded Arthur handed the giant's axe to Gawain."

"And could he lift it?" Stephen asked breathlessly.

"He could," Juliana said, "though the effort did make sweat spring out on his noble brow. Even more astounding, the Green Knight, after shamelessly teasing Arthur, went down on one knee so Gawain could strike his neck without leaping up."

"He did not kill the giant!" protested Helewis.

Ulric feared her outburst might nettle Juliana; Gawain was obviously the hero of this human tale. To his relief, Juliana broke into a wolfish grin.

"Gawain struck off his hideous head!" she crowed, then lifted her hands as Helewis groaned. "Mind you, the Green Knight did not die. Instead, gushing gouts of grass-green blood, his decapitated torso stood, walked across the hall to where his head had rolled beneath a bench, and picked it up by the hair. When he mounted his huge green warhorse, he tucked the gory trophy beneath his arm—presumably face forward, in order to see where he was going."

"Yay," said Helewis.

"Yay, indeed," said Juliana, clearly amused. "But not such happy tidings for Gawain. According to the bargain he had struck, one twelvemonth from that day, Gawain would have to let the giant smite him in return. Everyone in the hall knew such a blow would spell the young man's doom. 'For honor's sake,' the giant reminded as he spurred his horse around with a clatter, 'you must not fail to seek me out.'"

"Gawain had to go to him?" Bastien shook his head in disbelief. In Gawain's place, Ulric suspected Bastien would have stayed home.

"Yes," Juliana said, "and it would not be easy to find the Green Knight again. It was proof of Gawain's courage that he would overcome many perils just to face his demise."

"Ooh, perils," Ingrith said with a shiver of pure enjoyment. "Tell us about those."

Juliana bent confidingly across her book. "The year was drawing to a close," she said, "when Gawain at last departed on his quest. The dangerous wilderness of Wirral was in his path and many monsters opposed him—not to mention the hardships of a harsh winter."

As she described these obstacles, Ulric found himself caught up in the adventure, his blood quickening in his veins just as it did when he stalked prey. Gawain's terrors and triumphs became his own. When Gawain stabbed a dragon or wrestled a raging troll, Ulric's muscles tightened in sympathy.

"Finally," Juliana continued, "on Christmas Eve, exhausted by his journey, Gawain reached a fabulous castle perched on a lonely rock. The lord of this residence was nearly as gracious as Arthur. Inviting Gawain to stay, he assured the doughty knight that the Green Chapel, where he had promised to meet his foe, was very near. His lady wife seconded her husband's suit. Gladly, Gawain agreed to accept their hospitality until the appointed day.

"Little did Gawain suspect that this seeming stroke of luck would prove his greatest trial. The lady of the castle, though married in the eyes of God, had her eye upon Gawain. His reputation as a man of matchless vigor with the ladies went before him. Consequently, she vowed to try him for herself. No ploy was too bold for this wandering wife. Even into his private bedchamber she crept, then had the nerve to berate him for allowing her to steal in. He was, she claimed, too sound a sleeper to be a famous warrior."

"He had to give in then," Stephen said waggishly.

"He did not," answered Juliana, "for that would have stained both the lady's honor and his own. Instead, he put her off with flattering, golden words, claiming he did not deserve to touch one inch of her glorious person and that his dearest desire was only to be her knight."

"Huh," said Stephen, frowning in disappointment.

Soon, though, he was chuckling at Gawain's ingeniousness. The lord of the castle made a bargain with his guest. Each would spend the day hunting on their own, then trade each other for their best prize.

"Imagine the lord's amazement when he handed Gawain a stag and received but a kiss from his guest in return."

"His lady's kiss," Ingrith guessed, her eyes shining with amusement.

"None other's," Juliana said, and described how the lady—frustrated in her attempts to seduce the great Gawain—insisted that he accept a magic girdle, cleverly fashioned of green silk, which would prevent its wearer from being slain.

"That is cheating," Helewis huffed, obviously looking ahead to Gawain's battle with the Green Knight.

"Perhaps," said Juliana. "It certainly was not honorable of Sir Gawain to withhold the girdle when he and the castle's lord traded prizes at day's end."

"Withholding the prize was smart," Bastien objected. "Gawain knew the Green Knight had special powers. If that giant lopped off his head, Gawain could not walk away."

"That is true," said Juliana. "If Gawain resorted to magic tricks, one could argue he was only leveling the field."

From the way Bastien's mouth dropped open and then snapped shut, Ulric knew the Frenchman had betrayed himself in some way. One look at Juliana's small, satisfied smile made him glad she was not spying on him.

"The fight," Stephen demanded. "Surely it is time for that!"

"Ah, yes," said Juliana, turning the page and grinning all around, "the long-anticipated date with destiny. As you might imagine, Arthur's nephew awoke on the awful day with a heavy heart. Could the girdle save him, or was this to be the end of his short life? The Green Knight was magical himself. Perhaps the girdle would have no effect. Despite his fears, Gawain pulled on his armor, called for his horse, and rode to the Green Chapel.

"The giant awaited with his terrible four-foot axe, whose edge he teasingly tested with his big green thumb. 'You have come after all then,' he said derisively. 'On your knees, knight, and accept your just desserts, as I accepted mine in your uncle's court.'

"'As God wills,' said Gawain, and humbly obeyed. Alas, the giant had not tired of playing games. He pretended to swing at the good knight's neck, then mocked him when he flinched. 'You are not the Gawain whose fame all men admire. That Gawain would not have shrunk from my blow.' Gawain swore he would not do so again and set himself even more determinedly to meet his end.

"The Green Knight gathered his strength and swung, this time aiming true. For all his power, the blade merely nicked Gawain's neck and bounced away. Amazed, the giant tried to strike him again. Seeing his blood sprinkling the chapel floor, Gawain leapt up and sprang away. 'Enough!' he cried, 'I have kept the terms of our agreement, which was only for a single blow. You may not assault me more!'

" 'May I not?' said the giant. 'What of the assault I owe you for accepting kisses from my wife? What of the magic garter you took from her and failed to give back to me? Yes, Gawain'—the giant nodded at his growing horror—'I know about your deception. In addition to this monstrous form you see me wear, I am also lord of yon castle. I sent my wife to woo you as a test.'

"Mortified, Gawain covered his face, cursing his own cowardice and deceit. 'I confess,' he bemoaned to the giant lord. 'Requite my sins as you see fit.'

"At this the Green Knight laughed kindly. 'You have repaid your folly with your fear,' he said, 'and acted more honorably than most men. Most important, I can see your remorse is true. Accept my girdle as a reminder of our contest and go in peace to be wiser from now on.'

"This Gawain did, thereafter wearing the belt as a baldric across his chest, and confessing to whomever asked what faults it was meant to remind him of. So admired was he for this meekness that all Arthur's knights took to donning green sashes as a sign of their respect for him."

Thus saying, Juliana closed her book. For a moment, the pack was quiet. Ingrith was the first to release her breath. "That was wonderful," she sighed.

"Wonderful?" Stephen exclaimed, sitting up to stare. "How can it be wonderful when Gawain is wallowing in guilt and the giant was twice as dishonest as he? Plus, I refuse to believe that lady tried to seduce Gawain just because her husband told her to. If Gawain had given in, you can bet your sweet arse she would have enjoyed herself."

Helewis and Ingrith both snorted at this. Ignoring them, Stephen turned to Juliana and addressed her sternly. "Please admit you told the story wrong."

Juliana pursed her lips to hide her amusement and innocently spread her hands. "I read the words that were on the page, which I wrote down as the bard told them."

"Are you certain?" Stephen pressed. "Maybe you got some of them confused."

"Of course she did not," said Helewis. "Juliana reads very well."

"If you knew how to read," said Juliana, "you could confirm the words for yourself. In fact"—she paused to let her grin break free—"if you learned your letters, you could rewrite the story as you pleased."

Stephen narrowed his eyes, abruptly aware that he had stepped into a trap. "I will do it," he declared. "You can start teaching me tomorrow."

"Say 'please,'" Ingrith reminded laughingly.

"Please," Stephen said, then added a wolfish whine.

"You are a silly man," said Juliana, beaming as if she thought him quite wonderful. "But it would be my honor to help you learn."

She seemed so pleased with his brother wolf that Ulric felt compelled to squeeze her hand. The brilliant smile she turned on him did much toward easing his jealousy—though it could not erase it completely. That undertaking he would have to handle on his own.

Chapter 13

"I wish to speak with you," Ulric said, nodding for Stephen to walk beside him. The ground was damp from the earlier rain, the pine needles matted beneath their feet. Above them, beadlike drops of water plopped from the boughs.

Beyond these tiny noises, the life of the forest pulsed: things that flew and things that crawled, things that slept and things that hunted the dark like them. Ulric could even sense, like a distant ribbon of force, the protective barrier around his land, brought to life by Juliana's blood. *This is home,* said his heart. *This is safety.* For the first time, he really felt as if he were back. He did not worry that Gytha and Bastien had slipped away. For now, his world was in balance.

Ingrith, Helewis, and Juliana walked ahead of them on the path, their shoulders bumping as they whispered to one another and laughed as women have since the world was made. From Stephen's wistful expression, he would far rather be with them.

His gaze remained on Ingrith, whose steps were almost a prance. The only sign of her lingering trepidation was how close she stayed to the two females.

"It is funny how she trusts them to protect her," Stephen mused, "particularly Juliana. I am not sure what Ingrith expects a human to do if she is attacked."

"Talk her way around the threat," Ulric suggested humorously. "Or else convince Helewis she really is fierce enough to fight."

"I would not put either past her. Your Juliana has an odd assortment of gifts." With a smile as fond as Ulric's, Stephen shoved his side braids behind his ears. "Her presence makes me wonder who we all used to be when we were human. My guess for Gytha is that she was the wife of a marauding Viking warrior."

"Not a warrior herself?" Ulric said, supposing there must have been a few among the fairer sex.

"Nay. No woman gets that snappish except as a wife." Stephen grinned, baring teeth still sharp from the excitement of Juliana's story. Then he sobered. "Her husband probably beat her, come to think of it. Taught her only bullies were safe from harm."

"Or maybe she beat him," Ulric said, surprised to discover how easy it was to speculate. "Maybe her Viking spouse never rose to the heights her ambition craved."

"Mm," said Stephen, silent for a few more strides. "What was it you wanted to speak to me about?"

Now that they had come to it, Ulric found himself unable to answer as he had meant, shamed from it by Stephen's trust. How could he admit he wanted Stephen to try to seduce his lover, for no better reason than to prove she could not be glamoured by other *upyr?* How could he explain he wanted Stephen to do it because

Bastien, who was already making the attempt, did not so easily obey his rule? Scorn would be the least of the responses to which Stephen would be entitled.

Were Ulric in his position, he would have been outraged. The mere thought of the plan was childish, no better than that giant pandering his wife. Worse, given the timing, it was cruel. True, Ingrith had seen Stephen cast his lures at other women, but Ingrith needed to feel more secure now, not less.

Stephen's next words pulled him from his thoughts. "If you are concerned about my taking lessons from Juliana . . ."

"No," Ulric said. "That is perfectly fine."

"But if you wanted to take them first . . ."

The suggestion made him blink. He had said he would learn to read if it was important to Juliana, but he had not thought the promise through. Could he learn? Should he? He shook his head to clear it. "Do not worry," he said to Stephen. "I am certain she would make time for me if I asked."

Stephen nodded and scuffed his feet. Startled by the noise, a small, brown snake arced across their path.

"She cares about you," Stephen said as if uncertain the assurance was appropriate for him to make. "I have never seen a woman look at a man the way Juliana looks at you—except for Ingrith, of course."

"Of course," Ulric said, feigning seriousness. Stephen need not have worried his words would be unwelcome. Indeed, Ulric had to struggle not to ask for more.

"If that is not the problem," Stephen said, "why did you want to speak to me?"

Ulric took one last look at Juliana laughing up ahead and cast away his plan, though not without a silent sigh. "I wanted to ask if you think Ingrith will be over her fear by the time Gytha's fortnight is up."

Stephen fingered the end of one braid in thought. "She might be, though Gytha would probably prefer that she would not. A quick recovery seems a mite insulting."

"Maybe you can convince Ingrith to counterfeit some timidity. Out of kindness."

Stephen laughed outright, causing Ingrith to turn back and wave. "That truly would drive Gytha up a tree." He wiped at his eyes, then turned. "I should thank you," he said, "for asking my opinion."

Considering what Ulric had intended to ask, he could only shrug. "You are the one who knows Ingrith best."

"Many pack leaders would not care. *You* would not have cared before you came back. I simply want to say that it feels good to be consulted." His words must have required more courage than he was used to. Stephen blew out a breath. "There. Enough womanish talk of feelings! You should tell your Juliana that even Gytha enjoyed her tale. When she thought no one was looking, I saw her mimicking the fights with her fists."

"I shall," Ulric said.

For the second time that night, he did not object to Juliana being called "his."

⁓

He was tenderness itself as he slid inside her, his eyes like molten gold in the dark. The muscles in his chest and belly shifted rhythmically as he thrust, causing her locket to swing from his neck. His palms pressed hers beside her head, trapping them gently against the furs with their fingers twined.

"You shine when you make love to me," Juliana whispered, tilting her hips up to take him deep. "It is the most beautiful sight I have ever seen."

"Is it?" His smile was oddly melancholy. Colors fluttered like butterflies through his glow. She wondered if they were the colors of sadness, and why she could see them now. On a whim, she rolled him beneath her.

"There," she said, straddling him in his bed, copying his drawn-out strokes. "Now I shall ride you."

His neck arched as she slowly sank, his lips pulling back over sharp, white teeth. "Is that what you like? Being in control?"

She bent to lick the side of his throat. "I like everything I do with you."

"Wait." His hands smoothed around her bottom to hold her in place.

"Wait?" Her body quivered at the pause. She thought he had some game in mind, but he did not.

"I need to ask you something," he said, "before dawn makes me forget. Why were you so interested in Bastien's reaction to your story?"

Juliana shoved her hair back from her face. He was hard inside her, throbbing, but he wanted to ask her about Bastien. She wondered if she would ever understand this man.

"He defended Gawain's decision to keep the magic girdle to himself," she said. "He put himself in Gawain's shoes, rather than the giant's."

"But why is that important?"

"Because Bastien used magic on Ingrith, something your branch of the *upyr* forbids. Maybe the reason he left his pack was because someone else used magic to injure him. Maybe he learned it in self-defense."

Ulric struggled up on his elbows, his hardness shifting inside her. "That is a bit of a leap."

"Is it? He said he would follow you with all his heart if you were as honorable as you claimed. Apart from flirting a little, has he caused any trouble since?"

Ulric could not say he had. "If you ask me, he has been too virtuous. The only complaint I could make is that he eats more than anyone else on hunts. But that could be because he is French. Everyone says they enjoy their meals."

"Very well. Apart from being a flirt and a glutton, you have no complaints."

"No," he admitted reluctantly.

"I do not think he lays with Gytha anymore."

"It is true they no longer carry each others' scents, but that only proves he is willing to forsake his friends."

"Maybe," she said.

He covered her hands where they were playing idly with his chest hair. "Maybe you seek excuses for him on account of his silver tongue."

"Nonsense. Your clay tongue is the only one that interests me." The hurt that flashed across his face caught her off-guard. She expected him to have more of a sense of humor. "I speak in jest," she said, lifting of his knuckles for a kiss. "Truly, Ulric, I am flattered you are jealous, but there is no need."

"I am not jealous," he denied, then frowned at her raised eyebrows. "All right then, I am. What of it? I want you to belong only to me."

His expression held more grumpiness than romance, but her heart stumbled nonetheless. When she spoke, her voice was rough. "As far as any woman can belong to any man, I belong to you."

"Do you?"

Again, his manner held a challenge, choler struggling with anxiety. She stroked his face between her palms, waiting until the crease in the center of his forehead eased.

"Yes, Ulric. You have my word."

His response was a grunt of satisfaction.

How like a man, she thought with a private smile, to demand a promise and offer none in return.

Then he surprised her, his hand smoothing down the

curve of her spine. "You have *my* word," he said, "that you are the only woman I want." He rolled them onto their sides and arched her backward to kiss her breast, his hand shaping it closer, his incisors compressing either side of the swollen tip. His lips tugged it arousingly. "The . . . only . . . one."

The only one in his reach, she could not help but think as the flicking of his tongue made her shudder down to her toes.

"I do wonder about one thing," she said with her final scrap of rational thought. "If Gytha and Bastien no longer lie together, who is biting his neck? Certainly not Ingrith, and Helewis does not seem interested."

Ulric shut her up by nipping her skin. "Bastien's neck," he growled, "is not my concern."

Juliana's hand flew to her breast. She could not say whether her shock came from the fact that he would bite her there, or the way her body melted in response. Ulric's gaze slipped to the bead of red his teeth had set free. Fascination locked it there helplessly.

"I am sorry," he said even as his tongue curled over his upper lip. "I only meant to nip you, not break the skin. I have no wish to cause you pain."

As if to contradict his words, his ribs rose and fell like a bellows. His cock was only partially inside her, but suddenly it felt twice as thick. With his eyes still on her breast, her nipple was blazing hot.

"Never mind," she said huskily, reaching for the back of his neck. "Now that you have done it, there is no reason to turn back."

He fastened onto her with a moan, pulling deeply at the tiny cut, curving his back to thrust himself inside her at the same time. As he did, Juliana clutched his shoulder with so much force, her nails drew blood.

"It is all right," he said, moving his head to nuzzle the other breast. "It is all right."

His mouth was cool, wet fire, licking her, flicking her, suckling so strongly she gasped for air. His mouth fell away when he shifted her atop him and slid his hands up her sides. As he licked the last of her from his lips, fire gleamed in the depths of his golden eyes. She felt his fingers tighten on her ribs and then release, as if he were unable to decide what he ought to do.

Juliana knew she had to move on him or scream.

"Shall I ride you again?" she whispered.

He closed his eyes, seeming wracked by exquisite pain. "Yes. You do it. Take your desire."

She placed the heels of her hands directly over his tightened nipples, then pushed up her weight. She hesitated before she let it fall. She was not certain how to take charge.

"You cannot harm me," he said. "No matter what you do, it will not hurt."

She took him at his word, putting all the strength she could stand into every motion, driving her body against him just where she wished. His hands, now warm, smoothed and caressed her breasts before sliding down to put more pressure on her pubis. Beneath his fingers, her soft flesh squeezed against his hardness, her nerves keen enough to feel every ridge and vein.

The added provocation made her bite her lip, a gesture Ulric watched hungrily. Steadied by his hold, she dared to go faster. Her thighs seemed to hum as they rose and fell. She felt as if she were flying—that powerful and free. His expression tightened and his head rolled from side to side. With a grimace, he pushed his upper body up to meet hers. His mouth nuzzled yearningly at her neck.

"I will not trap you," he murmured, which she did not understand.

She had no time to. With this much stimulation, neither took long to reach their peak, both gasping sharply as the crisis came. Ulric's arms were wonderfully tight.

Knowing she had driven him to pleasure was almost, but not quite, as nice as being overpowered by him.

Only when she snuggled down against him, when she felt sleep begin to claim her as it claimed him, did she remember she had not yet told him about Bastien's morning jaunts. She knew the confession was overdue.

Bastien was too cunning to leave to his own devices. They had to discover what he was hiding.

⌒

Ulric roused, reluctantly, to the feel of someone shaking his shoulder hard.

"Get up," Juliana urged, grabbing his wrists and hauling him to the side of his sleeping niche. "It is just about the time Bastien usually comes back. I want you to see for yourself."

She handed him a long hooded cloak and a pair of boots. Then, failing to inspire motion, she began to stuff his feet into them herself.

Too confused to resist, Ulric rubbed his palms over his face. "Juliana, I am certain the sun is up."

"If Bastien can be awake now, so can you."

"Bastien?"

"Yes." She tugged at his hand. "If you do not hurry we will miss him."

More than half asleep, he let her pull him past a blissfully slumbering Helewis and down the passage to the entry ledge. The light was misty and indirect, a haze across the shadowy impressions of the pack's footsteps. No part of Ulric wanted to go near it.

"He comes," she whispered, pulling him behind a curve of the wall. "Be sure to look at his neck."

Ulric heard nothing, smelled nothing, his senses dulled by the risen sun. Sliding into a crouch beside Juliana, he pulled his hood over his head and began to doze. A sharp pinch on his arm jerked him awake.

"Watch," she hissed. "This is important."

He watched as Bastien stepped onto the rocky lip, his body muffled from head to toe in black. Ulric's eyes widened at his appearance. Even with the protection of his clothes, the *upyr* moved more vigorously than Ulric expected, seeming drained rather than sleepy. Clearly, this was not the first time he had been out during the day. He had built up a tolerance.

As he entered the cave, Ulric threw up a hasty glamour, but Bastien did not look around. Instead, he strode swiftly down the tunnel and out of sight.

"Damn," said Juliana. "That cloak covered his neck."

"His neck?"

"Where I told you I have been seeing bite marks."

Ulric could not contain a yawn. Vaguely, he remembered her mentioning this the night before. "Maybe he *is* meeting Gytha, only in secret. Maybe they are throwing off the mingling of their scents with power."

"I do not think that can be true. For one thing, Gytha is not acting like a woman who is being met. For another, I do not believe she is a good enough liar to pretend." Frowning with concentration, Juliana squeezed her lower lip. "I am afraid there is nothing for it. We will have to go out and retrace his trail. I would leave you here, but I need your nose to sniff out where he has been."

In spite of her earnestness, Ulric laughed. "Even if I were willing, at this time of day, I doubt I could track a skunk."

"Really? You cannot smell during the day?"

She seemed intrigued by this new fact. Ulric rubbed one hand across his smile. "No better than you."

"That is unfortunate. I have noticed Bastien's feet do not leave lasting prints. He must be almost as strong as you." Her brows drew together and went up as a new idea occurred to her. "You could change into your wolf form and smell him that way."

"I could," he agreed, "but I would rather not."

"I suppose you would look silly as a wolf wearing a cloak."

"I would not require a cloak," Ulric said. "As long as I had enough strength to change, the sun could not harm my other form."

"Then why not investigate?"

Ulric cupped her astonished face. "Juliana, I know you have taken it into your head that I simply order people to do things and assume they will obey. I cannot deny I never think that way, but being a leader requires more than that. My pack members have to trust me."

"But why would Bastien not trust you? Considering what he helped Gytha do to Ingrith, you have treated him more than fairly."

"I have tolerated him. Bastien knows he is being watched for mistakes. If I do as you say, I will probably find one, but I would rather give him a chance to undo it first, of his own free will. For that to happen, he must believe I will show him not merely justice but mercy."

"You have shown him mercy!" she exclaimed with a staunchness that made him smile.

"He holds himself aloof, Juliana. He hunts without joy and flirts without friendliness. He does not move against me, and yet I sense him seeking out weaknesses. As I watch him, thus he watches me. Maybe you are correct and he was abused by his former pack. If that is true, he will be slower to trust than most—and quicker to find causes for suspicion. Until he gives me a reason that I should not, I will show the same respect for his privacy that I would for Stephen or Ingrith. A pack lives cheek by jowl. We must give each other what room we can."

"But what if his secret is dangerous?"

Ulric stroked her sleeve down her arm. "I would know if there was malice in Bastien's heart. I would smell it."

"But—"

He hugged her to him until her frustration eased. "Trust me," he soothed, privately amazed that he did not resent the need to explain. "I have been through this process with every pack member I have. Loyalty cannot be forced."

"But I want to know," she murmured plaintively against his chest.

Ulric chuckled and kissed her hair. "I see that, love. You will simply have to be patient."

"Not patient," she mumbled.

Despite her denial, the way she held him spoke of acceptance. He knew she respected his position, even if she disagreed, an awareness that brought a curious mixture of peace and longing. We were made for each other, he thought. We are different but we fit.

She sighed as he rocked her from side to side, her body soft in his arms. The gentle weight of her was sweet and warm. In a moment, when he did not feel this sleepy, he would lead her back to his room.

"Ulric?" she said, her head tilting back from his chest. "I do not think I need until summer's end."

"Mm," he said, his thoughts hazy and relaxed.

"I know there are still things I need to learn and to get used to, but my life was never this interesting before. I want to be part of what is happening here. I want to be a member of your pack."

His lids flew open as if on strings. "Juliana! You want to become *upyr?*"

She laughed softly at his reaction. "Yes, if you do not think it is a bad idea."

"I think it is a wonderful idea! I will contact my sire and ask him to, er . . ." Ulric's voice trailed off as he remembered his previous omission.

"I know," she said, her fingers brushing his embarrassed wince. "Ingrith let it slip that you could not change me."

"I did not mean to mislead you, exactly. It seemed a lot to explain when I barely knew you."

"Quite a lot," she agreed with an indulgent grin. "And me a blackmailer to boot."

"I was reluctant to admit that I could not do it. It was flattering to have you think me that powerful. But are you certain of what you want? Being made *upyr* is a big decision."

She drew a short, broken breath as if she did indeed have reservations, then thankfully shook her head. "I would prefer that it was you who changed me, but if you think your sire will agree to help, I am certain that will be fine."

"He will agree. He has only to meet you to know what a perfect pack member you will be."

As she hugged him, he felt her smiling against his heart. "Perfect I do not hope for, only to be a useful part of your pack."

"They love you already," he said. "Most of them. And perhaps Gytha will, too, someday—though I would not hold my breath."

Juliana laughed, a wonderful sound.

If she had expressed an equal interest in being his queen, his happiness would have been complete.

⟿

Soon after sunset, Ulric ordered his pack to meet him in the hall of columns.

For his own taste, he would have chosen another room. Surely, there was something ridiculous in a space this grand being in a cave. The white-veined pink marble tiles were bigger than he was, the red porphyry columns too large to encircle in his arms. Their flowery capitals—which had been gilded and which loomed over them in the distance like titans' heads—were no possible use at all. What function this room had served in previous ages he could not guess. Did sufficient numbers of *upyr* exist to fill it? Even if they did, a ballroom for wolves struck him as nonsensical in the extreme. No doubt, it was due to Juliana's influence that the question even crossed his mind.

He was beginning to wonder why just like her.

For all its senseless grandeur, there were advantages to making his announcement here. The hall was a place Juliana felt comfortable. She had stamped it with her human slippers and her dusty books, with the friendships she had forged among his lesser wolves.

His pack watched him take Juliana's hand, their expressions open and interested—with the inevitable exception of Gytha. She stood behind the others, one shoulder propped on a column, her arms crossed sullenly. Ulric met her eye, both to warn and reassure. She might be under penance, but she was still a part of his pack.

"Tell us," Stephen said while bouncing on his toes. "What is your news?"

"My news," said Ulric, his own smile broad, "is that Juliana has decided to become *upyr*."

"Oh!" Ingrith cried, turning to Juliana, her hands clasped in excitement before her breast. "I am so glad. Just think of the fun we shall have!"

"Huh," said Gytha from the background. "I notice he does not mention making her his queen."

Leave it to Gytha to poke the sorest spot. Ulric could conceive of no good response, even if her punishment had allowed it. Juliana had ducked her head in an attempt to ignore the jibe, but a rosy flush swept up her neck. Strangely, when Ulric's glance fell on Bastien, he thought he saw the Frenchman looking at her with envy. If this was what he felt, he hid it quickly. A heartbeat later, his face was blank.

Stephen filled the awkward pause by folding Juliana

into a hug. "Welcome to our pack," he said, clasping her tight. The full press of his naked body heightened the color in her face. Presumably feeling this, Stephen pulled back and teasingly tapped her cheek. "You will have to get over this human modesty if you are going to be one of us."

"I am not one of you yet," she said, smiling through her blush. "Auriclus must agree to change me. From what I hear, he can be choosey."

"He will agree," Stephen assured her. "And if he does not, maybe Gill— Well, I am sure Auriclus will see you as we do, even if you have turned a few of the rules on their heads."

"There is that," said Juliana, rubbing her nose and trying not to look worried.

"It shall be well," Ulric promised, vowing to himself that it would. For many years he had kept his sire's children safe. Auriclus owed him a boon or two.

"We should have a howl," Stephen suggested, "to celebrate."

Helewis and Ingrith jumped at this. "Yes, yes," Helewis enthused. "Maybe we can coax the real wolves to join in."

"Stephen can teach you," Ingrith said to Juliana. "His howls are the best."

"Can that really be true?" Juliana asked with a secret smile. "I have, after all, heard your pack leader sing."

"Now that," said Ingrith, "is a tale I would like to hear."

They departed from the hall, leaving Ulric with Bastien.

"It is kind of them to welcome her," the Frenchman said to his fingernails.

"They enjoy her company. And she has earned their trust."

Bastien could not miss this implication. His gaze met Ulric's directly. "If I swear fealty to you . . ."

"You fear I will let you down."

"I fear that all this"—Bastien spread his hands to indicate what he had just witnessed—"cannot be as pretty as it seems."

"Your fear is of your own making."

Bastien closed his eyes and clenched his fists, his emotions obviously at war. "I cannot afford to guess wrong. If you knew what we . . . what I have come from . . . If I swore to you, I would be under your power. I would owe you allegiance."

"And I would owe you protection."

"Protection." Bastien wagged his head as if that were a joke.

"I will not press you," Ulric said. "This is a decision you must come to on your own, a decision you must be prepared to stand by once it is made."

Bastien nodded but did not speak. Ulric knew he was thinking hard.

Ulric and Bastien joined the others, shifting into wolf form with plenty of time to spare. Ulric had forgotten how much fun a howl could be. To Juliana's evident delight, they managed to get the true pack who lived in the neighboring valley to answer back. After a few laughing attempts, however, she gave up trying to imitate their song.

"I can almost see them," she said, her expression dreamy, her fingers buried in Ulric's ruff, "as if I were a pup listening from the den."

Glad she was enjoying this, Ulric leaned into her leg, mutely inviting her to scratch him behind the ears.

She did this as if it were natural.

When they tired of howling, Stephen and Ingrith reenacted the battle between Gawain and the Green Knight, after which Helewis and Bastien made a game of wrestling while changing forms. The two were evenly matched in strength, though Bastien had the advantage in aggressiveness. Ulric could tell he was holding back so as not to hurt Helewis, going as far as allowing her to pin him at the end.

"Cheater!" Helewis accused, pretending to bite his muzzle.

Bastien was laughing silently when he returned to his human shape. It was the first time Ulric could remember seeing him happy. He sobered soon after, almost guiltily, turning his head and frowning into the trees.

"Rabbit hunt!" Stephen shouted, possibly inspired by the direction of Bastien's gaze. He and the women tore off immediately. Bastien hesitated, then flashed into wolf form to catch up. His pelt was darker than the others, his stride a smooth gallop. Ulric could see how he might have caught Gytha's eye.

"You can join them," Juliana said.

Ulric smiled. "I was thinking you and I might enjoy having the rest of the night to ourselves."

Her slow, sweet smile told him she agreed.

He carried her to the chamber of the hot spring, making love to her in the steaming, mineral-laden water. For once he did not mind being gentle. This was precisely how he wanted to show his care. Their bodies were buoyant, their hair soon sleeking wetly around their heads. Pleasure rolled through them in slow motion.

"I love you," she said when it was over, her head nestled shyly against his neck.

He let her declaration ease him like the heat, not questioning what it meant or how long it would last. Instead, he pressed his lips to her damp temple.

I love you, too, he said, reaching for her mind. This alone could convey the truth of what he felt. A weight left him with the words—or maybe it was a ghost. Tomorrow would be soon enough for worries. Tonight he reveled in her answering sigh.

Emile

⌖

Emile had plenty of time to lie in his hole and listen—
and think, of course, but as listening provoked less worry,
he did that. He memorized the nightly routines of squirrels and spiders, of swooping owls and scurrying mice.
Sometimes, beyond the golden barrier, he heard the others hunt. Bastien hunted with them. When they brought
down prey, Emile sensed his old friend's joy.

The only pleasure Emile looked forward to was sleep,
and lately that had been slow to come. Bastien's morning
visits had trained him to stay awake.

Despite his misery, he knew Bastien had a right to those
moments of exultation. Forswearing them would not
change Emile's fate. Regardless of whether Bastien swayed
this pack in the end, Emile was almost certainly doomed.

The disappearance of all feeling in his feet had been
followed by that in his calves. Below his hips, everything
was blurred. The numbing effect seemed likely to
progress, but he could hardly bring himself to mind.

This is my destiny, he thought, one weary arm flung across his eyes. Who was he to question God's plan? Not a chosen creation, he did not think. More like an uninvited guest.

His mouth was twisting crookedly at his own black wit when he heard a crashing in the undergrowth—sounds too heavy, too deliberate to be made by any but mortal men. Back and forth the humans tramped near the spot where the golden wall had been brought to life. Snuffling noises accompanied the stamp of boots, along with the yip and whimper of hounds.

Emile welcomed his surge of fear as a sign of life, until he realized the searchers were not looking for him.

"The trail leads here," said the voice of an older male, "but I see no way through these thorns. Could the dogs be confused?"

A second human answered. "Perhaps they have been magicked to lead us the wrong way."

"Bollocks," said the first. "Perhaps you chose the wrong scent to track from Dunburn. Perhaps you were no more immune to that creature's thrall than my idiot sons."

"I assure you, master, my cross protected me—may God be blessed. Most of my memories have come back."

"Most but maybe not enough." Disgusted, the older human ground out a curse. "That thing stole not only my heirs' good sense but my future bride. I will have its secrets or the Almighty Himself will answer why not."

"Master . . ."

"Cease your puling, Captain. You are pious enough for us both. Let us go farther north. Maybe we can find a spot where this wall of thorns is thin enough to hack through."

Emile knew of no thorns that they might mean. He and Bastien had encountered none. But maybe they were a glamour generated by the barrier.

As he pondered this, the tramping and snuffling got

louder. He estimated a dozen men at the least—all coming his way.

"We should wait until full light," cautioned the second man.

"Nonsense," said the first. "Everyone knows these creatures become insensible at dawn."

Emile wished he were insensible. Then he would not be choking on his fear. He braced his hands against the earthen walls, blood-sweat prickling along his scalp. He could only hope the dogs would not smell it.

Dreading their approach, he squinted past his useless feet to the open end of his burrow. Bastien had blocked it with branches, but the barrier seemed horribly flimsy now.

They will find me, he thought, sureness tolling through him. Today is the day I die.

He was shocked to discover how much he wanted to live.

The discovery came too late. Better to grit his teeth and prepare. Despite his resolve, his heart seized as a hound barked once and began to dig. Branches were nosed away. Dirt was hitting his feet. He must have smelled like whatever *upyr* they were seeking, because he was also Auriclus's child. His lips moved in a long-forgotten prayer.

"Badger hole," someone scoffed, but the dismissal was no reprieve.

"Let her dig," said the older man when someone grabbed the dog's collar. "Something is here."

Two more dogs joined the first in throwing soil from the opening. The hole widened. Voices cried out in discovery.

Emile did not feel the hands that reached in to grab his ankles, only the drag and bump of his upper body along the dirt. Roots tore from his fingers as he clutched them to no avail. Smoke drifted thinly into the burrow, telling him his belly must be exposed.

A second later, he had to shield his face from the light.

"Christ," someone said, tight with fear. "They *are* more than a tale."

The thin, morning sun sapped what remained of Emile's strength. He was helpless to fight as the soldiers heaved him to his feet. His knees immediately collapsed. They had to grip his arms to keep him upright.

"Pull his hood forward," ordered the older man. "I do not want him going up in flames."

Emile's eyes streamed from their brief exposure as the man who led the others stepped forward. Frantically, he blinked to clear his sight. When he did, he was almost sorry. The human who confronted him wore the chilliest expression he had ever seen on a mortal man. Age might have robbed him of his vigor, but the willful set of his jaw seemed determined to deny the loss. Despite the seams of living in his skin, his eyes held no more life than stones.

All right, Bastien, Emile thought, though he doubted the words could reach his friend. *If you want to save me, now would be good.*

"Do not look into its eyes," the captain warned, a caution Emile wished was needed. At the moment, he could not have thralled a flea.

The cold-eyed human simply smiled. "I think this one is weak enough. Else, he would have prevented his being found. At any rate, with this many men he cannot bespell us all." A cool, gnarled hand slipped inside Emile's hood to trail caressingly along his cheek. Emile flinched but could not escape. The touch made him feel more like an object than a living being.

The older man did not react when his captain stepped to his side.

"This is not the creature who stole Buxton's daughter."

The old man snorted, his oddly bloodless finger sliding down Emile's jaw. "Juliana Buxton can go hang for the whore she is. She could never give me more than the illusion of restored youth. This one is going to give me its truth."

Emile doubted that declaring this was impossible would help his cause.

"Never," he said instead and felt an unexpected triumph at the angry narrowing of his captor's eyes.

Chapter 14

～

Bastien must have been more closely linked with the pack than Ulric guessed. Daytime sleep was a kind of stupor, thrown off only with great will. In spite of this, the mental echo of Bastien's distress cut through Ulric's slumber. He sat up before his mind sorted out what it had heard.

The motion woke Juliana.

"What is it?" she asked, going up on one elbow.

Ulric could not immediately answer. He swung his legs over the edge of his bed and tried to breathe alertness into his mind. "Bastien is in trouble," he said. "You stay here."

Juliana reached for her gown. "I cannot stay here. It is light. If something is wrong, you might need a helper who keeps her wits about her after dawn."

His head was too muddled for debate. Rather than try, he pushed through his door and stepped heavily over Helewis. An inadvertent jostling from his heel failed to make her twitch. If she was going to sleep this soundly, he probably ought to tell her not to bother to guard their room.

He was scratching his head over this quandary when Bastien staggered down the corridor. Though he wore his black cloak and clothes, his hood must have fallen back because his cheeks and nose were burned. Ulric marveled at the panic that could cause such heedlessness.

"Pack leader," the Frenchman gasped. "I need . . . your aid."

Still trying to marshal his thoughts, Ulric's eyes grew round as the other *upyr* fell to his knees. "I will swear to you," he said, clutching Ulric's hand to his reddened face. "Only promise not to let them kill Emile."

When Ulric blinked at him in confusion, Bastien threw himself to the floor. "I will be your wolf," he cried desperately. "No matter what you ask, I shall obey."

Ulric could see this was a terrible oath for the other man. "Bastien . . ." he said, hardly knowing what he was cautioning him against. He sank into a crouch beside the prostrate man with Juliana clasping his shoulder. Though her touch was light, it steadied him in a way he could not explain. "Who is Emile, Bastien? And who is trying to kill him?"

"You must accept my oath," Bastien insisted into the dirt. "You must give Emile the protection you claimed you would owe me."

"I will help you if I can, whether you swear or no, but you need to explain what you need my protection for."

Bastien's head lifted from the floor. "You accept me into your pack?"

Ulric sighed. Bastien might not be manipulating him on purpose, but he could tell he was not going to get answers until he agreed. As if Juliana sensed the moment he needed it, she stroked his hair. The sensation brushed as sweetly along his nerves as it would his wolf's. Whatever her doubts about Bastien, Ulric knew her inclination was to help. His was the same, though he understood better than she the responsibility involved in adding to his pack.

I must trust my instincts, he thought, *and I must trust hers. I cannot hope to make her queen if I do not.*

"Sit up," he said to Bastien. "Meet my eyes and promise you will serve with honor."

Bastien dragged his sleeve across his mouth, his body shaking. "I will," he said. "You have my word."

With the declaration, a shock snapped through the air between them, a sign that the vow had taken hold. The bond was breakable, but only at the cost of extreme discomfort to the forsworn. Bastien's word was genuine.

"Good enough," Ulric said. "Now tell me what has befallen your friend."

His oath accepted, it seemed Bastien's words could not tumble out fast enough. "Emile is my brother wolf. We escaped from our pack in Burgundy when our leader began using magic to shore up his power. He was getting old with no sign of becoming an elder, while some of the younger ones were growing into their gifts. Terror was the only way he could keep them down. Some of the punishments he imposed . . . He would have done worse than kill us had we not broken our oaths and run. I hid Emile in the woods while I waited to see if I could trust you to take our side. I was hoping—"

He stopped and shook his head; whatever he had been hoping was apparently too much to share. "Maybe I should have told you sooner when I saw you were not like Hugo. Or maybe I should have moved Emile within the barrier Juliana erected around your lands. I was afraid you would smell him if he came inside it. Now it does not matter because the English soldiers have dragged him from his concealment. Their leader wants Emile to make him immortal. I fear he will kill Emile when he cannot do what he wants."

"*English* soldiers?" Juliana said, exchanging looks with Ulric.

"Yes. A troop of them with an older man at their head. Emile was crippled by our former leader. He cannot defend himself. I wanted to stop them from taking him, but they were too many for me to fight."

Ulric knuckled his forehead, trying to arrange the jumbled pieces of this explanation.

"Could it be Drake's men again?" Juliana asked even as the suspicion formed in his mind.

"I do not know," he said, "and we might not have the luxury of finding out. Wake the others, Bastien. Whoever is strong enough to change will join us in wolf form."

"Thank you," Bastien breathed as he rose to hurry off. "I will not forget this service!"

Ulric imagined the day ahead would be memorable for them all. With a frown and a shrug, he turned to shake Helewis.

Juliana knelt beside him to help, her expression considerably more perturbed than his. "If these men are Gideon Drake's, then I have brought danger to you all."

"No more than I have," Ulric said. "For that matter, no more than Bastien."

"But I—"

"No," he said firmly. "Blame is useless. Save your energy for what lies ahead."

She bit her lip and nodded. "I will," she said. "I want to help however I may."

"Good," he said. "Just try not to help so much you get in the way."

It was his good fortune that Helewis's awakening grumble cut short Juliana's sputter of offense.

⟼

No matter what Ulric said, Juliana was determined to go along. This was her pack now—or nearly. If there was even a chance that she could help them combat this danger, she must try.

Of course, vowing to help was easier than keeping up with six fleet *upyr* wolves. All had woken eventually despite the hour, and none—not even Gytha—had protested being asked to fight for a stranger. They seemed eager to cross swords—or teeth, as it were—with whoever had abducted Bastien's brother wolf.

This was a side of the pack she had not seen before.

Willing though she was, Helewis was almost too wooly headed to change. Gytha solved that problem by slapping her briskly across the face. Juliana suspected the blow was not completely altruistic, but under the circumstances Ulric allowed it. Gytha also had the foresight to give Juliana a nasty-looking, forged-steel scythe. Pearls and rubies studded the handle, but the strong, curving blade was bright. Juliana could only assume Gytha had done some cave exploring of her own. Far deadlier than the knife she had brought from Bridesmere, which she had taken to wearing tucked in her purse, the scythe was the perfect size and weight for her human hand.

"For when you catch up," Gytha said with her usual derision, "because you have no proper defense."

Juliana bit back a smile as she thanked her, saying she appreciated her thoughtfulness.

"Hah," Gytha barked. "Try not to drop it on your foot."

Though no one said the words, it was obvious Gytha's shunning was suspended for the time being.

Armed now, Juliana's next challenge was following the pack's silent progress through the woods. Fortunately, their wolf forms did leave signs. Eyes sharpened by her tie to Ulric, Juliana was able to make out the trail of galloping paw prints and broken plants.

The time this took gave her plenty of chances to drink in the day. After her weeks in the cave, the sun cast a magic spell. Its beams were columns of bright green fire slanting through the leaves, dancing with golden motes, catching the colors of bird and flower. Even spiderwebs seemed like signs of a fairy realm. Never again would she take this wonderment for granted.

Once she was changed, she would have to take her wolf soul quickly. Only thus could she visit the daylight world.

Sadly, even with her improved sight to guide her, she made more of a racket than she wished battling through the trees. Branches caught at her clothes and bracken tangled her feet, but she could not slacken for fear of finding them too late. The noise was a risk she would have to take. These were humans they fought, and Juliana might know something the pack did not. Nerves taut with determination, she was dripping sweat by the time she reached the stones that marked the border of Ulric's land.

Apart from their carvings, the menhirs seemed perfectly ordinary as she passed between them, their surfaces white with bird lime and green with moss. Noting that the paw prints she followed were now coming closely placed, she moved more cautiously. She did not wish to accidentally overtake the pack, or to interfere with their strategy. Better that she concentrate on being quiet.

As it happened, Fate cared nothing for her good intentions. Juliana found the soldiers before she suspected how close they were.

A face surprised her as she edged around a tree: a human face with a dirty linen coif beneath one of mail. The mortal's breastplate was dented steel, his leg guards worn ox hide. A crude wooden cross dangled crookedly from his neck. Juliana had a second to register his startled eyes before his dagger pricked the soft spot beneath her chin.

He seemed not to care that she was female.

"Drop it," he ordered, nodding curtly at the scythe she had unthinkingly raised before her. Feeling stupid, but not knowing what else to do, she let it fall. Her only comfort was that it did not land on her foot.

This was precisely what she had hoped to avoid.

"Captain!" the soldier called. "There is a woman. Human, I believe."

You *believe?* Juliana thought, her brows rising. She could not fathom how there could be any doubt.

But he had called for a captain, probably the same she and Ulric had encountered in Dunburn. Ulric's thrall must not have taken, thwarted perhaps by the captain's cross. Now the others were wearing them, too.

We should have killed them when we had the chance, she thought, but was not certain they would have even if they knew. Racking her mind for some way out, she clenched her hands as she waited for a response. When the soldier got one, her worst fears came true.

"Bring her over by the other," said a steel-cool voice Juliana knew all too well.

Her shoulders hunched in revulsion. It was Gideon Drake, her would-be spouse.

The merchant broke into a smile as his man dragged her into view. Mailed like the others but dressed in silken raiment atop, Drake's garments bore the stains and creases of hard travel. Within them, he seemed as controlled as ever: tall and angular with long, waving gray hair whose fullness she knew was a source of pride. Unlike other men of his years, Gideon Drake wore no beard. He was handsome in his way, despite his slightly bulging eyes and his too-thin, too-small mouth.

It was not, Juliana thought, the mouth of a full-grown man.

He tapped his fingertips before it. "How convenient," he said, "we can question them both at once."

Juliana waited for him to say her name, to berate her for rebelling against her father and him. Instead, he flicked his fingers for his man-at-arms to take her away.

She did not think he was pretending not to know her. He simply did not consider her important enough to acknowledge.

"Tie her well," he said, "if they have begun to change her, they might have infected her with their strength."

She struggled wildly when she saw where the soldier was leading her. An unfamiliar *upyr*—Bastien's brother wolf, she presumed—had been bound from shoulder to ankle to the trunk of an ancient oak. From the way he sagged in the ropes, she concluded he was unconscious, though she saw no signs of the crippling injury Bastien had mentioned. To her surprise, the *upyr's* head lurched upward at her approach. Within his hood, she spied a gaunt and shadowed face.

Juliana knew it was daytime and his strength was low, but his skin did not glow at all. Rather, misery burned in his eyes like dun-brown flames, the purest suffering she had ever seen. Hell on earth took on new meaning as she met his gaze. If he were trying to send her some message, she could not read it. She did, however, stop thrashing in her captor's hold.

She could not leave this man to face the enemy alone. She might be useless, but at least she was company.

The tree they had tied him to was huge. They lashed her to it beside him, close enough that she could touch his gloved hand with her bare pinky. He jerked when she did this, then closed his eyes as if the contact hurt. Barely visible shimmers in the air around his head told her his hood was insufficient shelter. Turning those shimmers into smoke would not take much. She wondered if Drake knew he was in danger of incinerating his prize.

"You should shade him with a blanket," she said, "unless you want him to burn."

The *upyr* made a soft and indefinable noise. Drake stared at her, then snapped his fingers for his captain to comply. The captain moved off hastily, stepping between a pair of bloodhounds who had flopped tiredly to the ground. They were obviously the means by which Drake had trailed her and Ulric. Just as obviously, now that she had a chance to look around, she saw that she had stumbled into his camp. Easily two dozen soldiers guarded its perimeter. Her skin tingled with alarm to take in their demeanor. These were hardened warriors.

She did not know whether to be relieved or sorry that she did not see either of Drake's sons. If Ulric's thrall had permanently impaired his precious male issue, the man would be out for blood.

As she searched one more time for Milo and Milton, she spotted something she sincerely hoped no one else would: a single, black-pointed tail sticking out from a bank of ferns—Stephen's tail, if she did not miss her guess.

She looked away without delay, but not before a sudden knowledge flared in her mind. The pack was all around her. They had been lying in wait all along.

She wondered why they did not attack: if the soldiers were too numerous, or the sun too great a drain on their wolfish strength. Were they simply playing it safe? Would they move if presented with a more immediate threat than having their friends tied up? Or was a good distraction all they required?

This was why she needed to know everything—so she did not have to guess in an emergency.

Her frustration was worse than pointless. Shoving it aside, she tried to reach out for Ulric's mind. Her efforts gained her nothing but a mild headache. The realization that her own judgment was all she had to rely on impelled her to square her shoulders and lift her chin.

Whatever came, she would meet it as well as she could.

At her movement, Drake stepped close enough for her to smell his days' old sweat. After her time with the wolves,

who never smelled unpleasant, the scent was unnaturally
rank.

"Juliana," he said, finally deigning to say her name.
"My lovely, almost-bride. I wonder if you comprehend
the trouble you are in. Your father has disowned you, you
know. Told me I should not bother to chase you down. He
was trying to ingratiate himself, of course; our partner-
ship keeps him in slippers and venison. But I saw such
rage in that pettish old face, I am far from certain he
would care if I slit your throat."

Juliana was not certain, either. She knew how her
father got when his pride was wounded. Outwardly, she
was careful not to respond. Whatever hurt she might feel
was her own concern.

Drake responded to her silence with a subtle smile.

"You know these creatures," he said.

She shrugged, as cool in manner at least as he.

"They have shared their secrets with you."

"Some of them."

Impatience tightened Drake's childish mouth an
instant before he wrapped his hand around her jaw. By
chance or malice, he pressed the spot where the soldier
had pricked her skin. "I want you to tell me how they turn
humans into *upyr*."

"I am not privy to that mystery."

Giving her no warning, he backhanded her hard enough
to knock her temple against the tree. White exploded
behind one eye, then went away. Blood filled her mouth
from accidentally biting her tongue. She spat it out and
straightened. She was shaking now, shocked by his violence, though it was no more than she expected of a man
like him.

To make matters worse, the other *upyr,* Emile, had
turned his head slowly toward her, most likely attracted
by her injury. She did not want to look at him, but somehow she could not help it. A hint of fang glinted within

his hood. His breath came disquietingly harder than it had before.

Wonderful, she thought. My fellow captive wants to eat me.

Given her suspicions, he surprised her with his defense. "Leave her alone," he said in a dark, hair-raising growl.

Drake could not repress a shudder, though he recovered quickly enough. "I do not care which of you tells me, as long as one of you does." He examined a bit of soil caught beneath his nails, then offered the *upyr* a sly, man-to-man smile. "Perhaps you are in need of an incentive. She looks healthy, does she not? Living with monsters has given her a bright new bloom. Though by rights she should be mine, I would cede her to you, should you decide to cooperate."

This time the *upyr* shuddered—and not with fear. "If I . . . fed from her," he said, his voice gone thick. "My strength would be restored. I would break these bonds and kill you before you had the chance to use what you had learned. This is a bargain you cannot afford to make."

Drake's captain had finished propping up a blanket as an awning over both their heads. He shrugged at his master's inquiring glance. "It might be true. Frankly, I did not expect them to have any strength after dawn."

"Torture it is then," Drake said cheerfully. "Someone hand me a nice, sharp knife. We shall see how desperate for blood this creature gets once we let some of it out. I expect it will be willing to sell its soul for a sip or two."

Juliana's companion tensed in his bonds. She hardly liked the prospect of being a goad for his suffering, but what she sensed from him went deeper than horror. She worried whether, in his weakness, Emile might have little blood to spare. If that were true, his reluctance to harm her was all the more admirable.

Of course, what might be causing him to shrink in horror was his despair of resisting. Though she had never felt that kind of threat from Ulric, a maddened and starving *upyr* might be capable of causing death.

Lord save us, she prayed. I must find a way to help us both. She reached again for what sense of the pack she had, trying to drop whatever guards were keeping her from contact. If she discovered what they were planning, she could ensure her actions did not make their situation worse.

~

Ulric had no choice but to let Bastien lead the chase. Not only did the Frenchman know where the soldiers were, but only he, of all of them, was functioning at anything near full strength. Even in wolf form, Ulric felt as if he were half asleep. Though determination forced his feet to run, it failed to clear the fog from his brain.

This way, Bastien thought at him after snuffling around a recently dug-up burrow. *I can smell which way they have moved him.*

All Ulric could smell were clods of earth and pine sap.

Adding insult to injury, Bastien was skilled at mind speech, more skilled than Ulric. Between *upyr,* this was a tricky matter, depending on both parties being willing and attuned. To Ulric's chagrin, his inner hearing was as muffled as his nose, as if Bastien were speaking to him from a pit. Trying not to pant too loudly, he gathered himself to run where Bastien directed. The rest of his pack fell in behind him with wolfish sighs.

If nothing else, this experience was teaching him he had not been keeping his charges in fighting trim. From here on out, he would get them in the habit of taking a little sun—assuming, of course, that they survived this day.

They reached the camp in a shameful state of windedness.

Bastien had not exaggerated when he said there were too many soldiers for him to take, nor did their opponents display any shortage of weaponry. Ulric swore to himself as he counted swords, any one of them sharp enough to lop off their heads. If he had trusted his power to thrall, he would have lured the men out one by one. Regrettably, in his wolf form and in full daylight, he doubted the ploy would work—not when he could barely hear the thoughts of his pack. Ulric was no coward, but he had no desire to lose a single life if he could avoid it.

He signaled the wolves to stop behind a bank of blackberry brambles. He directed his thoughts to Bastien, confident that he at least would hear.

I think we must wait till sunset unless these Englishmen force our hands. See if you can get a message to your friend not to worry if we delay.

Bastien's head swung toward the tree where Emile was tied. *I am not certain he can hold out. Hugo put a curse on him, one that worsens progressively. Emile needs blood to stave off the growing weakness, more blood than most upyr. I am afraid I did not get the chance to feed him this morning.*

Now Ulric understood Bastien's greed and the bite marks on his throat. He cursed the mistrust that had kept him from confiding in Ulric before.

Can you reach him at least? he asked. *Let him know that we are here and find out how bad his condition is?*

Ulric did not think this an awful question, but Bastien sank down on his haunches and dropped his muzzle dolefully to his paws. *I have not been able to speak to his mind for days.*

From his half-pleading, half-woeful expression, Bastien clearly expected Ulric to pull some miracle out of his ear—despite Bastien being, for the moment, the strongest wolf they had.

This, Ulric thought in an ironic flash, was what came of encouraging people to obey you.

Very well, he said, bringing the rest of the pack into his thoughts with all the force of his concentration, trying to hold his sense of each in his head. *We will surround the camp in groups of two. If possible, we will wait for sunset. If Emile looks to be in urgent danger, I will give the signal and we will attack, bringing down whatever soldiers each of us can reach first. With luck, the confusion this causes will give us enough advantage to defeat the rest. Pairs, you are responsible for keeping each other awake.*

To his relief, everyone heard him. He kept Helewis with himself, Ingrith with Stephen, and sent Bastien off with Gytha. The two might be at odds, but together they would fight hard. Gytha's desire to show no weakness in front of her former lover would keep her sharp.

Ulric was settling in for a wait when Juliana's appearance as the soldier's captive turned his heart inside out. He had forgotten she was following and had not thought to caution her away.

Quiet, Helewis warned when his throat began to rumble.

Helpless to interfere and straining in every muscle, he watched them tie her to the tree. Drake's revelation about her father was cruel enough, but when the Englishman hit Juliana, Helewis had to bite his scruff to hold him back.

She is not truly hurt, Helewis soothed, her mind voice going in and out like a fitful wind. *Maybe, by . . . there, she . . . steady Emile.*

Ulric was more concerned that she would stir Emile's hunger. He tried to reach Juliana's mind, then fought panic when he could not. What if she thought she had been abandoned?

She will not think . . . such a thing, Helewis insisted. *Juliana might be human, but she is brave. It would be useful, though, . . . get a message to her.* Helewis panted quietly as she considered how to do this, her tongue lolling over her jaw. *Maybe Bastien can reach . . . not as drained by the sun.*

A wave of jealousy swept through Ulric, as blinding as a mirror's flash. For a moment, he could not breathe.

Never, he declared. Never would he let another man, much less Bastien, share that intimacy with Juliana. Ulric would not lose her!

You cannot lose her, Helewis said, *unless . . . hold on too tight.*

Coming from Helewis, this advice was unexpected, to say the least. With a crackle of undergrowth, he sat back on his hind legs. Helewis did not seem a bit intimidated by his amazement. When he agreed to improve her standing with the pack, he had not expected this end result.

She is your queen, Helewis said, as if this were a fact any pup should know. *I can see . . . even if you cannot. It is safe to let go.*

Ulric peeled back his lips in protest. *I am not going to let go so much that I am no longer holding on!*

Helewis grinned, both woman and wolf in the expression. *Why not?* she said. *Can you not trust . . . stay with you on her own?*

A sound of extreme mental disgust cut through their communication. *I know you are punishing me,* Gytha said, her words perfectly clear, *but must you make me this sick? We need to contact one of them. If you cannot do it, Bastien must try.*

Like it or not, Ulric knew she was right.

Chapter 15

❦

Juliana would not have guessed it, but being tied to a tree was rather exhausting. She was grateful she had thought to take care of her human necessities before she left. Now she was merely tired, thirsty, and a little frightened. The hour was nearing noon, and she had yet to see any sign of Ulric. She told herself he was doing exactly what she would have wished: waiting for an advantage. She did not want the pack to needlessly risk their lives. She had no real reason to believe that they had fallen asleep in the sun.

However anxious she was, her discomfort paled beside Emile's. He was sagging ever more limply in his bonds, responding ever more wearily to Drake's demands. He could not reveal what he did not know, he said—though this did not save him from Drake's knife.

For his part, Drake seemed fascinated by the way the cuts he made slowly closed. Juliana could practically hear him measuring this gift for himself. She did not like to think what would happen if he obtained it. The London merchant was both ambitious and sly. With the power of immortality added to that of his wealth, he probably thought his aspirations would have no check. She supposed it was just as well he was not aware that a strong *upyr* would have healed much faster. As it was, Emile was sweating with pain and weakness, his pale, smooth skin gone faintly gray.

"Do not be distressed," he whispered to her when Drake stepped away for a cup of ale. "I shall not hurt you no matter what."

He might have been trying to convince himself, but Juliana nodded as if she believed. "I shall not hurt you, either," she said, which seemed to amuse him.

This exchange would have pleased her more if the teeth he bared with his smile had not been so sharp.

Trying to act as if she had not noticed, she cursed a persistent buzzing between her eyes. All morning it had been bothering her, and naturally she could not scratch. She tried squinching her forehead, but found no relief.

Fine, she thought at the troublesome spot: Itch all you want.

With the surrender, she realized a voice was calling her name.

Yes, she thought as strongly as she could. *I am here.*

Someone sighed in relief. *Juliana. Raise one finger if you hear me.*

Juliana did, recognizing with some surprise that the speaker was Bastien. He must have been trying to reach her for a while.

Just listen, he said. *Do not react. I know, as a human, you are not used to mind speech. You must stall these soldiers. Give Drake a reason to wait until dark before doing anything dire. Then we can move on him with full*

strength. We will rescue you earlier if we need to, but the
chance of everyone coming through the fight alive will be
better when the sun has set.

Juliana moved her hand again to indicate she understood, though her eyes focused unswervingly on Drake's
return.

His lips curved gently in anticipation as he used one
fingertip to test his freshly sharpened dagger. "Well," he
said, "now that I am refreshed, shall we try my skill at
probing more sensitive spots?"

Juliana had never seen her father's associate look this
pleased. For Emile's sake, she did not want to consider
what spots he meant.

"Midnight," she burst out before he could inflict a new
torture.

"Midnight?" Drake repeated, his wispy gray eyebrows
cocking up.

"Yes," she said, the idea forming even as she spoke.
"Midnight is when the *upyr's* power is at its height. Only
then can they transform a human."

The captain had returned with his employer. "If that is
true," he mused to Drake in an undertone, "it would explain
why they are sometimes called the children of midnight."

"I do not care how they got their name. I want to know
how they share their gifts." Drake set the point of his
blade at Emile's groin, then turned coolly smiling eyes to
her. "Care to elaborate, Juliana, or would you like to hear
how loudly this wretch can scream?"

Hardly needing to pretend that she was scared, Juliana
moistened dry lips. Selling this tale would require all her
storytelling art. She sent a prayer to her mother to look
down from heaven and guide her now.

"The secret is in their blood," she said, "in an exchange
of vital essences. Three times they drink from your veins
and three times you drink from theirs. When this mingling takes place at the sacred hour, the change is done."

Drake slitted his eyes. "It cannot be that simple. If you are leaving anything out . . ."

Emile jerked as the knife pressed deeper into his clothes.

"They might say words," Juliana gasped, feeling terrified and brilliant in equal parts. "But I do not think they matter. The blood is what conveys their power."

"Woman," Emile growled, the sound disembodied within his hood. "You have broken a sacred oath."

Juliana said a silent thanks. Emile must have figured out what she was attempting and decided to play along. She did not dare meet his glare for fear of giving the game away. Instead, she shrank away from him in her bonds.

"Tut-tut," Drake chided. "Why scold her when she breaks her oath to spare you pain? Women can be such tenderhearted creatures. One should not trust them with important secrets. In fact, one should not trust them at all."

For once Juliana was grateful he was right.

"Maybe," she said hesitantly, "you should refrain from spilling more of his blood. I am not certain how much he needs for the rite to work."

"You had better pray it works," Drake warned, "or I shall kill you both as slowly as possible."

Sheathing his knife, he ordered his men to secure their camp against the dusk. Juliana watched their preparations, her emotions too numb for fear. She had done what she could. The rest was up to the pack.

~

The soldiers grew very quiet as the end of the day drew near. Some crossed themselves in superstition. Some fondled the hilts of their swords. All listened intently to the natural noises of the woods. The raucous cry of a jay set half of them atwitch. As the light turned from gold to blue, then from blue to smokey purple, a few exchanged laughing boasts.

"Our blades shall drink eternity," one of them joked.

Ignoring them, Juliana closed her eyes and rolled her head against the bark of the tree. She tried to look no different than she had during the day, but she was suddenly deeply aware of the pack—not so much in her head as along her skin. Currents of energy ruffled each tiny hair, filling her with the wolves' pent-up urgency. The sensation was so compelling she felt as if she could break free of her bonds and join them in wolf form. Her heart thumped with excitement, her thoughts taking on a painful clarity. Scents flitted distinctly past her nose: leather, steel, even one scent she could only call eagerness.

She marveled that the soldiers did not sense the impending threat.

A wolf in truth, Emile must have felt what she did. He touched her hand with his glove, either in caution or reassurance.

"Water," he rasped to Drake, calling the man's attention just as Ulric attacked.

Even without the distraction, the wolves were mere streaks of fur and teeth in the new twilight, nightmare shapes too blurred to discern individuals. The soldiers fell on every side, screaming, gibbering, raising their swords, and trying to fight back.

Juliana heard a wolf yelp in pain and struggled frantically against the ropes. One of the pack must have bitten partially through them, because she felt them snap. She stumbled forward and was free.

As she did, Emile teetered as well. To her horror, Drake caught him and began dragging him off, holding the *upyr* in front of him as a shield. Emile's legs appeared not to work at all. Desperate to thwart Drake, Juliana grabbed a dead man's sword.

For all its size, the weapon was surprisingly easy to lift.

"Behind you," Stephen shouted in human form.

She turned and, with what felt like the purest chance, spitted a soldier through the gut. While she stared in amazement at what she had wrought, Ingrith finished the man by ripping out his throat. This taken care of, she greeted Juliana with a bark and an incongruous wag of her tail.

Juliana was fortunate no one attacked her then, as she took a moment to shake off her daze.

"Emile is gone," she called to the dark wolf who was Bastien. "Drake dragged him away."

Bastien was circling two nervous soldiers who stood back-to-back. *I shall send Helewis to get him,* he said in a tone that reflected his distraction. *She is most ferocious when defending those who cannot defend themselves.*

Juliana agreed with this assessment but decided she ought to help as well. After all they had been through, she wanted to make certain Emile survived. Too, she seemed less likely to get in the way while searching for Emile than in the thick of the struggle. The camp was chaos as the pack fought those who had not been taken in the first assault. Ducking and weaving between combatants, four-legged and two-, she moved as fast as she was able in the direction she had seen Drake disappear into the trees.

Ulric barked at her in passing, and she sent as clear an explanation as she could. *Be careful,* he said, seeming to accept her choice.

Though she had no wish to repeat the morning's debacle, she felt much safer knowing she could call him at any time.

Gradually, as she penetrated the wood, the shouts and growls of battle began to fade. She halted and held her breath when the sound of Emile's voice drifted to her ear.

"Take it," he was taunting, "if you're man enough to dare."

She crept forward to find him on the ground with his back propped on a fallen tree trunk. Someone, perhaps

Emile himself, had torn his tunic open to the waist. He looked better now that it was dark. His skin was white as marble, shining faintly except for a slowly bleeding slash high on his chest. Drake knelt beside him. He was staring at the cut as if enspelled.

"Take it," Emile repeated. "Drink. Grasp the fate you have chosen."

Though Juliana suspected Emile was not thralling the other man, Drake fell on him as avidly as if he were. Juliana covered her mouth in horror as he drank. This could not be the way humans were changed. Juliana had invented the tale herself. Surely, if it were true, Emile would not allow his tormentor to be transformed.

Before she could solve the puzzle, Drake reared back. His mouth was wet and gaping, his skin beginning to scintillate with blue sparks. "Forever," he breathed as if he were drunk. "I shall live forever."

Then, with no more than a cough, he keeled face forward across Emile. His thick gray hair fanned across them like a cape. Once the last locks settled, he did not move.

"Good Lord," said Juliana. "He cannot be dead!"

"He can," said Helewis, stepping unexpectedly out from behind a boulder. "You chose your fiction well. Our blood is poison to humans. The moment he drank, he was doomed." Bending down, she pitched Drake's body aside as if it were made of straw. Juliana winced at the sight, wondering if Helewis thought she had planned for him to die. His demise seemed not to bother her in the least. She looked down at Emile, her hands propped on her hips like a Valkyrie. "Shall I carry you?"

"If you would," Emile said politely. "My legs are not much use."

Juliana felt odd leaving Drake untended behind them but did not wish to make a fuss. Nor did she explain that she had caused the death accidentally. It seemed a foolish cavil since she could not claim to be sorry. With no more talk, the three returned to the soldiers' camp, now eerily quiet.

To Juliana's surprise and—admittedly—her relief, the soldiers were not all dead. No matter how despicable she thought their employer, she did not feel comfortable seeing them slain. The ten who remained were lined up in two rows, kneeling in the dirt with their hands laced atop their heads. Drake's much-battered captain was among them, his eyes glassy with shock.

The pack, who were guarding them in human form, had come through the fight with little more than bruises.

"We have no choice but to kill them," Bastien was saying to Ulric. "I am not any happier about it than you, but your thrall failed once before. For the future security of the pack, you dare not release them. If even one of them regained his memory, they would return, most likely in greater numbers. Immortality is too sweet a prize not to chase."

Ulric rubbed his jaw. "They did not break through the barrier Juliana raised by feeding the standing stones."

"What of it?" countered Bastien. "Do you really want to be reduced to cowering inside your lands?"

"These are hired men, Bastien," Ingrith put in before Ulric could answer, her voice soft but steady. "Good or bad, but we cannot kill them in cold blood. If we did, we would be no better than the pack you and Emile fled."

"But the risk—" said Bastien.

Juliana stepped forward, turning all eyes to her. "I think I can ensure a thrall does not fail."

"Oh, you can, can you?" Gytha scoffed. Despite her sneer, her tone was not entirely skeptical. Perhaps watching Juliana hold up under pressure had won her respect.

"Yes," said Juliana. "I can because I understand why it failed before, at least for the captain. Evidently, the memory of Drake's sons remains a blank." She gestured toward the captain's neck, where glints of light danced along his cross. "The symbol of his faith protected him. Remove it and you rob him of his resistance."

"Heathen bitch," the captain burst out. "May you roast in hell for your treachery!"

Juliana smiled. Even if her claim was false, the captain believed it. She imagined his men would as well. Their credulity would be the key to Ulric's success. As she suspected had been the case when Bastien hurt Ingrith, the men would bolster Ulric's thrall by convincing themselves.

Spying Gytha's scythe lying in the grass, she picked it up. The captain flinched when it caught the moonlight.

"In these woods," she said, " 'bitch' is a term of honor."

"Hear-hear," said Helewis and gently set Emile down.

Bastien hurried over to gather his friend in his arms. The expression on their faces told a story of profound relief and regret. Juliana had to look away when Bastien pressed Emile to his neck to feed. Had she been able, she would have shut her ears to Emile's moan. The emotion it implied was much too private. With an effort, she returned her attention to Ulric.

"You are certain about this?" he asked.

Juliana nodded. His thrall would be strongest if he had no doubts. She could, after all, tell him the truth later.

"It is decided then," he said. "We will thrall these humans and send them home."

⧼⧽

Ulric wasted no time enforcing his decision, though it was not a process he enjoyed. To push through the horrors these soldiers had just faced, to see his darkest nature through strangers' eyes was more than a little disturbing. Though the soldiers would not recall the beasts who had attacked them, Ulric would. From this night forward, he would know how he looked when he killed.

Even with Bastien's help, even with the advantage of removing the humans' last defense, Ulric was exhausted when they were done.

He sensed his influence was firm. Drake's men would know they had fought a battle, but not where it had occurred, nor precisely why. Too much drink was the explanation he and Bastien had devised, a long debauch that started the day they were hired and ended in being set upon by ruffians. Maybe they would have nightmares or dread leaving home again. Possibly they would shudder at tales of wolves. He and Bastien ordered them to cross the border to England as fast as they could. Every one of them plodded off obediently.

Relieved but weary, Ulric fell to his knees by the nearest stream and tried to wash their taste from his mouth. Again and again he cupped the water. Again and again he pushed someone else's terror from his thoughts. When he finally sat back trembling on his heels, Juliana was beside him.

He wished he had taken the opportunity to embrace her earlier. Now it seemed too far to reach.

"I am well," she said with a little smile, answering the question he did not have breath to ask, "and I can see how you are." Her hand reached up to smooth his dripping hair back from his face. "I imagine your head is full of them. Their fear, their pain. Bastien had anger to shield him, but you faced it all."

"It is the last respect," he said, the words rough in his throat. "To read what you are about to destroy. And I could not be as careful otherwise. I wanted to leave them with a memory of those who fell. Their kin deserve to know they are gone."

Her eyes shone with understanding. When he reached for her, both of them kneeling in the squelching mud, she held him as tightly as he held her.

She was warmth itself, as comforting as he had wished he could be to her. Her words stirred softly against his neck. "I am sorry I let myself get captured."

Her confession released his. "I was afraid," he said into her hair. "I did not want to lose you. I hated having to leave you there all day. When that Englishman struck you . . ."

"You did the right thing," she crooned, rubbing his back in sweeping strokes. "The wise thing. You brought everyone through the battle safe. I am grateful"—she hiccupped and caught her breath—"so grateful that you trusted me not to break."

He kissed the bruise where her cheekbone had hit the tree, tasting solace and salt. How could she break when her heart was this strong?

"I trust you with my life," he said, feeling the words in his bones, "just as you trusted me with yours."

Chapter 16

Ulric was the last of the pack to climb the cliff, his way of ensuring all arrived safely. He found Ingrith waiting at the entrance, looking stronger and happier than he had seen her in some time.

"That was good," she said as she turned to walk with him. "Nothing pulls a pack together like a fight."

Ulric squeezed the back of her neck through her silky hair. "I am glad you are feeling yourself again."

"How can I not when your Juliana proves even a puny human is not helpless?"

"She was resourceful," Ulric agreed, watching his lover—his queen, said his heart—move down the passage beside Stephen, "and this was the longest day of my life."

Ingrith rubbed his arm with a sympathy rare in a subordinate. "Maybe we should help the others with Emile. His weakness makes them uneasy."

Ulric had noted this himself. Now leading the way with Emile between them, Bastien and Helewis had conveyed the ailing *upyr* up the cliff in a makeshift sling. Though Bastien had assuaged his hunger, Emile did not appear much improved. The pack was unaccustomed to seeing injuries that did not heal. Because of this, the atmosphere was tense as they laid him on the floor in Bastien's room.

"I will get more furs," Gytha volunteered, which would have been kind had she not seemed so eager to leave.

"My condition is not catching," Emile called after her with rueful humor. "If it were, Bastien would have succumbed long ago."

At the moment, his friend looked tired and worried.

"Are you still hungry?" Helewis asked, hovering near, no doubt prepared to offer herself as his next meal. Ulric could tell Emile called to her protective urges. He suspected she was disappointed when he shook his head.

Stephen knelt, lifting the *upyr's* arm to check its veins. He ran his fingers along them to the elbow. "I do not think he needs blood," he said. "I think he needs energy." He turned his gaze to Ulric. "If you made him pack, we could share ours."

It was a statement, not a plea, but Stephen appeared unafraid to make it. He waited quietly for Ulric's decision. Just as quietly, Juliana slid her arm around Ulric's waist. Oddly, though Emile might end up presenting a burden, Ulric was less concerned about accepting him than he had been about Bastien. Maybe it was because Emile was not a dominant wolf, or maybe the slaughter they had left behind them made him wish to be kind.

"Is that what you want?" he asked Emile. "To join my pack?"

Emile's eyes flicked to Bastien and back. "Yes," he said, then broke into the sweetest smile Ulric had ever seen. "The quality of your queen convinces me you lead with honor. Her courage kept me from despair."

Gytha returned with the extra furs in time to sigh. A sigh, however, was an improvement over a snort.

"I am not his queen," Juliana clarified, "merely a future pack member like yourself."

"You are *my* queen," Emile said, kissing her hand.

Ulric fought a twinge of irritation. The man was not flirting, simply being gallant, and Juliana more than deserved his homage. All the same, he was not sorry when Gytha spoiled the Frenchman's gesture by dumping the furs in his lap.

⥊

Emile's oath took place with more ceremony than Bastien's, but—in Juliana's opinion—the rite was still quite plain: an exchange of promises, an odd concussion of the air to mark their acceptance, and it was done. Ulric's pack was seven instead of six.

The process of sharing power involved even less ritual. Everyone lay down close to Emile, their limbs tangled together like a pile of pups. Emile immediately closed his eyes and fell asleep. For Juliana, who had not shared a bed with anyone but Ulric since she was a child, such casual intimacy was awkward.

"Come," Ingrith urged, waving her down. "This is about giving comfort. No one will be forward."

"Speak for yourself," Stephen laughed, then winced at Helewis's buffet.

"I should wash," Juliana said, though she was not as filthy as she might have been.

"No, no," said Stephen. "To us, you smell good."

To him, she probably smelled like dinner, but she wriggled into the space between Ulric and Ingrith. She was wearier than she had realized, her muscles seeming to sigh in relief as she lay down and wrapped her arm around Ulric's ribs. His back was broad and firm, and he kissed her palm before pressing it over his slowly beating heart. Ingrith was right. There was comfort in this. For the first time since Bastien had staggered panting into the cave, she felt completely safe.

"Ooh," said Stephen as a flare of heat moved around the circle. "The human is nice and warm."

"The human has a bit of extra energy," Bastien commented blandly. "Your pack leader must be good at sharing."

"Enough," said Juliana, hiding her face against Ulric's neck. Comforted or not, she decided she was extremely thankful for her gown. She was "sharing" enough as it was.

Not much longer, Ulric teased, *before you will have to relinquish your modesty.* His mind-voice happy, he took her hand and shifted it to Emile's chest. Every member of the pack was touching the *upyr's* skin, but when Juliana's palm met his bare flesh a spark leapt up. She tried to ignore the sudden prickling at her nape. The air must have been dry.

"Hmpf," was Gytha's succinct response.

"I think it is time you told us your story," Ulric said to Bastien once the general snuggling down subsided.

Bastien lay on his side at Emile's head with his hand curled loosely over his friend's neck. Stephen's cheek rested on Bastien's calf, while Helewis spooned his back. Bastien seemed comfortable with the contact but reserved. He did not, Juliana surmised, ever wholly let down his guard. He frowned slightly before he spoke.

"There is not much more to tell than I have already. Our leader, Hugo, established his pack in Burgundy. Like Ulric, he served as guardian to Auriclus's children, those humans Auriclus changed on the Continent.

"Hugo was, I believe, four or five centuries old. Four is generally when indications that one might become an elder appear, but Hugo showed no signs. That potential," he said to Juliana, "to change humans, to master the higher powers, must be inborn. All *upyr's* gifts develop as we age, but after a certain point our strengths plateau. Hugo seemed to have reached that point, which would have been fine except some of the younger members of his pack, myself included, were getting strong enough to nip at his heels.

"Rather than lose his place to a challenger, Hugo decided to use magic to keep us down."

"Where did he learn it?" Juliana asked.

"From one of Nim Wei's children, an *upyr* named Damiano who was trying to establish his own empire. The magic is based upon the science of the stars."

"Nim Wei is another elder," Ulric explained. "A rival of Auriclus. There has always been a divide among the *upyr* between her children and his—not unlike the English and the Scots. Nim Wei's broods live in the cities and cannot take animal form. They are, however, allowed to practice the darker arts. Nim Wei tends to keep a tight rein on those she begets. This Damiano might have been acting without her knowledge."

"It is true Nim Wei's children are not famed for their loyalty," Bastien agreed. "But to each his own. Damiano probably hoped Hugo would teach him the secret of turning wolf. Whether he acquired it, I do not know. I heard rumors that Damiano was killed by a human monk shortly after he left us—some other plot gone bad. Whatever his fate, Hugo took Damiano's magic and turned it on us."

As if it soothed him, Bastien combed his fingers through Emile's hair, the strands a berry-black that matched his own. A moment later, he went on. "Hugo was hardly a saint before, but his new powers seemed to warp him. Cruelty became an end in itself. He would hurt his people even when they did nothing wrong. Our queen was no better. She spurred him on. I suppose she knew the next king would discard her. She never was well liked."

"And you tried to stop the abuse," Juliana said.

"Emile and I both. We tried to convince the others that if we stood together, Hugo could not win." He swallowed hard and his hand shook against Emile's cheek. "They said I spoke from ambition, that I would be no better if I ruled. They claimed Hugo was only instilling discipline—as if the outrages he committed could possibly be called that!" His voice broke with remembered anger, causing Emile to stir in his sleep. Helewis stroked Bastien's arm.

"Our brothers and sisters betrayed us," he said more quietly. "We were trying to save them, and they chose Hugo's side. When he heard what we were planning, he cast the spell that crippled Emile. I think he feared I might be able to resist his magic, but knew I could be controlled through a threat to my friend. Hugo promised he would remove the curse if I stopped rebelling, but I knew he lied. My only choice was to watch him closely and try to recreate his spells. Alas, I never found the secret to the one he used on Emile."

Without warning, tears spilled from his bright green eyes. "I am sorry, Ingrith," he said. "I thought if I could control your pack, I could make myself king and summon all the wolves of this realm to fight Hugo. I could compel him to heal Emile. But there was no excuse for doing the same to you."

Ingrith considered him in silence. Whatever she was thinking, she was keeping it to herself. Strangely enough, Bastien calmed beneath her scrutiny.

"It is done," she said at last. "You did not know you could trust us. Now you do. You also know that as a member of this pack, you will be held to a higher standard."

Bastien drew breath to speak, but Gytha broke in. "*I* am not apologizing."

Ingrith responded with dignity. "I would not expect you to, Gytha. If I decide to forgive you, it shall be for my own benefit."

This brought a grin to Helewis's face, though she was cautious or—perhaps—kind enough to hide it.

"I am grateful to you all," Bastien said seriously, "for Emile's sake as well as my own. Even if we cannot cure him, I know that, here, the time he has will be happy."

"We will cure him," said Helewis, her chin tucked around his shoulder. "Juliana will find a spell."

Her confidence was flattering but misplaced. Juliana began to deny the possibility, then thought better of saying a word. Even if there was no magic in Lucius's books, she could pretend. At worst, she would raise false hopes. At best, the pretense would work as well as Ulric's thrall had on the soldiers whose crosses they had removed.

She decided she would try, then confess what she had done if Emile improved. Better the pack know their own power than think she was a sorceress.

The resolution inspired the last of her tension to seep away. Closing her eyes as trustingly as Emile, she gave herself to the balm of sleep.

⌐

Sunrise woke Juliana, along with the alteration it brought to her companions. Huffing a bit to shift their heavy limbs, she squirmed out of their hold and stood looking down.

The pack was pale and lovely: statues twined among the furs with faces as blank as stone. Signs existed, however, that they were living beings. Her lips twitched to see that Stephen had stretched his leg across Emile and Ulric to touch Ingrith with his foot. Seeing this, seeing them all, she experienced a bit of what she would have watching children sleep.

The recognition that she was different, and maybe

always would be, did not inspire loneliness. Despite the bonds they shared, the members of the pack were also individuals. They held mysteries inside their hearts that Ulric would not disturb. This morning, safe and sound, that seemed a boon. Part of her would belong only to herself even when she joined them.

Content that it should be so, she left Bastien's chamber to head for the cold fountain. A splash of icy water across her face was just what she needed. Halfway down the passage something stopped her—neither sound nor sight, but an abrupt awareness of the world outside the cave.

Though she could not say how, she knew that a fine, warm rain—almost a mist—fell on the forest. The dampness lulled the animals into a doze but brought the growing things awake. The soldiers who had died the day before were beginning to be reclaimed, as if they had always dwelled in this place. Rust would take their armor, predators their blood and flesh, until no trace of their deaths remained.

Their families will miss them, she thought, then rubbed her face. The soldiers must have known the risks they were taking when they signed on with Gideon Drake. For him she experienced no regret; no rejoicing, either, just a sense of unreality that he was gone. The man she had run from, the man her father had schemed for her to marry, was no more.

Added to the knowledge that her father had disowned her, this made her feel as if she had cut the final ties to her human life.

She could not claim she was entirely comfortable with that idea.

She started to walk again, unsettled by her vision but unable to doubt its reality. Figments of the imagination were not that detailed. She was still shaking off the effects when she reached her destination.

The chamber of the cold fountain was ringed by three

mosaics: one of wolves hunting deer, one of an island breaking into pieces while being swallowed by the sea, and one of *upyr* flying against a backdrop of stars. Juliana assumed these were illustrations of events in the *upyr's* past but had no way of being sure. Stephen had mentioned Gillian often wondered at their meaning and had liked to sit here for hours on end. That had been enough to stop Juliana from making it her favorite spot.

She had no desire to feel any more haunted.

The fountain itself bubbled up from an unknown source, its waters glowing an uncanny blue that reflected off the mosaics and made them dance. Glow aside, the water was free of taint—sufficiently pure for Ulric and the rest to drink. Dirty water disagreed with them even more quickly than it did with humans.

Juliana stepped through the arched door in full expectation of having the room to herself. Instead, she came to a startled halt. An unfamiliar *upyr* sat on the fountain's rim with his legs extended and his ankles crossed. He was slim and quick-looking, even though he was motionless. His hair was closely cropped and brightly silver, his garb a rich, dark green. His hose clung to his legs like a second skin. His doublet, of equally exquisite fit, quite obviously required no padding. Atop one leanly muscled thigh he held a large, bound volume: the Aristotle she had dug out of a cache. He did not look sleepy, as most *upyr* would, but like a man who had had a nice, long walk and now savored sitting down.

His stone gray eyes met hers with the faintest smile, their sparkle the only part of him that moved.

"You must be Lucius," she said, oddly unafraid.

He conveyed a sense of stillness, inside as well as out, which precluded any sense of threat. Or perhaps his confidence was what calmed her. He would not attack because nothing could threaten him.

"I am Lucius," he conceded after a pause that seemed,

to her, a few breaths too long. "I am afraid I do not know you. Sadly, I arrived too late for proper introductions."

"I am Juliana Buxton, a friend of Ulric."

This elicited another pause and then, after Lucius finished thinking whatever he thought, a slow, white smile. The smile brought an unearthly beauty to his face, making her heart beat faster for strictly feminine reasons. She did not believe this had been his aim. Unlike Stephen and Bastien, this man did not strike her as a flirt.

"I feared Ulric would be unhappy after recent events in which I played a part," he said. "Thus, I returned. I am glad to see I wasted my time."

He rose as if he meant to go, as if the idea of speaking to Ulric himself after journeying specifically to see him were now pointless. Juliana's jaw dropped in disbelief. Of all the *upyr* she had met, this was the most peculiar.

"You cannot leave," she said, finding her voice.

"No?" said the *upyr*. He tilted his head unsurely, as if he truly did not know what courtesy required.

"No," Juliana said. "Ulric might have been worried about *you,* or he might want to wish you well in your new life. If I am not mistaken, you were with the pack a long time."

"That is true," said Lucius. "It was rather long." He pursed his lips in a thoughtful frown. "I suppose the others will want to greet me as well."

"Most assuredly they will. And I"—Juliana gathered her nerve—"should very much like to ask you some questions."

Lucius lifted his elegant silver brows and assumed a receptive pose, both hands crossed and gripping the book he held against his thighs. She tried not to be distracted by the fashionable shortness of his tunic. Apparently, he expected her to ask her questions then and there.

"I need a spell," she said, the first topic that came to her mind.

"A spell?" he repeated. His manner suggested no explanation in the world could take him aback. Before she knew it, she was telling him everything that had been happening to the pack. He listened with great attention, only breaking in occasionally with comments like: "*Two* new wolves?" and "Thought you were an *upyr*, did they?"

She told him a great deal more than she intended. In fact, now and then during her recitation, she felt as if she were not speaking at all, but that he was lifting the words straight from her mind. He seemed to understand whatever she said without explanation, until it was like a dream of a conversation, rather than a conversation itself.

"Interesting," he said when she finished, then spent a good three dozen heartbeats—her sort of heartbeats—staring at the wall. During that time, Juliana neither saw him breathe nor blink. He was so motionless, he practically disappeared, like a chameleon freezing on a rock. The fountain's glow slid over him in waves.

"You should not assume," he said, reanimating without warning, "that the Christians' cross has no power over our kind beyond an individual owner's faith. Symbols become invested with the energy of many believers and can carry that energy even in the face of doubt, like a flagon carries wine. The English captain might have expected more of his cross than it could deliver—that it be an invincible weapon rather than a modest shield—but that does not mean it had no real strength.

"Too, if such entities as gods exist, I see no reason why they cannot bless their tokens. No doubt these tokens' protective powers are smaller than they would be if they spoke in the original language of the *upyr*, but the effect might well be more than a trick of the mind. Or that is what I believe. I could be completely wrong. I have seen *upyr* who wore crosses themselves, who did not bat an eye at having one shoved in their face. Maybe it is a matter of power turned to a specific purpose by belief: of

latent force activated by human will. If the *upyr* knows
what to defend against, his will can reign supreme."

He smiled as if bemused by the workings of his mind,
a sentiment Juliana shared. She recalled Ulric mentioning
that Lucius had only recently regained some of his memories, that he had forgotten he was an elder. If this were
true, it might account for the eccentricities of his speech.

She rubbed the bridge of her nose. "I do not suppose
you remember any spells."

"Not a one," he said cheerfully, then thought again.
"No, actually, I did remember how to call a fog. Pretty little charm. Latin. But I am sure I could invent a spell to
help this Emile. Perhaps in a language no one understands? I would be interested to test your theory concern-
ing inherent power versus mere belief."

Then he yawned and she realized she had kept him
long after dawn.

"No matter," he said before she could apologize. "I
will seek my old room and we shall talk again after I have
slept."

He offered her the Aristotle as if he had borrowed it
from her, rather than the reverse. When she declined, he
smiled and left by the farther doorway, leaving her to
shake her head.

He was not what she imagined an elder would be.

Dazed, she turned her footsteps toward the hot spring
chamber for a soak. She needed time to consider what
she had learned.

⇌

Lucius was back.

The elder was sitting on Bastien's bed when the pack
awoke, as if there could be no question that he belonged.
The moment Ulric saw him, his heart sank to his gut. *Not
again* was all he could think. Juliana had never felt more
like a member of his pack, and now the *upyr* who had

helped Ulric's last lover run away from him had returned.

Ulric had changed. For Juliana, he had stopped trying to hold on so hard. He had been gentler, less controlling. He had taken the time to learn who his beloved was, as opposed to who he wished her to be. He did not deserve to have to confront this specter from the past.

Fighting to hide these thoughts, he watched Ingrith and Helewis greet the prodigal with shrieks of pleasure. Stephen hugged him and clapped his back. Because Gytha rarely waxed sentimental, her nod of welcome did not insult.

"It is good to see you," Lucius said, seeming surprised by his own delight. "You all look very well."

Then he turned to Ulric.

"Lucius," Ulric said, unable to refrain from crossing his arms.

Lucius ran his hand down the front of his dark-green tunic, a gesture that for one strange instant reminded Ulric of a human.

I do not know this *upyr,* he thought. And maybe I never did.

Lucius blinked, went down on one knee, and inclined his head. "Forgive me, pack leader," he said gravely. "I should have asked your permission before I returned."

Ulric let out his breath, realizing how conspicuously he must be bristling if Lucius felt obliged to kneel. "You do not need permission. You did what you believed was right by helping Gillian. You will always be welcome among my pack. Not that I could stop an elder like you."

"You are an elder?" said Emile, who had been waiting along with Bastien in wary silence.

"It appears I am." Lucius turned to the newcomers as he rose. "Juliana told me you might be in need of a spell."

"You met Juliana?" Ulric demanded, an inadvertent growl darkening his voice.

Lucius smiled faintly. "I did. While you were sleeping.

She was kind enough to share what has been happening in the pack. An interesting woman, and most attractive. I can see why you are more inclined to forgive me for Gillian."

"Ulric," Ingrith cautioned, catching his arm as he stepped forward. "Lucius is teasing you. He means no harm."

"No harm in the world," Lucius agreed. "In truth, I hope to pay off a debt. I enjoyed the hospitality of your pack for many years and, though I did not mean to, under false colors. Would you allow me to see if I can help Emile?"

Only a cur would have refused him, but Ulric was not given a chance.

"Oh, can you?" Helewis breathed. "That would be marvelous!"

Lucius tipped his head to the side, gazing at the sturdy *upyr* as if she were the marvel.

"What?" said Helewis, touching her throat nervously.

"I am wondering," Lucius said, "why you all seem different when I am the one who has changed."

⁓

Juliana had not felt comfortable returning to Bastien's chamber after her soak. Sleeping *upyr* could be unsettling company. Instead, she spent the rest of the day reading and napping in Ulric's bed. When she rose, some time past nightfall, to see how Emile was doing, she found a scene that caused a brief stab of hurt.

Lucius had not waited for her to perform his experiment. The pack were all in Bastien's room, gathered around Emile with varying expressions of wonder. His complexion gleamed white and clean as he sat upright on the floor wiggling his toes.

"I can feel my feet," he cried, "and I can move them!"

Then he burst into tears.

"It was nothing," the elder demurred, clearly uneasy. "You would be amazed what you can find in these old books." He patted the volume he held at his side, the Aristotle, conveniently scribed in indecipherable Greek.

"How interesting," Stephen commented softly, "that Juliana found no mention of magic in her searches."

"This text is in the tongue of Alexander," Lucius said with a passable imitation of affront. "Hardly any humans read that these days."

"And maybe some people"—Stephen leaned closer—"do not want word to get out that they can heal curses by laying on their hands."

"Nonsense," Lucius began to say when Bastien engulfed him in a bone-crushing hug.

He was crying, too, and noisily slapping Lucius's back. So much, Juliana thought, for Bastien's reserve.

She was not the only one grinning at his effusiveness.

"You have saved my friend!" he declared, seeming for once thoroughly French. "If I had not sworn to Ulric, I would follow you. The good Lord bless you, *mon ami!*"

Lucius freed himself gingerly. "No, no," he said, raising his hands and backing away. "I do not wish to lead anyone."

He retreated all the way to where Juliana stood in the door, so disconcerted he jumped when she touched his arm. Elder or not, it was impossible to be intimidated by this flustered man.

"Did you cure Emile with your touch?" she asked in an undertone.

Lucius wagged his head like a worried dog. "I cannot say. I thought the made-up spell was working, but perhaps I do not know my own strength."

"You will know it. Give your memories time to come back."

He grimaced as if this prospect failed to fill him with joy. "Speaking of strength . . ." he muttered to himself. He lifted his hand to catch Ulric's eye. Ulric was helping Emile see if he could stand, but he let Helewis take his place when Lucius beckoned.

"Come with me," the elder said. "We need to speak privately."

Juliana pressed her lips together to hide her smile. For someone who did not want to lead, Lucius was not shy about giving orders.

Chapter 17

Emile was sleeping again, with Bastien and Helewis watching over his bedside. Juliana could see their newest wolf had a gift for winning people's affections. Since Stephen and Ingrith were reluctant to leave his vicinity—in case he required more help—Juliana was working with Stephen on his letters in the hall outside Bastien's room.

This was the first chance they had gotten to fulfill her promise to teach him to read. Like all *upyr*, he was quick to learn, though it did take some doing to keep his mind on the task at hand. For Stephen, the attention of two living, breathing females meant it was time to play.

"No more 'cat' and 'hat,'" he said. "I must learn to write 'Ingrith is beautiful.'"

"Only beautiful?" Ingrith inquired. "What about clever and brave?"

His response was cut short by Ulric's appearance. The

pack leader had returned from his talk with Lucius looking grim.

Juliana's eyes widened at his frown. "Is everything all right?"

"Fine," he said, not seeming it at all.

"He did not make you lose your temper?" Ingrith asked worriedly. "I know you never liked when he forgot his place."

"No." Ulric rubbed his brow with the heel of his hand. "Not that I know what his place is now."

"Did he have a message from Gillian?" Stephen asked with his usual dearth of diplomacy.

Ulric shook his head as though his thoughts needed dislodging. "He did not mention her. He wanted to speak to me about Juliana."

"About me?" Juliana set down the stick with which she had been drawing letters in the dirt.

As she did, Ingrith jumped to the worst conclusion. "He cannot be trying to prevent her from becoming pack!"

Again Ulric shook his head. "He had no objection to that." His tone implied that Lucius had objections to something else. He turned to Juliana. "Walk with me. I will share what he revealed."

Juliana rose to her feet and shook out her skirts. "It is not bad, is it?"

"No, love." Ulric petted her cheek. "It is not bad."

But he sounded as if it were. With some anxiety, Juliana accompanied him down the passage to the entry ledge. There, in privacy, they sat with their legs dangling over the rock. Juliana lifted her hair from her neck. The outside air was warmer than she expected, a true hot summer night. Crickets sent their song in waves through the sea of trees. In the distance a lone wolf howled.

Ulric smiled to hear it, but to her the smile looked sad.

He must have seen her concern because he wrapped his arm around her shoulder. "What would you think," he said, "if you did not have to be changed?"

"Not be changed? What do you mean?"

She thought he was going to withdraw his invitation to join the pack, that despite his denial to Ingrith, Lucius had given him some reason why she could not be one of them. Her throat tightened, her mind already searching for ways to argue against she knew not what.

"It is not what you fear," Ulric said, his mouth pressing briefly into a line. "Lucius tells me that changing you might not be necessary, that your transformation has already begun. He says that when a human and an *upyr* are especially well matched, the normal sharing of power becomes something more. They actually begin to blend their essences. The process is slow, but in ten or twenty years, you would be *upyr*."

A tingle of shock streaked down her spine. Was this why Drake's soldiers had wondered if she were human: because in truth she was not?

Her reaction to the possibility took her by surprise. Perversely, it was more disturbing than being refused a chance to become *upyr*. That she could have fought. This had been thrust upon her without her knowledge.

"No," she breathed. "It cannot be."

Ulric shifted on the ledge to face her, his gaze intent. "Look at the evidence, Juliana. You are stronger than you were when I met you. You woke the menhirs and can climb our cliff without aid. Emile said you broke the ropes you were tied with all by yourself. You can see in the dark almost as well as I, and I cannot remember when I last had to uncrease your clothes. Those are not things the average human can do."

Juliana pressed her hands together over her mouth, her emotions in a turmoil she could not explain. "This morning, right before I met Lucius, I had a vision in which I saw the forest, even though I was inside. I knew it was misty. I could feel the growing things."

"Maybe that is your gift, to sense the life of the land."

"My gift . . ." She laughed, the muted nature of the sound failing to hide a hint of hysteria. "I read. I cipher. I bargain well in the market. Those are my gifts."

Ulric stroked her hair behind her ear, his hand as gentle as it could be. "Those are human gifts. All *upyr* have special talents. Some excel at thralls, some at feats of physical prowess. Do your abilities really trouble you that much?"

"How can Lucius know?" she demanded, evading his question. "I thought he had forgotten his past."

"He said he remembered that kind of changing when you described the reaction of Drake's guard. He said he thought it used to be more common, but now mortal and *upyr* live too much apart. He claims you smell too much like us not to be altered."

"His memory cannot be reliable!"

"According to him, skills come back more readily than life events. He was certain, Juliana. He would not have spoken if he were not."

Too agitated to sit, Juliana pushed to her feet and began to pace across the passage. Her prints pressed deeper than the *upyr* who had trod before her. In that, at least, she was human.

Ulric watched her from where he was. "Why does this upset you? I thought you wanted to be one of us."

"I did. I do. I simply thought it would be my choice, that I would have time to prepare. I thought you would summon Auriclus and he would judge if I was worthy and only then would I be changed."

"You are worthy," Ulric said. "You should not doubt that. But perhaps you did not truly think your decision through. Perhaps you made it in a weakened moment."

She could tell he was forcing steadiness into his voice, that he was no calmer than she. Her throat squeezed out a tiny noise she did not mean to make. The panic that surrounded her made no sense. Yes, she had told him she did not need to wait until summer's end because she thought it would make him happy, because his handling of Bastien had filled her with admiration. That said, she did want to be *upyr*. She was as ready as any mortal could be. She had seen how they lived. She could accept both best and worst. She ought to be grateful to join his pack—no matter what the means.

She would have been grateful if she were not terrified. It was all she could do not to wring her hands.

"I do not suppose," Ulric said with a touch of dryness, "that I would improve matters by relaying Lucius's other offer."

Juliana commanded herself to be still. "What other offer?"

"That he could change you himself as soon as you wished. Tomorrow, if you pleased. He is powerful, Juliana. Whatever his loss of memory, you could not want for a better sire. I doubt Lucius would ever force you to his will. You heard him with Bastien. He has no desire to rule. You would be indebted to someone who would probably never claim recompense."

Juliana thought this was true. So why did she feel as if she could not breathe? Why should being changed tomorrow be any different than a month from now?

Ulric rose, approaching her as carefully as he would a trembling hare. "There is another choice," he said, then exhaled heavily. "You could leave me before the change goes any further."

"No—"

"Hear me out, Juliana. You are stronger, but you are still human. If you lived among your kind, in some town where no one knows you, I doubt you would ever be at anyone's mercy. You could marry or not as you chose. Lucius said you might even have a little power to thrall. You are better at mind-speech than most humans. If you decided to go into trade, as you once said you wished, you would have a definite advantage."

His face was now totally unreadable, a perfect alabaster mask. But this could not be what he wanted. She knew he cared about her. Even if he did not love her as he loved Gillian, she knew he wanted her to stay.

"Think it over," he said. "You owe it to yourself to make a careful choice. Forever is a long time for regrets."

She dropped her head. Her indecision shamed her, but he was right. "I will think, Ulric, because I owe it to us both."

———

Ulric waited until Juliana had disappeared down the passage to slam his fist into the wall. Damn playing fair and damn Lucius for convincing him he had to.

"You must give her a choice," Lucius had said, "a true choice, to stay, to be your queen because her heart yearns toward yours, not because she believes she has nowhere else to go. If you love her, you must put her happiness before your own."

Ulric wanted her to be happy. He understood that if being with him did not lead to that end, he should be willing to let her go—truly willing, not just willing to say the words. He simply had not realized it would be the hardest thing he had ever done.

He had not believed she really might change her mind.

He clenched his hands on the stone, pushing it in his frustration, feeling the cold, rough surface begin to crack.

Helewis claimed he would only lose Juliana if he held on too tight, but Helewis had not seen her fear. Juliana was not as ready to be one of them as he hoped. Now that Drake was dead, maybe she felt she dared return to her own kind.

A shard of granite split off beneath his fist.

I gave up too easily, he thought. I should have fought harder. Surely he was entitled to argue for what he loved.

He pushed from the wall to seek her out, then commanded himself to stop. This was the same mistake he had made the last time. Juliana needed room to breathe, room he never gave Gillian.

A love he forced would try to escape.

~

Juliana moved through the darkened tunnels in a daze, struggling to understand the storm in her heart. Did she not trust Ulric? Had he not proved he would treat her well? Was she so set on being loved better than Gillian that she could not appreciate what the pack leader offered her? Every woman could not come first. That was simply a fact of life. Some had to settle for second best.

She stopped at the rubble-strewn entrance to another passage, this one too narrow to traverse. She shook her head at the stony floor.

Listen to her talk of "settling"—as if Ulric's love, second best or no, were not better than what thousands of women had. Compared to the dutiful misery she would have shared with Drake, it was a blessing. If she became *upyr,* she would be strong and cared for, not just by Ulric but by his pack. They would be her new family, and together they would live an adventure such as few dreamt. She would run as wolf and explore as woman, blessed by the company of a man she adored. Surely that was what mattered most. Love was about the gifts one gave, not those one got. Juliana had known that since she was young. How else could she have loved her father? That exchange had never been equal.

She pressed her palm to her heart. From its sudden ache, she realized she had stumbled onto the reason for her distress.

Ever since meeting Ulric, she had been trying to make

herself as indispensable to him as she had made herself to her father, offering her body and her blood just as she had once offered Henry Buxton a nice, hot meal. Even her human learning she had placed on the altar of usefulness. How different was searching for magic spells from helping her father with his accounts, or entertaining the pack with stories from pouring her father's port?

She trusted Ulric to protect her. What she did not trust was that he would love her for herself. That gift she had never been given by any man.

With Lucius here, no one needed Juliana to seek the secrets of the *upyr*. With Stephen learning to read, no one needed her to tell tales. Helewis and Ingrith were beginning to stand up for themselves. Once, she had envied the *upyr's* beauty, but as soon as Juliana became one of them, she would lose her last distinction: her human warmth. She would be the same as every female Ulric knew. Nothing would bind him to her but whatever affection she could inspire by being who she was.

It seemed a paltry weapon when he had won all her heart. After all, as soon as she lost her usefulness for her father, he had disowned her, had told Drake not to "bother" to chase her down. Little though it surprised her, the betrayal hurt. A parent should love a child no matter what. Knowing that Ulric was a very different kind of man could not ease her dread of being cast aside.

Clenching her hand before her breast, she forced herself to walk again. Enough of this self-pity! She did not wish it said that her mother had raised a coward. Her mother, after all, was the parent who had taught her how to love.

Juliana had the chance to live out a truly extraordinary fate with a truly extraordinary man. She would not shy away because she feared Ulric would never care for her as much as he had for Gillian. If he loved Juliana, however much he loved her and for however long, it would be because his heart chose, not because she made his life comfortable. That was the sort of love she wanted, the sort she deserved.

If he asked her to be his queen, so be it. If not, she would take pride in sharing his bed. Never would he doubt she was thankful for what she had or that he had been right in asking her to be pack.

Then again, she thought with the beginning of a wolfish snarl, if he *ever* took another female—as queen or lover—that would be the last he slept with Juliana. There were limits to what even a second-best love would stand!

Despite her satisfaction with this decision, she should have known it would not smooth every obstacle from her path. Through chance or unknowing intent, she had made a circle in her wanderings, returning to a finished section of the tunnels. She recognized the rosette carvings on the door up ahead. This was one of the entrances to the Hall of Columns, most likely the shortest route back to Ulric. She heaved at the door with her shoulder to overcome the ancient hinges' tendency to stick.

Inside the hall, lights sparkled on the polished pink marble floor, reflections from the two functioning chandeliers. It was a pretty effect, like jewels strewn on a pond. Distracted, Juliana did not at first see the person curled into a ball on the tiles.

Then Gytha lifted her head.

All at once, Juliana remembered she had not seen the *upyr* since Emile was healed.

Gytha's tears dried in a twinkling, but not before Juliana saw their tracks. She suspected more than a few had been shed in rage. The pack's acceptance of Emile and Bastien—formerly Gytha's ally—must have pushed her past the limit of what she could bear, a limit Juliana did nothing to restore by walking in on her suffering.

"Come to gloat?" Gytha said, her voice darkened by

defiance. "I suppose you think you have everything you want. Ulric's love. The pack's loyalty. Why, that Emile can hardly stop singing your praises. If Helewis were not so busy cosseting him, Ulric might take offense."

Unfolding her long, lean body from the floor, Gytha stalked closer to Juliana, completely unashamed of her nakedness. Truth be told, she had no reason to be ashamed. The black-haired *upyr* was as perfect a female as nature—or art, for that matter—could create.

"My intent was never to hurt you," Juliana said cautiously, aware of the weight of the purse that hung at her hip. Her knife was in it, along with Gytha's scythe. She decided now was not the time to return it.

"I believe you," Gytha said, flashing an alarmingly sharp-toothed grin. "Now ask me if I care."

Juliana could see no benefit in that. "Do not do this," she said instead, shifting position as the *upyr* began a slow and ominous circling. "If you could learn to control your temper, you would have a chance of earning back everything you lost."

"Not Ulric."

"Ulric was never yours to lose."

She had said it gently, but the *upyr* was crouched now, heartbeats from attack. Juliana's pulse pattered in her throat. She dared not assume Gytha intended anything but to kill her. Gytha had not earned her position as lead female with empty threats. The *upyr* paused long enough to gather her leg muscles for a leap. Without a moment for second thoughts, Juliana seized her chance.

She did not waste time opening her drawstring purse. She grabbed it and thrust as Gytha jumped, snapping the cord that held it to her waist with the same strength that had surprised Emile earlier. Gytha jumped back and danced away, her reflexes too quick for Juliana to take more than a glancing cut out of her belly—even with both blades splitting the chamois cloth.

Frankly, she was impressed she had managed that.

Wrenching the knives free of the purse, she took one in each hand and barreled toward the *upyr*. Juliana had no training in knife play; Gytha could have evaded her as before. Instead, she laughed, braced her feet, and stuck out her arms to halt the rush. As Juliana had hoped, the *upyr* underestimated her speed.

When Juliana hit her, Gytha lost her footing. Even so, as she fell with Juliana atop her, she was able to sweep the scythe aside. The knife was a different matter. Held in Juliana's stronger right hand, it stabbed through Gytha's palm and pinned it to the floor.

Gytha did not bother to scream. Though her lips peeled back at the pain, she was already preparing to tear free when Juliana stopped her. Thanks to Lucius, she had one more trick the *upyr* did not expect.

Do not do this, she said with all the force of her mind.

Gytha froze, either with shock that Juliana could speak in her thoughts without Ulric there to help, or because the order held an edge of thrall. Juliana prayed it was a bit of both.

"Think, Gytha," she said, her knees planted stubbornly on the *upyr's* ribs, her voice surprisingly hoarse. "If you kill me, you lose. Even if you hurt me, Ulric will banish you from the pack. He will do so not because he loves me, but because as long as I am human, there can be no equal battle between us. After what you did to Ingrith, you are already on your last chance. The only way to win is to stop fighting. Maybe one day you will find a pack you like better, one where you can rule, but if you become known as someone who preys incessantly on the weak, who do you think will allow you in?"

"The weak!" Gytha laughed shakily. Blood puddled on her palm around the blade, her fingers twitching in little jerks. Juliana swallowed, striving neither to wince nor let up. Gytha's wolf instincts drove her to dominate. The slightest sign of hesitation might inspire an attack.

Juliana did not want this fight to have more consequences than either of them could survive.

"I caught you unawares," Juliana said levelly. "I doubt
you will give me that chance again."

The *upyr's* gaze locked onto hers, narrow and searching. Juliana knew her firmness was being weighed. "You
could call the pack leader," Gytha said, "using your mind.
You could tell him of my assault."

"I could. Whether I do is up to you."

"I could bide my time until you are *upyr* and challenge
you then."

At this suggestion, Juliana flashed her own toothy grin.
"Lucius has agreed to change me. I could be wrong, but
I suspect he is older and more powerful than your sire.
Because his strength would determine mine, you might
not find me easy to subdue."

Gytha spat out a pithy curse. "I am not exactly 'sub-
duing' you now." She rolled her eyes and shook her head,
her fangs retracting as Juliana watched. The *upyr* heaved
a disgusted sigh. "It is done. I acknowledge your superi-
or rank. I would offer you my throat, but you do not have
the teeth to bite it."

"That will not be necessary," Juliana said, "as my knife
has already tasted your blood."

A muffled thump in the air between them startled
them both. This was followed by a flash that signaled the
unexpected lighting of a third chandelier. With the
added illumination, the pink of the marble paving edged
closer to red. Juliana fought a superstitious shiver.
Grudging or not, queen or not, the outcome of this infor-
mal challenge had been accepted by whatever forces
ruled the *upyr*.

"Wonderful," Gytha said sourly. "Now you can let me
up."

This Juliana did, bracing her weight on Gytha's palm as she withdrew the knife. To her relief, the blade came out cleanly. Gytha immediately cradled the wound to her chest, gripping her left hand with her right until the bleeding stopped. The slash on her belly was already closed. All that marked where it had been was a line of puffy red across her muscles.

When the worst of the pain seemed past, Juliana offered her hand.

"Pull it back before I bite it off," Gytha snapped. "We are not friends."

"As you wish," Juliana said, turning away before the other saw her amusement. Shameful though it was to admit, she had enjoyed getting the better of this *upyr*.

⌘

Ulric waited in the entrance to his chamber, one hand propped on either side of the open door. The light shone from behind him, outlining his naked form. Ropelike muscles stood out in his arms, and his torso was taut with impatience.

As was usual, her portrait locket hung around his neck, a belonging he had never asked leave to keep. The sight of it touched her, but just as inspiring was the tapering of his chest down to his hips. Juliana bit her lip. One of his legs was cocked, the other straight, the hair on both gleaming gold. Even the hang of his sex was arrogant, his shaft a bit too substantial to be at rest.

I am king, said the pose, *and woe betide anyone who denies it.*

She could see he had been fuming since she left.

He truly did not want her to leave.

Though her clothes were straight, Juliana felt disheveled and breathless, heat moving through her in heavy waves. Tonight Ulric resembled the *upyr* she had met in

Bridesmere, the *upyr* who pursued his desires without apology.

When he spoke, his words did nothing to contradict that impression.

"I do not care what you have decided," he said. "I will not lose you—at least, not without a fight."

Juliana bowed her head to hide her smile. "If you do not want to lose me, you should probably stop blocking the doorway and let me in."

His look was wry as he stepped aside. "This is no game, Juliana. I told you what Lucius said, that the two of us are unusually well matched."

She moved past him to the other side of his chamber, shy of letting him see her pleasure, wanting to be certain she understood. With restless fingers, she touched the seat of his unbroken stool. To its left was a new malachite-topped table, which he must have carried from one of the storerooms to hold her books. To its right— Her heart stuttered for a moment. To its right, above the level of her head, a pair of thick bronze hooks were screwed into the wall. They were also new, though less obvious in their use.

She turned her back on them hastily, embarrassed to betray the ideas they stirred. No doubt Ulric had a lamp he wanted to hang up.

As he followed her into the room, the door swinging shut behind him, she searched his solemn face.

"One match in thousands," he said, "and we found each other, not by looking but by fate. That tells me we were meant to be together."

"We are together," Juliana said.

He took her by the shoulders and gave her a little shake. "As mates, Juliana. Bonded. Like a marriage among your kind."

"Like king and queen?" she said very softly.

A subtle flush flooded his face as he crowded closer,

almost close enough to kiss. "I will not deny that is what I mean. I want you to be mine. Not like Stephen and Ingrith, not like Gytha and Bastien, but mine as in my other half for as long as our lives shall last." His wonderful scent grew stronger as his body warmed. "If you insist you need more freedom, I will concede, but I will not pretend for one more night that complete possession is not my aim. It is my nature, Juliana, to hold what I love."

"Ulric, I—" She meant to assure him their wishes were in accord, but he cut her off.

"Just listen," he said, and she hushed instinctively at the authority of his tone. "I know I have made mistakes in the past, that I held too tight when I should have given freer rein. I will try not to repeat those errors. I will try to be gentler, to listen, but I will not hide who I really am."

"I would not want you to," Juliana cried, lifting her hands to caress his forearms. "Ulric, love, I think you are laboring under a misapprehension. Whatever Gillian wanted from you, I am different."

"Yes," he said. "You are." He looked into her eyes and drew a chest-swelling breath. "She was the love of my pride, Juliana. You are the love of my heart."

For a moment, she was speechless, blinking against the burn of tears. To have had what she wished for all along . . .

"I thought—" She swallowed, scarcely able to speak the words. "Everyone told me how much she meant to you. You told me yourself. I always felt I was in her shadow, that even if you wanted to, you would never let yourself love me as much as you loved her."

A smile lifted one corner of his mouth. "I did not want to love you more," he admitted, his hands sliding over her shoulders. "I simply could not help it. You were like her in too many ways, with your books and your questions. I thought I would lose you if I did not change. But I can only change what I do, not who I am."

"I love who you are! I think . . ." She wrapped her arms behind his waist. "I think some of the changes you have made are good, but I loved you before you made them." She hid her face in his shoulder. "I even love your arrogance. Helewis said something that first night when you wounded Bastien and I ran away. She asked me not to fight you. She said when the leader is strong, everyone feels safe. Maybe I am less of a follower than I believed, but part of me, an important part, only feels safe when you are in charge. I like it when you are gentle, but that is not all I like, and it has never been what I like best."

Her voice sank to a murmur at the confession. To her relief, he appeared to understand what she meant. His pulse sped up and his shaft surged strongly against her gown. She hugged him tighter rather than let it rise.

"Is that so?" he asked huskily. "In that case, I think you will like how I planned to treat you tonight."

His eyes were dark, his irises a ring of burning gold.

"Planned?" she repeated as his fingers trailed shiveringly down her spine. "You mean you did not intend to ask?"

"Not this time. Not when asking might have meant letting you slip away."

His hands caught her wrists and pulled them from behind his back, not hurting her, but not letting her refuse. With the release of her embrace, the crown of his erection brushed up her dress. She wanted to see it, to measure the starkest evidence of his need. When she began to lower her eyes, his grip turned hard.

"No," he said. "It is my turn to admire you. Remove your gown, Juliana. I cannot treat you as I wish until it is gone."

The order turned her liquid deep inside. Unable to speak, she fumbled with her laces, only with difficulty able to pull the bodice down. As she wriggled it over her hips, a vein beat noticeably in his jaw.

She felt a surge of triumph when he wet his lips.

"Chemise, too," he said, "and then stand still."

She did as he demanded, aware of the heat and throb of her body as never before. Ulric backed up to watch, his erection as hard as horn. He clucked his tongue at her disobeying his order not to look, but since his penis jumped a fraction higher, she thought he was not displeased. His gaze centered on her nipples, hard now and tight, then slid to the apex of her thighs. His perusal was like the most delicate touch, making her swell and dampen, making the bud of her pleasure push between her folds.

When Ulric saw it, his teeth slid out.

"It is almost worth letting you wear clothes," he said hoarsely, "to watch your body react when you take them off."

She could only manage to gasp his name.

"Do you want me to kiss you?" he said, seeming determined to make her speak. "Do you want me to shove my tongue in your mouth?"

Juliana shuddered. "I want you to do exactly what you please."

The air shimmered around him as a growl rumbled in his chest. She thought he was going to change, but he held on. A trickle of arousal ran down her inner thigh. His nostrils flared when he caught the scent.

"Back up and lift your arms," he rasped. "I want you to hold those hooks."

She had known what they were for as if she had read his mind, but having the guess confirmed was like stepping into a dream. Though the bronze was colder than the chiseled wall, her body felt as sultry as the night outside. With bated breath, she awaited what would come next.

Ulric did not keep her in suspense. Simply gripping the hooks was not enough for him. He bound her to them with two long strips of fur-lined hide, wrapping her wrists tightly enough that even with her enhanced strength, she was unable to break free.

She hung on them for a moment just to be sure.

"There," he said, "now I can pleasure you as I wish."

He was breathing especially hard for one of his kind, and across his belly his cock cast a shadow that pulsed and surged. The air around him seemed to vibrate, the force of his lust too great to contain.

"You are my prisoner," he said, the words as rough as sand.

She could not help wondering if he were not one as well.

Chapter 18

❦

Ulric had never been this aroused in his immortal life. His body was pounding so hard he felt as if he were shifting form. When Juliana moaned, he nearly did. Gone was his fear that she could not love him, leaving him elated and light of head.

She wanted to be his prisoner.

Triumph soared through his veins like heated wine. Everywhere he faced her, his skin felt tight.

"All this time," he whispered, wrapping his hands behind hers on the hooks. "All this time I wasted trying to keep my beast in check when I could have been running wild."

"I liked watching you struggle," she whispered back.

He laughed low in his throat and kissed the tip of her nose. Unnaturally hot though he was, her flush was a trembling fire. "I wanted to tie you up to show you what you would be missing if you left."

"Show me," she said, "what I have to look forward to."

He shifted his hands until his fingers twined with hers, the interpenetration a reminder of what would come. Other than this, there was no contact between them: only the mingling heat of their bodies, only the rapid brush of their breath. Their energy was so high her hair had begun to dance and his prickled on his chest. He moved his hips forward just enough for the throbbing tip of his hardness to strafe the silk of her abdomen. She jerked at the contact, then settled as he drew the crown right and left. He was damp with excitement, heating and cooling by turns.

Her lower lip whitened delectably beneath her teeth.

"There," he said on a puff of sound. "That is what you have to look forward to. My cock driving inside you, pushing, rubbing, filling you up until you want to howl."

Stirred by his own words, he tilted his head and kissed her hard, his fangs making it awkward, though neither of them seemed to mind. Her tongue curled between them, tickling and tempting until his hunger to bite her slim, smooth neck squeezed his ribs around his lungs. Panting uncontrollably, he pulled free of her mouth. The pad of his thumb drifted up her strongest vein.

She must have guessed what he longed for, because she wet her lips.

"Not yet," he said, though he reveled in the knowledge that her desire echoed his. "If I feed, my lust will drive me too fast. I want to savor teasing you first."

He palmed her breasts in both hands, smoothing the rich curves upward, squeezing her rosy nipples between his pale fingers.

Only when her head lolled back did he bend to kiss them.

"Ulric," she gasped, then murmured a broken prayer.

Suckling her was his prayer, tormenting himself with the way her blood rose sweetly beneath her skin. He moved his hold to her back to press her closer, spreading his fingers out. One breast enthralled him, then the other, her muscles tensing and relaxing under his hands.

Sighing, he sank to his knees and kissed her belly, softly at first, then hard enough to leave a mark. Her thighs trembled as he caressed them, as he pushed them gently apart. Her excitement smelled like his idea of heaven.

"Ulric," she said, trying to close her knees.

He drew his tongue up her hipbone, then kissed the crisp, warm triangle of her hair. "You do not have my permission to hide. All of you belongs to me."

"Ulric—"

"Hush, love, unless you want me to believe you have forgotten every word but my name."

He spread her secrets and kissed her tenderest bud, delighting in her rising tension, exulting in her broken gasps. She was satin and cream and hot, swollen folds of plumpness that were perfect for pulling against his tongue—now gently, now with groan-inducing force. She squirmed beneath his ministrations, his fangs a pressure he knew how to wield to excellent effect.

He heard his name moaned more than once as he coaxed her to the brink and then backed off.

When he rose, shaking slightly from his own unmet needs, the knuckles with which she gripped the hooks were white.

"Take me," she said, her frustration giving the plea an edge.

Ulric shook his head and leaned in to lick her full, red lips. "Not yet."

"You want to."

"I do, but first I want to feed."

"You could lose control from that. You could spill."

"I could," he said, knowing it was true, especially with her, especially tonight. "But I will not. You cannot be king unless you know how to rule your desires."

She craned forward to catch his mouth in a kiss. He let her, delving deep, drawing and being drawn until he could barely think. She lifted one knee to caress the side of his leg.

He knew his eyes were glowing when he pulled back.

"Ul-ric," she complained with an expression so close to a pout, it threatened to break his control. Instead, he smacked the curve of her bottom, relishing the way it shimmied beneath the blow. Caught by surprise, she squeaked and went on her toes.

"First one hunger," he said, "then the other. I want to swive you slowly tonight."

"But—"

"I will take you hard, Juliana, bruising hard . . . and slow . . . and deep until neither of us can keep from exploding."

Her eyes widened and her cheeks grew pink. He knew he had voiced her wish. Smiling softly, he cupped her mound. For a moment, he simply enjoyed her heat, then slid two fingers between her folds and curled them inside her, holding them tight to the front of her passage with an opposing pressure from his thumb. She made a broken sound as he rubbed a circle on both sides.

"That should keep you," he breathed close to her ear, "until I shove what you really want up in there."

He licked her lobe and made her shiver, then mouthed the salty skin beneath. Gradually, her neck relaxed and her hips began to rotate against his palm. She smelled like musk and felt like oiled velvet.

"Tell me when you want it," he said. "Tell me when I should bite you."

He knew from her smile that he should not have given her the power. She used his exhortation to take revenge, waiting until he had nuzzled the length of her collarbone, until he had tugged her nipples between his teeth and buried his face in her breasts. His breathing grew labored, his muscles tight, while her sexual scent curled maddeningly up from his hand.

"Now," she sighed just as he was sure he would lose his mind.

His mouth was at her neck before the word faded.

When he pierced her skin, he almost brought her to pleasure. He could feel her passage clenching around his fingers in soft spasms of greed. His peak was just as close, plucking with dangerous insistence at his nerves. His promise, or mayhap his boast, was all that kept it back.

Tightening his arms around her, he lifted her until her wrists slid off the hooks. With her bonds for bracelets, her hands plunged immediately into his hair, holding him to her as he fed.

The connection between them nearly stopped his heart. Her pulse, her very life, beat in his mouth, offered freely and with love. He himself could hold nothing back. His soul was open, his nature bared. That he could trust her with both was a miracle. He drank her in tiny sips, wanting the closeness to last, pulling the ecstasy through her veins like golden fire.

Her thighs rose smoothly to wrap his waist. The moment his mouth released her, she slid her creamy warmth over his cock. Speechless with the sensations, he planted his legs a little wider to help her sink.

"Promise," she murmured next to his ear. "Promise it shall be hard."

She had no doubt he would oblige.

Groaning, he eased her closer, one arm like sun-warmed marble beneath her bottom. He did not move, as if he did not dare, carrying her squeezed tight against him and lowering her to the bed. He lay her crosswise in his sleeping niche with her hips positioned on the edge. He was kneeling between her thighs, hard and thick inside her, almost grinding her in his need.

She stretched her arms above her head until they touched the wall. The sound she made as she arched her back could only be called a purr. His cock quivered in response.

"You want it hard," he said.

Though it was not a question, she nodded and braced her hands on the stone.

He drew back, slowly, his expression tight. Her body clung to his hardness, as if it could not bear to let go. She sucked in a breath and held it. Then he drove in, every bit as forceful as she wished, all his frustrations in the shattering thrust. At her cry of helpless pleasure, he did it again. The blows were perfect: deft, determined, gradually gaining in speed as he built up a strong rhythm. The tautness of his muscles, the grinding of his teeth told her how badly he longed to spend. The night's first coupling was, for him, always the most intense. Sweat began to roll down his straining body, now as hot as hers.

King or not, he was not used to waiting this long.

"More," she moaned, feeling delightfully cruel.

He gripped one of her thighs and pushed it wider, opening her completely to his long, hard thrusts. She clenched around him to pull him in.

"Juliana," he said in warning, a muscle in his jaw ticking for control.

"More," she whispered, betraying herself with a grin.

The grin, or maybe the fact that she dared to give him instruction, turned him wild. He made a sound between a growl and a grunt, his motions suddenly too quick for human speed. Sensation swelled between her legs like a wailing wind, causing her to clutch at him and gasp, narrowing her awareness to the places their bodies met. In heartbeats, he cried out, bringing her with him in a spangling flood.

"Juliana," he groaned. "Lord Almighty."

Before she could catch her breath, he flipped her over and slid into her again, for once seeming even more desperate for a second ride. Glassy smooth and hot, he pumped into her from his knees, rubbing the front of her passage, taking full advantage of the slickness he had made.

His thumbs pressed the cleavage of her buttocks, stirring sensations she did not expect.

"You . . . are . . . mine," he said in time to his movements. "You shall never refuse me again."

Her nerves already primed, Juliana came twice more before he thrust one final time and held. His orgasm hit him with brutal force, his arms tightening around her while his prick gave up its burden as deep as it could reach.

Her pleasure flared like a tinder tossed on a fire.

Ulric groaned, finally relaxing, his cheek coming to rest against her sweaty back. Gently, he nuzzled her nape. From the tiny sting and the glow that even now spread through her body, she knew he had bitten her again at the end.

"Good," he said, the word coming out on a heaving breath. He had softened inside her, but not enough to slip out. "That was the way it should be."

At her wriggle, he eased back enough to allow her to turn around. With her calves crossed comfortably behind his thighs, she drew one finger down the side of his face. His hair hung toward her in a spill of lamplit gold, increasing her sense of their bond. For this moment, he was all she wanted in the world.

She knew he felt the closeness, too. He turned his head just enough to kiss her wrist where her pulse had begun to slow. His lashes fell, hiding the glow of his eyes, despite which his happiness was plain to see.

"Speak to Lucius soon," he said, his lids lifting slowly to meet her gaze. "I want you safely settled in your new life."

Juliana smiled, half to herself and half to him. Autocratic though it might be, the order suited her to the ground.

Chapter 19

An upwardly sloping tunnel with rough-hewn walls led Juliana and her two companions to their goal: the octagonal chamber with the marble benches, where the natural chimney let in the sun. Lucius had chosen this isolated spot as the setting for her transformation. As the hour was close to midnight, the light would pose no problem for him or Ulric—assuming, of course, that Lucius could be harmed.

Because the elder led the way, Juliana was able to observe that his footwear left no marks, not even briefly, as if he were more ghost than man. She could not imagine how it would feel to possess more power than anyone you knew, much less what it would take to hide that power even from yourself.

The passage ended at a door capped by a triangular pediment. None of them spoke as they walked beneath it. The room seemed ancient to Juliana—because of its parchment smell perhaps, or the well-worn mellowness of its sand-colored stone. At the junctures of the walls, unknown masons had carved the rock into grooved pilasters. The eight half-columns gave the room the air of an ancient chapel, one that followed unfamiliar rites. Plain, beveled squares incised the walls between. A single torch leaned out from each.

Once closed, the door was thick enough to block all sound.

"Privacy," Lucius explained as she and Ulric moved farther in. "We cannot have that Frenchman adding to his repertoire of tricks. You, of course," he said to Ulric, "must be included, though Auriclus would have my hide if he knew."

The pack leader pulled a dubious face. "I am no longer certain my sire could take your hide."

Lucius's smile was pure, boyish joy. "True," he said, "and how nice it is to realize that likelihood."

From this and other comments the pack had made, Juliana concluded Ulric's sire could be a bit of a prig. Maybe it was better than she knew that she was not waiting for Auriclus to change her.

She and Ulric took a seat on the bench opposite the door, while Lucius lit the ring of torches with a flint. They all burned smoothly in their metal sconces, a soft, rich blue that did not sputter or smoke. Like the chandeliers in the hall, Juliana suspected these were part of the cave's oldest furnishings. They did not work like human creations.

Her excitement rose as the strange, clean flames brightened the room. She was going to take part in a mystery.

"Atmosphere," Lucius said when he had finished his circuit. "In case, as Juliana posits, our success can be enhanced by faith—not that I have any doubts about the result."

"I am wondering what you need me for," Ulric said. "Since this process is supposed to be a secret."

"You are here to open Juliana's heart. As closely bonded

as you two are, her spirit might resist me if I tried to change her on my own." Lucius rubbed one finger across his lips and turned to her. "There is a question I should ask you first. As Ulric knows, traditionally a new *upyr's* memory of the change is erased as soon as it is complete. The elders, in their wisdom, did not think our population should increase indiscriminately. As a pack leader and his future queen, however, you might have a need to know. I thought I would leave the choice up to you."

"I want to remember," Juliana said without hesitation.

"I as well," Ulric added behind her.

Regardless of their agreement, Lucius had a caveat. "Knowing how the change is accomplished does not guarantee that either of you would be able to perform it. That gift depends on age and inborn power. Besides, it might be risky knowledge to have, should someone learn you possess it and want it for themselves."

"I want to know," she repeated, leaning earnestly over her knees. "I am sure we can be discreet."

"As you wish," Lucius said. "You have shown tolerable judgment up till now. I will leave your memories intact."

Though euphoric over his concession, Juliana tried to conceal her feelings. Responsible people did not leap about excitedly.

"Do we need to do anything special?" she asked.

"As in hop on one foot chanting prayers?" The elder smiled gently and shook his head. "I see no reason to engage in empty ritual with you. No, I think you should simply sit in the center of the floor—tailor fashion, as the humans say—and we will do the deed without more ado. Ulric, you sit behind her and put your hands on her waist. That should reassure her spirit that I do not mean to tie it to mine."

Somewhat unnerved by his talk of spirits, as if hers might be doing something behind her back, Juliana and Ulric arranged themselves as the elder wished. Lucius sat

directly before her, his hose-clad knees bumping hers. At
his instruction, he and Juliana grasped each other's wrists.

Her contact with the elder's skin did peculiar things to
her heart, which seemed unable to decide whether to slow
down or speed up. She swallowed back a touch of alarm.

"Breathe with me," Lucius said, "and relax."

Juliana did her best, though her nerves were jumping
like field mice. In time with Lucius, she filled and emp-
tied her lungs while Ulric did the same behind her. The
procedure did relax her. Soon Lucius looked as still as all
upyr did in sleep, more statue than living being. He was
as lovely as a statue, one carved by an expert hand. High
brow. Straight nose. Lips like a Roman coin. His jaw was
as lean as a fasting saint's. She noted, too, that his glow
was brighter than before, rolling over his skin in gold-
white waves.

Watching it made her eyes want to cross.

Relax, said Lucius in her mind, reassuring her he was
awake. She only wished she did not have an itch on her
nose.

Thankfully, Ulric rubbed it for her.

Maybe you should close your eyes, he suggested with a
hint of acerbity. He must have sensed her admiration for
the elder's looks. She would have been glad to allay his
concern, but feared she would miss the most exciting part.

Then, as if to justify her desire to watch, Lucius's glow
began to flow down his arms like smoke. Over his wrists
it curled and up and through her sleeves. As soon as the
smoke-glow reached her neck, her skin went numb. The
feeling was unexpectedly pleasant, similar to being about
to drop off to sleep. Her eyelids grew so heavy she had to
struggle to keep them up.

A moment later, she was glad she had. A body formed
of light—this one supremely naked—detached itself
from Lucius's solid form. As sinuous as a cat stretching its
spine, the figure rocked forward on its hands and knees.

Then, before she had a chance to be shocked, the light-
body slid effortlessly into hers.

The invasion was accompanied by a ferocious tingling
and the very odd impression of being stretched.

Heavens, she thought. He is inside me.

She had only an instant to comprehend this. Her heart
gave one great jolt as the edges she had always known
herself to live within disappeared. The floor of the chamber, the soft blue light of the torches, Ulric's hold on her
waist—all dissolved to black. On every side, even under
her now-invisible feet, stars whirled and bobbled like
drunken moths. She felt as if she floated high in the air,
both immense and inconsequential, the forest and the
beings who lived within it beating far beneath.

Though she was afraid, it was the kind of terror that
brings delight. Somehow, beyond any promise, she knew
she would be safe.

Where is this? she thought, the question echoing in the
spaces that were her head. *How did I get here?*

This is the nothing place, answered someone who was
not quite Lucius, the voice so close it seemed to resound
inside her, as if she spoke and listened at the same time.
*This is where everything comes to change and where every-
thing remains the same. The void gives birth to the spark.*

Are you Lucius? she asked.

I am—the other trembled on a hesitation—*the Lucius
at the heart, the Lucius who remembers the beginning.*

This pricked up Juliana's ears.

Tell me where you are from, she asked eagerly. *Tell me
how the* upyr *came to be.*

The stars swelled hugely, swallowing the velvet sky, then
dwindled to pinpricks. *I can,* he said, *only show you a piece.*

～

Through the heavens a ship was sailing, silver sleek and
arrow light. It had no mast or oars, no portholes, and no

deck. The only reason Juliana called it a ship was because
that was how Lucius thought of it. He rode in a tiny com-
partment shared with two other men, deep within the
needle-shaped hull. He was young—no king, no elder, but
a cleaner and fixer of broken things. He barely understood
the voyage he had been conscripted to embark upon.

The ship, such as it was, circled ever closer to a planet
of deep-blue waters and swirling clouds. Though she had
never seen it from this perspective, Juliana knew the
planet was Earth.

As the vessel approached the surface, flames danced
along its skin, creating a beautiful, white-pink glow.
Juliana was afraid, but the fire did not burn. Still cool as
snow, the ship landed like a feather on an island in an
unnaturally placid sea. With wonder and fear, humans
rushed out to greet the intruders. Many in the ship were
carrying weapons, but not Lucius. He was not sufficiently important. Despite his defenseless state, his mind
buzzed with interest as he descended a sloping, silvery
ramp in the midst of a murmurous crowd.

His surroundings came as a surprise.

The sun was brighter than he was used to, and peculiar
on top of that, creeping like spider silk along his arms.
Nearly blind, he had to shield his eyes to see where he
and his shipmates had ended up.

To his astonishment, once his vision cleared, the
natives' city appeared as marvelous as the ones he had
left behind—spires of stone and glass rising from a shim-
mering net of canals. The architecture was unfamiliar but
pleasing, and the scent of many gardens perfumed the air.

"Greetings," said Lucius's captain in a gentle but carrying tone. "We are the *upyr*. We come in peace to trade
knowledge with your people. If you allow it, we hope to
live among you for a time."

Though little more than a serf, Lucius knew the captain
lied. He hoped to live here forever. He was an exiled

prince who had headed a failed rebellion. He and his
crew could never go home.

He is desperate, Lucius thought. We do not even know
if this place is safe.

As if to underscore his fears, the bright-yellow sun
seemed to glare at him from the sky, glinting off the
glassy towers, burning balefully from the sea. Lucius
could feel the alien light bouncing all around him, poking here, prodding there, like a living being who was not
sure it liked this planet's new guests.

The light felt as if it wanted to change them, to warp
the very particles that made them up.

He shivered strongly at the foreboding, then just as
strongly shoved it aside.

I do not care, he thought with the rebellious optimism
of his youth. Here all started fresh. Whatever came, he
would make the best of it that he could.

❧

A roaring like the ocean filled Juliana's ears, shaking her
from the dream.

"You had no special powers," she breathed, the sound
of her voice an oddity. "The *upyr* were like humans when
you first came."

Whatever had just happened, she was back in the
eight-walled chamber, back in her body and her mind.
She was not, however, satisfied. "Where was that city?"
she demanded. "And how long ago did you arrive? I am
sure I never heard of a place like that, not even from merchants' tales!"

Before Lucius could answer, she covered her mouth
with both hands. "Oh! Those people who were in the flying ship with you must have been the first elders. The sun
must have changed them just as you feared. How horrified you must have been when you had to start drinking
blood . . . unless you did that before?"

Lucius gaped at her as if her face had grown a second nose. "Flying ship?" he said weakly.

Still behind her, Ulric chafed her arms. "You are babbling, love. Are you all right?"

"Of course I am all right. I saw one of Lucius's memories." She turned to the elder for confirmation and met a blank. "You do not remember, do you? Oh, Lucius, I am sorry, but I would be happy to share what I saw."

"No," he said, putting out a forestalling hand. "I . . . lost my awareness when I slipped inside you. If you told me what you saw, it would be meaningless."

"I cannot believe you do not want to know."

The elder's arm fell to his side. "If I were ready, my past would come back to me on its own."

"Hush," said Ulric when she drew breath to speak again. "Everyone is not as curious as yourself. What matters is that you came through the change with no ill effects."

"Came through—" Struck speechless, Juliana turned on her hip to face him. "Do you mean to say that was it?"

Behind her, Lucius snorted out a chuckle. "Loss of memory notwithstanding," he said, "I wager you are the first *upyr* not to realize she was changed. But I am certain you two have many things to discuss. I shall leave you to it and wish you well."

Before she could open her mouth to protest, Lucius bowed and withdrew.

"Well," said Juliana. "I wager I am the first *upyr* to frighten off her sire. He might have stayed to say 'congratulations.' "

Ulric hugged away the sting of the elder's hasty departure. "Lucius has always been very private. No doubt the closeness involved in the change was a bit too much. And better you frighten him than the reverse."

"Did you understand what he did?" she asked. "Because I am convinced I could never tell anyone what it was."

"I believe I understand, in principle at least. Lucius let go of his physical form, somewhat as we do when we turn wolf, but instead of altering his body, he left it behind. Then he merged his spirit form with yours. I suppose he must have left an essence of himself inside you when he drew out, and that was what allowed you to become *upyr*." Ulric buried his nose in her hair. "You do smell a bit like him now, like snow that is about to fall. Auriclus's children tend to smell like the forest."

Remembering Ingrith and Stephen's argument about whether Lucius had a scent, Juliana smiled. How long ago that seemed, and how unimportant. Tonight, she was content to let Ulric hold her as she tried to decide if she felt different. More sensitive perhaps, and quieter deep inside. The effect of Ulric's hand stroking her hair was like a drug.

"The light has more colors," she said as Ulric pressed his lips to her cheek.

He was warmer than she remembered—unless he merely seemed warmer because she was cool, like a basin of tepid water that feels hot when one's hands are cold . . .

Before she could reason her way through the puzzle, a hot, thick flush uncurled from her core. She would have thought it an aftereffect of the change, except for it centering unmistakably between her legs. In instants, her flesh was pulsing. Had it been possible to get any warmer, she would have blushed.

Embarrassed, she fanned her face.

"That is normal," Ulric said, his amusement clear as he hugged her closer. "Your new body is eager to be tried. Shall we slip into the hot spring chamber where we can see to its needs comfortably?"

She wanted to say something witty, but the strength of her arousal robbed her of speech. The best she could manage was a definite nod.

They made it through the door before she tore her clothes over her head, pushed Ulric to the floor, and fell on him like a madwoman. Touching him, kissing him, and most of all, taking him inside her seemed like a matter of life and death. Happily, he let her do it, only rolling her beneath him once she had accomplished her first climax. Its spine-wrenching nature banished all doubts that she was more sensitive, not to mention more greedy. She had not caught her breath before his quick recovery made her writhe again.

To her relief, Ulric did not need to be told to pound her with all his might.

Once this second struggle was satisfactorily concluded, he managed to coax her into the steaming pool. There, face to face, with the hot mineral water seething all around them, they experienced their first truly equal coupling.

To know one's partner could withstand whatever one asked was wonderfully freeing, but to know one could do the same was utter bliss. Juliana hardly recognized the woman who met her lover with such abandon, who clutched his buttocks and nipped his shoulder and murmured hoarse encouragements in his ear. Similarly inspired, Ulric wedged her against the side of the pool for his lightning thrusts, right where the spring gushed out from its narrow channel. The combination of pressures rocked her body with ecstasy.

It seemed natural to bite him at the final moment, to feel the spicy richness of his life overflow her tongue.

He groaned and shook and she knew that this, as much as anything, had pushed him over the edge.

"Juliana," he said on a sigh. "Juliana, I love you so much."

For long, panting minutes, she could only stroke his water-slicked back. Her body was sated, her spirit peaceful, her intuition—or perhaps her new *upyr* senses—telling her he felt the same.

"I thought you did what you wanted last night," she said when she found her voice, "but you must have been holding back."

Against her neck, Ulric's lips curved in a smile. "A little. Now that you can keep up with me, I think you had better be on your guard."

"Mm," she hummed, not worried at all. From under heavy lids, she gazed idly around the chamber. While she had enjoyed its amenities before, tonight she saw it through different eyes. The grotto had been left rough by whoever found it, but it was naturally beautiful. Above her, a bank of black and yellow crystals twinkled and zinged in the dark, now colorful and defined. Her ears were also sharper. The rushing, bubbling water cocooned them in sound, making them seem the only *upyr* in the world.

"Ulric?" she said as something occurred to her. "Please do not tell the others I did not realize I was changed. They would never let me live it down."

"Your secrets are safe with me—until I need to hold them over your head." When she punched him at his joke, he rubbed his ribs. "Take care," he teased. "You would not want to injure your new king—although, strictly speaking, you have not accepted the post as queen."

"Strictly speaking, you have not asked."

"Most certainly I have."

"You demanded. That is not the same thing."

"Very well." He gathered her in his arms until her front floated against his. "Juliana Buxton, heart of my heart and light of my soul, keeper and sharer of important secrets, would you do me the honor of being my queen?"

"I would," she said, "gladly."

She expected the same sort of thump that had greeted Gytha's surrender and Bastien's oath. Instead, a bouquet of green and golden sparks sprang into being around their heads. Startled, Juliana gave a little shriek. Ulric laughed and batted them as if they were gnats. "Really, Juliana, I know you are happy to rule at my side, but there is no need for such fireworks."

She twined her arms around his neck, his chest and hands supporting her easily. "You started a few yourself a little earlier."

"Just a few?" His mouth whispered over hers.

"An excellent beginning," she assured him and kissed him for sheer pleasure. When she released him, it was only to trade that pleasure for snuggling close.

"Thank you for letting Lucius change me," she said, her body as limp as if it had been steamed. "I imagine it must have been difficult being left behind while he and I, er, while we did whatever in the world that was."

"As to that," Ulric said, sounding vaguely uncomfortable, "I saw a snippet of his mind myself."

"You did?" Juliana pushed back to see his face. "Tell me what you saw."

"Well, not a flying ship. I saw him here, in this cave in the hall of columns, dancing with a dark-haired woman."

"Really?" Juliana's brows shot up with interest. "Did it seem as if it was a long time ago?"

"I think it must have been. The cave was . . . shiny. Not like it is now, half preserved and half gone to ruin. I got the impression that many *upyr* lived here, that the rock was riddled with sleeping rooms."

His gaze was distant as he remembered what he had seen.

"Tell me," she prodded. "If he was dancing, was it a ball?"

"I think so. A formal one, with simple, elegant gowns and some sort of uniform. The oddest thing is that more than half the guests were human. None of the *upyr* acted as if that was strange. The woman Lucius danced with was a human. She was . . ." He searched for a word. "She was a diplomatic liaison, appointed to ease tensions between the races. I think by then our kind must have been what they are today. Blood drinkers. And maybe wolves, as well."

Ulric wrinkled his forehead before going on. "I think Lucius was in love with the woman. At least, she felt very dear to his heart. She was sick, though, and refused to let the *upyr* change her. He did not have the power he has now. Every moment he had with her seemed precious. It made me realize how fortunate we are."

He clasped her face in his hands. "We should live like that, Juliana, like the humans, as if every night were a gift. We should not take for granted what we have been lucky enough to find."

"All humans do not live that way. Only the wise ones."

"Then let us be wise."

His seriousness made her smile. Despite his years, at that moment, he seemed achingly young. She prayed she would never disappoint him.

"I shall make you a bargain," she said lightly, one hand lifting to smooth his golden hair. The locks slid through her fingers like the finest silk. "Whenever you please, you may remind me how lucky I am—preferably in more than words."

Undistracted by her wagging brows, he saw the tears that burned in her eyes. His own glittered dangerously in response.

"I shall remind you any way you wish," he vowed. "From now until the last midnight."

After the end

The new queen had a way about her that Emile liked.

He and Bastien stood among the encircling trees, watching the packs approach the clearing. From Juliana's bemused expression, she had not expected to be made queen of quite so many. Nonetheless, she stood calmly beside her king, the moon a hammered coin above her, the upyr slowly filling the open ground—hundreds, all told, every one of them wondering what her accession would mean to them. It had been the wolf called Stephen's idea to channel her subjects to her between the standing stones—for drama's sake and to at once establish her credentials.

Emile considered it a stroke of genius.

No *upyr* who felt that wall of force break prickling across his skin, who sensed the new queen's personal blood magic twined within it, could doubt this female was born to lead. Emile saw more than one hand rub the back of a neck where tiny hairs were standing on end.

By the time the crowd had gathered, Ulric's formal introduction was somewhat moot.

"Thank you for coming," she said, her hand locked tight in his. Her voice was soft but steady, both richer and sweeter now that she was *upyr*. "You honor us by joining our celebration. I only hope that, with Ulric's guidance, I shall be able to contribute to the future well-being of the packs."

Emile smiled to himself, having heard a few of her plans. Their guests had a treat in store if they thought this pretty queen was just for show. She had learned to trust her strength as a human. By becoming *upyr,* that strength won a wider scope.

"Tomorrow we discuss mutual interests," Ulric said, the warmth he felt for his mate spilling over to touch them all. "In addition to our own concerns, a situation exists in France which, together, we might see a way to address. For tonight, I ask only that you enjoy. Once the ceremonies are dispensed with, we shall hunt and dance and be happy that we are pack. Each of you please come greet my queen. She is beautiful, as you can see, and very gracious. When you know more of her, you will realize how much we have to celebrate."

Because everyone knew this was an order and not a request, there were no complaints at what was sure to be a lengthy business. One by one, the crowd began filing forward. Though they tried to hide it, they seemed impressed by the small green sparklers that met their oaths.

"She looks well," Emile commented to his companion. "Regal."

"Anyone would in that cloak," Bastien scoffed, crushing an old, dry pinecone in his fist. "I am surprised Ulric let her wear it."

Emile considered the sweep of scarlet velvet draping Juliana's back. It was trimmed—appropriately enough—in spotted ermine that Ulric himself had caught. "He wanted her to be comfortable, I expect, and to signal the old ways are passing."

Not passing entirely, of course. Beneath her sop to modesty, Juliana was gloriously bare. She had been a pretty human; now she was a goddess: her figure strong, her carriage confident. Emile felt a flush of pride at their queen's good looks—though he suspected they were in part responsible for Bastien's sourness.

Bastien had been born to rule himself. His nature dictated that he desire the lead female.

"Her eyes are twinkling too much," he groused now. "She looks as though she would rather laugh than fight."

"Would that more queens embraced that attitude," Emile muttered under his breath, then caught himself when Bastien's head snapped around. "I said you should laugh more, old friend. We are safe here, and our pack stands first among them all."

"There is that," Bastien admitted, letting his shoulders sag on a sigh. "And I suppose she cannot be too pacific, or Gytha would not be serving as her right hand."

In tandem, their gaze went to the scowling, black-haired *upyr* who stood next to their queen, radiating every ounce of intimidation Juliana did not. Emile, who was surprised by little, had been stunned by Gytha's determination to hold that job. Not even Juliana's demand that she give Ingrith an overdue apology had put her off.

People can change, he thought, then smiled as Gytha insisted the pack leader from Skye bow a little lower. Thankfully, they did not change too much.

"She would take you back," he said to Bastien, eyeing his brother wolf at a slant. "You only need to smooth her hackles."

Bastien grimaced and waved his hand. "That female is too much trouble. A man hardly dares close his eyes with her in his furs."

"Then you would not mind if I pursued her?"

"You? And *Gytha?*"

Emile grinned at Bastien's open mouth. "She appeals to me. I understand how she feels, always standing just a little on the outside."

Bastien shook his head, though not in refusal. "It is your back that will feel her claws. But you have my blessing if that is what you wish."

Emile confirmed this, pleased he could proceed without offending his friend. Gytha did not know it yet, but she was about to discover how irresistible a brown-eyed Frenchman could be. As for Bastien . . . Emile paused to study his companion's habitually cool, stern face. Despite their acceptance into the pack, Bastien remained on guard. Emile dreaded what might happen if Ulric discovered he had spied on their queen's transformation, literally pressing his ear to the ground beside the opening for the sun.

"Knowledge is power," Bastien had said when Emile expressed dismay. "If nothing else, Hugo taught me that."

But Emile refused to worry tonight. He doubted Ulric would give Bastien cause to move against him. His rule was too fair and his power too firmly established. It might be centuries before Bastien had the strength to use what he learned. Until such time, he would be more than careful to hide his ambitions—especially with Emile keeping Gytha out of his hair.

Bastien would be better off, for now, with Helewis. That the mothering redhead would approach him seemed assured. She had lost interest in Emile as soon as he was hale. Bastien, on the other hand, still had healing to do.

His world arranged to his liking, at least in his own mind, Emile turned his attention to the dancing that had begun in the trampled dirt. The patterns were dizzyingly intricate, involving wolf form and man and great bursts of *upyr* laughter when the inexperienced missed their steps.

Ingrith and Stephen added to the merriment by trying to redirect those who got lost.

In the center Juliana and Ulric spun, part and apart as lovers are wont to be, their cheeks aglow with humor, their eyes as dazzling as the sun. Juliana's cloak whirled with their movements in bloodred arcs. On the other side of the clearing, the elder, Lucius, clapped. He and Helewis sang the instructions that led the dance, their voices twining melodiously. The elder almost looked normal with his face split into a big, wide grin.

This is good, Emile thought, feeling the waves of enjoyment flow through the crowd. This is what our kind was meant to be.

"Come." He nudged Bastien's arm. "Everyone is at peace here. Let us join the fun."

Bastien hesitated, his muscles stiff.

"We need to celebrate," Emile insisted, "because we survived."

He smiled at his too-serious friend, putting his understanding into his eyes. *Your turn will come,* he promised Bastien silently. *Someday, when you are ready to admit you want it, you will have your own pack.*

"Plenty of pretty *upyr* out there tonight," he coaxed aloud. "If you do not claim them, your rivals will."

"Oh, very well," Bastien surrendered, answering his friend with a flash of sharp, white teeth. "I suppose I could manage a dance or two."

Emma Holly

Beyond Innocence
0-515-13099-0

When her beloved father passes away, Florence Fairleigh
finds herself alone in the world. All she wants is a man who
will treat her kindly and support her financially—and she's
come to London to find him…

Edward Burbrooke thinks marriage is the only way to save
his brother Freddie—and their family—from scandalous ruin.
As head of the family, Edward has vowed to find Freddie a
bride—and fast.

Beyond Seduction
0-515-13308-6

To avoid marriage, Merry Vance has concocted a sinfully
scandalous scheme: to pose for Nicolas Craven, London's
most sought-after artist. No man in his right mind would
marry a woman who posed nude for this notorious rogue.

But Nicolas has his own plans for the feisty young woman—
and Merry has no idea how hot it can get in an artist's studio.

From
USA Today and *New York Times*
bestselling author

SUSAN KRINARD

To Catch a Wolf
0-425-19208-3
When Athen Munroe falls in love with a werewolf,
she must fight her desires—or face her
own extraordinary destiny...

The Forest Lord
0-425-18686-5
Lord Hern, a woodland guardian spirit, has but one
chance to escape his forest prison and one hope for
love—the very woman he has vowed to destroy.

Secret of the Wolf
0-425-18199-5
The story of a tortured man with werewolf blood,
and the beautiful hypnotist who vows to heal his
wounded soul.

B095